Driven

The Night Guardians Series

Book One: Vigilant
Book Two: Guarded
Book Three: Driven

Driven

The Night Guardians Series

By

Sara Davison

Dedication

To every mother and father who has known the incomprehensible pain of losing a child. May you be deeply aware of the presence of the Father of mercies and may the God of all comfort be with you every moment as you travel that road.

And always and above all to the one who leads and guides us down every unknown path—it is all from you and for you.

Acknowledgements

As always, I am indebted to so many for the creation of this book. I am deeply grateful for the support of my family. Michael, Luke, Julia, and Seth, thank you for your patience and understanding when I disappear into my office for hours (sometimes days) on end or retreat to the cottage to write. I couldn't do what I do if you weren't fully on board.

To my extended family, friends, and readers who encourage me and tell everyone about my work—you not only keep me going, you help me to remember why I write.

To Miralee Ferrell and the amazing team at Mountain Brook Ink, thank you for believing in me and my stories. I am proud to be part of a family whose work glorifies God and provides such powerful, entertaining, and uplifting books to our readers.

To Greg Johnson and everyone at WordServe Literary—it means so much to me to have you standing behind me and my work.

A special thank you to early readers who provided such encouraging and helpful feedback and to Ines Jimenez who read the manuscript to ensure the Spanish was accurate—gracias!

And first and foremost, deepest gratitude goes to God, who gives me the stories and who has a plan and a purpose for every one of them. All honor and praise go to You, always.

I know now, Lord, why you utter no answer.
You are yourself the answer. Before
your face questions die away.

What other answer would suffice?

~ C.S. Lewis

Chapter One

Holden bolted upright at the sound of a loud groan. "Chris?"

His wife was curled on her side, facing him. Her eyes were screwed tightly shut and both her hands were pressed to her royal blue T-shirt, over the place where her belly rounded above the top of her flannel pajama bottoms.

"What is it? Are you having contractions?"

Without opening her eyes, she nodded, slightly. "Really bad." The words came out in a breathless whisper.

It's too early. Holden threw off the covers. "I'll take you to the hospital."

She shot out a hand and grasped his arm. "No. I can't move. Call 911."

Holden snatched the cell phone off his bedside table. With a trembling finger, he punched in the three numbers. "Come on, come on, come on." When she groaned again, he reached behind him and grabbed his wife's hand.

It seemed minutes before a calm, cool voice came over the phone. "911. What is the nature of your emergency?"

He described Christina's condition quickly and gave the woman their address and the front door code. Not bothering to listen to her reply, he tossed the phone onto the table and searched his wife's face. His chest clenched. Her eyes were open now, but in the dim, early morning light, they were wild, unfocused. Her white-knuckled grip on his fingers nearly sent him to his knees beside the bed. Although he was ready to drop to them anyway, and beg God to spare his wife and child.

"It's too soon." She gasped out the words.

"I know, love." Holden stroked her wrist with his thumb, fighting to keep the panic out of his voice. As she was only thirty weeks along, his wife's intense contractions were the last thing he thought he'd be dealing with today. For once, he'd have been happy if all he'd had to face was some kind of domestic dispute or even the never-ending pile of paperwork stacked on his desk at Child Services headquarters in downtown Toronto. "It's going to be okay."

The words he hadn't meant to say sent remorse coursing through him. He shouldn't make a promise he had no idea if he could keep. *God forgive me.* Still, the wildness in her eyes eased and the fingers clutching his loosened their grip enough that blood began to flow again, so he couldn't bring himself to feel too repentant. *Please make everything be okay so that I didn't just lie to my wife.*

For the eighteenth time in the last ten minutes, he shot a glance toward the hallway. Where was the ambulance? They only lived a few minutes from the hospital—how long could it take the EMTs to get there? He pressed his lips together to keep the angry questions from spewing out of his mouth and attempted to offer his wife a reassuring smile. Judging by the look on her face, the attempt fell short. Vastly short. "Please Chris, let me take you to the hospital." Holden tried to gently extricate his fingers from hers so he could get up, but she tightened her grip again. He hid a wince.

"It's too late. I won't make it. Where—?"

Her question was cut off by the shrill wail of an alarm cutting through the early-morning silence of their neighborhood. "Holden. I can't lose him. Please …" Pain contorted her face as another contraction gripped her.

He had no idea what to do. *God, show me how to help her.* More words of reassurance rose in his throat. *He'll be fine. You'll be fine. We won't lose him.* He bit them back as he brushed the long auburn hair, damp with sweat, away from her forehead. "Chris, listen to me." The doorbell rang. Seconds later the door creaked open. Holden called out, "We're upstairs." He cupped his wife's flushed cheek as boots thudded on the wooden stairway. "I'll be with you every second. We'll do this together. Okay?"

She nodded and let go of his hand as two EMTs, a man and a woman, burst into the room. They carried a stretcher that they lifted onto its wheels next to the bed. The woman rounded it and stopped at the side of the bed. "Ma'am, we're going to get you to the hospital."

Christina shook her head against the pillow. "No time." She pushed the words out through clenched teeth.

Holden's heart pounded hard against his ribs. Another contraction? What had it been, thirty seconds? A minute? At Lamaze class they'd told them to go to the hospital when they were five minutes apart. How had this come on so fast?

The female EMT took her blood pressure then rested a hand on her shoulder. "Don't worry. I'll ride with you and if anything happens, we can take care of it on the way." She squeezed Christina's shoulder and nodded at her partner.

The tension in Holden's muscles eased slightly at the confidence in the woman's voice. Maybe everything *was* going to be okay. At least the professionals were here now.

The paramedics moved his wife from the bed to the stretcher in one quick movement. Holden followed them as they wheeled the bed to the top of the stairs, pressed the button to release the legs and swing them into place, and carried it down. He passed them at the bottom and whipped open the door, holding it until they had passed through. He grabbed Christina's coat from the hook behind the door and shoved his feet into his tennis shoes before slamming the door behind him and hurrying along the front walk. A brisk autumn wind swept past him, sending leaves swirling around his calves. Holden caught up with the gurney and tossed Christina's coat over her, trying to protect her from the chill in the air. From the corner of his eye, he caught a glimpse of several of their neighbors peering out red-flashing-light-splashed windows.

Holden didn't ask before hauling himself into the ambulance after they'd slid the stretcher inside and the woman had climbed in.

The male EMT didn't comment, or try to stop him. Which was wise. Enough adrenaline coursed through Holden that if the man had tried to keep him from his wife and child, Holden might have put *him* in the back of an ambulance.

Holden's entire body shook as he settled on the bench across from the woman and reached for Christina's hand. Her fingers were as cold as a … He slammed up a wall in his brain before it could allow the word *corpse* to fully form. He wouldn't associate that image with his wife, not even for a second.

Sirens wailed again as the driver squealed out of the driveway in reverse, then shot forward in the direction of the hospital. Through the rear window, Holden caught a glimpse of Mrs. Barrows, self-appointed keeper of the neighborhood's affairs, stepping out onto her porch, clutching a lavender-colored robe to her throat. He tried to smile at her to staunch the flow of grim speculation on their situation that she'd spread around the street before they could return, but his mouth refused to cooperate.

Let them talk. He tore his gaze from the window to study Christina. Her eyes were screwed tightly shut and her lips had gone thin and white. Holden glanced over at the EMT, hoping for more reassurance, but with Christina's eyes closed, the woman had lowered her guard. Concern was etched across her face. After attaching a clothespin type of monitor to one of his wife's fingers, the EMT grabbed a starched white sheet from a cubby bolted to the wall of the vehicle and shook it open. Holden snatched Christina's coat so the EMT could spread the sheet over her before moving to the foot of the stretcher. She fired questions at Holden as she examined his wife. How many weeks along was she? When had the contractions started? How far apart were they? He had no idea what he said in response, if his answers were accurate or even intelligible. He kept his eyes fastened on the woman's face. Whatever she was seeing only deepened the concern that lined her forehead. She lowered the sheet and turned her head to speak into the mic on her shoulder. "Hurry, Darryl."

Through static, Holden caught the words, "Almost there."

Christina moaned. The sound ripped the air from Holden's lungs, but he forced himself to draw in a ragged breath. It wouldn't help his wife any if he passed out. The grip on his hand had weakened. Had the pain lessened, or was she losing strength? Holden swallowed hard and cupped her face again. She shifted her head slightly on the rounded mound at the head of the stretcher, until she faced him. Her eyelids fluttered for a few seconds before opening. The terror in her hazel eyes sent fresh panic coursing through him. *God help her. Please.*

"Something's wrong."

Everything's wrong. He didn't voice the thought. "We're almost at the hospital."

He could see in her eyes that those weren't the words she'd been looking for, but she nodded slightly.

The ambulance careened into the hospital parking lot and screeched to a stop under the awning in front of the emergency room. The EMT leapt to the doors and flung them open. Her partner appeared in the opening and the two of them slid the stretcher out. Holden jumped from the vehicle after them and jogged beside the stretcher as the automatic doors slid open and they wheeled Christina through.

In seconds, they were swarmed by men and women in gowns and masks. His wife disappeared through swinging doors. Holden pushed through after her and followed the horde into a room. A gloved hand appeared before his face and he stepped back. The door swung shut in front of him and he moved forward to peer through the small, round window, clutching Christina's coat to his chest. The faint aroma of the floral scent she wore drifted on the air, and he took his first deep breath in what felt like hours.

Holden watched, pulse pounding in his neck, as people worked frantically on his wife, calling for instruments, reaching for towels. A crimson stain spread across the crisp white sheet at Christina's feet and the hallway spun around Holden. Blindly, he groped beside him for the wall and pressed splayed fingers across the smooth, cool surface of it, attempting to stay on his feet.

God. God. God. It was the only word that would emerge from the fog swirling around in his mind.

The woman working at the end of the stretcher, facing him, straightened, clutching a tiny, red-smeared body in both hands.

My son. He held his breath, shoving the door open a couple of inches with his shoe so he could hear the tiny wail when it came, but there was only a sudden, deafening silence in the room.

The woman's eyes met Holden's through the glass.

And he knew, with an absolute certainty that gripped his gut like a vise, that he was not going to be able to keep the promise he had made to his wife.

Chapter Two

Six months later

Holden had to catch up to him. The tiny blond boy who scampered through the woods ahead of him was so light the twigs barely crunched beneath his feet as he ran. Holden stumbled over a tree root and nearly fell. He caught himself with a hand pressed to the rough bark of a large maple and stopped to catch his breath. His free hand on his hip, he bent forward slightly, willing the pounding in his chest to ease.

A crow in the branches high overhead cawed, but he kept his eyes on the little boy who was almost out of sight. Through the thick brush, Holden caught a flash of red—the ball cap the boy wore—before that too, disappeared.

With a grunt of frustration, he shoved himself away from the tree and took off again. For several minutes he made his way through the woods, leaping over fallen logs and avoiding the deep ruts carved out by the rain that had fallen for the last three days, anything he could twist an ankle on. He strained to see into the distance. How fast could a little kid run, anyway?

At last he was rewarded with another glimpse of red. The sight sent fresh adrenaline coursing through him and he bounded forward. A branch, slick with rain, slashed across his cheek and he bit back a curse word as he swiped it away. He could see the boy ahead of him—navy shirt damp with mist and pressed to the little shoulder blades.

Holden opened his mouth to call out. For a moment he thought he knew the boy's name, but before his tongue could form it, it was gone. "Hey," he shouted, feebly, his voice raspy from exertion.

If he heard, the boy gave no indication. The toe of Holden's running shoe caught the tip of a rock sticking out of the ground and he went down hard on both knees. His palms hit cold, wet mud and for a moment he couldn't move. The shock of the impact emptied his lungs and he concentrated on dragging in one jagged breath after another. *I have to get to him. I have to make sure he's safe.*

The thoughts propelled him to his feet. He made an attempt to wipe the mud from his knees, but his palms were so caked with it he only made things worse. There'd be time to clean his clothes later. The boy was all that mattered now.

Holden ran until his heart thudded so hard against his ribs he was sure they would crack, but drew no closer to the boy. The bobbing red of his cap stayed as far ahead of Holden as it had been before he'd fallen. No matter how fast he ran, or how long, he couldn't catch up to the child. He couldn't save him.

The thought crushed him. Completely spent, Holden stopped running. The boy slowed and turned to look behind him, as if he could sense that Holden was no longer following. When he squinted for a few brief seconds, Holden could almost see the boy's face, the features that always eluded him no matter how hard he tried to make them out in the distance.

Before they could come into focus, a man, dressed in black from head to foot, suddenly appeared in the path of the child. Tingles of shock rippled across Holden's skin as every muscle in his body tightened. *No!* He had no idea if he shouted the word, or only thought it.

It made no difference either way. The man grabbed the boy's hand and yanked him along the path, faster than the boy had moved before. His cry drifted to Holden, swallowed by the flapping of wings as a murder of crows lifted from the branches and flew away, a black cloud swooping above the tops of the trees. Still, the cry spurred him into action. Leaping forward, he crashed through the underbrush, ignoring the branches that whipped mercilessly against his cold, raw cheeks and arms.

The man and the boy disappeared from view. Holden ran for several more minutes without catching a glimpse of them. Even the crashing of branches, the sound that had kept him going far past his body's ability to continue, had died away.

I can't do it. I can't get to him. Pressing his back to the trunk of a tree, Holden slid to the ground, ignoring the pain as the rough bark scraped against his spine. He drew his knees to his chest and propped his elbows on them. *He's gone.* Dropping his face into his hands, Holden let out a loud moan.

The sound woke him.

Sweat had plastered his T-shirt to his chest. Beneath the damp cloth, his heart continued to thud wildly, bouncing like the silver metal ball in a pinball machine. Turning onto his side, he stared at the back of Christina's white T-shirt. For a moment he took her in, the faint floral scent of her shampoo, the gentle rise and fall of her shoulder, the soft exhalations of breath.

He needed her. Needed warmth. Comfort. Solace.

Tentative, he rested a hand lightly on her hip, the flannel of her plaid pajama bottoms soft beneath his fingers. Even in her sleep—or maybe she wasn't actually asleep, he could never tell anymore—she shifted, enough for his hand to slide off. Holden clutched it to his chest. She still grieved the loss of their tiny son. He did too, but they grieved differently. His instinct was to draw closer to her, to wrap his arms around her and hold her tightly against him so he wouldn't lose her too.

Hers was to pull away.

He understood. She couldn't think about it yet, think about being with him, about doing anything that would put her in danger of having another child growing inside her. Another child that could be ripped from her and tossed away.

He understood, but still he missed his wife so badly he ached with it day and night. Not even the physical loss so much as the severing of their emotional closeness, the lightness they'd always shared. A lightness that had enabled them to laugh, and tease, and finish each other's sentences, and know what the other wanted before the request could even be made. He missed the joy of simply being with her, of yearning to come home and see her after a long day at work.

All of that had vanished the day they'd stood around a hole in the ground watching a tiny wooden box being lowered into the darkness.

They'd advised against watching—the funeral home people and the minister and their family and friends. Even his psychiatrist had warned the sight could cause irreparable damage. But Christina wouldn't leave their son to the care of strangers. She had to be there, had to know they would be gentle, respectful, as they lowered him to his final resting place. Only then was he able to slide an arm around her trembling shoulders and lead her away.

That was the last time she had allowed him to touch her.

Holden tossed off the covers and eased out of bed, not wanting to disturb her. After tugging on his slippers, he padded to the window and stared out at the gray, misty morning. That part, at least, he hadn't dreamed.

He drove his fingers through already-disheveled curls. Who was that boy? And why couldn't he get him out of his mind? He'd been dreaming about him for weeks now. Was it his son? Was he subconsciously chasing after him? Trying to rescue him and bring him home?

The blond didn't necessarily fit. Holden's hair was almost black, like his brother Gage's had been, and both their parents. Christina's was brownish-red. He'd seen pictures of her as a child, and she hadn't been blond then either. Neither was anyone in her family, that he could recall. The color represented innocence, maybe. Or purity. Both reflected the baby that had died before taking a single breath on this cursed planet.

The man in black could be death. That made sense. Except that he'd seemed familiar, somehow, as though Holden had met him in the past. Not that he didn't know death—he'd become far more familiar with it in his lifetime, especially in recent months, than he'd ever hoped to be. Still, it didn't feel like that was it.

If only he could see their faces. He couldn't shake the idea that he knew them both, or had seen them before, anyway. When and where, he couldn't say.

All he knew was that, when the boy looked over his shoulder, he was sending Holden a message.

That message was the only thing that was truly clear about the dream, and it echoed through his mind for days after he'd woken from it. The three words haunted him, drove him to try and find out who the boy was and how he could help him.

Don't give up.

Chapter Three

Christina kept her eyes shut and concentrated on keeping her breathing deep and even. If she didn't move, gave no indication that she was awake, he'd go to the kitchen and put on coffee and she could relax. Not that he would push her, that wasn't Holden. But every time he reached out for her, touched her, something deep inside her—that dry, crypt-like place where everything she had to give him used to be stored—forced her to shrink away.

Not that she didn't want them to be close. Most of the time she longed for his touch, ached with the desire for things to return to the way they used to be. To the time when that well within her was so overflowing with everything she wanted to share that she couldn't touch him enough, be with him enough, or tell a joke for the sheer joy of hearing him laugh often enough.

When he moved toward her now, the bucket she dropped down to retrieve something, anything she could give him in return clunked against the hard, cracked bottom of the well and came up empty.

And so she withdrew, praying that, if she did so often enough, he would stop reaching for her, stop touching her. And she could stop seeing the hurt and confusion in his eyes when she couldn't give him what he wanted.

Not that praying did any good. Had God heard her when she begged Him, over and over that terrible day, to spare the life of her son? Why had He allowed her to get pregnant in the first place? To carry that precious life inside her month after month, her heart becoming more inextricably entwined with the little heart beating inside of her with every passing day? Why allow that and then cruelly rip that little life away from her? If there was some master plan, a grand design, a way that God was working this out for her good and His glory, she certainly could not see it. And she didn't want to.

The bedroom door clicked shut softly behind her husband. Tears pricked Christina's eyes. The only well that wasn't empty inside her these days was the one that held her tears. That one appeared to maintain a never-ending supply. Impatient, she swiped at one that had started to slide down her cheek. *Enough. You have to get a hold of yourself, Christina.*

How many times had she admonished herself with those words over the last few weeks and months? More than she could count. But as much as she knew in her head that the words were true, as often as she warned herself that she had a good, good man whose patience would have to run out at some point, she couldn't seem to bring herself to take her own advice.

Would Holden's patience run out? It had so far proven to be as never-ending as her supply of tears, but even the best of men had their limits, didn't they?

How long would he stay?

Christina swung her legs over the side of the bed. She couldn't go there. Couldn't even think about how, one day, she might wake up and he would be gone. Although she recoiled every time he got close, the thought of him not being there was more than she could bear.

She strode to her closet and yanked out the first pair of jeans she laid her hands on. The blue T-shirt she'd tossed on a shelf was a bit wrinkled, but it would do for a Saturday spent hanging around the house. She wasn't going to have tea with the queen. Or see anyone at all if she could help it.

Given that it was mid-April, winter should have released its grip on their corner of the planet by now, but spring was late in coming this year, even by southern Ontario standards. Still, in spite of the cool, damp day, Holden would putter around outside, tuning the lawnmower, getting the seed ready to toss over the lawn as soon as the last of the snow disappeared, digging through old paint cans in the garage to find the right one to touch up the window frames that the long, cold winter had left cracked and dingy. He'd stay out of her way. Which she was grateful for.

And hated.

Christina tugged on the shirt and jeans, pausing for a few seconds to press a hand to her flat belly before tugging her shirt in place and wrestling her hair into a messy bun. She threw a glance in the mirror. *Good enough.*

She traipsed down the stairs, following the aroma of coffee drifting in the hall. The long day stretched out before her. What should she do? She could clean, of course, although in fits of rage against God and the world in general she had scrubbed every surface in the house free of any trace of dirt, dust, or varnish over the last few weeks.

Cooking was a waste of time, as neither she nor Holden had much of an appetite these days and were content to grab whatever canned, packaged, or frozen food they could prepare and eat without a lot of effort. They'd gone through more boxes of cereal in the last six months than they had the first seven years of their marriage. Besides, if either of them could summon the energy or the interest to choose something and defrost it, the freezer was still stocked with enough of the casseroles and lasagnas that various church members had brought over to keep them going for ages.

Reading, then. Christina sighed. Since she'd come home from the hospital, reading, one of her favorite activities in the world, had become next to impossible. Words tended to dance across the page when she looked at them. If they did stay still long enough for her to make them out, their meaning was pretty much lost to her. She couldn't seem to concentrate on anything for more than a few seconds at a time. The novel sitting on the table beside her armchair in the living room was the same one that had sat there for months, the marker only a few pages farther along than it had been the day she came home.

She snatched the carafe off the warming pad and sloshed coffee into the chipped mug she always used. The one Holden had given her on their first anniversary. The black lettering, bold against the yellow ceramic, spelled out *World's Greatest Wife*. Although the words mocked her, sent pin-pricks of heat, like fire ants, crawling across her skin, she forced herself to drink out of it every morning. A kind of penance. Maybe, if she drank enough cups of coffee to read the words a thousand times, or a million, it would start to sink in that she needed to start doing whatever it was she should be doing to earn the right to that moniker again.

She was tired of herself. Tired of the pitying looks of friends and co-workers. Tired of remembering her boss's expression when she went into the Children's Services headquarters where she and Holden were both employed as social workers to cancel her maternity leave. That had been a cruel blow, one of the hardest things she'd had to do, but forcing herself to stay afterwards, to stand in front of him as pity filled his eyes and leached into his words, had been even harder. In the end, all she'd been able to do was nod and head to the office she'd been away from for a month.

Christina grabbed the cream from the fridge and splashed a little into her mug. Wrapping the fingers of both hands around its warm sides, she carried it over to the window and slid onto a stool in front of the bar Holden had installed beneath the glass.

He was chopping wood, his back to her. Piles of melting snow still littered the yard, but he'd shed his hoodie and tossed it over a stump. The royal blue, long-sleeved shirt he wore clung to him. Christina bit her lip as he lifted the axe, muscles across his neck and shoulders tightening, and brought it down with all his might on the hapless piece of wood. He'd chopped a lot of wood over the winter, far more than they needed. She suspected the motivation behind the activity had long since ceased to be the need for kindling and become all about releasing pent-up emotions. And desires.

The phone on the kitchen counter vibrated. Christina hopped off the stool and reached for it. Nicole. She hit the button and lifted the phone to her ear as she returned to her perch in front of the window. "Hey, Nic."

"Hey, yourself. Miserable day, isn't it?"

Christina doubted her friend had called to talk about the weather. "Yes. Definitely."

A short silence followed. Was she expected to say more? Small talk was not her forte these days.

Before she could compose a fumbling comment on the rising temperature, or how nice it would be when they could stop bundling up every time they went outdoors, Nicole rescued her. "Daniel has a buddy here visiting for a couple of days, one of the PI's he worked with in London for a few years. Tonight's his first dinner with us and we wanted to make it special, so we invited Mikayla, and I wondered if you and Holden would like to come."

The question crackled in the air for a moment, as though still making the journey from Nicole's condo through the miles of city streets between them and out the speaker of Christina's phone. She ran it through her mind, attempting to process the words. A dinner party? Could she do that?

Not that she didn't get out. Of course she went to work every day, but other than that first awful day, that was doable. She could lose herself completely and utterly in the chaotic lives of others there. She could even, occasionally, allow that what was happening to them was as bad or worse than what had happened to her, if suffering could be measured in terms of fear, or physical pain, or numbers of lives being threatened.

She'd gone to Nicole's condo plenty of times too. The place was a sanctuary for her. Usually she went when Nicole was home alone, although she didn't mind seeing Nicole's husband Daniel or her son Jordan either. Daniel was the strong, silent type who didn't try to ease her pain with platitudes or advice, only wrapped his arms around her and hugged her, or kissed her cheek or her forehead like the older brother she'd always wished she had.

And Jordan was a high-energy, wise-beyond-his-years kid who'd lost his dad before he was even born. He understood more than he should have to about death and what it was like when the person who should be there, kissing you good night or playing catch with you or making you feel as though you were part of a real family, wasn't there. He was the only one who'd been able to make her laugh, even to forget about the gaping hole in her life, if only for a few minutes here and there. So she had no trouble spending time with them.

But other people? She adored Nicole's sister, Mikayla. Even though Nicole had only found out a year ago that Mikayla existed, Christina had recognized a kindred spirit the moment she had met her. They'd both experienced great loss recently and, as the Psalms put it, deep called to deep. Mikayla seemed to have an innate ability to know the time to speak and the time to simply sit with her, when to give her space and when to offer her a hug. Nicole was the same, likely the whole twin thing. So Christina could handle being around Mikayla too.

But this friend of Daniel's was a complete stranger. What would she say to him? Would he be able to see, at a glance, that she'd recently suffered a trauma? Did she carry the aura of that around like some kind of supernatural shroud? That thought haunted her at times, when she was in the grocery story or the bank or walking along the street. Every once in a while she was sure someone had cast a furtive glance at her then looked away, as if they somehow knew.

The silence grew heavy. Nicole must know the invitation had sent her reeling and was giving her time to process. Christina chewed on her thumbnail. Maybe she and Holden *could* sit and eat a meal with other adults, possibly make conversation. Be witty, even. *God, will I ever be witty again*? Occasionally, her mind had been able to work quickly enough to conjure up a humorous response to something Holden or a co-worker said. Each time, the words died on her lips before she said them, as though she'd bitten into something that looked good but tasted bitter on her tongue. Each time it had struck her, right before she spoke, that it wasn't right to joke or laugh. Not when she was in mourning. What would that mean, that she had forgotten her son? That his death no longer mattered, or didn't bother her? That she was doing what seemed to her to be that most loathsome of things—*moving on*? Whatever that looked like.

But dinner was different. They didn't have to laugh, but they did have to eat. There was nothing disrespectful in that, was there? They used to do those kinds of things all the time, before, when they were fully part of the land of the living, not hovering between this world and the next with one foot still stuck in that tiny hole in the ground. Was it possible they could do it again? Would they even remember how?

Christina cleared her throat. "Nic, I—"

"Don't say no."

"But …" Nothing would come to mind. No argument strong enough to justify denying a request from the person who had been there for her, night and day, for months now, never once asking for anything in return.

"Christina Diane Kelly, listen to me. I know you don't particularly want to do this. And I know it will be hard. But if I didn't believe with all my heart that it would be a really good thing for you, I wouldn't ask. Besides, if you and Holden don't come, Mikayla will be furious with me as it will look like a complete set-up."

"Isn't it?"

"Of course not. It's—"

"A really good thing for her, or you wouldn't ask."

"Ha ha. You're hilarious. Now, are you coming or not? And while that might sound like it's optional, to clarify, it's actually not."

Hilarious? Christina reflected on her comment. Not hilarious, exactly—Nicole was being generous, as always—but maybe she hadn't lost her sense of humor entirely, even if it did creak a little as she trotted it out, like a gate that hadn't been pushed open in years. "Then there's nothing more for me to say, is there?"

A rush of air sounded over the phone, as if Nicole had been holding her breath. "Excellent. Come at seven. No need to bring anything." She disconnected the call, no doubt afraid Christina would change her mind if she didn't.

Which she might have. She exhaled a breath of her own and set the phone beside her mug. What had she agreed to?

She peered out the window. Holden had stopped chopping and was stacking the pieces on top of the already towering pile of wood leaning against the side of the garage. He did look more relaxed, as though he'd blown off all the steam he'd needed to. For now.

Maybe she should head outside and try chopping a few pieces of wood herself.

Chapter Four

Rain teemed from a platinum sky, and Natalya tugged the hood of her jacket over her head as she picked her way around the puddles dotting the gravel parking lot. When she reached the warehouse, she entered the code and then pressed her thumb to the security pad next to the entrance. The green light flashed on, and Natalya pulled open the heavy metal door and slipped inside, the sound of trucks rumbling through the Chicago industrial area fading behind her. Since it was Saturday afternoon and no one in their building was working, the interior was dark and still. Lights attached every few feet along the outer walls made a weak attempt to push back the gloom of the place, but with the overhead fluorescent panels switched off they fought a losing battle.

"Don't move." The harsh command was accompanied by something hard and round jabbing into her back, between her shoulder blades. Natalya froze and lifted her hands, elbows bent. "Turn around slowly. Keep your hands where I can see them."

She complied, pushing back her hood to reveal her face to the person who'd issued the orders. The hulking, bearded man in front of her lowered his assault rifle to his side. "Sorry, boss."

Natalya dropped her arms. "It's all right. You're doing your job. I should have told you I was coming in this afternoon."

"Need help with anything?"

"No, I'm fine. Thank you, Rourke. I'm going to my office, but I won't be long. I'll let you know when I'm leaving."

"Yes, ma'am." He inclined his head in her direction before fading into the shadows near the door.

Natalya strode down the long aisle between two rows of shelving that reached nearly to the metal ceiling, the rubber soles of her wet shoes squeaking on the cement floor. Offices lined the back wall at the rear of the building. Another security pad was mounted outside the one she used, and she entered four numbers then pressed the star button before touching her thumb to the pad. The green light glowed and she stepped into her office, closing the door firmly behind her.

The reason she hadn't let Rourke know she was coming was that she hadn't realized it herself. When excess adrenaline had propelled her from her penthouse condo downtown and behind the wheel of her car an hour earlier, Natalya had no plan in mind other than taking a drive. Somehow she had ended up here, at the headquarters the organization had set up after Ted Stiller had been arrested and Gage Kelly killed nearly eight years earlier. Many of her colleagues had also been arrested after Stiller gave them up to the police, but she and a remnant of co-workers had eluded capture. Eventually they regrouped and began their new mission of protecting the children the organization had rescued from their abusive homes and placed with new families who loved them and kept them safe.

Natalya had dedicated her life to ensuring they stayed that way. For several years now, all had been quiet. For the most part, every active case had grown cold and been abandoned. As far as she knew, only Detective Daniel Grey in Toronto continued to make calls or follow up on leads once in a while, but nothing too serious. Still, he was a good cop and Natalya was determined not to grow complacent or underestimate his ability to uncover a clue that could lead him to one of the kids.

Which was why they watched him very closely, prepared to move in if it appeared he was getting too close. Maybe use his pretty little wife or his step-son—Gage Kelly's son—as collateral to convince him to abandon his efforts.

Still, none of her people had notified her of any breakthroughs in his investigation, so why was she so restless today? Natalya had woken in the night, a strange uneasiness circulating throughout her body. Even with no clear reason, she had learned over the years never to discount the sense she got occasionally that something was about to go terribly wrong. The tingling spread across her scarred arms and torso—the constant reminder of a childhood lived at the mercy of a mentally unstable mother. That sixth sense had kept the organization going as long as it had and kept her out of prison at the same time.

Shoving away thoughts of her childhood so she could think clearly, Natalya crossed her office and stopped in front of the sliding security door covering the back wall. A chain hung around her neck, and she reached inside the collar of her blouse and tugged the necklace free. Natalya bent forward and slid the small key attached to the chain into the lock on the sliding door, turning it until the rounded metal bar popped open. She removed the lock and clutched it in one hand as she shoved open the sliding door with the other.

Natalya stepped back to survey the contents of the metal cabinets that had been hidden behind the door. The organization's carefully-amassed stash of assault rifles, pistols, and ammunition lined the interior of every cabinet. A row of shelves separating two of the cabinets contained boxes of latex gloves, dark bottles of chloroform, rags, plastic ties, jugs of bleach, and plastic sheets. Everything they could possibly need to deal with unwanted problems.

Or uninvited guests.

Water dripped from her sleeves and the hem of her jacket, leaving dark stains on the carpet at her feet. The tension quivering through her since she had woken in the night settled a little. If Detective Daniel Grey or anyone associated with him thought they could track down one of the children and not pay a heavy price for their interference, they would quickly find out how mistaken they were.

Natalya ran her fingers along the smooth, gleaming black barrel of an AK-47. *Let them come.* If they did, she and her security team would be ready.

Chapter Five

Mikayla stepped through the doorway of Daniel and Nicole's condo. One hand still on the knob, Daniel gave her a one-armed hug as she came inside. Jordan barreled over from the living room to throw himself at her. She dropped her multi-colored bag on the floor and flung her arms around him, the force of his greeting sending her stumbling backwards a couple of steps.

"Easy, Jord." Daniel closed the door behind her.

Jordan stepped out of her embrace, a look of chagrin on his freckled face. "Sorry, Aunt Mikayla."

She ruffled her seven-year-old nephew's dark curls. "No problem, buddy. I'm happy to see you too."

"Can I take your coat?" Daniel held out his hand.

Mikayla slid the long, cream-colored wool coat off her shoulders and handed it to him. She smoothed the front of her shimmering black sleeveless top and black pants.

"Is that you, Mikayla?" Nicole's voice drifted from the kitchen, over the tops of the swinging doors.

Daniel hung her coat in the closet and came over to rest a hand on Jordan's shoulder. Mikayla loved how they were together, like father and son. Jordan clearly looked up to his step-father, and why wouldn't he? Daniel was a great role model for her nephew and couldn't love Jordan more if he were his own.

Mikayla shot her brother-in-law a rueful look. "She's going to put me to work, isn't she?"

"I believe she has more planned for you than that."

Her eyes narrowed. "What does that mean?"

He inclined his head toward the kitchen. "Best ask her yourself."

A niggle of apprehension working its way through her stomach, Mikayla pushed through the French doors. Her sister was pulling a pan out of the oven. The tantalizing aroma of roasting meat swirled around Nicole as she set the pan on top of the stove and closed the oven door.

Mikayla breathed it in. "Hey, Nic."

"Hey." Still wearing oven mitts, her twin offered her a hug. The scent of mingled spices—cinnamon and cloves and nutmeg—clung to her.

Mikayla contemplated her. It still threw her a little, seeing someone who looked so much like her, only with long blond hair instead of a short bob, the way Mikayla wore hers. Tonight Nicole had arranged hers in a neat bun at the nape of her neck. She tended to wear lighter colors than Mikayla, and the peach blouse she had on gave her a breezy, spring-like look. Mikayla took another deep breath. "Mmm. Everything smells amazing. What have you been baking?"

"Apple pie." Nicole's cheeks were flushed from the oven. She tugged off the mitts and tossed them onto the island. "Want to help?"

"Sure." Mikayla wandered over to the sink and washed her hands. "What can I do?"

"Everything's almost ready. I've peeled the carrots, but I need them cut into pieces and thrown into the water." She nodded at a pot steaming on the stove.

"Done." Mikayla sat on a stool at the island. Nicole had already set out the cutting board and knife beside the carrots, as organized at home as she must have to be at the diner she owned downtown. Mikayla reached for the knife and grabbed the first carrot out of the bowl. When she'd finished chopping them all, she carried the pieces over to the stove and scraped them off the cutting board and into the boiling water with the knife. "Daniel said you had something planned for me. Any idea what he was talking about?" She walked to the island and picked up the knife and board to rinse them off.

Nicole didn't glance her way, only kept stirring the gravy on the stove. "None whatsoever."

Mikayla recognized her sister's guilty voice when she heard it. "Nicole."

Her sister turned around, gravy dripping from the spatula onto the floor. "I was going to tell you. A friend of Daniel's is staying with us for a couple of days, so he'll be here for dinner."

"What friend?"

"No one you know. His name is Jax Rodriguez. He's a private investigator. Daniel worked with him in London for a few years when he was suspended from the force."

Mikayla dropped the knife and cutting board into the sink with a clatter. "I just remembered I have something important to do tonight. At home." She headed for the doors.

Nicole dropped the spatula into the pot and grabbed her arm before she could reach them. "Kayla. Don't go. Please. I'm not trying to push the two of you together—I only wanted to have a small dinner party for Jax's first night here. Holden and Christina are coming too."

Mikayla's eyebrows rose. "They are?"

"Yes. And you know how huge that is for Chris. She's going to need us to help her through tonight. Both of us."

Mikayla pursed her lips. Her sister had played the trump card. Worst part was, from the faintly triumphant look in her green eyes, Nicole knew it. Mikayla's heart had broken for Christina when she heard she'd lost her baby. Her own parents had been killed in a car accident a year and a half ago, so she knew all too well what that bottomless ache of loss felt like. If Christina was pushing herself to come tonight and be with people, Mikayla would have to suck it up and stick around. "Fine." She tugged her arm from her sister's grasp and stalked to the sink. Grabbing the knife, she waved it in Nicole's direction. "But I am only staying for Christina's sake. I am not interested in meeting some random guy who makes a living out of sticking his nose into other people's business."

Nicole ripped a few paper towels from the roll mounted beneath a cupboard and wiped the gravy off the floor. "He's not a random guy. I really like him and he's a friend of Daniel's, so you know he's okay."

Mikayla had to give her that one. Grudgingly. "Even so. I am not looking to get involved with—"

The doors swung open and a tall man in black jeans and a fitted gray, V-necked T-shirt under a light khaki leather jacket stepped into the kitchen. His long, dark hair was pulled back in a ponytail, and even from across the room, his eyes appeared so dark they were almost black.

Mikayla pressed her lips together to stifle a groan. *You have got to be kidding me.* This was the random guy? In addition to the extra effort God had clearly put into him, the man definitely knew how to dress. Weren't private investigators supposed to be good at blending in, not drawing attention to themselves? If so, he had to be the worst PI in the world. She sank onto the stool at the island.

"Hey, Nicole. I wanted to see if there was anything I could do to help."

Was that a Spanish accent? Made sense, given his name and the whole Latino thing he had going on. Mikayla shifted on the stool, but he didn't glance her way. *Hmm.*

Nicole turned off the burner below the pot. "Thanks, Jax. Could you grab the gravy boat off the island and hold it for me so I can pour this in?"

Jax walked over to the island. Reaching past Mikayla, so close she practically had to lean out of the way, he grabbed the white ceramic dish. A faint hint of tantalizing cologne hung in the air when he straightened.

Seriously?

The corners of his mouth twitched, as though he could feel her ire and found it amusing as he turned away and carried the gravy boat to the stove. "Here you go." He held it so Nicole could tip the pan and carefully pour the gravy into it.

"Thanks." Nicole wiped the edge of the pot with the spatula before returning it to the stove. "As you can probably guess, that's my sister Mikayla Grant. Kayla, this is Jax."

The guilt in Nicole's voice was gone, replaced by repressed laughter. Mikayla frowned. *Is that why I've been brought in tonight? To be the appointed entertainment?*

"Ah." Jax's face brightened, as if he was noticing her for the first time. He wandered to the island and set the gravy boat on the marble surface.

Mikayla started to hold out her hand, but he leaned in and kissed her on one cheek and then the other. The light stubble that covered the lower half of his face brushed against her skin. "That is how we do it in my country."

Heat crept up her neck. "And what country is that?"

"Canada." Daniel pushed through the French doors. "Don't let the whole fake accent, this-is-how-we-do-it-in-my-country thing fool you. Dude was born in Toronto."

Mikayla contemplated the two of them. If their third partner in the PI business looked anything like the two of them, no doubt they'd been overrun with business. The irony of all those wealthy women banging on their doors, clamoring for appointments so they could spend time in their company while complaining about their husbands' wandering eyes, wasn't lost on her.

Jax appeared completely unfazed as he lifted his broad shoulders. "My body may have been born and raised in Canada, but my heart will always belong to Puerto Rico." The accent had abated a little, but didn't disappear completely. Even if he'd been born here, his first language had to have been Spanish.

Daniel snorted. "Only because it helps you get …" he shot a look at Mikayla, "… better service in Latino restaurants," he finished lamely.

Mikayla hopped off the stool. "If you'll excuse me, I'm going to see what my nephew is doing." Without a glance at either Jax or Nicole, she shoved through the doors of the kitchen. She half-expected a burst of laughter to follow her, but only silence accompanied her to the living room. Which, for some reason, felt worse.

Jordan sat on the couch watching an episode of *The Three Stooges*. When Daniel had reconnected with Nicole and met her son, he'd introduced Jordan to the classic comedians, starting with Laurel and Hardy. Jordan had been hooked from the start.

Mikayla dropped onto the couch beside him and slid an arm around his little shoulders. Shortly after she and Nicole had been reunited, Jordan was abducted, and she'd been terrified they would never see him again. Since that awful day, she had never taken time with him for granted.

He looked at her and grinned impishly before turning his attention to the antics of Curly, Larry, and Moe.

Less enamoured by those three than Jordan, Mikayla idly ran her fingers through her nephew's dark curls. What was Nicole thinking? There was no way Mikayla would ever get involved with a guy like that.

A silent voice inside rebuked her. *And how do you know what he is like? You've only spent three minutes with him.*

Mikayla shifted. A guy who looked like that? She knew exactly what he'd be like. Shallow, way too sure of himself, used to having everything in life handed to him. Certainly used to women throwing themselves at him. He'd likely cruised through school, captain of this, president of that, had his pick of girls every weekend and for prom. It was doubtful much of what he'd learned had stuck, especially since there was probably always someone willing to do his homework for him. He likely hadn't cracked a book since leaving high school. Why would he? You didn't have to know much to get by in life when you looked like that. People bent over backwards to do everything for you. The whole PI thing was likely for kicks, because he was bored. He'd have no strength of character because he'd never had to endure a moment of hardship. Life for people like that was like meandering along an endless, shaded, golden road with no twists or turns or detours along the way.

Did she need that in her life? Someone who would expect her to cater to him like everyone else always had? She slumped against the couch cushions. Absolutely not.

Get a grip, Mikayla. She wasn't here for herself, she was here for Christina.

Which was too bad, because otherwise she could have walked out that condo door and never had to give Jax Rodriguez another thought.

Chapter Six

Holden speared the last bite of roast beef and gravy on his plate and stuck it in his mouth. Nicole was a fabulous cook and dinner had been amazing, as always. He shot another look at his wife, as he'd been doing all evening, Was she okay? He'd been shocked when she came outside this morning to tell him she'd accepted Nicole's invitation. Shocked and thrilled, although he tried to keep that in check. They still had a long journey ahead of them, but this was a tiny leap forward, at least. He'd take as many of those as he could get.

Christina was clearly trying. She'd responded whenever anyone spoke to her, even questioned Jax a little about himself. The effort showed in the lines around her eyes and the tightness of her lips. Still, she hadn't asked him to take her home yet, and he was immensely proud of her for that.

He forced himself to look away from her and focus on the other people at the table. Jax seemed nice enough, although there was something weird going on between him and Mikayla. He'd been glancing over at her all night, eyes gleaming as if he was on a mission to try and get a reaction out of her. She was offering him nothing, unless the fact that she was clearly aware of his glances and studiously ignoring them could be considered a reaction.

Only Nicole and Daniel were themselves, initiating conversation and making everyone as comfortable as possible by laughing and teasing each other. The way he and Christina used to do.

Before that thought could get away from him, Nicole reached for an empty bowl in the middle of the table. "I'll clear these dishes away and then we can have dessert. Chris? Want to help?"

His wife managed a smile for her as she stood and reached for the platter of roast beef. "Sure."

"I'll help too." Jax started stacking everyone's plates.

Mikayla blinked but didn't say anything as she grabbed four glasses and carried them into the kitchen.

Nicole came out bearing a chocolate ice cream cone that she presented to her son. "It's past your bedtime, Jord. Eat this and then go brush your teeth, okay?"

Jordan nodded, sticking out his tongue to catch a drop that had slid down the side of the cone. Holden watched, amused in spite of himself by how quickly his nephew inhaled the ice cream and crunched the cone almost to the bottom before popping the tip into his mouth. Jordan had barely finished before he yawned loudly.

Daniel rose and clapped a hand on his shoulder. "Come on, little man, let's get you to bed."

"Okay. Good night, Uncle Holden."

"Good night, J-Man."

Jordan gave him a hug, sticky fingers grasping Holden's neck, before traipsing alongside Daniel into the hallway that led to his room.

Holden watched them for a moment. He was deeply grateful to Daniel for taking his brother's place in his nephew's life, but it hurt too, witnessing another man father Gage's son. Blowing out a breath, he rose and headed down the other hallway to the guest washroom. He splashed cold water on his face then pressed both hands to the cool porcelain on either side of the sink and drew in several long, deep breaths. When he felt composed enough to join the others, he pushed away from the sink and yanked open the door.

On his way to the dining room, he passed the open door of Daniel's office. The dark-paneled room with half-drawn burgundy drapes was dim and quiet, a beckoning oasis. A burst of laughter rolled down the hallway toward him and he sighed. *I need another minute.* He ducked into the office, stumbled to the plush black chair behind the large wooden desk, and sank onto it.

Pressing the tips of his fingers to his temples to try to push away a nagging headache, he closed his eyes and rested his head against the soft leather.

Holden had no idea how much time had passed before he jerked, dragging himself out of the oblivion he'd drifted into. He opened his eyes and blinked in the dull light. *What time is it?* He'd left his phone in the living room. Daniel's laptop sat open on the desk and Holden reached for the button. Partway there, he froze, hand hovering above a cream-colored file folder. *What is that?* An eight-by-eleven-inch drawing had slid part way out of the folder. Holden glanced at the door. More muffled laughter filtered into the room, but no footsteps sounded in the hallway.

He grasped the corner of the paper and started to tug it out. A surge of guilt struck him and he stopped. *What are you doing?* Whatever was in the file was not his business. It could be part of an official police investigation, classified, even, which would mean that his snooping might get not only himself, but Daniel in trouble. He let go of the paper but continued to stare at it. The drawing was obviously of a person. He could see the top of the head sticking out, covered in … blond hair?

With another glance at the door, Holden grasped the picture and slid it out a little farther. His heart beat out an uneven rhythm in his chest. Was that …? He pulled the paper out the rest of the way and bent closer to examine the face of the boy staring at him. The room was too dark. Casting caution to the wind, Holden hit the button on the desk lamp, flooding the work area with bright light. Squinting, he examined the picture for a few seconds before setting it on the folder. The room spun around him.

He had never seen the face of the boy in his dream, but he knew he was looking at it now, as strongly as he'd known anything in his life. And he knew who the boy was.

At least, he had known him, years ago, although in the picture he had aged as many years as had passed since that time. The boy in his dream was three or four, the age he'd been the last time Holden saw him. Which would make him what, twelve now? Holden closed his eyes. *What do you want me to do with this?*

The words hit the ceiling and crashed down around him, as they always did these days. As they had done for the last six months, ever since …

"Holden?"

Holden straightened so quickly the black chair slammed into place. Daniel stood in the doorway, a palm pressed to either side of the frame, peering in at him. Holden glanced at the folder. No way to hide what he'd been doing. "I'm sorry. I was …" Nope. No excuse was good enough to explain digging around Daniel's private files.

Daniel pushed away from the frame and came into the room. "It's okay. I shouldn't have left that folder out. I was looking at it before you came and then Nic called me and I meant to come and put it away and didn't get around to it."

Holden touched the corner of the page. "Is this Matthew Gibson?"

"An artist's rendering of what he could look like now, eight years later, yes."

His stomach twisted. "So you're continuing to look for him."

"The cases are all still open. I don't think there's a lot of active investigating going on, other than sending these updated photos out on the wire every year or so."

"Then why were you looking at it?" Holden jerked his chin toward the file.

Daniel sighed and dragged a chair from the corner over to the side of the desk. He sat and lifted the photo. "When I was with that PI firm in London, I continued on with the investigation in my spare time, sort of a hobby. I still haul the files out now and again and look them over, sometimes make a few phone calls. Not much more than that."

"Any leads?"

"No. None. The organization Gage worked for was incredibly powerful and well-connected. We were able to arrest a lot of those involved, but no one we brought in would talk. We didn't get a thing out of any of them, even though it meant longer sentences for them. It's as if those kids disappeared off the face of the earth, like they no longer exist. Although there's absolutely no evidence they've been harmed, either."

He cocked his head and studied Holden.

Holden shifted on the black chair. "What?"

"When I came in, your face was white as a sheet. What was that about?"

"Guilt, I guess. And you startled me."

Daniel shook his head. "No, I watched you for a few seconds before I said your name. You looked like you were in distress already, before I came in."

"Seeing this photo brought it all back. What Gage did, how he died."

Daniel didn't respond to that.

He knows me too well. Holden blew out a breath. "All right, it was more than that. I've seen this kid." He tapped a finger on the edge of the paper.

"I know. He was in the system, right?"

"Yes, but I don't mean years ago. I've seen him recently."

Daniel's eyebrows shot up and Holden raised a hand. "Not in person. I've been having strange dreams for weeks now. I'm chasing this blond kid through the forest, but I can never catch him, and I never see his face. Then a man in black appears and takes him away and I stop because I realize I can't save him. The kid looks over his shoulder at me and he's sending me a message: *Don't give up.* As soon as I saw this picture, I realized the kid was Matthew Gibson." He lowered his hand to the desk, resting it on the photo. "What do you think that means?"

"What does it mean to you?"

Holden shot him a look. "You sound like my shrink."

"Bottom line is, it doesn't particularly matter what either your shrink or I believe it means. Only you can say why you think you are having this dream over and over and what you're going to do about it. Especially now that you've identified the boy."

"What *can* I do?"

Daniel offered him a wry grin. "That's entirely—"

"Up to me, I get it. Although a little brotherly advice would be nice, since you're the closest thing to a brother I have now."

"I think you know where I'd tell you to start."

Everything in Holden rebelled at the thought. His fists tightened on the arms of the chair. "Let me guess, pray about it."

"Exactly. Looked like that might have been what you were doing when I walked in, actually."

"I was. Well, trying, anyway."

"Trying?"

"Yeah. My prayers seem to be going unanswered these days. Actually, it's worse than that. They're going completely unheard. It's as though a barrier has been erected between God and me, and I can't seem to break through."

"Are you really trying?"

Holden frowned. "What are you suggesting?"

Daniel rested his forearms on the desk. "You're mad at God. I get it. He took your child. You and Christina should be enjoying these days as the best time of your life. You should be closer than ever with a healthy newborn at home, starting out as a family. Instead, there's no baby, and the two of you are …"

Holden grimaced. "It's okay. You can say it. I'm getting a little tired of pretending anyway. Nothing's the same as it was. We share the same house, the same bed even, but we're so far apart we might as well be living on different planets. And I guess you're right. I am mad at God. When I'm alone I question him all the time, even yell at him."

"And?"

"Nothing. The long, loud silence of heaven, as I like to call it."

"Any chance the problem could be on the other end?"

"Meaning?"

"Maybe God's talking, only you're not willing to listen."

Holden grabbed a pen and tapped it on the desk. "I suppose that could be it. I'm not very disposed to hear what God has to say these days. I know he's unlikely to explain himself or his decision to take my child, and frankly, that's all I want to hear. I definitely don't want him to ask me to do anything for him, I can tell you that."

Daniel pressed the tips of his fingers to the picture of Matthew Gibson and slid it a little closer to Holden. "I hate to tell you, *brother*, but it appears that's exactly what he is doing."

"And what am I supposed to do with that?"

"Well, you could keep sitting here talking to me, going around and around in circles and arriving back at the same question every time, or you could stop yelling and start listening to what it is God is trying to tell you."

"And if I don't like what he has to say?"

"In my experience, that's pretty much never a prerequisite for obedience."

"Even so—"

A feminine voice interrupted the protest he was about to utter. "There you are."

Holden and Daniel glanced over at the doorway. Mikayla had propped a shoulder against the frame. "Nicole sent me to find you two. Dessert's ready."

Daniel nodded. "Thanks, Mik. We'll be right there."

Mikayla pushed away from the frame. She took a step into the hallway, then stopped and walked into the office, her gaze fixed on the picture in front of Holden. Her forehead wrinkled. "Why on earth do you have a picture of Andrew Thompson on your desk?"

Chapter Seven

Holden's head jerked. "You know this kid?"

"I think so. I mean, it's not exactly like him, but close."

Daniel grabbed the picture and held it closer to Mikayla, as though that might help her provide him with concrete answers. "Where do you know him from?"

"If it is the same kid, he lived in my neighborhood in Chicago. I saw him at the park sometimes, walking home from school. Why? Is he in some sort of …?"

Holden caught a movement from the corner of his eye and grabbed Daniel's arm to keep him from tugging the phone from his pocket. "Daniel, wait."

"You know I have to call it in, Holden."

"Can we talk about this first? He's been missing for eight years. A few more minutes isn't going to make any difference."

Daniel contemplated him for several seconds. Holden held his breath until Daniel dropped the phone into his shirt pocket.

Mikayla's face had gone pale. "Missing? He's not missing. I saw him a few months ago."

Daniel stood and cupped her elbow to guide her onto his chair. When she was settled, he thrust the picture into her hands. "Look closely. Seriously try and figure out if this is the same kid you saw in Chicago."

She scrutinized the picture. "I don't know for sure. It's definitely close, but Andrew's hair was darker and his face was thinner. Maybe this is only someone who resembles him."

Daniel strode around behind the desk. Holden wheeled the chair a little to the left so his friend—who'd clearly gone into full cop mode—could slide open a drawer and withdraw a notebook and pen. He lifted both in Mikayla's direction as he shut the drawer. "Can you sketch him?"

"Who, Andrew?"

"Yes. Please, Mik. This is important."

Her gaze shifted to Holden's. "This is one of the kids your brother took, isn't it?"

His chest tightened. "Yes. The last one. The one that got him …" Eight years later, he still couldn't say the word.

She rested a hand on his arm. "They never found the boy?"

"They never found any of them." He angled a glance at Daniel. "Not for lack of trying."

"So this picture is an artist guessing what he would look like now."

"That's right." Daniel took the paper from her and handed her the notebook and pen. "Do you want to work from this picture, or would it be easier for you to go from memory?"

"Memory, I think. I can imagine him in my head."

Daniel stuck the paper inside the folder.

He perched on the edge of the desk and folded his arms over his chest. He and Holden waited in silence as Mikayla made the first strokes of pen on paper then stopped. "This would be a lot easier if you both weren't staring at me. Why don't you go get dessert and I'll bring this to you as soon as I'm done. Nic will be wondering where we all are, anyway."

Exhaling, Daniel uncrossed his arms and nodded at Holden. Holden shoved the chair away from the desk and followed his friend across the room. At the door, he glanced back. Mikayla was bent over the notebook, sketching madly. At that rate, it wouldn't take her long. Which was good, because he had no idea how much time Daniel would be willing to give him before calling his detective-sergeant with this new information. Holden had only known his friend to keep vital information from someone twice. The first time he'd ended up suspended from the force for five years, and the second time Nicole had broken their engagement and he'd come very close to losing her and Jordan forever. Judging from the taut neck muscles above the collar of his black T-shirt as he led the way to the dining room, Holden guessed he was seriously struggling with the idea of holding on to this bit of information any longer than absolutely necessary.

Christina carried a tray laden with cups of coffee and tea out of the kitchen. Her long hair was caught up in a gleaming ponytail. The dark green blouse she wore over gray dress pants brought out the red highlights. She was thinner than she'd been before she got pregnant, and there were dark smudges beneath her eyes that showed a little, in spite of the makeup she'd used to try and cover them, but the sight of her still took his breath away. "Here." Holden reached for the tray. His fingers brushed hers and she surrendered the tray.

The ache in his chest that hadn't gone away in six months—only deepened or eased a little, depending on the day—intensified now. Holden carried the tray into the dining room and set it on the table. He breathed deeply, inhaling the rich aroma of fresh coffee as he tried to push away the shadows that threatened to overtake him. The shadows he'd wrestled with since spending almost every night of his childhood hiding in the bedroom closet with Gage, trying to stay out of the path of their alcoholic, abusive dad.

Nicole tucked a strand of hair behind one ear and slid an arm around Daniel's waist when he came over to stand beside her. "There you both are—I thought you'd gotten lost."

Daniel kissed the top of her head. "Sorry, hon, we were talking."

"About?" She gazed at him, green eyes sparkling.

Holden pressed the heel of one hand to his heart. When was the last time his wife had looked at him like that? He glanced over at Christina, but she busied herself with setting plates of steaming apple pie and ice cream in front of everyone and didn't meet his gaze. He repressed a sigh and distributed the hot drinks around the table. Would Daniel tell them what was going on? If Mikayla was about to come out with a picture of one of the missing kids, it might be better to launch a pre-emptive strike and prepare everyone. Especially Nicole. Gage had been her husband and the father of the child she'd given birth to months after his death. His decision to kidnap those children had affected her more than anyone. Although it would be great if Daniel could tell the story without letting everyone know Holden's part in bringing that picture into the open.

Jax came out of the kitchen, a dish towel over one shoulder. He passed out the last two plates of pie and took his seat, removing the towel from his shoulder and draping it over his chair.

"Actually," Daniel held a chair out for Nicole and she settled onto it. He took the one next to her. "We might have gotten a break in the case of one of those missing kids."

Nicole blinked. "You mean the ones Gage took?"

"Yes."

"What break? What did you find out in the last ten minutes in your office that you haven't been able to discover in eight years?" The sparkle had faded from her eyes.

"It wasn't so much me as Mikayla. Holden and I were studying the latest artist's sketch of what Matthew Gibson might look like now, and your sister saw it. She thought she recognized Matthew as a kid who lived in her neighborhood in Chicago."

"Wow."

The tightness in Holden's chest eased. He should have known his friend wouldn't throw him under the bus and tell anyone he'd been poking his nose in where it didn't belong. Christina pulled out the chair beside him. Holden joined her at the table and nudged a mug of coffee closer to her plate.

"Thank you." Her voice was strained. She lifted the cup and peered over the top of it at Daniel. "So what now?"

"Mikayla said the picture isn't exactly like Andrew Thompson, the kid she knew, but it was close. She's drawing us one that might be more accurate."

"And what will you do with it?" Nicole clasped her hands in her lap.

Daniel's eyes met Holden's. "I'm not sure yet. We still need to talk about that."

Jax cut into his pie with the side of his fork. "Is this the case you always used in London as an excuse when Chase and I tried to set you up with someone on the weekends?" He started to lift the pie to his mouth, then glanced toward Daniel's office and lowered it to his plate.

Daniel shot his wife a sideways look. "It's the one I was working on in my spare time, yes."

"And you've finally found one of the kids? That's great, right?"

"It's … complicated."

Nicole rose abruptly. "I'll get the cream and sugar."

Christina stood too. "I'll help."

The two of them disappeared into the kitchen.

Holden tossed a helpless look in Daniel's direction.

Jax rested his fork on the edge of the plate. "I am trying to keep up with all the subtext happening around here, but it is not easy."

"Sorry, man." Daniel wiped his mouth with a napkin and tossed it onto the table. "You're right, there's a lot going on with us tonight."

Jax shook his head. "No need to apologize. It has been fascinating. Although, what is the deal with your sister-in-law?"

"You mean why isn't she throwing herself at you like every other woman you've met? Don't expect her to. That's not Mikayla."

Jax shook his head. "That is not what I meant. I am trying to figure her out, that's all. She is beautiful, of course, like Nicole. I have been watching—"

Daniel punched him in the upper arm. "Keep your eyes to yourself, buddy. I catch you checking out either of them and you'll be spending the next few nights at a shelter downtown. Or the hospital."

Holden winced. He'd been on the receiving end of one of Daniel's *light* punches before and he'd felt it for days afterwards.

Jax didn't flinch. He did reach out and clasp Daniel's arm. For the first time since Daniel had introduced him to Holden, Jax's face went serious. "I do not *check out* women, Daniel.

Especially not the wives or family members of my closest friends. You know me well enough to know this, right?"

Daniel hesitated a couple of seconds before the tension left his shoulders. "I guess I do. I'm sorry."

Jax squeezed his arm before letting go. "It is no problem. I understand." He held both hands in front of himself in a *check this out* gesture. "I know I can be intimidating to other men."

Daniel snorted a laugh. "Yeah, that must be it."

Holden laughed too. It felt good. *When was the last time I did that?*

The gleam had returned to Jax's eyes. "Still, your sister-in-law. She is a piece of work, no?"

Daniel threw him a look. "Easy."

Jax shrugged. "It is a compliment."

"What's a compliment?" Mikayla came into the room, brandishing the notebook Daniel had given her. He pushed his plate and mug out of the way and she set it in front of him.

Holden couldn't resist. "Jax was telling us what a piece of work you are. He claims it's a compliment."

Mikayla dug a fist into one hip. "How, exactly, is that a compliment?"

Jax looked completely unrepentant. "I meant it like art. A piece of *art*work. Whistler's Millie Finch, maybe."

Holden had to hand it to him. The guy could think fast on his feet. Even when he was sitting.

"Millie Finch had dark hair. I look nothing like her."

"That is true. Da Vinci's Female Head then. She was blond."

Mikayla rolled her eyes, but Holden suspected she was more than a little impressed. He certainly was.

Daniel touched her elbow. "This is great, Mik."

"I hope it helps. Andrew's a really sweet kid. I remember him, partly because of that white-blond hair, but also because he always smiled and said hi to my dad and me when we saw him walking home from school. If he was alone, he'd stop and talk for a while, which isn't that common for a ten or eleven-year-old boy. Most of the time he was with one or the other of his parents, and while they were definitely not as friendly as he was, nothing raised any red flags for me. I'd hate to think I might be causing anyone trouble."

"Keep in mind that, however good they are as parents, if this *is* Matthew Gibson, they didn't get him through legal channels."

"Neither did my parents." Mikayla's voice had gone quiet. "And if someone had come along and ripped me away from them, I never would have gotten over the trauma."

Daniel set down the sketchpad. "You're right. Thank you. That puts things in perspective."

Jax's dark eyes settled on Mikayla's face, but he didn't say anything.

Holden cleared his throat. "That's kind of my point. I think we should talk about the best way to handle this, not make any snap decisions." He rested a hand on Mikayla's back. "No one wants to make this situation worse than it is."

She managed a wan smile. "I know you don't."

"Excuse me for a moment." Jax sent Mikayla a look that she didn't return before disappearing into the hall in the direction of the washroom.

Daniel grimaced. "Sorry, Mik. Jax is a really great guy, just not opposed to stirring up trouble whenever possible."

"I gathered that," she said dryly.

Holden turned his knife over and over on the napkin. "Is he a believer?"

"Not yet. He was raised Catholic so he knows the truth, but something is keeping him from making it personal. He's curious though, asks a lot of questions."

Nicole came through the swinging kitchen doors, a creamer in one hand and a sugar bowl in the other. Christina came after her with spoons and more napkins, which she set in the center of the table before taking her seat beside Holden.

Jax wandered into the room and slid onto his chair.

Nicole stopped behind Daniel and peered over his shoulder. "Is that Matthew?"

"Maybe. Only DNA testing would be able to tell us for sure, but this Andrew definitely looks an awful lot like the sketch the police artist did."

"What are you going to do with it?"

He pointed to her chair with the notepad. "Why don't you and Mikayla sit before your ice cream melts and we can all discuss it."

Holden waited until everyone was well into pie and coffee before clearing his throat. "Someone should go to Chicago and check out this Andrew, see if we can find a way to prove whether or not he actually is Matthew Gibson. Then, when we know for sure, we can tell the police and let them take care of it. I think that would be the best way to handle this." He reached for his cup of coffee.

"No, you don't." Daniel held up his fork, crumbs flying.

Holden stopped, the mug halfway to his mouth. "What do you mean, I don't?"

"You don't think telling the police would be the best thing to do, not if everything looks good with his home life. As Mikayla pointed out, that would mean ripping a happy, healthy kid away from the only parents he knows and dragging him here, where his loser of a biological father is rotting in jail so he'd only go straight into the system. You'd never want to subject him to all that, would you, even if from a legal standpoint it's the right thing to do?"

Nicole clutched the spoon she'd used to stir her tea in a white-knuckled grip. Keeping his eyes on Holden, Daniel reached over and covered her hand with his. That loser of a biological father had not only abused his young son, he'd pulled the trigger and fired the bullet that had killed Gage that horrible night eight years earlier, and later abducted Jordan in an attempt to exact revenge on his dead father for taking Matthew from him.

Daniel's eyebrows rose.

Holden set his coffee on the table. "All right, no. I wouldn't."

"Okay. If we're going to figure this thing out, we need to be honest with each other—and ourselves—about what we believe would be the best thing to do here, for all concerned."

"I could go," Jax offered. "As a PI, I could poke around, do a little investigating. With Chase recovering from knee surgery, we've closed the business for a month, so it is good timing."

"Mik, maybe you and I should go too." Nicole let go of the spoon she'd been clutching. "You know the neighborhood where the Thompsons live, if they're still there. And you'd know Andrew if you saw him. It would go a lot faster if you went along to show those places to whoever else was going."

Daniel closed his fingers around hers. "Hold on now. What about … Jordan? And even if I do agree to this crazy plan, it likely wouldn't be wise for my wife to be involved in it."

Holden tapped a finger on the handle of his mug. What had Daniel been about to say? Was there another reason he didn't want Nicole to go that he wasn't willing to share with the rest of them? His stomach twisted. *God, don't let her be pregnant.* The prayer was an instinct, muscle memory, more than a heartfelt cry to the one he'd once felt so close to. It didn't matter. As usual, there was no response. Not that he didn't wish Nicole and Daniel every happiness, he did. But he wasn't sure Christina would be able to take watching her closest friend make plans to bring a baby into the world while her arms remained empty.

Nicole nodded. "You're probably right."

Daniel let go of her and picked up his fork again. "It's a big decision. It could take days or even weeks to find him and gather the evidence needed to prove who he is. If you can find him at all. That organization was good, not to mention highly connected. It won't be easy to uncover the trail of one of the kids, even if we have stumbled upon a big lead. Everyone should take time to think about this, and pray. I will too. And if I decide I can wait before handing over this information to my DS, we can figure out at that point who is going to go. Let's give it twenty-four hours then we'll talk again."

Everything in Holden screamed at him to volunteer, but he clutched the edge of his chair until his palm hurt to keep from speaking. It wasn't that he wanted to go so much as he felt he *had* to. Whether or not it was God sending him those dreams, they'd come to him for a reason. Someone was calling him to go find Matthew, to make sure he was okay. Even if his biological father didn't deserve it, Holden did feel for him. He knew what it was like to lose a son and no one deserved that kind of pain. On top of all that, he needed to know that his brother hadn't died for nothing. He had to go. But Daniel was right. He should pray about it. For all the good that would do. And, more than that, he should talk it over with Christina.

If she didn't want him to go, nothing would induce him to leave her side.

Chapter Eight

Natalya pressed her cell to one ear, plugging the other ear with a finger so she could hear over the murmur of voices and the whooshing of the subway as it sped through the network of tunnels beneath the city of Chicago. "Yes?"

"He suspects Andrew Thompson is Matthew Gibson."

Her heart skipped a beat. "Who does?"

"That detective, Daniel Grey."

Ah. That explained the uneasiness that had woken her several nights in a row. Natalya concentrated on the images whirring past the glass, broken into window-sized chunks of flashing pictures. "How?"

"His sister-in-law was there tonight, in his office. She recognized an aged drawing of Matthew Gibson as a kid who lived in her former neighborhood."

Natalya shifted her gaze to the old man across the aisle from her, his face nearly hidden by a *Chicago Tribune*. Huh. Did people actually still read newspapers? She lowered her voice. "Did the detective call it in?"

"No. Holden Kelly was there as well. He talked him into holding off."

Her chest tightened as the name of Gage Kelly's brother drifted over the line. "Why?"

"He said they should talk about it first, figure out the best thing to do."

"So no indication of what that might be?"

"Not yet."

She sighed. "All right. Thank you for letting me know."

"Do you want us to do anything else?"

"Only stay on top of this—let me know the moment you hear if they've decided to act on their suspicions."

"I will."

Natalya disconnected the call and cradled the phone in her lap with both hands. Her fingers trembled slightly, but she tightened them around the device to still them. *This isn't happening*. After almost eight years, she had begun to relax her guard, to believe that the children they had rescued might be safe. Daniel Grey was their only wild card. The one person who still seemed to have any interest in the cold cases. For years she had suspected he might still be investigating the cases on his own after he'd been suspended from the force. She hadn't been able to prove it, not until a few months ago when he'd made a call to the Denver P.D. where a member of their organization worked. That person had reported the call to her to confirm that, while he had nothing concrete to go on, Detective Grey hadn't stopped trying to find the kids Gage and his predecessor on the Toronto missions, Ted Stiller, had rescued.

Three days later, Natalya had sent someone into Nicole's condo when none of them were there to tap his phone and wire his office. Only his office. She did have some scruples. It would be entirely unethical of them to listen in on conversations or activity taking place in any other part of the condo.

The detective often worked in his home office. And he was as squeaky-clean as they came. Although he hadn't reported the possibility that Matthew Gibson might have been located to his superiors. Not immediately, anyway.

She rested her head against the side of the subway car. That was uncharacteristic of the by-the-book Detective Grey. The only other time she'd known him to bend the law was the night he had sent the police in the wrong direction when they were chasing after Matthew Gibson. The night Gage Kelly had been gunned down in the street. Natalya bit her lip, fighting the surge of emotion that still rose when she thought of Gage. She lifted her head, her jaw tight. She wouldn't think of him. If all the good they had done over the years was being threatened, she needed to keep a clear mind. She would request the transcript of the conversation between the detective and Gage's brother. Holden must have done some pretty fast talking to have convinced Grey to hold off on making that call. What was Holden's stake in this?

She sighed. Her men were good. Before the detective, or Holden, or anyone else could ever act, she would know about it.

And when she did, she could decide what she was going to do to counter whatever move any of them might be foolish enough to make.

Chapter Nine

Holden found Christina the next morning in the nursery they'd set up when she was five months pregnant with their son. His chest squeezed as he leaned against the doorframe and watched her. She stood, both hands gripping the rails of the crib, staring into the vast quiet emptiness of it.

A month after their son's death, he'd asked her if she wanted him to remove the baby things from the room. "No," she'd said curtly, with no more explanation than that as she rearranged the teddy bears propped against the colorful cushions on the window seat. He didn't push her.

Two months later, when she sat in the rocking chair in the corner, her tear-stained cheeks a sickening contrast to the cheerful, prancing farm animal decals they'd stuck onto the freshly-painted blue walls behind her, he'd broken the vow he'd made to himself not to ask her again. Kneeling in front of her, he rested his hands on the arms of the chair, not quite touching her. "Please, Chris," he'd begged. "Let me take this stuff away. I won't get rid of it, I'll put it in storage."

She hadn't said no this time. She hadn't said anything. Her fingers continued to knead the white blanket in her lap, the one her grandmother had made for her when she was a baby. The one she'd long dreamed of tucking around her small son when she put him to bed at night, smelling of talcum powder, curls damp from his bath.

The silence had dug into the still-raw wound in his chest and he'd nodded, pushed to his feet, and left her alone in the room.

So Holden hesitated in the doorway today, reluctant to disturb her when she was in the company of her memories, but needing to speak with her about traveling to Chicago to try and find Matthew Gibson. "Chris?"

She glanced at him over her shoulder. She wasn't crying, but her eyes were rimmed with red, as though she had been, or was fighting the urge. "You're going, aren't you?"

Holden stepped into the room. "I'm thinking about it, but I wanted to talk it over with you."

"Why?" She reached out and straightened the soft white blanket.

He took another step closer. "Because I care what you think. If you want me to stay here, I won't leave you." Two more steps and he stood beside her. His elbow brushed hers lightly.

Christina turned and leaned against the rails, crossing her arms over her chest. In jeans, a light pink T-shirt, and a ponytail, she looked like a teenager. "Why haven't you?"

"Why haven't I what?"

"Left me. I know I'm hurting you, Holden. I know I'm not being any kind of wife to you. But I can't seem to let go of …" Her voice broke and she unfolded her arms and pressed a fist to her mouth.

He felt sick. On top of everything, she'd been worrying that he would leave her? *Don't you know me better than that?* He faced his wife, resting a hip against the bars of the crib. Everything in him longed to pull her to him and hold her until the invisible chasm between them closed. When his arm started to move, she stiffened. Holden gripped the top of the railing to keep from reaching for her anyway. "I'm not going anywhere. Even if I do go on this trip, I'll come back to you. You're my wife. I love you, and I will never give up on us." The words struck him with the force of a hundred-mile-an-hour fastball to the head. Was that what the message in the dream was about?

"Never is a long time," she said flatly.

Holden had to get through to her somehow. He released the wooden bar and took her face in his hands. Every muscle in her body remained tense, calcified, but she didn't break away. "I can't tell you how to grieve, love, or for how long. That's something you have to work out for yourself. In the meantime, whether I'm here or in Chicago, I'll be waiting for you."

Christina bit her lower lip. When her eyes met his, for the first time in six months a shutter didn't drop over them and she didn't turn away. Holden froze, aware of the fragility of the connection, a veil of bubble stretched across the small round hole of a wand, breathtakingly beautiful but vulnerable to the slightest movement.

She gave him five seconds before she drew in a shuddering breath, stepped away, and the bubble shattered.

Holden lowered his hands, still warm from her skin, to his sides. "So are you okay if I go?"

"Why do you want to?"

It wasn't much, but that single question reflected more interest in his life—in anything, actually—than she'd shown in months. Holden would take it. "It's not that I want to, more like I need to. I've been having these dreams for weeks …"

"I know. I hear you some nights, talking in your sleep."

"What do I say?"

"Not a lot. 'Hey', sometimes. Or 'Stop'. Enough that I've figured out you're chasing someone. Is it him? Matthew?"

"I think so. I can't make out his face when I'm dreaming, but as soon as I saw that picture last night, it clicked that it was him. Even though I'm not able to catch him in the dream, he seems to be telling me not to give up."

"On him?"

Or on you. "Maybe. I haven't quite figured that part out yet."

"And you think this trip will help you to do that."

"I hope so."

A shudder moved through her. "Then you should go."

"Are you sure?"

Her laugh didn't hold a trace of humor. "I haven't been sure of a single thing since Tristan …"

A fiery dart ripped through him. The last time she'd said their son's name was before they had lost him. She'd written it once, numbly and in shaky handwriting, on the form they'd set in front of her at the funeral home. *Tristan Jacob Kelly.* Holden had offered to fill it out, but she'd waved him away with a trembling hand.

Christina swallowed hard. "Can you get the time off?"

"I think so. I've got a few weeks of vacation time coming."

"So you're set."

"Will you be all right?"

She lifted slender shoulders. "I'll be working. And Nic will come if I text her."

Which didn't answer his question. "I'll be a phone call away at all times. If you need me, I'll be on the next plane."

The shutters did drop over her eyes then. Her nod was wooden, perfunctory. She hadn't moved, but she was withdrawing again, to some place deep inside herself where he couldn't follow. He felt the ending of their brief, tenuous reunion like another death.

"I hope you find what you're looking for, Holden." Christina pressed her stomach to the bars and stared into the perfectly-made up, never-been-used crib.

Holden contemplated his wife another minute, caught in a beam of sunlight that made her hair glow like fire. *I hope we both do. Before it's too late.*

Christina stared into the crib until Holden's footsteps sounded on the stairs. Her throat ached, but she refused to allow another tear to slip from beneath her eyelids.

He was going then. For a few days, or weeks, maybe, he would be free of her. Out from under the thick blanket of tension and silence that had draped itself over their house the day they returned from the hospital, empty-handed. The day Holden had tried to sneak the baby seat from the car to the closet in the nursery without her seeing. The day she had pretended not to.

Would he come back?

That was the question. Once he had escaped this house that had become a mausoleum—got out and breathed fresh air again, spent time with people who laughed and touched and talked about mundane things that still mattered to them—why would he willingly choose to return?

In spite of his reassurances, it was possible he wouldn't. And she couldn't blame him.

Christina lifted her face to the bright sunlight streaming through the window. *God, help me. I don't want to lose him too.*

No response. Not even the slightest breeze to ruffle the red and white striped curtains that hung on either side of the glass.

She turned from the light and wandered over to the dresser she and Holden had brought home from a thrift store and finished and painted themselves. After hours of work, failed attempts, do-overs, and laughter, they'd stood and admired their achievement. Holden, grinning broadly, had tapped his paint-laden brush against the tip of her nose then grabbed her brush and held both of them above his head to keep her from retaliating.

A smile tugged at the corner of her mouth at the memory. The movement felt strange, foreign, and she dropped it quickly as she riffled through the stack of cards on the dresser. They were full of condolences, which she appreciated, and advice, which she resented. She understood the sentiments, had offered them to others herself on numerous occasions. Encouragement from Scripture, assurances that this too would pass, that God was in control and had a plan, that all of this would only make her stronger. Assertions that God had taken their son because He needed another angel in heaven, that they would have more children to replace this one. Chills swept through her and she scooped up the pile, shoved it into the top drawer, and slammed it shut.

Christina wandered to the side of the crib, ran her fingers over the spot where Holden had gripped the bar.

Lifting her hand to her face, she stood for a long time, pressing it to her cheek and clinging to the memory of the strong, warm touch of his skin against hers.

Chapter Ten

Mikayla paced the studio she'd set up in one corner of the living room in her tiny apartment on the west side of Toronto. Should she go? Leigh, her agent, had been pressuring her to come to Chicago for weeks now. Her first art show had been such a success that it had spawned several others, including one being held at the Windsong Gallery this spring. The owner had called Leigh several times, asking if Mikayla planned to make an appearance at some point, but she had been putting it off. Maybe she should go—schmooze a little—for the sake of her career.

And it did make sense for her to accompany Holden on his quest, given that she knew the neighborhood and was the only one of them who had seen Andrew Thompson in the last eight years. But still …

She stopped and turned a slow circle in the middle of the room. Half-finished canvases filled the space, their splashes of bright color bringing a smile to her face in spite of her inner turmoil. Leigh was likely thinking of her coming to Chicago for a couple of days, not a couple of weeks. She might not be happy if Mikayla took off for an extended period of time and didn't complete at least a few new pieces soon. Mikayla stopped turning. To be fair, it wasn't Leigh who pressured her to produce, it was herself. Leigh always told her to let her muse guide her or something to that effect. Mikayla grimaced. She preferred to say it was the Holy Spirit guiding her, since she believed God was the one who had gifted her with any artistic ability she might have. When she said things like that, however, Leigh tended to stare at her blankly for a few seconds before shrugging, as if to say, *whatever gets the work done.*

So work wasn't an insurmountable barrier. The fact that Jax

Rodriguez would probably be going might be. Mikayla bit her lip. Spending days or weeks in the company of a man who clearly delighted in driving her crazy did not sound like a productive use of her time. She'd drawn the picture—Daniel could send it with Jax. If the man did have any actual PI skills, which she doubted, he could track down one young kid on his own after she'd given him a picture and pointed him in the direction of Andrew's neighborhood. Right?

With a loud exhalation of breath, Mikayla reached for the brush sitting in water and dabbed it in red paint. For a long moment, she stood in front of the easel, staring at the blank canvas. No inspiration came to her, not from a muse or the Holy Spirit or anyone else. *Paint something, anything. It'll come to you.*

Mikayla touched the tip of the brush to the canvas. The loud buzzing of the phone startled her and her hand jerked. A three-inch line of red streaked across the white. She pressed her lips together tightly to keep a word she shouldn't be saying from spilling out as she tugged the phone from the back pocket of her jeans and stabbed at the button. "What?"

"Mik?"

Mikayla sighed. "Leigh, hi. Sorry." What were the chances her agent would call her at the exact moment she was debating about going to Chicago? She glanced at the ceiling. *A little on the nose, don't you think?*

"No worries. Did I catch you at a bad time? Were you working?"

"Trying to." She set the phone on a nearby table and eyed the canvas warily. She'd have to start over. Unless she could use the streak somehow, in a sunset, maybe, or a field of flowers. She studied the line of paint. Yes, she could probably …

"Hello? Mik?"

Mikayla blinked. Was she still talking to Leigh? She grabbed the device, turned off the speaker, and pressed it to her ear. "Sorry. Got a little distracted there."

"I understand. And if you're that deep into something I

definitely don't want to disturb you. But I did want to let you know that Greg Myers at Windsong called me again. He would appreciate you coming by in person. Ideally, he'd love for you to show up for one event that they would invite the press, investors, and critics to a week before the show opens. And if you're there for opening night, they'll play it up in the media, do a fancy wine and cheese thing, the works. I know you're still trying to get your new life going in the wilds of Canada, but I truly believe this is a valuable opportunity you should not miss at this stage of your career."

A thought struck Mikayla and she frowned. "Did Nicole put you up to this?"

"Your sister? Of course not. What would she be doing arranging for you to be part of an art show?"

Mikayla chewed on the inside of her cheek. Leigh sounded genuinely confused. She could play innocent like nobody Mikayla knew, but even she wasn't that good an actor. "So you didn't know I was considering coming to Chicago?"

A clacking sound came over the line. Mikayla grinned, picturing her agent's multiple earrings knocking against each other as she shook her head emphatically. "No, I had no idea. But I'm absolutely thrilled to hear it." The delight in her agent's voice did sound genuine. This call, and the invitation to appear at an art gallery in her home town, had to be completely unrelated to the Andrew Thompson situation. A coincidence. *Or is it?*

Mikayla dropped the brush into a jar of water and massaged her temples with her free hand. "When is the opening?" *Say June. Say June.* If the opening wasn't for a month and a half, it would make no sense for her to go to Chicago now.

"They haven't confirmed the date yet because they've been waiting to see if you were coming. He's hoping for the second week of May, as he's planning on displaying your watercolors from then until the end of the month."

She bit her lip, calculating. Since today was April 25th, it was pushing it, but the timing might work out. As Daniel had suggested, it could very well take two or three weeks for them to find Andrew. And Jax did say he had a month off. She repressed a sigh. "All right. I'll come." *No changing her mind now.*

"Wonderful, darling. I'll send you all the details. And Mik?"

"Yes?"

"Apparently there's already a lot of buzz around this show. Can you bring more pieces?"

Mikayla glanced around the room. "I have a few here that might work."

"I can't wait to see them. Or you." Leigh ended the call.

Mikayla set the phone on the table. If Daniel agreed to let them go on this crazy search for Andrew Thompson, they'd likely leave within a couple of days, say by Tuesday. That meant, if the opening was the Friday or Saturday of the second week in May, they'd be in the States almost three weeks. A lot of time for her to be in the company of a man she barely knew. Maybe this wasn't such a great idea after all. Although it sounded like Holden wanted to go too. Her shoulders relaxed a little.

For several minutes she stood staring out the window at the gray day, the drizzle trickling down the outside of the glass and pooling on the sill. It might be nice to go to Chicago. She hadn't been there since she'd moved to Toronto four months ago. She could visit friends and her favorite haunts, and of course Leigh's advice was right, if characteristically self-serving. Mikayla grinned wryly. The art show was a great opportunity. Sales had slowed a bit since she'd left the windy city—maybe this was the impetus she needed to kick-start her career.

An image of Jax Rodriguez's face flashed through her mind, his dark eyes teasing, challenging. Mikayla rested her forehead against the cool glass, barely resisting the urge to bang her head against the window a few times.

Or it could be the biggest mistake she had ever made.

Chapter Eleven

Holden tossed his bag into the trunk of Jax's metallic-black Porsche 928. He let out a low whistle as he ran his fingers lightly along the side of the classic vehicle. What was it, a '94, '95? *Must be pretty good money in the investigating business these days.* He shoved the slightly resentful thought away. His job was a calling. He was a social worker because he wanted to help kids, not because he wanted to get rich. Which was good, because between his salary and Christina's, that wasn't going to happen any time soon.

A strong hand clamped onto his shoulder and Holden jumped. "All set?"

He turned to face his brother-in-law. Given the circumstances, Daniel was being incredibly supportive of this crazy venture. "I think so."

"Good." Daniel's blue eyes met his. "No pressure, but I'm placing a lot of trust in you here."

"I know."

"I want daily reports on what is going on. If you do find Matthew Gibson, I need your word that you will let me know right away so we can figure out the best way to handle that. And if you encounter a remotely dangerous situation, you are to remove yourselves immediately and contact me, or the local authorities if it's urgent. Understood?"

Holden nodded. "Understood."

Daniel dropped his hand. "Mik." He enveloped his sister-in-law in a bear hug. "I appreciate your help with this, but I want you to be careful, okay? Nicole will never forgive me if anything happens to you."

She moved out of his embrace and brushed the hair from her face. "I will."

Daniel looked at Jax and jerked his head toward the sidewalk. "Can I have a word?"

"Sure." Jax followed him a few feet away and the two of them huddled together.

Holden watched them for a few seconds. *What's that about?* He blew out a breath. They were the experts—no doubt they were talking shop, devising a strategy. Either that or Daniel was warning him about crossing any kind of line with Mikayla. A wry grin crossed his face. If Jax did and Daniel found out about it, he wouldn't want to be in Jax's shoes, even given the cool vehicle and the whole exotic Latino thing.

Mikayla touched his elbow. "Should we wait in the car?"

Since he couldn't hear anything Daniel or Jax was saying anyway, Holden nodded and held out his hand. "You want shotgun?"

"No." The word came out forcefully and her cheeks colored. "I mean, I didn't sleep well last night, so I might try to grab a nap in the back seat."

He glanced from her to Jax. It was doubtful lack of sleep was her motivation for wanting to sit as far from their resident PI as possible. *This is going to be interesting.* Holden pulled open the door of the car and waited until she had climbed into the back before jumping into the passenger seat. The car was small and his knees banged the dashboard as he settled onto the leather seat. Their eight-hour drive to Chicago—not including the time it would take to cross the border and stop to eat and use the facilities—was not going to be a terribly comfortable one, especially since he couldn't move the seat back with Mikayla behind him.

Not that anything in his life was comfortable these days. He sighed and propped his knees against the glove box. Christina had still been asleep when his alarm had gone off that morning and he'd silenced it quickly. Although he'd studied her for a few moments, her breathing had stayed deep and even, her face half-covered by the thick duvet on their bed. Everything in him had longed to wake her, to tell her how much he'd miss her and kiss her good-bye, but she looked so peaceful he couldn't bring himself to disturb her.

The driver's side door flew open and Jax slid behind the wheel. "Ready to hit the road?"

"Yep." Holden reached for the seat belt.

Mikayla mumbled something that Jax must have understood as assent, because he nodded. "Good. Then we will roll, yes?"

He appeared to be waiting for a response, so Holden obligingly gave him a thumbs up. "Yes, let's roll."

Daniel stood on the sidewalk outside his window and Holden offered him a small salute as the Porsche pulled away from the curb. For better or worse, they were on their way.

Fifteen minutes from the border, Jax grew quiet. Holden cast several sidelong glances at him, but Jax gripped the steering wheel tightly and stared straight ahead. *What is that about?* When they crossed the bridge to the States and pulled into the security checkpoint line-up, his hold on the wheel tightened until his knuckles grew white.

Holden retrieved their passports from the glove box. "You okay, man?"

Jax released the steering wheel with one hand long enough to yank off his sunglasses and toss them onto the dash. "Fine."

After a few minutes' wait, the light turned green and Jax pulled the Porsche to the booth and hit the button to lower his window. Mikayla leaned over and did the same. The border protection officer, a male in his early thirties dressed in a navy shirt and ball cap, stared at Jax a moment before holding out his hand. Holden passed Jax their passports and he handed them over to the officer, who scrutinized them before lifting his gaze to Jax again. "Reason for entering the States?"

Jax pointed over his shoulder with his thumb. "We're taking our friend to Chicago. She's part of a show there."

The man ducked his head to study Mikayla. "What kind of show?"

"An art show." Mikayla held a piece of paper over the seat. Jax took it and gave it to the man. Thankfully, Mikayla's art show was a good cover, since they couldn't explain the other reason they were heading to Illinois. Her agent had managed to get her name and pictures of several of her pieces inserted into the pamphlet on short notice before scanning it and sending it to Mikayla so she'd have it to show at the border. Helpful, since she'd couriered her work to the gallery so they had no physical evidence they were telling the truth.

Holden studied the man questioning them. His job, part of the last line of defence for his country, was tough. Given the hard set of his features, he took his responsibilities seriously. Good thing they had the pamphlet for the art show, since it looked as though he was not going to let them go through easily, even with it.

The officer returned the brochure to Jax, along with two of the passports. Jax passed them over to Holden. He glanced at them. His and Mikayla's. Was the guy not going to give Jax his?

The man focused his attention on Jax, his eyes cold. "Are you a Canadian citizen?"

"You have my pass—"

"Answer the question," he said sharply.

Jax's jaw tightened. "Yes."

"Place of birth?"

"Toronto."

The officer looked skeptical. His gaze swept the vehicle. "Nice car." It was an accusation, not a compliment. Jax didn't respond.

"Ownership."

Jax sighed and nodded at the glove box. "In there, blue folder." He'd toned down the Spanish accent, but couldn't lose the trace of it that threaded through his words.

Holden opened the box and withdrew a small plastic folder. He held it out to Jax, who tugged the piece of paper loose. "Here." He reached through the window to give it to the officer.

The man typed something into his computer, his eyes darting from the paper in his hand to the computer screen. After a few seconds, he returned the ownership to Jax and said something into the microphone on his shoulder. Holden couldn't hear most of it, but he caught the word *dogs. Seriously?*

"Looks like you cross the border often. Attend a lot of art shows, do you?"

"No, I travel to the States for work."

"And what kind of *work* is that?" The man didn't make air quotes with his fingers, but he may as well have. Holden frowned.

"I'm a private investigator, specializing in missing persons cases, which takes me across the border several times a year."

"Ten."

"Pardon me?"

"You crossed ten times last year. Six already this year. Seems excessive."

"A lot of people go missing every year."

The officer couldn't have appeared less concerned about that. "Do you have your PI license?"

Jax leaned forward to tug the wallet from his pocket. After flipping it open, he removed a plastic card and handed it through the open window.

When he had finished perusing it and Jax had returned the card to his wallet, the officer lifted his gaze above the car and signaled to another border protection officer approaching from Holden's side. The newcomer held the leashes of two dogs tightly as he led them around the vehicle.

"Any other papers?"

Jax shook his head. "No. I was born in Canada. I have no other papers."

What is going on here? Holden contemplated the officer. He'd crossed the border a hundred times and never been interrogated like this.

"What are you coming into the US for?"

Jax took a deep breath. "I told you, we're taking our friend to her art show in Chicago."

The man shifted his gaze to Mikayla again. "So you're going with these men of your own volition, ma'am?"

She frowned. "Of course. Like he told you, they're friends of mine."

"And you are an American citizen?"

"Yes, but I live in Toronto now."

The man with the dogs flipped his hand at the one in the booth, presumably an all-clear signal, before walking away. Although Holden didn't think for a second that Jax had drugs stored anywhere in his vehicle, the muscles in his shoulders still relaxed a little as the man guided the dogs into the low brick building that housed immigration.

The officer in the booth pursed his lips, clearly disappointed. He swung his gaze back to Jax. "How long do you plan to be in the country?"

"About three weeks."

Holden held his breath. They hadn't decided how long they would be in the US, not exactly. The date of Mikayla's show opening hadn't been set yet, but according to her agent it would be sometime the second week of May. What would Jax say if the man pushed him on that?

The officer's eyes narrowed. "That's mighty vague. What day do you plan to return?"

"We're not sure. The opening is sometime the second week of May, and we'll leave shortly after it happens."

The man reached out and gripped the window frame. "If you can't offer me anything more definite than *sometime* or *shortly*, maybe you need to go in and talk to immigration. Is that what you want to do?"

Jax's jaw worked. "No."

"Then give me a straight answer. What day do you plan to leave the United States?"

For a moment, Jax didn't speak. When he did, he ground out the words. "May 15th."

Holden pursed his lips. The Saturday at the end of the second week of May. That gave them almost three full weeks. Should be enough time. Hopefully the opening would happen before that or Jax might need to drive home and leave the two of them to fly. He was tempted to glance at Mikayla for confirmation, but he probably shouldn't risk it.

The officer stared at Jax for a few seconds. "May 15th. No longer." He entered something into the computer. "I'm putting it on your record that you will leave the United States by that date. See that you do." He smacked the passport on the window frame. "Have a nice day."

Jax didn't respond, only took the passport, flipped it into Holden's lap, and eased past the guard's window. As they pulled out from under the cover and followed the signs for I-69 west, Jax shot a sideways look at Holden, probably anticipating the questions he was dying to ask. "It happens sometimes. I'm used to it." He shrugged, as though it didn't bother him. *Which is clearly not true.* Getting used to something wasn't the same as being okay with it. Before Holden could probe further, Jax stabbed at the button to turn on the radio.

Holden took the hint—the man didn't want to discuss it. He crossed his arms over his chest. Maybe he'd get a bit of sleep himself. Not long after Holden had closed his eyes, Jax turned the music off, and the three of them traveled in silence for the next couple of hours.

Chapter Twelve

The phone on her desk vibrated and Natalya snatched it up, impatient. "Yes?"

"They are on their way. They crossed into the US thirty minutes ago."

"Who is coming?"

"Holden Kelly, Mikayla Grant, and Jax Rodriguez."

Her eyes narrowed. "Jax Rodriguez?"

"Yes, a PI and former partner of Detective Daniel Grey. They definitely suspect that the boy is in Chicago."

Natalya propped an elbow on her desk and rubbed her temple with the fingers of her free hand. Was their carefully-constructed tower of cards about to come crashing to the ground around them? "Where are they now?"

"Six hours from Chicago. Still driving, so they are likely planning to arrive this evening."

She mulled that over. Was there a way to stop them from reaching the city? They could arrange an accident easily enough. Likely their best bet. Still, someone could be hurt. The thought made her weary. So many had been hurt …

"Would you like us to stop them?"

She sighed. "No. For now we will only watch them. Andrew Thompson is largely out of sight these days. It is unlikely they will be able to find him. But keep a close eye on them. If you believe they have spotted him, let me know immediately. We will take whatever actions are necessary to stop them at that point."

"So we won't remove him from Chicago?"

She resisted the urge to sigh again. The people who worked for her, who were as committed to the cause as she was, were looking to her for decisive answers and directives. And the children they had rescued needed her to be strong as well, to protect them from ever being discovered and removed from the homes where they had found happiness and security after years of abuse and neglect. Natalya straightened. She wouldn't fail them. She couldn't.

"Not yet. As you know, his situation is uncertain at the moment. I don't wish to add to his distress by causing more upheaval in his life. Not unless it becomes absolutely necessary. Watch his house carefully and report any activity, either by him and his father or this new threat. I wish to hear of anything as it happens."

"Yes, ma'am."

"And let me know where they will be staying in the area."

"I'll call again as soon as I know."

"Thank you." Natalya disconnected the call and set the phone on the desk. Holden Kelly. Somehow she had known he would come, that one day the two of them would meet. Since the moment she had read his file, and the one of his brother Gage, her life had somehow become intertwined with theirs, so tightly entangled that, even now, she struggled to deal with Gage's death and her part in it. As expert as she was in compartmentalizing her feelings, Gage Kelly was the only person she had encountered in her life who hadn't allowed her to do so, not completely. She suspected she would have the same strong reaction to the brother who was so like him—in character and in appearance.

How and when their paths would cross in person was yet to be determined. But it was only a matter of time. If Holden was as determined as his brother, it would take a great deal to stop him from accomplishing his mission.

Sooner or later they would meet. The only question that remained to be answered was which of them would survive the encounter when they did.

Chapter Thirteen

Mikayla woke when the steady thrum of the engine that had lulled her to sleep suddenly cut out. She opened her eyes and blinked against the bright sunlight streaming through the window. Leaning closer to the glass, she stared at a stand of trees with picnic tables scattered between them. "Where are we?"

Jax twisted to look at her over the seat. "At a rest stop one hour from Lansing. There is a service center here so we can get something to eat. Are you hungry, Grant?"

Mikayla swallowed. Somehow everything the man said rang with double entendre. It had to be that accent. And *Grant*? Did she mind him calling her by her last name? No one ever had before. The idea of him being the only one sent an odd rush of warmth through her chest. "I could eat something, yes."

When Holden flipped the seat forward and held out his hand, Mikayla took it and clambered out of the vehicle, grateful for his support as her legs were stiff from sitting so long. A cool breeze whistled through the trees and she stopped and tipped up her face, allowing it to flow across her skin and drive away the last of the drowsiness clinging to her from her nap.

"Beautiful, no?"

Jax's voice yanked her back from her reverie and she opened her eyes. It *was* beautiful here, with rolling green lawn extending past rows of maple trees beginning to bud in the warmth of the sun. Birds trilled in the branches, no doubt thrilled that winter appeared to be over and spring had come once again.

As it always does. In the dead of winter, it was easy to believe that it might not return, that the snow would never thaw and the arctic wind would howl around buildings and trees and people forever. Still, spring did come, every year, a reminder that all hard things did pass, with time. Mikayla's throat tightened. Grief over her parents' death almost two years before still washed over her without warning sometimes. The desperate ache in her chest, the gaping void in her life, had not yet eased and she couldn't imagine it ever would. At best, the time between onslaughts of emotion was gradually lengthening.

"Grant?" Jax spoke so close to her ear that she could feel the warmth of his breath brushing against her cheek. "You are okay?"

"Of course." Her gaze found Holden's. He stood on the far side of the car, hands clasped on the roof as though waiting for her. Her cheeks warmed. How long had she been standing there, lost in thought? "I could use a coffee. Shall we go in?"

Inside the service center, they ordered food and drinks and carried their plastic trays out to a picnic table in the sun. Mikayla settled on the bench. "It's so lovely here. I could pitch a tent under those trees and spend the night."

Jax paused in the process of unwrapping the plastic from a roast beef sandwich and raised an eyebrow. "You camp?"

"I haven't for years." Mikayla unwrapped her own ham and cheese sandwich. "But my dad used to take me when I was a kid and I loved it."

"Why did you stop?"

She took a bite of the sandwich and chewed thoughtfully before swallowing. "I got older. As a teen, it didn't seem as cool camping with my dad. Then I got busy with my artwork and now he's gone so …" She cleared her throat to rid it of the lump that had formed there. "I guess my camping days are over."

Jax touched the side of his hand to hers. "I'm sorry."

Mikayla waved her sandwich through the air. "Me and Holden. A couple of orphans." It took everything she had to keep her voice light.

Holden paused, the French fries he'd been about to shove into his mouth hovering in mid-air. The smile that crossed his face was grim. "That's right, a regular Oliver Twist and Annie, that's us."

It helped to joke, although technically Mikayla wasn't an orphan. The parents who had raised her, whom she believed to be her biological mother and father, weren't her parents after all, something she had found out after their deaths. Her birth parents had long believed her to be dead after she'd been abducted from a park shortly before she and Nicole turned three. Mikayla had spoken to them by phone several times since the Toronto P.D. had found her in Chicago six months ago, but they had a long way to go in restoring the relationship that had been lost for so long. The fact that they had essentially abandoned Nicole after the abduction because the sight of her was too painful for them was not helping the healing process in any way.

Mikayla tugged a piece of wilted lettuce from her sandwich and dropped it onto the plastic wrap. "How about you, Jax? Any family?"

He hesitated, a slight shadow flickering over his face before he responded. "Only *mi mamá*."

"Where does she live?"

"She is still in Toronto. I come see her as much as I can."

Mikayla nodded. "That's good. Don't waste a moment. I promise you'll regret it if you do."

She didn't look at him as she reached for her bottle of water, but she felt his eyes on her. They'd rested on her at Daniel and Nicole's the other night too, when she'd mentioned that her parents hadn't gotten her through legal channels. For a man who knew how to talk, when he did choose to stop—and somehow, he always seemed to know the right time—his silence, and those intense eyes contemplating her, said far more than most people did with words. Mikayla shoved her sandwich into the paper bag, her appetite gone. "I'm going to take a short walk while you guys finish. I'll meet you at the car, okay?"

Before either of them could answer, she scrambled off the bench and strode to a nearby garbage can. Empty cups and crumpled take-out bags littered the ground around the can, a stark contrast to the natural beauty around it. *People ruin everything.* Mikayla grimaced at the cynical assertion. Cynical, but in many ways true. That drunk driver had definitely destroyed the beautiful family she'd grown up in when he'd decided to climb behind the wheel that day. She tried to push the thought—and the sour smell—away from her consciousness as she shoved her bag into the receptacle and stumbled through the trees toward the rolling lawn beyond.

Her heart thudded in her chest. *No. Not here. Not now.* A wooden fence bordered the property. Mikayla stopped when she reached it and gripped the top rail in both hands as she drew in several long, deep breaths. *It's okay. You're fine. This is in your head. It's not real.* Through a thickening fog, Mikayla summoned every phrase her counselor had instructed her to say to herself when emotions crashed through her with such intensity she felt as though she must be having a heart attack. *You're fine. Breathe.*

After several long minutes, her heart rate slowed enough that blood no longer pounded in her ears. Mikayla turned and slumped against the fence. *Father, help me. I miss them so much. Thank you that they're with you. That they're with each other. That they will never suffer or be sad again.* Another strategy, expressing gratitude, almost always proved effective at keeping the darkness at bay, and as she listed one thing after another, the heavy clouds slowly lifted.

Through the trees, she caught a glimpse of Holden and Jax walking to the car. Drawing in a final deep breath, Mikayla pushed away from the fence and went to join them.

No one spoke for the next few miles, until Jax slid an arm along the top of the seat. "I used to camp too. Many times as a child. I was excellent."

Mikayla snorted a laugh. No one could accuse the man of being short on confidence, that was for sure. "Of course you were. Who did you camp with?"

"The boy scouts. Me and my … friends, we were scouts."

Her eyes narrowed. What had he been about to say? "So you

can build a fire with two sticks, construct rabbit traps, catch fish with your bare hands, that sort of thing?"

"Naturally. I learned all of that. I had to, because they would dump us in the woods miles from our destination and we had to survive for days with no shelter or supplies as we made our way to the site."

"That doesn't exactly sound legal." Holden shifted in his seat. Poor guy. Jax's car was cool, but it definitely wasn't designed for passengers over six feet tall. Mikayla would switch places with him, but her position was even worse, especially since both men had pushed their seats back as far as they would go.

"Maybe not, but it was a lot of fun. And, as you can see"— Jax pointed a finger at himself— "I survived. Those days in the woods, they made me a man." His eyes, gleaming with mischief, met Mikayla's in the rear-view mirror.

Time to bring him down a peg or two. "Prove it."

"Prove what?"

"Your superior outdoor training. When we get to Chicago, let's camp. It would save us a lot of money, and it would be a shame to waste all those skills of yours on a hotel room."

Holden twisted to look at her. "It still gets pretty cold at night. And we don't have any supplies."

Jax studied her in the mirror. Clearly he understood her words to be the challenge she'd intended them to be. "We could buy a few things. We would not need so much, some warm sleeping bags, a camp stove, food, and two tents. We'd be all set." He swatted Holden's arm with the back of his hand. "Let's do this. It will be fun. I can teach you what you need to know, city boy."

"Hey," Holden protested. "I know how to camp. Gage and I had a set of foster parents for a few years who were actually pretty cool. They used to take us camping every weekend in the summer."

"It is settled then." Jax returned his hand to the wheel. "When we get to Chicago, we will camp."

What had she done? In an attempt to call Jax's bluff, she'd ended up committing herself to sleeping on the hard ground and foraging for meals for the next few days or weeks. *Three at the most.* Mikayla's grin faded at the memory of the grilling Jax had endured at the border. She reached for her phone. Might as well find a good camping spot while they were driving. Preferably one with good shower facilities.

After all, she did need to look presentable. She shot a look at the front seat. Not for anyone she knew, of course, but for the art show. So she could look like a professional when she went to the gallery to schmooze with potential customers.

No other reason than that.

Chapter Fourteen

Mikayla followed Holden into the biggest outdoor warehouse she'd ever seen in her life. It was called The Great Nature Adventure Store, and she could see why. Somehow, she felt more like she was outside after walking into the building than she had when she was in the parking lot. Trees appeared to be growing out of the cement floor everywhere she looked, and animals peered from branches and the tops of shelves. Fake ones, she hoped, although they looked disconcertingly real. Bird calls played over the speaker system, punctuated by the occasional clap of thunder, the pattering of rain, or the growl of what she could only assume was a bear, given that the store was located in Illinois where wild cats were at a minimum.

She felt like a child, staring in wide-eyed wonder at the wilderness they'd wandered into. For a city kid, the place felt like a foreign country.

Jax clapped his hands. "Ah, the great outdoors. Feels like coming home."

Mikayla resisted the urge to roll her eyes. "Didn't you grow up in Toronto?"

"*Sí.* Mostly." He lifted a compass from a box on a shelf and examined it. "But as I told you, I also spent a lot of time in the woods. I did not know how much I missed it until this moment."

Holden pointed to a long row, past a massive waterfall that fell into a pond filled with goldfish that all looked to be at least six inches long. "I see a sign for cook stoves. I'll grab one of those and some propane if you guys want to look for the tents."

Before Mikayla could protest, he had ducked around the rocks lining the fish pond and taken off in search of a stove. Exhaling, she scanned the signs, carved out of wood, that jutted out the end of each aisle.

"There." Jax touched her back lightly. "Looks like camping gear is in aisle three."

Mikayla nodded and started past the waterfall. The spot where his hand had touched her still felt warm. *What is the matter with you?* Without waiting for him, she stalked to aisle three, turned the corner, and stopped. "You have got to be kidding me." The aisle stretched as far as she could see. Thick vines looped around the metal framework, making it almost impossible to read any of the labels. Planting her hands on her hips, she turned to Jax, who had stopped at her side. "All right, Bear Grylls, do your thing. Or will the fact that there are no stars in here to guide you throw you off?"

An easy grin slid across his face. "Cute. But no need to worry." He tapped his temple. "I have the compass right here. I will find the tents." He held up a finger, as though testing for wind, before holding out his hand, turned sideways, in the direction of the gaping aisle. "I am confident we should go this way." He started off in the direction he'd indicated. Which was the only available direction if they planned to stay in aisle three.

Mikayla bit her lip to keep from laughing. What was with this guy? It was maddeningly impossible to stay irritated with him. Not that he was the one she was necessarily irritated with.

Shoving away that thought, and any inclination she might have to analyze the truth behind it, Mikayla followed him.

Ten minutes later they had traversed the aisle twice and seen every possible piece of camping equipment known to man. Except a tent. Jax stopped and ran his fingers through his dark hair. "I am thinking that the tents are not in this aisle."

Her lips twitched. "Not lost, are you, Grizzly Adams?"

"Lost? Of course not. I am never lost. Thanks to my extensive outdoor survival training, I know exactly what to do in this situation."

"Search for a salesperson?"

"No. Stay calm. The most important thing to do when you are not sure where you are is to keep your wits about you. If you don't, chances are good you will not survive. Or, in this case, find what it is you are looking for in the vast wonder that is this store."

"Well, my wits are telling me that all we need at the moment is a store employee."

As if the words had conjured her, a young woman in her early twenties with a short, dark cut that perfectly accentuated her pixie face, turned into their aisle. She sported a green T-shirt, camouflage pants, and a tag with her name—Brittany—scrawled over a background of trees and mountains as she walked toward them, pushing a cart filled with boxes. When she saw Jax, she skidded to a stop so abruptly the top box toppled off the cart and onto the floor at his feet. Jax picked it up and handed it to her. The girl swallowed as she took it from him and set it on the cart, so close to the edge it nearly fell off the pile again. Color rose in her cheeks as she grabbed for it, settled it more securely on the pile, and whirled to face him. "Can I help you with anything?"

Mikayla pressed her lips together to hold in a snort at the way the woman emphasized the word *anything*. Given how she was looking at Jax—as if Mikayla had thrown on a cloak of invisibility—there likely wasn't much she wouldn't have done for him if he asked.

"Yes, actually. *Gracias*. We are looking for a tent. Which aisle are they in, and can you recommend one that is not too expensive but would be good for this time of year?"

Mikayla contemplated him. It was actually pretty impressive, the way he could make the Spanish accent wax or wane at will, like the tide. Clearly it was now high tide.

"Sure!" The woman actually bounced a little on the balls of her feet, obviously thrilled to be given the opportunity to wait on him hand and foot. "Come with me." She left the cart where it was, in the middle of the aisle, and grasped Jax's elbow. "Tents are this way, aisle nine. I understand why you are confused. It would make sense if they were here, with the camping equipment, but there are so many of them that they fill an entire aisle, which is why …"

Although she was clearly still talking, the words faded to indistinguishable as the two of them made their way to the far end of the aisle. Jax shot a look over his shoulder and motioned for Mikayla to follow. Shaking her head, she moved the girl's cart closer to one of the shelves so other shoppers could get by before traipsing after the two of them, who had disappeared around the end of the row. Good thing the woman had mentioned the aisle number or Mikayla might have roamed the rows indefinitely, like Jax's scout troop, left on their own to struggle for survival as they attempted to make it to their destination.

A little melodramatic, don't you think? It bothered her how much it bothered her to catch a glimpse of the two of them walking close together ahead of her. Not that it appeared Jax had much of a choice. The woman had hooked her arm through his like one of those plastic monkeys Santa had given Mikayla for Christmas one year. Once Jax did appear to be making a polite attempt to extricate himself, but the salesgirl only tightened her grip. *Professional.*

By the time Mikayla caught up to them, the woman was pointing to a box on a shelf above her head. "I think that's the one you're looking for. It's on sale this week. Sturdy and weatherproof, of course, and sets up easily. And it sleeps two comfortably." She lowered her arm and shot a dark look at Mikayla as she said those last words.

Heat rose in Mikayla's neck. She caught Jax's amused look from the corner of her eye but refused to look at him. "Perfect. We'll take two of them."

The woman's face lit. "Great. I'll go grab the stepladder." She bounced her perky little self to the end of the row and disappeared.

Mikayla stole a glance at Jax to see if he was watching the girl, but his gaze was firmly fixed on her. She rolled her eyes.

He lifted both hands. "What?"

"Nothing."

"Don't do that. As they say in my country, *Sin pelos en la lengua.*"

Mikayla gritted her teeth. She absolutely hated when he spoke in Spanish. And hated even more that she found it incredibly attractive when he did. "What does that mean?"

"Basically, if you have something to say, say it."

She drew in a breath. *Don't do it, Mik. Keep your mouth shut or you'll regret it.* "It must be nice having women so incredibly anxious to serve you everywhere you go. It has to make life nice and easy." She'd meant it to come out light, teasing. Instead, the words carried a sharp edge and a shadow crossed his face. One of these days she needed to learn to take her own advice.

Where is that girl? Unable to look at him, she rose on her tiptoes and grasped the bottom corners of the box. She tugged on the corners, but it refused to move. *Come on.*

Jax came up behind her. He stopped short of touching her, but the warmth of his body and the light scent of his cologne sent shivers skittering across her skin. He reached for the box. "Come on, Grant. Are you going to pretend that you were some kind of wallflower growing up? Can you honestly tell me men haven't tripped over themselves your whole life to do whatever you wanted them to do? I can't imagine your life has been all that difficult."

The accent had abated considerably, which she was coming to realize was not a good sign.

She let go and ducked out from under his arms. "You have no idea what my life has been like." Blood crashed through her veins like white water between narrow riverbanks, and she stepped away from him and struggled to rein in a breath.

Jax slid the box off the shelf, lowered it to the floor, and rested a palm on the top of it. "You are right, I don't. *Lo siento.* I'm sorry. I should not assume anything."

She didn't miss the unspoken words in the dark eyes that met hers. *And neither should you.* Her chest tightened. "I'm—"

"Here you go." The saleswoman stepped between them and dropped the stepladder to the concrete floor with a clatter. Mikayla had to move to avoid being shoved out of the way. Seriously? She glanced around the aisle. Could anyone else see her? "Oh. You got one already. Impressive. Most customers aren't that strong."

From the adoring gaze the woman leveled at Jax, Mikayla half expected her to reach out and stroke his upper arms, but thankfully she managed to remember herself enough to keep her hands to herself and start climbing the ladder. Mikayla felt Jax's gaze like the heat of the sun against her face, but she kept her eyes on the box on the shelf above them. The woman slid it out far enough for Jax to grab it and set it on the floor beside the first one.

"I'll go get us a cart." Grateful for the reprieve, Mikayla spun around and headed to the front of the store. At the waterfall, she paused for a moment and pressed her hands to her flushed cheeks. For a few seconds she concentrated on drawing in one steadying breath after another. When she felt composed enough to face Jax again, she hurried to the long row of carts, jerked one free, and wheeled it to aisle nine.

Holden stood beside Jax. He'd set the box containing the stove and a small tank of propane on top of the tents. The salesgirl was nowhere to be seen. Mikayla focused on Holden as she pushed the cart towards them. His warm smile eased the angst that had tightened every muscle. A little, anyway.

When she reached them, the men loaded the boxes into the cart, and Holden took the handle. "What else do we need?"

Jax shifted his attention to Holden. "Three sleeping bags and pillows, three air mattresses, and a frying pan should do it. We can stop at a dollar store and grab a few utensils and disposable dishes and purchase food and water at a grocery store and we will be good to go."

"Great." Holden performed a three-point turn so the cart was pointed in the right direction. They returned to aisle three where they'd seen sleeping bags and mattresses. Holden snagged a sleeping bag and squeezed it between his hands. "I spotted frying pans in aisle seven where I found the stove. I grabbed a pot, but I wasn't sure which pan to get." He returned the bag to the shelf and reached for a different one. "I can go pick one out if you two—"

"I'll go." Mikayla tossed a pillow into the cart. "Pick any sleeping bag for me. I don't care."

Before either of them could respond, she started for aisle seven. Three minutes later she stood in front of a wall of frying pans. Thoughts whirled and tumbled through her mind and the last thing she felt capable of was figuring out the pros and cons of thirty different pans. Everything in her wanted to close her eyes and pick one. Holden would be fine with whatever she got, but even though Mikayla had never seen Jax cook, somehow she knew he was good at it and would want a quality pan. It would be great if she could leave this store having done at least one thing right.

"Can I help you?"

Mikayla's eyelids dropped shut at the sound of the overly cheerful voice behind her. Pasting on a bright smile, she turned around. "Hi again."

The girl's shoulders slumped, as if Mikayla had pricked her with a pin and now the perkiness was leaking out of her like helium from a balloon. "Oh," was all she said.

Mikayla heard the *it's you*, as plainly as if the girl had tacked it onto the end of that sentence, like she clearly wanted to. She decided to press on. "I need a frying pan. Which one do you recommend for cooking on a camp stove?"

"That depends." The salesgirl's tone had turned decided frosty. "How many people are you cooking for?"

"Personally? None. I don't cook. But whoever will be doing the food prep will be doing so for three people."

"Adults?" She peered around Mikayla as though she might have a small child hidden behind her.

"Yes."

"Hmm." The girl moved to stand beside her, tapping her finger on her chin as she contemplated the rows of pans. "So what's his story?"

Mikayla blinked. "I'm sorry?"

"That man with you. Is he single?"

She almost choked on the breath she'd taken. Was the girl serious? "Umm, yeah, I think so." Her own words gave her pause. *Was* Jax single? She'd assumed so, since her initial impression was that Nicole had some idea of trying to get them together, but now she wasn't sure that had been the case. Maybe he did have a girlfriend, or even a fiancée, in London. It was almost impossible to believe he didn't have at least one woman on the hook. For all she knew, he kept several of them dangling on a stringer, like the professional fisherman he'd no doubt claim to be. All of that was decidedly more than she wanted to get into at the moment, standing in front of a wall of frying pans in aisle seven of The Great Outdoors Adventure store with a stranger who struggled to comprehend the basic rules of human propriety and professionalism.

"Is he straight?"

Case in point. Time to end this conversation. Mikayla cleared her throat. "About that frying pan?"

"Here." The girl reached for a large pan and lifted it from the hook. "Cast iron. Lasts forever, cooks food evenly, and it's naturally non-sticking. Better than stainless steel, titanium, or aluminum, unless you're planning on hiking long distances because it weighs a ton." She hefted it in one hand, eyeing Mikayla as she did as if contemplating using the thing as a weapon.

Mikayla reached for it. "Nope, no hiking. This will be perfect." The girl didn't let go of the handle, and for a few, ridiculous seconds, they stood there glaring at each other, the frying pan between them.

"Find one?"

Mikayla turned at the sound of Holden's voice. He'd parked the cart at the end of the aisle and both he and Jax strolled toward them. She tugged on the pan. The salesgirl let go of the handle, reluctantly, as if lamenting the lost opportunity. Then her gaze flicked from both men to Mikayla and she raised her eyebrows.

She didn't voice the question splashed all over her face—*seriously?*—but she may as well have.

Take the high road. Mikayla couldn't help herself. She lifted her shoulders in a *what-can-I-say?* gesture, flashed the girl a smug smile, then forced her features into a neutral expression as she faced the two men. "Yep. Got it." She hoisted the pan, which had to weigh close to five pounds, into the air to show them.

"Hey." Jax took hold of it and lifted it two or three times. "Good choice." He pointed it at the saleswoman. "Thank you for all your help."

"My pleasure." The words came out more like a squeak and her cheeks grew pink which, unfortunately, only made her look more adorable.

"Shall we?" Mikayla gestured toward the exit.

"Yeah, let's get going so we can set up camp before it gets dark." Holden fell into step beside her as they headed to the cart. To her relief, Jax's shoes thudded on the cement floor behind them.

After they'd paid and wheeled their purchases to the door, Jax tugged the keys from his pocket. "I will get the car."

He was halfway across the parking lot when Holden slid an arm around Mikayla's shoulders. "Want to tell me what's going on?"

"What are you talking about?"

He cocked his head, and she sighed and swung her gaze to the black sports car headed in their direction. "I wish I knew, Holden." She rested her head on his shoulder and he tightened his grasp. "I really wish I knew."

Chapter Fifteen

Holden paced behind the red brick building that housed the public washrooms, his phone clutched in his hand. He desperately needed to hear his wife's voice, to know that she was okay. But what would he say to her? They'd been home so much since their son had died that they had rarely needed to speak by phone, and he had no idea how it would go. Even their face-to-face conversations were tense and strained. How much worse would a long-distance one be?

He smacked the wall with the palm of one hand. *This is ridiculous. She's your wife. Call and ask how her day was. You can handle that.* Pressing his back to the cold, hard brick, he punched in her cell number before he could lose his nerve.

It rang seven times with no answer. Not sure whether to be relieved or disappointed, Holden reached for the end call button but stopped when her voice rose from the device. "Hello?"

He lifted the phone, fingers trembling slightly. "It's me, love."

"I know." Her voice was soft, and he pressed the phone harder to his ear.

"How was your day?"

She paused. "Fine."

Holden gritted his teeth. Seriously hated that word. "Work was good?"

"You know, tough at times, but okay."

She was going to make him work for it. "Did you have dinner?"

One of the many things he worried about was that she wouldn't eat enough while he was gone. The last few months he'd had to remind her to have a meal, and even then she'd only picked at what he set in front of her.

"Yes. I had some of the leftovers Nic sent home with us the other night."

"Okay, good."

Another pause then, as if she'd suddenly realized she should ask, "How are you?"

"I'm all right. We've decided to camp at a park outside Chicago."

"Camping? Like in a tent?"

The hint of surprise in her voice, curiosity even, caught at his chest. "Yes. It's expensive to stay in the city, and Jax was going on about what an expert camper he is, so Mikayla called him on it. We bought tents and a few supplies and here we are."

"Oh."

Silence stretched between them. A movement in the trees in front of him snagged his attention. A red squirrel, bushy tail brushing the branch behind him, chased another squirrel down the trunk to the ground and up another tree, unable to close the gap between them no matter how fast he ran. Holden knew exactly how he felt. "Are you still there?"

"Yes."

"What are you thinking?" Would she tell him? He studied the squirrels. They'd stopped on branches a few feet apart, gazing at each other as if trying to figure out their next move.

"That I hope you don't run into any bears."

He let out his breath on a short laugh. "I'm pretty sure the only bears around Chicago are the ones in Soldiers Field."

The joke went over like a line from a stand-up comedian playing to a tough crowd. Her monotonic voice didn't even hold sympathy laughter when she replied, "I guess that's true."

"Will you be able to sleep?"

"Better than you on the hard ground, I'm sure."

He did detect a little sympathy that time, which might have been wishful thinking. "I'll be all right. Talk to you soon?"

"Okay. Good night."

"Good night, love." He lowered his free hand until his palm grazed the rough brick. "I miss you."

She was already gone. He pulled the phone away from his ear and stared at the device. The five hundred miles between them felt more like the length of the galaxy. Would they ever find their way back to each other? Holden tipped his head to gaze at the sky. Pinpricks of light penetrated the darkness, stretching as far as his eyes could see. He hadn't been out of the city in so long he'd almost forgotten what stars looked like. If he wasn't already struggling to draw in air after the terse conversation with Christina, the sight might have stolen his breath away.

The heavens declare the glory of God. The verse he'd learned in childhood came, unbidden, into his mind and his jaw clenched. In spite of the awesome spectacle in the night sky, the glory of God did not impress him at the moment. God might be the master designer of the universe, but He had done nothing for Holden but take everyone he had ever cared about away from him. His mother, Gage, Tristan, and now Christina. Even if she still breathed in oxygen on this planet, at the moment she was as lost to him as any of the others.

What did I ever do to you? Anger and grief coiled together in his chest like snakes fighting for dominance. A tear pricked the corner of his eye and a revelation struck him. He'd never cried for his son. How could he have? Every bit of his time and energy had been focused on comforting his wife since that tragic night. He'd fought the urge to weep along with her, afraid of adding to her grief if he did. And when he wasn't with her he was at work. There, he'd learned to compartmentalize his feelings to keep from losing his mind over the things he saw every day, the heart-wrenching way people treated each other, especially kids. The very experiences that had driven his brother to try and help and, ultimately, to sacrifice his life.

The anger that had billowed inside him dissipated as quickly as a flame flaring in response to a single shot of gasoline, leaving only the grief. A grief that, for once, he didn't resist when it came for him.

Holden slid down the brick wall as wracking sobs gripped his body. *Tristan.* Thoughts of all he had lost along with their little boy—the joy of feeling those tiny fingers wrapped around his, of hearing his son's first words, helping him take his first steps, teaching him to ride a bike, taking him to school, watching him graduate, get a job, marry the love of his life, give them grandchildren—assaulted him.

Lying in bed at night, his head resting against her stomach, the rapid, steady heartbeat of their son thudding against his ear, he and Christina had talked about those moments and laughed, imagining how wonderful each one would be. Those images they had created in the night as surely as God had created the scene above him now flashed through his mind, a montage set to morbid, dissonant music.

Death didn't only steal a person—it stole moments that hadn't yet happened, memories that hadn't yet been made. It stole the future with all the sorrow and joy and everyday events it should have held and replaced it with a black, gaping void.

Holden lowered his head into his hands, weeping not only for the loss of all of those moments with his son, but for the moments he should have been able to spend with everyone else he had loved. He couldn't have stopped the weeping if he'd tried, which he didn't have the strength to do. Finally, after several long minutes, the sobs subsided to rasping breaths.

Footsteps sounded along the path that ran the length of the building and Holden lifted his head. He swiped the moisture from his cheeks with both hands as Jax lowered himself to the ground beside him and rested his arms on his knees.

Holden stared into the bush in front of them, surprised at how much he didn't resent Jax insinuating himself into this private moment. Or catching him with tears on his face. Although he didn't know the man well, his strong and, for once, quiet presence made Holden feel less alone than he'd felt in a long time.

Neither of them spoke for a moment, until Jax nudged him in the shoulder. "Life can really kick you in the butt sometimes, bro."

Holden almost laughed. Yeah, life really could kick you in the butt. And sometimes, when it did, that was the only thing you needed the guy beside you to say.

Chapter Sixteen

Christina picked at the cold tuna casserole for several minutes before dropping the fork onto her plate with a clatter. The sound bounced off the cupboards, echoing through the room like words shouted into a valley. *It's so quiet in this house.*

That's what it was—that's why she felt as if she was slowly going out of her mind. She'd watched a movie once where someone was trapped in a room with the walls closing in. The space grew smaller and smaller until the person had a hand pressed to two of the walls and was pushing on both at the same time in a vain attempt to stave off the inevitable. That's exactly how it felt, being in this house alone. Not that it had been much better when Holden was home.

Not for the last six months, anyway. Before that, whenever he'd walked through the door, the house had come alive, ringing with his teasing voice and laughter. Since their son's death, the house had felt more like a funeral home, the type of place where people tiptoed and spoke in hushed voices.

Christina had always dreamed of a house filled with noise— a dog barking, a baby crying, a toddler calling out for her, "Mama." For a while, it had seemed those dreams were about to come true. Now she could barely hold a conversation with the one other person occupying this space with her.

Why was it so hard to talk to her own husband? She'd stared at her phone for several long seconds as it rang, debating about even answering it before berating herself for being a coward. This was Holden, the man she'd been so crazy in love with when she'd married him that she couldn't imagine ever not wanting to talk to him. She had lived for the sound of his voice because it meant he was thinking about her or, better yet, home with her.

How could that have changed so completely? Her hands shook and she wrapped ice-cold fingers around her water glass.

Now his voice drove daggers through her heart, because she could hear in it how desperately he was trying to reach out to her, how much it hurt him that she couldn't respond the way he wanted and needed her to. Maybe it would be better for both of them if they didn't talk at all for a while.

Or ever.

The thought, not a new one but one that filled her with a strange mixture of excitement and horror every time it flitted through her head, consumed her now. She knew where her precious baby boy was. And she knew how to get to him. *Maybe this is the time.* There was a bottle of Tylenol in the kitchen. And another one in the bathroom. A few sleeping pills in her bedside table drawer from her last prescription. She could consume every drug they had and then simply crawl beneath the covers of their bed and close her eyes. She would welcome the silence then, the oblivion as it came for her. Since it already felt as though they were living in a funeral home, might as well make it official.

No, beloved.

The trembling stopped as rage coursed through her, so thick and strong it burned in her throat. Christina hurled her drink against the wall. The glass shattered into pieces on the floor. "Why not? You're the one who took Tristan and destroyed my life. You're the reason I have nothing left to give my husband, the reason I push him away and break his heart over and over and over. How dare you tell me that I have to keep living this way?" She pushed herself off the stool and flung open the cupboard doors. Glasses lined the lower shelf and she snatched two of them and pitched them onto the gray tile floor. "Why do you want me to keep suffering? Don't you feel any compassion at all?"

Shaking and nearly blind with fury, she grabbed the glasses one at a time and smashed them at her feet. Crash after crash echoed through the house. "Why can't I end this now?" She stood on her tiptoes and thrust her arm into the far corner of the cupboard to capture the last glass and send it to join the others. "I can't keep going." Christina eyed the next shelf, filled with mugs. Lunging for a black and white one, she knocked the chipped yellow one onto its side. The anger drained from her as quickly as it had exploded, and she closed shaking fingers around her coffee mug and lifted it from the shelf.

Completely spent, she slumped against the counter. "I have to, don't I?"

No answer this time, yet the truth seeped deep into her bones. Yes, she did.

The part of her that throbbed with the hurt of all that had happened the last few months screamed at her that she was alone in this, that no one else understood, that the pain would never end. Still, she did know in some small corner of what was left of her rational mind that none of that was true. She wasn't alone. Someone did understand, not only God—who had watched His son die like she had—but Holden too, who was suffering as much as she was. And as impossible as it was to believe from where she stood, ankle-deep in pieces of glass, she understood that the darkness would begin to lift, sometime in the future. Even now it occasionally seemed a little more gray than black, and once in a while, for a few seconds, the thick fog parted enough to offer her a sliver of light, even if it was quickly swallowed again.

Christina studied the mug. The words danced in front of her eyes. *World's Greatest Wife*. Holden had believed that once. Would he ever believe it again?

She couldn't go. She couldn't do that to Holden. He'd blame himself for leaving her and he might never get over the guilt of that. If she loved him at all, she couldn't add to the burdens he already carried, not only his but her own.

Christina's head jerked. How had that never occurred to her before? Her own burden felt so suffocatingly heavy that somehow she had failed to see that Holden carried it too, at least as much of it as he could. Anything more added to his load might break him, and she couldn't be the one to push him to that point.

She cradled the mug to her chest as if it was the most precious possession she'd ever owned. Maybe it was. If it was how Holden had seen her—and he knew her more intimately than any other human being—maybe that's who she truly was, deep inside, buried under layers of grief and loss. And maybe that's who she could be again.

For several long minutes she stood, clutching the mug to her T-shirt, before turning and gently setting it on the shelf. "I *will* be her again."

Christina whispered the vow fiercely, her jaw set, then gingerly stepped over the pieces of glass, tiny shards grinding beneath the toes of her sneakers. She made her way to the closet and tugged out the broom. It would take a while to clean the kitchen, and she'd have to buy more glasses, but it had been worth it. Breaking everything in sight had been incredibly cathartic, and she felt as though the load she carried had lightened, somehow.

And the best part was—the ghost of a smile flitted across her lips—for a few minutes at least, the house hadn't been quiet at all.

Chapter Seventeen

Natalya tapped the speaker button on the phone and left it lying on her desk as she wandered over to the large window in her office. "Yes?"

"They are staying at a campground, Riverside Acres, fifteen minutes south of Chicago."

Although the person on the other end of the line couldn't see her, Natalya nodded. "Good work."

"We are still only watching them?"

"Yes. But carefully. They must not suspect anything."

"Of course."

"Continue to report any activity to me. I will let you know if I feel we need to move in. They are in tents?"

"Yes. The two men in one, Nicole Kelly's sister in the other."

Natalya stared out the window at the bare oak tree on the edge of the gravel parking lot. The last vestiges of ice still dripped from the branches, although the sun was warm and she could hear the chirping of birds even through the glass. It was early in the season for camping. Clearly they did not have any idea they were being watched, or that anyone might try to stop them from finding Andrew Thompson, or they would never have left themselves in such a vulnerable position. "All right. If we need to get to them, they will be easy to reach. Monitor the situation and let me know what is happening."

"Yes, ma'am."

The phone clicked and she faced the window, chewing on her lower lip. What were they thinking? Did they have any kind of plan for tracking Andrew? Certainly the PI must have some idea of what it would take to find him.

She rested her forehead against the cool glass. The fact that someone was on the verge of discovering one of the children was entirely her fault. Her research into the Kelly brothers hadn't extended far enough for her to discover that Nicole Kelly's long-lost sister lived in the same neighborhood the Thompsons had moved to after acquiring Matthew Gibson. The random kidnapping that had taken Nicole's twin from her family had occurred long before the organization had begun its work and had nothing to do with them, so Mikayla Grant had never even been on Natalya's radar. That constituted serious negligence on her part, one of the very few times she had failed to prepare for any eventuality with enough rigor to remove the possibility of something like this happening.

She blamed it on her one weakness—Gage Kelly. Not that she had been romantically interested in him. She had no ability to love another person in that way or likely any other. Although there was a physical attraction—on her part, for he had eyes only for Nicole—it was more than that. No, the connection she felt to him was something much harder to define. She couldn't have put it into words if she'd had to defend it to another person. Which she didn't.

Natalya pushed herself away from the glass and straightened her shoulders. She was in charge. She defended neither herself nor her actions to anyone, and no one questioned her orders. Only Gage had pushed back, occasionally. And it had taken everything she had not to give in to him when he did.

Which had made her weak and vulnerable to mistakes. And the ones she had made with Matthew Gibson might cost her. In fact, before all of this was said and done, it might cost everyone involved a very great deal.

Chapter Eighteen

Holden stepped over a tree root and ducked below a low-hanging branch. Birds chirped in the upper branches as a chipmunk scampered under the picnic table and out the other side. The site Mikayla had picked out offered a lot more nature than he'd expected to find this close to Chicago. No electricity yet, this early in the year, but they could live without that. When Mikayla had proposed the idea, Holden had been a little leery, but now he was kind of excited about it. He'd always loved camping, and the idea of paying for a hotel room for three weeks had concerned him. This might be a little more rustic, but it would save him a lot of money so it was worth it. A maintenance worker in forest green overalls raked leaves under a tree on a nearby lot. Holden lifted a hand and the man nodded.

Ahead of him, Jax flipped a pancake with the plastic spatula they'd purchased at a Dollar General the evening before. The pancake landed in the frying pan on the cook stove with a hiss of hot grease and a waft of fried batter. Holden breathed deeply as he walked toward the picnic table. "Smells good."

"Everything smells better outdoors. Tastes better too." Jax waved the spatula at Holden. "That Mikayla, she has good ideas sometimes, no?"

Holden chuckled as he slid onto the bench. "Actually, she has them quite often. Don't get distracted by the outside, my friend. There's a lot going on in that woman's head."

"I have gathered that. A lot going on in here too, yes?" Jax tapped the spot over his heart with his fist.

"Yeah, I guess that's true. She's been through a lot the last year and a half." Holden shot a look at Mikayla's tent, but it was a good twenty feet away and she didn't appear to be stirring inside yet. Still, he lowered his voice. "She has a strong faith—that's what gets her through. And family, of course."

Jax flipped another pancake and tilted his head. "I have heard people say that a lot and I have never understood it. How does faith help you get through anything? I have never found it to be much help."

Holden let out a humorless laugh. "I'm not the one to advise you on that, unfortunately. It hasn't done a lot for me the last few months either."

Jax lowered the flame on the stove and shoveled pancakes onto two plates. He slid one across the table to Holden and handed him a plastic fork before sitting across from him. "It is none of my business, but you and Christina are going through something tough, no? I felt it the other night at Daniel's."

Holden blew out a breath, dumped syrup onto his plate, and stabbed at a pancake. "You could say that." The bite he shoved into his mouth tasted like sawdust. He tossed the fork onto his plate and reached for the carafe of coffee. "We lost our son six months ago. He was stillborn. We're both having a hard time working our way out of that. And, as you likely gathered the other night, and from seeing me after I talked to her on the phone yesterday, we're not doing much better at finding our way to each other."

Jax propped his fork on the paper plate and fixed his dark gaze on Holden. "I am truly sorry. I have lost people, but I cannot imagine losing a child."

Holden focused his attention on the steam rising from his coffee. "Yeah, it's been rough. This trip kind of came at a good time. I think we both need a little space to see if we can somehow get our heads on straight."

Jax nudged a small container of cream closer to Holden. For a moment he tapped a finger on the top of it, as if debating whether or not to say something. "*Mi mamá*, she lost a son too, my older brother."

Pain darted through Holden's chest. It seemed pretty much everyone had lost someone so incredibly precious to them that life without that person barely felt worth living. Shouldn't such a widespread, collective human experience somehow temper the pain of each individual loss? Instead, if anything, the pain only magnified with every story told, every heart broken. Magnified and diminished at the same time. Knowing Jax understood, a little at least, of what he was going through saddened him, even as it lightened his own load a bit. He wasn't alone, which eased the ache in his chest slightly. "I'm sorry."

Jax picked up his fork and idly steered a piece of pancake through the syrup. "I was fourteen. She cried every day for months, although she tried to hide it from me. And every night, through the thin wall between our rooms, she would sob into her pillow. And then I woke one morning and realized I had not heard her crying in the night. She wept that night and for the next few nights, but then not for two nights in a row. It took many, many months, maybe a year or more, but finally she did not cry herself to sleep more nights than she did. And she started to smile again and even laugh sometimes. Life does return, slowly and by going forward a few steps and then back one or two. But it does return."

Holden unscrewed the lid of the cream container. "Thanks. That helps, actually." He splashed a little of the thick liquid into his coffee and grabbed a plastic spoon. "I have seen that with Christina, a bit. Her going to dinner the other night, especially with someone there she didn't know, was a huge step for her. Definitely not something she could have done a few months or even weeks ago."

"That is good." Jax lifted his fork. Syrup dripped onto the plate but he didn't take a bite. "What was your son's name?"

Holden stopped stirring. No one ever asked that. It was almost as though they were afraid that hearing his son's name would make his loss all too real, like it was easier somehow not to think of him as having had a name, of being an actual person. "Tristan." He paused, assessing. That had hurt a little less than the last time he'd said it.

"A good name. I like that." Jax stuck the piece of pancake into his mouth.

Holden resumed swirling the spoon around his cup. The sound of a zipper running along its tracks broke the silence and he glanced over at Mikayla's tent. She lifted the flap and straightened as she came out the opening. She wore a pale blue sweatshirt and gray sweat pants, and her short blond hair was tussled. Clutching a small bag and a rolled-up towel under one arm, she shot a brief look in their direction, clearly a warning not to attempt to engage her in conversation. "When I'm done, coffee."

Jax must have gotten the message too, because he lifted the pot without speaking. Mikayla gave him a sarcastic thumbs up before heading for the trail that led to the public washrooms. A smirk crossed his face. "She is not a morning person, I take it?"

Holden snorted. "Not even a little bit. She's a true artist. She can stay awake all night painting, but don't ask her to leave the house before noon. She told me once that the only time she ever saw a sunrise was if she hadn't been to bed yet."

Jax chuckled. "Is she any good at the art?"

"Actually, she's very good. I think so, anyway. Art is subjective, of course, so you'll have to judge for yourself when we get to the show, but she's gotten glowing reviews from previous shows. Daniel said when he first saw it, the night he flew to Chicago to tell her she had a twin sister in Toronto she knew nothing about, he was blown away by it."

The smirk disappeared from Jax's face. Holden grimaced. "You don't know about any of that yet, do you?"

Jax shook his head. "Since Daniel brought me to his home to meet all of you, I have been feeling as though I have fallen into the middle of some kind of telenovela. One I am so far behind on that I am struggling to follow the storylines. So no, I do not know about that part of it, but I don't think there is much any of you can reveal now that would surprise me." He pushed away his empty plate. "Tell me, how did she not know about Nicole?"

Holden glanced at the pathway where Mikayla had

disappeared. "It's really her story to tell. Basically, she was abducted from a park when she was little and raised by a couple in Chicago she thought were her parents."

"Ah." Jax propped an elbow on the table. "I wondered what she meant the other night when she said her parents did not get her through legal channels. That makes sense now." He rested his head on his hand and pressed his fingers to his temple. "It is almost too much to take in."

"Tell me about it."

"Is there more I should know?"

"Well, there's more. Whether or not you should know it is up to Mikayla, I guess."

"Fair enough." He reached for the coffee pot as sneakers padded along the packed earth trail. By the time Mikayla had tossed her towel over a branch beside the one Jax had hung there earlier and walked over to the table, her hair still damp from the shower, Jax had filled a cup with the steaming liquid.

"Here you—"

She held up a hand and he clamped his mouth shut.

Mikayla took the cup and rounded the table to step over the bench and sit beside Holden.

Both men watched as she lifted the cup to her mouth and took a sip. Closing her eyes, Mikayla let out a contented sigh. "Ahh. So good." She opened her eyes. "Thank you."

Jax hesitated, until she circled her hand through the air, giving him permission to speak. "You are welcome."

Holden passed her the cream. "How did you sleep?"

"Not bad, actually. The air mattresses we bought helped."

"So you're not ready to check into a hotel? Even with no electricity on the grounds?"

Mikayla drew in a long, deep breath. "And sacrifice all this fresh air? Not on your life. We can charge our phones when we go into town, otherwise we don't need power. Besides, while I have to admit this coffee is impressive, Jax hasn't had a chance to truly show off his skills yet. Tonight I want to see him start a fire without a lighter or matches."

He waved a hand through the air. "Child's play. I can do much more impressive things than this."

"Such as?"

His dark eyes gleamed. "You will have to wait and see." He stood and walked over to the camp stove. "Pancakes?"

"One, please. If there's real syrup."

"After your ten-minute lecture last night in the grocery store on the evils of table syrup, I would not dream of serving you anything but the real thing." Jax handed her a plate and produced the jar of maple syrup with a flourish.

"*Gracias.*"

His smile went deep into his eyes. "*De nada.*"

Holden felt suddenly as though he was intruding on a moment he was not meant to witness. He swung a leg over the bench. "Thanks for breakfast, Jax. I'm going to hit the shower before we leave for the city."

Jax nodded, his eyes still on Mikayla.

"I'll see you both soon."

Neither of them responded. Holden waited a few seconds then, with a grim smile, left the table and headed for the tent to grab his towel and supplies. *Yep, definitely going to be interesting.*

Chapter Nineteen

Mikayla removed the lid from the bottle of maple syrup and poured a healthy dose over her pancake. Her fingers shook slightly. *Neutral topic. Neutral topic.* "The pan works okay?"

Jax settled onto the bench across from her. "Yeah, it is great. You and your little friend made an excellent choice."

She set the bottle on the table with a thud. "*My* little friend? It wasn't me she wanted to go on a play date with, believe me."

"Play date?" Amusement swept across his face as he reached for his cup of coffee.

"Yeah. She asked me if you were single. And if you were straight."

He almost spewed out the sip of coffee he'd taken. With a wry grin, Mikayla handed him a paper towel and he wiped his mouth. "What did you tell her?"

"That I didn't know."

"About which one?"

"Either."

He tossed the paper towel onto the table. "Well, I am not gay."

Yeah, she'd pretty much figured that out on her own.

"As for the other …"

Mikayla shook her head. Imagining him with a girlfriend or a fiancée in London actually helped her set boundaries around him in her mind. Maybe not as many as it should, but better than none. "You know what? Don't tell me. It's not my business."

The amusement faded. "I see. All right then. My personal life shall remain personal. I actually prefer to be a man of mystery anyway." He lowered his gaze to the coffee in his hand.

Like she'd intended with her words the night before, he'd

clearly meant his to come out light, but a faint hurt threaded through them. Mikayla's chest clenched. Wounding him had definitely not been her intention. Which reminded her … "Actually, I'm glad we have a moment alone. I wanted to apologize to you for what I said in the store last night."

He looked up, forehead wrinkled. "Which part are you talking about?"

Had she said more than one thing she should be sorry for? Given the tendency she'd exhibited to lose control of her mouth—and her brain—around him, it wasn't impossible.

"The part about life being easy for you because of the way women treat you. That wasn't fair of me."

He waved a hand dismissively. "It was nothing. Forget it."

"No, really. How do you say *I didn't think before I spoke?* You know, in your country?"

His lips twitched and the knots in her stomach loosened. "We have an expression: *Hablar sin pensar es tirar sin apuntar.* It literally means: Speaking without thinking is like shooting without aiming." He reached over and touched the side of her hand with his. "And I *hablé sin pensar*—spoke without thinking—too. I should not have accused you of having an easy life. I know that you have not."

Her head jerked. "How do you know that?"

"I …" For the first time since she'd known him, he appeared to falter a little. "That is, I already knew your parents had died. Then Holden and I were talking this morning and he told me a little about you, that you were abducted as a child and only recently found out they were not your real parents."

Mikayla shot a heated glance in the direction Holden had disappeared. Why had he been talking to Jax, a man she barely knew, about her private life?

"Please, it was not Holden's fault. I was asking him about you. He told me very little, and said if I wanted to know more I needed to ask you because it was your story to tell."

Her shoulders relaxed a little. That did sound more like Holden. "Why were you asking about me?"

Again, he seemed to hesitate. Then he straightened his shoulders. "I like to know about my friends, Grant. Who they are and what they have gone through in the past. And we are becoming friends. I believed so, anyway."

That stabbed through her like a knife thrust between her ribs. "You're right, we are. And I do want to know about you and your life. Only maybe not your love life."

He tilted his head. "Why not? It is all part of who I am, no?"

"I think …" Her stomach churned. The few bites of pancake she'd taken, as good as they had been, weren't sitting well. "Sometimes, with certain people, under certain circumstances, it's better to leave that part of their lives off the table, you know?"

"The certain people being you and me, and the certain circumstances being that we will go our separate ways in a few weeks."

Among other things. Like your lack of faith. "Exactly." He got it. That helped settle her stomach a little.

He contemplated her in silence for several seconds. It took everything Mikayla had not to squirm under his intense scrutiny. Then he speared another piece of pancake. "Fine. If that's the way you want it." He raised his fork in her direction. "Very smart. Far better to think with your head than with your heart, I always say." He stuffed the bite into his mouth.

Somehow she doubted that was true. Mikayla repressed a sigh. So he didn't get it. But he did get her. She was being a coward, and he'd called her on it. The irritation she'd felt the night before gripped her again. "As a matter of fact, I agree. And for the record, the people who raised me *were* my real parents, even if they weren't my biological ones."

He set his fork on the table, a stricken look on his face. "Of course they were. I am sorry."

Like it had the last time, the irritation slipped through her fingers. "It's okay. You shot without aiming. I understand."

He laughed. The sound did something to her insides, and she

pressed a hand to her stomach. Where was Holden? How long did a shower take, anyway?

Jax's face grew serious. He grasped his fork and tapped it on the plate.

Mikayla blew out a breath. "What is it?"

"What happened to them?"

She blinked. "What?"

"You said you were an orphan, that the people who raised you are gone. What happened?"

An almost hysterical giggle rose in her throat. "Not much for small talk, are you?"

"Not much, no. *La vida es demasiado corta.* Life is too short."

How many topics could she rule off limits and still claim she wanted to be friends with him? Mikayla reached for her paper cup. "I'll need more coffee if we're going to go there."

Jax grabbed the pot and filled the cup with the steaming liquid. She splashed cream into it and sat for a moment, breathing in the rich aroma of mocha that swirled around her. It wasn't until he covered her hand with his that she realized she'd closed it into a fist on the table. "It is okay. You do not have to talk about it if you are not ready."

She drew in a quivering breath. "No, it's all right. First of all, while they didn't get me through legal channels, I don't believe my parents knew I had been kidnapped. They were beautiful, godly people who would never have supported that, no matter how badly they wanted a child. Daniel thinks that whoever stole me told them that my birth mother was young and alone and couldn't take care of me and that she needed the money to start a new life. Even then, knowing them, I'm sure it was an incredibly difficult decision, but they must have been desperate. They were older, and my dad had health issues that likely prevented them from getting a child any other way." Mikayla rubbed a drip of coffee from the side of the cup with her thumb. "Unfortunately, I'm guessing at all of that, because I never had a chance to talk to them about it. They were killed in a car accident a year and a half ago."

He winced and withdrew his hand. "That must have been horrific."

"It was. Still is, actually. At the time, I believed I was an only child and had no other family. It had always been the three of us, and we were extremely close. They were my best friends. So yeah, after they died, I spiraled pretty good. I struggled to find a reason to keep going. If it weren't for God, my church, my agent, and a few other close friends, I'm not sure I would have."

"How did God help?"

Mikayla analyzed the question, and the way he'd asked it. He didn't sound sarcastic, or even skeptical, only genuinely interested. "Lots of ways. He sent people into my life who showed me compassion, directed me to verses in the Bible that brought me comfort and strength, that reminded me that even if everyone else in my life left me, he would always be with me. And he spoke to me at night when I cried out to him, asking him why. Basically, he surrounded me with love and mercy and kindness."

"He spoke to you?"

"Yes. Not out loud, in words, but deep inside."

"And did he answer that question? Did he tell you why he allowed that to happen to your parents?"

"No. But eventually I was able to get to the point where I could stop asking that question so often and trust that he was in control and loved me. That was enough. Most days." Mikayla took another sip of coffee, possibly the best she'd ever had. Her chest pricked. It was so easy to say those words. They were the right ones, she knew. Truths her parents had raised her with. Lessons preached week after week in the church she'd attended with them. But did she truly believe them? *Had* God been with her every step of the way? Would He always be, no matter what she faced?

She swallowed. Until the death of her parents, she'd had no reason to question that. But now …

Jax appeared to have more questions, but the sound of whistling drifted on the air between them and he lifted his cup to his mouth instead.

Holden strode along the pathway. He hung his towel on the branch beside the other two and walked over to the table. "Should we head into the city, see if we can find this Andrew Thompson?"

Mikayla tossed the last swallow of coffee into the bushes. Jax watched her but didn't say anything as she stood. "Yes, let's. Time to stop sitting around and start doing what we came here to do."

Chapter Twenty

Mikayla scanned the playground as they walked by, following the path that meandered through the park in her old Chicago neighborhood. The sky had clouded over and a thin mist hung in the air. No kids climbed the jungle gym or slid down the bright red slides. The only other person in the park was an elderly gentleman walking a black lab on a leash. When the pair reached them, the dog went straight to Jax, who crouched to pet it, speaking softly to the animal in Spanish. The dog responded with a wagging tail and a lick to his cheek. Jax laughed and straightened as the man coaxed the animal along the path.

They reached a wrought-iron bench, and Mikayla sat and tugged off her gloves. "We should wait and see if Andrew comes by here. He used to walk through the park on his way home from school. I know that because our house overlooked this park, and my dad arrived home from work around 3:30. I'd often meet him here and we'd walk or get a drink at the coffee shop or sit on a bench and talk. Most days Andrew would pass us shortly after I joined my dad." She tugged her phone from her pocket and glanced at the screen. "If he does come this way, it should be soon."

Jax sat beside her, but Holden stood, gazing across the park and rubbing his hands together to warm them. "So there's a coffee shop nearby?"

A smile tugged at Mikayla's lips. "Yes, Michelangelo's. Fabulous pastries and the best coffee in Chicago." She pointed to the street that bordered the far side of the park. "See that red sign hanging in front of the little stone building? That's it."

"Got it. I might go grab a hot drink. Do either of you want anything?"

Mikayla nodded. "I'd take a green tea."

"Nothing for me, thanks." Jax stretched his arm along the back of the bench. "Do you need help?"

Holden shook his head. "I'll be fine. Keep Mikayla company. I won't be long." Abandoning the path for a more direct route, he strode across the grass toward the building she'd indicated.

Birds chirped in the tree branches hanging over the bench. Mikayla took a deep breath. The air was clean and fresh and smelled of blossoms and rain. A breeze swirled around them, lifting the last of the fall leaves from the ground and sending them twirling across the pathway at their feet. Jax brushed a dark lock of hair off his forehead. "I can see why they call this the windy city."

Mikayla laughed. "This is nothing. Downtown, near the water, the wind can howl so loudly between the buildings it sounds like an orchestra tuning its instruments. I've had more than one Marilyn Monroe moment while walking around there."

Jax grinned. "That I would like to see."

"Well, you won't. I stopped wearing dresses downtown or pretty much anywhere in the city years ago."

"Too bad." The corners of his mouth twitched and warmth suffused her neck.

Mikayla pulled one sneaker-clad foot onto the bench and wrapped her arms around her knee. If he took the same path home he used to, Andrew would come toward them from the east. She scanned the houses that ran along the tree-lined street at that side of the park. When her gaze fell on the red brick house with the white window frames, her chest clenched. Although she braced herself, tiny prickles skittered over her skin like electric shocks. She'd been so distracted since they'd left Toronto that she hadn't prepared herself mentally for the memories that flooded over her in waves. She breathed deeply to stave off the grief that rose in her chest. *Not here. Not now. I'm fine.*

Jax touched her shoulder. "Is that it, the red one?" His voice was gentle, which was not helpful in terms of maintaining her composure.

She risked a look at him. As he so often did, he was watching her intently, as if he could read her mind and wanted to let her know that he was there if she needed him. The thought was as disconcerting as it was comforting. Still, peace flowed over her like a warm sweater wrapped around her shoulders and the tidal wave of emotion abated. "Yes."

A mischievous glint entered his eyes. "Which room was yours?"

"The top left corner." She contemplated the window of the old brick house, envisioning the room on the other side of the glass, the way it had looked when she'd last seen it. "Why?"

"I'm trying to picture little eight-year-old Mikayla peering out one of the windows, watching for her friends. Or you as a senior pulling back the curtain to see if your prom date had arrived yet."

Her stomach twisted. The word *prom* always did that to her, brought memories of one of the worst nights of her life crashing through her.

"Don't tell me you did not go to prom. A dozen guys must have asked you."

They had, and she'd chosen the one who was the cutest. And the biggest jerk of them all. "Of course I went."

"With whom?"

More than a dozen years later, and a cold chill still gripped her at the sound of his name. "Kyle Martin." Mikayla forced a dreamy expression. No need to let Jax know the entire evening had been a nightmare. Not when he'd likely been the king of his prom.

He leaned forward and studied her for several long seconds. Then he shook his head. "Nope."

She choked back a laugh. "What do you mean, *nope*?"

"You can't fool me—Martin was a jerk and you had a terrible evening."

Her mouth dropped open. "That is so not true. The theme was Under the Stars, and it was a magical, enchanted …"

He shook his head again. "Give it up, Grant. All these years later, you're still mad about it."

"*All* these years? How old do you think I am? And what makes you think it was terrible?"

Before she realized what he was planning to do, he'd reached out and grabbed her hand. "Look. As soon as I mentioned the word prom, your fingers clenched into fists, and now they're ice cold."

Mikayla forced her tight muscles to relax and tugged her fingers from his. "That means nothing."

"You sat straighter, your jaw tightened, and your eyes went dark. Basically, your sympathetic nervous system kicked in, and within seconds your body had performed every instinctive response on the fight or flight spectrum short of fleeing the area. So, you can smile and inject as much wistfulness into your voice as you want, I am not buying it."

All right, maybe the man did have a few PI skills tucked away in his pocket. Given their current situation, that was a good thing, but it didn't mean she appreciated him turning them on her. "Fine. It *was* a terrible evening. Are you happy?"

"Happy that you had a terrible evening when it should have been the highlight of your high school career? Umm, no. Not even a little bit. What happened?"

"For starters, he pulled to the front of the house in an old cab instead of the limo he'd promised me. The dress I'd scrimped and saved for months to buy smelled like smoke and vomit the entire night."

Jax pressed his lips together. "And?"

"And the second we stepped into the gym he started drinking out of a flask he'd strapped to his chest. He clearly had one thought on his mind. He spent the whole evening trying to get me to go out to the football field with him and hang out under the bleachers, if you know what I mean."

He grimaced. "I have a pretty good idea, yeah. So what did you do?"

"I finally called my dad to come and get me. By the time I arrived at school the next day, Kyle had spread vile rumors around about me. Suffice it to say, I spent the last month fending off guys sniffing around my locker after every class and praying for high school to be over."

Jax blew out a breath. "Ah, Grant. On behalf of seventeen-year-old guys everywhere, I am sorry."

Mikayla shrugged. "It's been five years—I'm over it now." Her hand had clenched again and she opened her fingers and rubbed the palm that had gone damp over the front of her jeans.

"Clearly." He cocked his head. "And somehow I think we need to land somewhere between *all* those years ago and five, if we're going to be honest with each other."

"Apparently I have no choice but to be honest with you."

His face grew serious. "Maybe not. But I will make you a deal. If you will be honest with me, I will be honest with you. Okay?"

"Okay." *So much for not talking about our love lives.* She swept an arm through the air. "Can you picture me here, growing up?"

He paused, as though debating whether or not to allow her the subject change, and she held her breath until he nodded. "Yeah, it fits. I can see it."

She exhaled. "It was a wonderful house, full of good memories. I miss it."

"Tell me about them."

"Who, my parents?"

"Yes. What were their names?"

Mikayla swallowed. Was she ready to share the people who had meant the most to her in the world with this man—the ones whose loss had left a deep gash across her heart that still ached at unexpected moments? She'd hardly talked about her parents since they had died. So few people asked about them, as if they were worried it would only cause her more pain to hear them mentioned. Which it did. But it brought relief too, and joy, and healing, all mixed in with the horror and sadness in strangely beautiful swirls, like paint on her palette. "Mark and Rose."

He smiled. "Rose. *Nombre bello*. Beautiful name."

"It suited her. She was lovely and kind and had a wonderful sense of humor. So did my dad. The three of us laughed a lot."

The tips of his fingers brushed below her temple, barely grazing her. "I thought you must have, since you have such incredible lines around your eyes."

Mikayla's breath caught in her throat. Even after he withdrew his hand, she felt the touch of his skin against hers. In an attempt to erase the sensation, she made a face at him. "Wrinkles, you mean?"

"No, lines of laughter. It is not the same. Wrinkles age. Laugh lines soften, add beauty."

"Oh." Mikayla drummed her hands on her knee, trying to release a little of the emotional adrenaline roiling inside her. "Anyway, my parents. My dad was a professor, so of course he loved to read. He was the one who told me stories at bedtime, and I definitely inherited my love of books from him."

"And your mother?"

"She was an artist too. I always assumed any talent I might have came from her, and maybe it did—from watching her work anyway. That's how I inherited her love of color and her desire to capture the perfect portrait on canvas, the curve of a neck, age spots on a hand. I would sit for hours and study her. I'm not even sure she was aware of my presence most of the time, she would get so lost in what she was doing, as if she'd fallen into another world."

"Do you do that?"

"I do, actually. When I lived here, Leigh, my agent, would come by almost every night to make sure I remembered to stop and eat dinner, or go to bed. Hours can go by while I'm painting and I have no idea. When I do stop, it takes me a few minutes to get my bearings, as if I need to reorient myself to this world, to my life."

"And who does that now?"

"Who does what?"

"Checks on you, makes sure you are eating and sleeping and going out into the real world once in a while?"

"Oh. Nicole, I guess. She phones me most evenings and I'm usually deep into my work, so her call draws me out of that."

"So as much of a shock as it was to find out she existed, it was a blessing too, no?" Jax's arm was still stretched out on the bench behind her and his fingers brushed her shoulder again.

Mikayla bit her lip, his touch making it difficult to think clearly. "Yes, it was. A shock and a blessing, you're right. For a year I truly believed I was all alone in the world. It's impossible to describe that feeling. The closest I've come is comparing it to an astronaut who has become untethered from his spaceship and cast adrift to float around in the infinite dark emptiness of space."

"Actually, that describes it pretty well." His words were tinged with sadness, and she tilted her head and contemplated him.

"You sound like you know what I'm talking about." Somehow she couldn't imagine Jax ever lacking for company. Company for the sake of company, however, was no substitute for true relationship, as she well knew.

"I guess I do, a little, anyway."

"How——?"

"Here you go, Mik." Holden thrust a large paper cup in front of her.

Mikayla blinked, returning with an effort, like she did after she'd been lost in her painting. "Oh. Thanks, Holden." Steam curled out from under the lid and she inhaled the acrid scent.

"Any sign of Andrew Thompson?"

She lowered the cup to her knee. No one had walked by while she and Jax had been talking, had they? Surely one of them would have noticed. Her cheeks warmed. If she was being honest, like she'd promised to be, a herd of elephants might have thundered by when they were deep in conversation and she likely wouldn't have seen them. She glanced at Jax and he shook his head slightly. "Nope. Nothing yet."

She tugged out her phone again. Four o'clock. Andrew used to walk through the park around 3:45. He could have been delayed at school, of course, but it was equally likely that he had taken a different route home or one of his parents had driven him. "Should we wait a little longer?"

Holden sat beside her. "Let's give it a few more minutes. Do you know which part of the neighborhood he lived in, which house or even which street?"

Mikayla lifted the plastic tab on the lid of the cup and snapped it into place. "I'm not sure which street. To be honest, I never paid that much attention. His parents weren't exactly rude, but they didn't go out of their way to speak to anyone either. I said hi to his mother one time when she was walking home with Andrew. She nodded and said hi but didn't stop walking. If her son is actually Matthew, I guess that makes sense. She wouldn't want to get too close to anyone who might identify him. And actually," she frowned, "now that I think about it, I haven't seen her in a long time, a year or more. His dad started walking him home around that time, but he was even harder to talk to, didn't even look at anyone as he strode through the park." She lifted her free hand, palm up. "Sorry I can't be any more helpful than that. All I know is that he must live in walking distance of the park, and that he headed east in the morning and west in the afternoon."

Holden patted her arm. "Don't worry about it. You got us this close. We never would have known what city to look in, let alone which neighborhood, if you hadn't been able to get us here. We'll keep our eyes open, watch the area for a few days. If he still lives around here, he has to come out of his house sometimes, right? I'm sure we'll spot him."

He leaned forward a little to peer past her at Jax. "This is more your area of expertise, Jax. Any idea how we can track him from here?"

Jax clasped his hands between his knees. "We could go into

the school and ask about him, but I hate to arouse any suspicion at this point. It would be better to have one of us at the school at the end of the day, see if he comes out and which direction he goes. If he gets into a car, we can get the plate number. Daniel should be able to find an address for us that way." He glanced at Mikayla. "You would be the best one to wait at the school. A guy with no kids loitering anywhere near the building at that time of day might arouse suspicion."

Holden tipped his coffee cup in Mikayla's direction. "Good point. Plus, you're the only one of us who's actually seen him in person in the last year."

"That's fine. I can do that." She took a sip of the green tea. The steaming liquid burned her tongue a little, and she rested the cup on her knee again.

"You would have to be discreet." Jax nudged her lightly in the arm. "Parents do not take kindly to strangers—men or women—hanging around the school with no apparent connection to any of the kids. You will need to stand as far away as you can, as out of sight as possible without looking like you are hiding, try different locations on different days, stuff like that."

The cup warmed her fingers and knee, but the rest of her felt damp and chilled. "All right."

"It is always iffy waiting around a school. Today is Wednesday—my suggestion is we come here morning and afternoon for the next couple of days, see if we can catch him walking home. If not, we revisit the idea of staking out the school next week."

"Makes sense." Holden tipped up his cup to take another drink of coffee.

Jax stretched out his long legs, crossing them at the ankles. "I went online, trying to find a phone number or address for a Thompson in this area, but could not find anything in this exact neighborhood. Not surprising. If they are trying to lay low, they likely would not have a landline or any kind of online presence. We have time. If you hang out at the school next week and

Holden and I cover the park in the afternoons, sooner or later one of us is going to spot him."

A large splotch of water landed on Mikayla's jacket, followed by another. She glanced at the sky. The clouds had thickened and grown darker as they'd been talking.

"We might want to head for the car before it starts raining in earnest." Holden pushed to his feet.

Jax stood too, and held out his hand to Mikayla. After a brief hesitation, she slid her fingers into his and he pulled her up. "Thanks." She tugged her hand free and concentrated on pushing the tab closed on the lid of her cup.

"Tell you what." Jax zipped his jacket. "Let's drive around the surrounding streets for a few minutes, see if we catch anyone outside, which is not that likely, given the weather. At least we will get an idea of the area, and if the rain stops by tomorrow we can come again and watch for Andrew."

Holden flipped his hood over his head. "Sounds good."

The three of them started along the path they'd taken into the park earlier. Mikayla lifted her hood too as the drops began coming thicker and faster. She grimaced. Whose crazy idea had it been to camp instead of staying in a hotel anyway?

Chapter Twenty-One

Natalya steered her silver Camry south along the Skyway, heading for her office in the warehouse. Their most vulnerable child was Matthew Gibson, so after everything had fallen apart, most of the active organization members who hadn't been arrested had settled in Chicago to keep an eye on him and to be relatively central to the rest of the country in case they needed to put out any other fires. So far they hadn't, but that appeared to be about to change.

Her cell phone chimed and she tapped the screen set in the dashboard. "What's happening?"

"They are in the boy's neighborhood. Today the three of them waited in the park for an hour, but we intercepted Andrew on the way home from school so they wouldn't see him. When they gave up on that, they drove around the area for a while before returning to the campground."

Natalya's chest tightened. "All right. Thank you for letting me know."

"What do you want us to do?"

"You and Walters start driving the boy to and from the school, following the protocol we used when we first brought him to the city. Otherwise, simply monitor the situation for now. Keep me informed. If they do happen to find the boy, we will take immediate action."

"All right. We'll wait to hear from you."

"Someone is watching them at the campground?"

"Yes. Clark and Fernandez are there, posing as park employees. They are reporting on all movements to and from the grounds."

"Excellent. Any other campers on the property?"

"Very few. I can find out how many, exactly."

"Let me know. We'll need to take that into consideration before we put any plan into action."

"Yes, ma'am. I'll be in touch shortly."

"Thank you." Natalya tapped the screen to end the call and touched her brakes to avoid hitting the cement truck that veered in front of her without warning. City traffic. No matter how long she lived here, she would never get used to it, which was why she took the subway occasionally when she didn't feel like dealing with the gridlock. She signaled and guided the car onto the ramp that would take her to the warehouse on the outskirts of Chicago. As soon as she got to her office, she would make a few calls, ensure that every detail of her plan would come together perfectly.

In the meantime, she'd wait and see how close Mikayla Grant was able to lead the men to the street the boy lived on. Natalya had been holding out hope that, with no clear connection to the Thompson family, Ms. Grant would have only a vague idea of where their home was located, and so far that appeared to be true. If Doug Thompson did as he was told—and that had become less of a given as the years had gone by—and kept his son out of sight for a few days, the danger may pass and they might all be able to return to living their lives in peace, if still in constant vigil.

If not, and the three of them did spot Andrew Thompson and identify him as the missing Matthew Gibson, they would have to be dealt with. Quickly and decisively.

Children weren't the only ones who could disappear.

Chapter Twenty-Two

Mikayla propped the heel of her running shoe on the bench of the picnic table and bent forward to slide her hands along her shin, stretching her calf muscles. The rain hadn't amounted to much more than a few drops. As soon as they'd arrived at their campsite, Mikayla had changed into her running clothes, anxious to move around after doing so much sitting lately. Holden had gone for a walk. Mikayla watched him as he wandered through the empty camp sites surrounding theirs and disappeared into a stand of trees. Her heart ached for him. He worked hard not to show it, but he was clearly worried about Christina and trying to figure out how to deal with their loss and the struggles they continued to face in their relationship.

With a heavy sigh, she lowered her foot and propped the other one on the bench. She and Jax were at the campsite alone. His response to the story she'd told about her prom night, and the fact that she hadn't been able to hide her reaction to the memory of that horrible event from him, had disconcerted her. Enough that getting a little exercise seemed like a better idea than hanging around here when Holden wasn't available as a buffer.

"You are going for a run?"

She dropped her foot to the ground and spun around. Dressed in track pants and a black T-shirt, Jax exited his tent and zipped it closed behind him.

"I was thinking about it." *And you.* She kept that part to herself.

"May I join you? I was about to go out, as well. Too much sitting around in cars lately."

"That's how I was feeling." Did she want him to go running with her? She typically went alone, usually using ear buds to listen to music. Still, it would be rude to refuse. "You can come if you want. Assuming you can keep up."

He grinned. "I have never had trouble with that before."

She believed it. "Let's go then." Before he could respond, she had jogged across their lot and onto the gravel road that ran around the outside of the campground. The crunching of gravel told her he was not far behind and catching up quickly. Hopefully she wouldn't have trouble keeping up with *him* or she likely wouldn't hear the end of it.

The two of them fell into stride next to each other and managed to stay that way at a decent pace for twenty minutes. When they reached the edge of a large field, by unspoken agreement both slowed their pace to a walk. Mikayla rested her hands on her hips as she concentrated on breathing deeply and slowing her heart rate. It was disarming, how in sync the two of them were. When they were running, anyway.

An old band shell sat at one end of the overgrown field they'd passed by once already. Paint hung off the sides of it in strips and part of the roof had collapsed. Graffiti covered the front of the stage, some of it surprisingly artistic. Although it clearly hadn't been used in years, likely a lot of shows and concerts had been performed there. It would have been kind of cool to be able to sit outside, under the night sky, and watch them.

"That would have been fun, no?"

"What?"

"To sit out here and listen to a concert."

Seriously? Could he actually read her mind? "I guess so. Looks like no one has done that for a long time. The place is a dump."

He glanced over at her. "Only because it has been neglected. There is still much potential."

Mikayla shook her head. "I don't see it." She jogged on the spot. "Ready to go?"

"Of course." They took off running again and fell into easy step beside each other. After a few minutes, he nudged her arm.

"When do you need to go to the gallery?"

"Next Friday evening. That will be a pre-show event with media and investors. The official opening will be the week after that."

"Can Holden and I come with you next week?"

Her stomach tightened. Was she ready for this man to see her work? So much of her heart went into her pieces. While she deeply appreciated galleries showing them, and people coming to see them, it was hard for her too. As though something deep inside of her was on display at the same time. "If you really want to."

They had nearly reached their site, and Jax touched her arm to slow her. When she stopped at the edge of the road, he did too, and faced her. "I really do want to. Unless you would rather I did not."

Mikayla pulled her foot up behind her to stretch her quads. "No, it's okay."

"It is hard, no?"

"What?"

"Putting yourself out there like that."

She repressed a sigh as she switched to the other foot. "It can be."

"I promise to be kind."

Her eyes met the dark ones that were watching her intently. "I'd rather you be honest."

"Do you believe I cannot be both?"

"I guess we'll see."

He studied her a few seconds then smiled. "Would it help if I put my skills on display for your critique first? I will show you how I start a fire with two sticks, as you have requested."

"I would very much like to see that, yes."

"Come, then." Jax nodded toward the fire pit. Mikayla sank onto a stump and watched him get ready. He'd already gathered moss and leaves and twigs to use for tinder, and he and Holden had stacked a pile of dried wood next to the pit. He reached for a piece and propped it on another stump. Mikayla's eyes widened when he pulled a serious-looking knife out of one of their boxes of supplies. "Where did that come from?"

"I found it at the store the other night. When you were chatting with your friend about frying pans."

Mikayla rolled her eyes. "Ah." For several minutes she watched him as he removed the bark from a piece of wood and trimmed the sides until it looked like a flat board. Sweat dripped between her shoulder blades. "Will this take long?"

He glanced up from his task and swiped an arm across his forehead. "Do you work better when someone watches you and asks how long it will take?"

She laughed. "No, I guess I don't. Should I take my shower now and see how you're doing when I'm done?"

"Probably a good idea."

She stood and took a few steps in the direction of her tent before turning around. "How do I know you won't use the lighter while I'm gone?"

Jax exhaled loudly and set the knife carefully on a stump. "One of these days you will understand that you can trust me, Grant. Until then …" He pulled a lighter from the box and held it out to her.

She took it from him. "Do we have any others?"

"There is one over by the cook stove. That is it." A gleam sparked in his eyes as he straightened and held his arms out to his sides. "Unless you would like to search me for a pack of matches?"

Mikayla bit her bottom lip. A challenge. He was intentionally embarrassing her, making her pay for not trusting him. "No, that's okay. I believe you." She wished with all her heart that she could control the flush that spread across her cheeks to keep from obliging him.

From his triumphant expression when he lowered his arms, she'd failed miserably. "That is a nice change."

She whirled around, grabbed the other lighter, and carried both to her tent. After stuffing them into a bag along with her towel and a change of clothes, she crawled out the opening.

Without looking at him, she stalked toward the washrooms. Even though he hadn't made a sound, she knew he was laughing at her. Somehow that didn't bother her as much as it would have a few days ago.

When she returned to the stump, there was still no sign of Holden. Jax had set the flat board he'd made in the fire pit. A small crater had been dug in the board and he set a stick into the opening. He'd carved a notch in the wood beside the crater and stuffed some of the kindling beneath the notch. A thin rope attached to something that looked like a crude bow from a bow and arrow set was wrapped around the stick. The rocks had been cleared away from the side of the fire pit closest to him and, as she watched, he knelt on one knee in the opening and held the flat board in place with his other foot. Gripping the stick in one hand, he moved the bow back and forth, as though sawing the stick. After several minutes, a tendril of smoke furled upwards from the board, and bits of coal dropped through the notch onto the moss and leaves below.

Caught up in the moment, Mikayla let out a tiny squeal before clapping her hand over her mouth. Jax glanced at her and grinned but didn't stop the sawing movement. After another minute or two, he tossed the drill and stick aside and blew onto the notch in the board. More smoke poured out and a tiny spark dropped onto the tinder. Jax blew on it again and added kindling. In seconds, the spark had become a flame. He tossed on more moss and twigs and gradually built a teepee of wood around the fire. When it was going strongly, he replaced the rocks to complete the ring. Strands of long, dark hair had escaped his ponytail and clung to the sides of his face. He tugged the elastic out and pulled the loose strands in before tying it back again.

"All right." Mikayla clasped her hands between her knees. "I have to admit, I am very impressed. That did not look easy."

"The best things in life rarely are, Grant."

Her chest tightened a little. Everything the man said seemed to imply something deeper than the words appeared to on the surface. "I suppose that's true. But that was amazing."

"You see?" He held his arms out to the sides again. "It is possible to be both kind and honest at the same time. You are kind to say I am amazing, plus it is true. I am."

She pressed her lips together to keep from laughing. "I said what you *did* was amazing, not you."

Jax dropped his arms. "Same thing." He gestured to the flames. "Can you keep this going while I have a shower?"

"Sure." No way she was going to let the fire go out, not after all the work he'd gone to in order to light it.

"Thank you." He pushed to his feet. "I will make dinner when I return."

His shirt clung to his torso and he looked exhausted. Guilt niggled through her. "Or I could." The words came out tentative.

Jax laughed and brushed a finger lightly across her cheek as he passed by. "I will do it when I return. If you keep the fire from going out, I will be happy."

Her skin, where he had touched her, burned like the flames curling around pieces of wood as he walked to his tent. Did he know he had that effect on her? Mikayla suspected that he did. And that he thoroughly enjoyed that fact. Still, she would definitely keep the fire going. Although she hated to admit it, the idea of making Jax happy, even at her expense, was becoming more important to her with every day that passed by.

And she had no desire to analyze that fact to try and figure out why.

Chapter Twenty-Three

"Please sit, Mr. Thompson." Natalya held out an arm toward the chair across from her desk. He dropped onto the plastic seat and shoved the hair out of his face. Her eyes narrowed. When was the last time the man had gotten a haircut? Or taken a shower? "Is everything all right with you and Andrew?"

Doug Thompson shoved his hands into the pockets of his windbreaker. "No."

She blinked at the abrupt response. "What's wrong?"

He let out a short, humorless laugh. "What isn't wrong? I can't go on like this much longer."

"Like what?"

"Pretending that everything is fine. That the two of us are still a happy little family. I don't even know who the kid is."

"He's your son, Mr. Thompson."

For the first time since he'd entered the office, the man met her gaze. His eyes were red-rimmed and bloodshot, and the wildness in them shook her deeply. He was unraveling. Rapidly. "Is he?"

"Of course. When you agreed—"

"That's the thing. I never did agree."

Her eyes narrowed. "What are you talking about?"

"I'm talking about when my wife first came to me with this crazy idea that we could somehow buy ourselves a child. I thought it was the most ridiculous thing I'd ever heard at the time, and I only believe that more strongly now."

"Are you telling me you never wanted to adopt Andrew?" Her mind whirled. How was that possible? They had been so careful with the prospective parents they approved. Of course, Matthew Gibson's case had been unique.

"Oh, I would have been happy to adopt him, if he'd come to us through legal channels. This back-alley, black market, baby-trading like these kids are a commodity on the stock exchange didn't sit right with me at the time and it doesn't sit right with me now."

Her stomach churned, but she forced her features to remain neutral. "But you signed the papers."

"I did, after weeks of my wife crying and pleading and begging. I couldn't see any other way to make her happy or to shut her mouth. And where did it get me, going along with her insane scheme? Got me a kid now that rightfully belongs to someone else, and no wife."

Natalya swallowed the bile that rose in her throat. "I'm very sorry about what happened to your wife, Mr. Thompson." Pamela Thompson had died of cancer almost a year ago, something none of them could have foreseen when they chose her to be a parent to Matthew. "But Andrew is such a sweet boy. And he believes you are his father. Do you not have any feelings for him at all?"

"I've got lots of feelings. None of them you want me expressing to you right now."

"You do understand that Matthew Gibson's birth mother is dead and his father is in prison for kidnapping another child, don't you? And that he also served a sentence for killing a man."

Doug Thompson scrubbed his face hard with both hands, the several days' worth of growth rasping beneath his fingers. "CAS could find him a good family. The legal way."

"You want your son going into the system? He could end up in a far worse situation than he is in now."

He lowered his hands. The look he offered questioned her assertion more eloquently than words could have.

Natalya rearranged a pile of papers on her desk before folding her hands on top of them. "Someone might have figured out that Andrew is actually Matthew Gibson."

His head jerked. "Really?"

"Yes. Three people are in the area now, from Canada, searching your neighborhood trying to find him."

"Bad people?"

She repressed a sigh. Such a subjective question. "No. A private investigator and the brother and sister-in-law of the man who took Matthew from his home. They don't mean Andrew any harm, but if they find him, they will either take him or report the situation to the authorities. That would mean that a lot of people, including you, could get in trouble, and that Andrew would be removed from your home and will enter the system."

"Maybe it's time for all that."

Maybe it is. Natalya pushed the thought away impatiently. She had to get through to Andrew's father somehow. "You will go to prison."

"That would only require a shift from one kind of captivity to another."

Which might also be true. For her as well as for him. Her jaw tightened. "All you need to do is keep your son out of sight for a little while, until these people give up and leave the country. Alternatively, we could move you and Andrew to—"

"No." The word exploded from him and Natalya blinked again. "I'm not going anywhere with you or this crazy organization you work for. You aren't driving me from my home."

She reached for a pen and clutched it in her fingers. If Andrew's father refused to leave the city, it would be that much more difficult—and traumatizing—to transport Andrew anywhere else. And even if they were able to, the three people who had tracked Andrew this far might still find the house and speak with Doug Thompson. With his son gone, he would have nothing left to lose by telling them everything he knew about the organization. That could do far more harm than keeping the two of them out of sight until the PI, Gage's brother, and the woman returned to Canada.

Natalya set the pen on the desk. "Very well, then. Do as I have asked and lay low until I contact you to let you know it is safe. After that you and I will meet to discuss our options. Whatever we decide, we will give you more support than we have in the past. You won't have to do this alone any longer. Can you do that?"

A heavy silence followed before the man heaved an enormous sigh. "I'll try."

"That's all I ask." Natalya rose. "A few days. Stay inside the house this weekend. My men will continue to drive Andrew to school in the morning and drop him off at home afterwards. The rest of the time he needs to stay indoors, until you hear from me."

He nodded curtly as he stood. "Has it been worth it? All this?" He waved a hand through the air, indicating, she supposed, everything she and her organization had accomplished over the last decade.

Good question. She'd never wondered that during the years they were rescuing children, but uncertainty had been creeping into her mind more and more lately. *Had* it been worth it? She squared her shoulders. She had to believe it had been, or she would unravel too, likely much more quickly and thoroughly than him. "Yes. Many children are safe now and in happy, loving homes as a result of our work."

When he shrugged, his shoulders barely moved, as if the weight pressing on them was too heavy to budge. "Good for them."

Natalya followed him out of her office and into the warehouse they used as a front for the scaled-back work the organization continued to do. After Doug Thompson slunk out of the building, she pulled the door closed behind him. His last words still hung in the air when she returned to her office. Their work *had* been good for the children. Which made every sacrifice worth it.

In any case, she had to continue telling herself that. Maybe, if she did, she would be able to keep believing it.

Chapter Twenty-Four

Christina waited until the singing began before slipping into the sanctuary and finding a seat in the last row. She and Holden hadn't gone to church for a month after Tristan's death. When they finally did, Christina insisted they arrive late and leave early, unwilling to talk to anyone who might ask questions she wasn't ready to answer. She hadn't been sure she'd be able to go without Holden, but when she woke up this morning, she felt the need to be here. That didn't mean she wanted to allow the opportunity for any conversations with anyone before the service began.

The final hymn before the sermon was one of her favorites. Christina closed her eyes and let the words of "Be Still My Soul" wash over her.

When the last note faded away, she sank onto the chair, perusing the program before opening her Bible and keeping her eyes on it to avoid catching anyone's attention who might glance in her direction. Which, even though it felt as though everyone was watching her, probably no one did.

As the pastor began speaking, the words of the hymn continued to play over and over in her mind. She winced a little at the admonishment to bear the cross of grief or pain patiently. Was she doing that? What did that look like in real life, anyway? Her thoughts flitted to Holden. No one in the world was more patient than he was. Should she be more like him? They had definitely handled their grief differently, but he had never made her feel she was somehow doing it the wrong way.

The promise that all that was now mysterious and dark would someday be bright captured her attention. She'd struggled for months with so many questions, with a longing for answers that no one could give her. The idea that someday maybe she would understand, even if it wasn't until she was face to face with Jesus, did provide a measure of comfort.

Mostly, what swirled through her as the words sifted through her mind and finally settled in her core, was a feeling of peace. Although she hadn't put a name to it until this moment, it was peace that had come to her the night she broke the glasses. The night she had contemplated ending her life and had been stayed by a gentle, compassionate voice. It was that gentleness, that compassion, that had finally allowed her soul to still after months of torment.

The words the pastor was saying broke through her musings. He was speaking on the story of the crippled man whose friends took him to Jesus. Unable to push through the crowds, they climbed to the roof, cut a hole, and lowered their friend down. Now those were good friends, people who knew exactly what to do when someone they cared about was hurting.

Lost in thought, Christina didn't realize the service had ended in time for her to slip out early, as she'd planned. She gathered up her bag and Bible and stood, but before she could exit the row she spotted Marlene Brown, a woman who had been in a small group study with her the year before, wending her way through parishioners and heading straight for her.

Panic wormed through Christina. Marlene had sent a card and flowers and dropped off several meals to her and Holden over the past few months. Like so many, her heart was in the right place and her intentions good, but somehow everything she said managed to prick Christina's chest like needles in a pin cushion.

Behind the woman, Christina caught a glimpse of Nicole trying to make her way through the crowd filling the aisle. Obviously her friend had seen her standing there caught in Marlene's crosshairs and was making a valiant attempt to head the woman off. It struck Christina then how many people had been doing that for her. Holden, Nicole, Daniel, Mikayla—each of them had been stretcher bearers for her when she hadn't been able to make her own way through the pain and grief that had assailed her.

Maybe it was time for her to stand on her own two feet, even if she did stumble a bit as she picked up her mat and tried to walk—to mix up her stories and beat a biblical metaphor to death. She hid a grim smile and forced herself to wait until Marlene had reached her and grabbed both her arms. "Christina! It's so good to see you here."

"Thanks, Marlene. It's good to be here." That was the truth. It had been good to be here today, even if she hadn't been able to process everything that had been said from the pulpit. Something about this place had always brought her comfort when she'd walked through the doors, even over the past months of slipping in and out and trying to avoid encounters like the one she found herself in now.

"I've been praying for you and Holden so much."

Christina met her eyes. Those words were easy to say. She knew, since she'd said them more often to people in her lifetime than she could begin to recall. More often than she had actually prayed—she had to acknowledge that truth and the sting of guilt that accompanied it. Somehow, looking into this woman's earnest face, Christina knew she hadn't said the words lightly. Marlene *had* been praying for her. This woman whom she'd attempted to evade had, in reality, been another stretcher bearer for her, lowering her to the feet of Jesus when she'd been incapable of crawling there herself.

Tears pricked her eyes. "Thank you, Marlene. That means so much to me."

The woman hugged her briefly before releasing her. "You call me if there is anything you need, you hear? I can be at your door in ten minutes, night or day."

Her throat had tightened, so Christina merely nodded before watching her friend walk away. Then she scanned the sanctuary, seeing everyone around her in a new light. Yes, maybe they hadn't always said the right thing to her or Holden. Maybe they'd been awkward or fumbling when dropping off food or cards. But they had been there, trying. And no doubt countless of them had spent time—possibly a great deal of time—on their knees asking God to comfort her and Holden, to shower them with mercy and to make His presence real to them as they worked through their terrible loss. Overwhelmed, Christina rested a hip against the back of the chair in front of her as Nicole reached her.

"Are you okay?"

Christina ran down a checklist in her mind, evaluating her emotional and mental state the way a paramedic might examine an unconscious patient for injuries. "I am, actually."

The worry cleared from Nicole's face as she slid her arm through Christina's. "Come out for lunch with us?"

"Sure." She allowed her friend to guide her through the throngs of people in the lobby, many of whom smiled and greeted Christina as she walked by, appearing genuinely happy to see her and to have her there with them.

Be still my soul. The words from the hymn drifted through her mind as she followed Nicole out to the parking lot. Her soul *was* still, and that had a lot to do with the people milling about in the building behind her, the ones who had gathered around her and Holden and lifted them up, even when Christina hadn't realized that's what they had been doing.

Yes, their attempts had faltered at times, but still they had persevered. Like the friends in the story. And even with plaster and dust raining down around him, Jesus hadn't complained. He'd only greeted the man with love and compassion and done what the man's friends had asked him to do—He healed him.

And He had done what Holden and Christina's friends and fellow church members had asked too. He'd walked alongside them throughout these long months of darkness and given them the strength to make it through every day. And if sometimes that had looked a little messy, Jesus wouldn't have minded that.

And suddenly, neither did she.

Chapter Twenty-Five

Mikayla sat on the cold metal bench in the bus shelter a block away from the school Andrew Thompson had attended when she last saw him several months ago. Did he go there still? Were he and his family even in Chicago anymore? After waiting in the park three times last week and then staking out the school for the third straight day this week with no sign of him, she was beginning to wonder.

Four city buses had come and gone from this stop while she'd been sitting here. The last one she'd had to wave off as the kids and parents taking buses home had all left and she was the only one in the shelter. Any more like that and someone was definitely going to start getting suspicious. A gust of wind swept through the shelter and Mikayla zipped her jacket higher. She should probably think about calling it for today. The school bell had rung almost twenty minutes earlier and only the odd straggler was coming out of the building now or hanging around the playground.

Jax and Holden were waiting a few blocks away from her, at a Laundromat she and her mother used to take their clothes to. Midway through their second week in the States, they'd all agreed a laundry run was a good idea. If she'd spotted Andrew after school, she was supposed to have texted Jax who would have driven over right away. Mikayla pulled out her phone and glanced at the screen. Her battery was nearly dead anyway. She sighed and pushed to her feet. Might as well walk over and help them with the clothes so at least she'd have done one productive thing today.

Wandering along the streets between the school and the home she had grown up in brought a tidal wave of memories sweeping over Mikayla. A tidal wave that might have drowned her a few months ago but now brought more warmth and gratitude for the wonderful life she'd had than sadness. That was still very much there too, woven throughout the good memories like silver threads through fabric.

When she pulled open the door of the Laundromat and stepped inside, the past enveloped her as strongly as the warmth of the dryers and the smell of fabric softener and damp clothes. The plumbing in their old house was unreliable, so she and her mother had come to this place most Saturday mornings when she was growing up. Mikayla could picture her standing there now, shaking out a sheet she'd pulled from the dryer and handing one end to Mikayla so they could fold it together. She stopped and stared at the spot, hearing them both laugh as Mikayla tried and failed to master the art of neatly folding a fitted sheet.

"Grant?"

Jax's voice, and the puzzled look on his face when she blinked away the mist that had drifted across her vision and focused on him, drew her back to the present. "Yeah. Sorry." She glanced around the room lined with washing machines on one wall and dryers on the other. "Where's Holden?"

As usual, Jax refused to be redirected. "He decided to walk around the neighborhood a bit, see if he happened to spot Andrew in case you didn't. But you look like you need to sit down." He took her hand and guided her to the table at the back. Mikayla sank onto one of the worn folding chairs. He relinquished her hand and pulled out the chair next to her. "Is everything okay? Did you see Andrew?"

In the close air of the space, she unzipped her jacket. "No, unfortunately. I'm starting to wonder if he even goes to the school anymore."

"So what has upset you?"

"I'm not upset, only … remembering." Mikayla ran her hand over the rough, splintered surface of the wooden table. "My mother and I used to come here every Saturday to do our laundry. When I walked in I could almost see her standing here."

"Ah." A shadow flickered over his face. "*Mi mamá* and I took our clothes to a Laundromat too, on Thursday evenings. They had a few arcade machines there and she always let me play while the clothes were washing."

The image of a young Jax standing in front of a machine yanking on the joystick and yelling in triumph made her smile. "What did you play?"

"Asteroids and Pac-Man, mostly."

"Let me guess, you got the high score every time?"

"Of course. Someday I should go back and check. I am sure I still have it on both machines."

"No doubt."

When they met hers, his dark eyes were laughing. Any lingering sadness drifting through Mikayla dissipated as she stilled, caught up in their depths. Then the dryer let out a long, shrill buzz and the spell was broken. "I'll get those."

Another buzzer sounded and Jax pushed his chair away from the table. "I will help."

He tapped the top of the first machine that had buzzed as he walked by it. "This one has your clothes."

How did he know that? Her cheeks warmed a little as she mentally ran over the items in the bag she'd handed Holden before she left to go to the school. She shrugged off her embarrassment. Camping together meant sacrificing a few boundaries and a fair amount of privacy. And it had been her idea, after all.

Jax tugged a towel from the dryer and folded it before setting it on top of the machine. "What did you do?"

She swiped the side of her hand across the top of the machine to rid it of a layer of lint before setting a T-shirt on it. "What did I do?"

"Yes. When you and your mother were here and the clothes were in the washing machine or the dryer."

"Oh." Mikayla worked a pair of track pants loose from the tangled mass of clothes. "Mostly we sat at the table in the back and drew or painted in our sketchbooks."

Jax craned his head to look at the table where they'd been sitting. "Same table, do you think?"

"I don't know. It's been a few years." Mikayla dropped the track pants on top of the folded T-shirt and walked over to it. It was an ancient piece of furniture, and it definitely looked familiar. Maybe it was the same one she and her mother had used. If so … She dropped to a crouch at the end of the table and peered beneath it. Her heart flip-flopped in her chest. They were faded, but she could still make out the letters. And the images.

Jax's legs appeared in her line of vision before he squatted at the opposite end of the table. "What is it?"

"Here." Mikayla pointed to the underside. "I got bored of my sketchbook one day and crawled under the table and painted a picture of my mother and me. I added our initials underneath. R. G. and M. G."

"I see them." Jax reached over and lightly ran his fingers over the drawing of the mother and daughter. "How old were you?"

"Maybe eight or nine?"

"Even then you had talent." Jax pulled the phone from his jacket pocket, held it under the table, and snapped a picture. He pushed to his feet, came around to her end, and crouched beside her. "See?" He held out the phone.

He'd captured the picture she'd drawn perfectly. "Will you send it to me?"

"Actually, I thought I might try to sell it on the dark web. I am sure I could make a great deal of money."

Mikayla laughed. "I seriously doubt—"

Another pair of legs appeared at the side of the table. "You two might be the worst hide and seek players in the world."

Bracing herself with a hand on the table top, Mikayla stood and offered Holden a sheepish smile. "My mom and I used to come here to do laundry. I was showing Jax a drawing I made of the two of us one day."

"Here." Jax held the phone out to Holden.

Holden bent over the device to take a good look. "Wow. That's still here?"

"Believe it or not," Mikayla said dryly.

Jax laughed and tucked the phone into his pocket. "Yes, I will send the picture to you."

"Thanks." She made her way to the dryer and finished folding the rest of her clothes. That had been thoughtful of Jax, taking the picture. Clearly he recognized how important it was to her. The man definitely had a knack for keeping her off-balance.

Holden joined her and grabbed a sweatshirt from the machine next to hers. "I don't suppose you saw anything at the school today?"

The question sounded casual, but she knew it wasn't. Everything in her wished she had more to report. "No, sorry."

"It's okay." Holden folded a few more items before lifting the pile of clothes and sliding it into the garbage bag Jax held open for him. "I didn't see anything either. This is all a long shot, I know. I appreciate you guys hanging in with me as long as you have."

"Hey." Jax clapped a hand on Holden's shoulder. "We are not giving up yet. Why don't we take a break from the school tomorrow and go to the park again? Then, if Mikayla is okay with it, she can wait at the school again on Friday. If nothing happens that day, maybe we regroup, try to think of anything else we can do while we are still in the area. We have another week and a half. If Andrew still lives around here, we are bound to catch a glimpse of him sometime between now and then."

Mikayla reached for the bag Jax held out to her and deposited her clean clothes inside. "Sounds like a plan."

Holden slid an arm around her shoulders. "All right then, if you're both sure. In the meantime, I'm taking the two of you out for dinner tonight as a thank you."

Part of Mikayla wanted to protest that he didn't owe them anything, but a hot dinner in a warm restaurant definitely sounded appealing. Besides, she needed to recharge her phone.

Even if she had thought to take a picture of her drawing beneath the table—which she hadn't—she likely wouldn't have been able to. Which made Jax's gesture all the more considerate.

She followed the two men to the door. Before heading outside, she craned her neck for a last glimpse of the table along the back wall of the Laundromat. A vivid image of her mother, head bent over her sketchpad, and seven-year-old Mikayla gripping a paintbrush and lost in another world next to her, flashed through her mind, remaining there like an imprint as she tore herself away and stepped outside, zipping up her jacket against the cold Chicago wind.

Chapter Twenty-Six

Christina knocked on Daniel and Nicole's condo door. She could hear voices and laughter inside, so when no one came to the door, she tried the knob. It turned easily in her hand. She pushed open the door and slipped inside. A childish squeal wafted between the French doors. Christina slid her green coat off, tossed it over a chair, then made her way to the kitchen.

"Thanks for lunch, Nic. Everything was amazing."

Christina paused outside the doors. Was that Becca? She hadn't seen Daniel's sister or her three kids in months. Olivia and Josh were in school, so that must have been two-year-old Ava she'd heard when she first came in. Drawing in a deep breath, Christina pushed through the swinging doors. "Hi, all."

Daniel and Nicole swiveled on their stools at the island. "Hey, Chris." Daniel motioned toward a free stool. "Come join us."

Becca was wiping Ava's face and hands with a cloth. Ava's soft curls were damp and one was matted with something that looked like banana. She was squirming to get away from her mother's ministrations. She looked so adorable the urge to sweep her into her arms gripped Christina with an intensity that shocked her. Becca looked over at Christina and smiled as she shoved a strand of long brown hair that had come loose from her ponytail away from her face. "Hey, Chris." She straightened, tossed the cloth into the sink, and bounded over to pull Christina into a hug. "Good to see you. It's been way too long."

"It definitely has." Christina glanced past her at the toddler twisting in her child seat. "Ava's getting so big."

Becca let her go. "Yes, she is. They all are. You and Holden need to come for dinner soon so you can see everyone."

The idea of another dinner party tightened Christina's stomach, but she forced a smile. "We'd like that."

Nicole undid the strap on Ava's seat and lifted the giggling girl into her arms. "Hi, Chris."

"Hey. Sorry to barge in. I knocked but no one answered, so I let myself in."

Nicole waved away her apology as she came over and gave her a one-armed hug, Ava settled on her other hip. Christina touched the little girl's red cheek. So sweet.

Becca held out her arms and Ava leaned toward her. "Better get this little one home so she can have a nap before the other terrors arrive." She kissed Nicole on the cheek. "You should get some rest too. Take care of yourself, okay? And this little one." She inclined her head toward Nicole's abdomen.

The knot in Christina's stomach tightened to the point of pain. Nicole was pregnant? She worked to hide her shock as Nicole glanced at her, a look of chagrin on her face. Daniel hopped off his stool. "I'll walk you two to the door." He took Ava from his sister's arms and lifted her high in the air. "Come on, little girl."

Christina watched them, avoiding Nicole's gaze. Daniel would be an amazing father. He'd already proven that with Jordan. Holden was great with his nephew too, which is why Christina had been so sure he would also be a wonderful … She banished the thought, already dealing with enough emotions at the moment.

Daniel lowered his niece and rested a hand between Becca's shoulder blades to guide her to the door. Becca waved at Christina. "'Bye, Chris. I meant it about dinner. When Holden's home, give me a call."

"Sounds good." The words came out in a croak and Christina cleared her throat.

Her legs felt weak, so she walked over to the stool Daniel had vacated and sank onto it. Nicole took the one beside her, and rested her hands on Christina's knees, her cheeks ashen. "Chris. I'm so sorry. I didn't mean for you to find out like that."

"It's okay."

"No, it's not. I've been meaning to tell you for weeks, but it never seemed like the right moment."

Christina nodded woodenly. "I get it. Honestly, I do." She reached out, tentative, and lightly touched the front of Nicole's shirt. "How far along are you?"

"Four and a half months." Nicole bit her lip.

What did she think Christina was going to do, lash out? Burst into tears? Storm out of the condo? She reached for Nicole's hands and held them. "I'm happy for you and Daniel, Nic."

"Truly? Because I would totally understand if the idea upset you. You don't have to pretend you're perfectly fine with this."

Christina let go of her and grabbed a mug and the pot of tea sitting on the island. "I'm not pretending. I mean, it's a little hard, of course, thinking about you having a baby so soon after losing one, but," she filled the cup with hot liquid, the smell of peppermint drifting from the spout, "a baby is always good news. Always."

To her surprise, she realized she meant the words. Was that why she had experienced peace lately, and been overwhelmed by the realization of how much others cared for her and Holden? Had God been preparing her for this moment, for this news?

Nicole's face softened. "We are pretty excited, but we've had mixed feelings about sharing this with you and Holden. It doesn't seem right, somehow, to experience this much joy when you guys are still going through so much."

Christina used her finger to wipe off a drop of tea sliding down the spout of the pot. "I don't want you to think like that and neither will Holden. I know we won't technically be an aunt and uncle to this little one, but it will definitely feel that way. Please don't let what we've been through spoil your excitement in any way." She lifted her mug and took a sip of the calming liquid.

"If you're sure ..."

"I am. Now tell me everything. How have you been feeling?"

"Not too bad. Daniel's been wonderful, running out at any time of the day or night, whenever I have a craving. He loves his sister's kids so much and Jordan, of course. He's ecstatic at the idea of having one of his own."

Christina ran a finger around the rim of the mug. "Yeah, Holden was the same. He spent two hours one night searching four different all-night stores trying to find Häagen-Dazs® caramel corn ice cream, because that's what I felt like. By the time he came home I was fast asleep, so he stuck it in the freezer and crawled into bed to grab an hour or two of rest before work." She started to laugh at the memory, but it caught in her throat and she lifted her mug and took another sip.

"He's a good guy," Nicole said softly.

"Yes, he is."

"How are the two of you doing?"

She shook her head slightly. "Not great. I'm sure he's happy this trip came along when it did so he could be free of me for a little while."

"Hey," Nicole grasped Christina's upper arms. "That man loves you. I was watching him when you were here for dinner and he never took his eyes off you."

"That's because I've become a crazy lady, and he was likely worried about me losing it in the middle of your amazing roast beef dinner."

"He's worried about you, yes, but not because he thinks you're crazy, because he knows you're sad, and it's killing him. He'd do anything to make you feel better, to ease your grief somehow."

Christina pressed a palm to the cool surface of the island. Two of her fingernails were broken and a spot of pink polish clung to several of them. She needed a manicure. When was the last time she'd indulged in one? "The question that's been haunting me the last few days, is what about his grief? I've been so wrapped up in myself the last few months, I'm only now starting to realize that he's hurting as much as I am, only he's been so busy trying to comfort me, he hasn't been able to express it."

Nicole tilted her head. "Well, that's hopeful."

"What is?"

"That you're beginning to think about him and what he's going through. That's a real breakthrough, Chris. A definite move forward."

"Maybe. For every step forward though, I take at least two back. One night last week I smashed every glass in my cupboard."

"How did that make you feel?"

Christina shot her friend a wry grin. "Pretty good, actually."

"Then that's not a step back, that's another step forward. You're not keeping everything bottled inside anymore."

"No, I think it's safe to say I am not doing that."

"There you go." Nicole lifted her mug. "To progress."

Christina clinked her mug against Nicole's before taking another sip. The soothing drink had begun to ease a little of the tightness in her stomach. "You don't have any cravings now, do you?"

Nicole's forehead wrinkled. "I hadn't thought about it, why?"

"All that talk of Häagen-Dazs® ice cream got me thinking."

Nicole grinned. "If you can't take advantage of your husband's good nature when you're pregnant, when can you?"

"Exactly."

Nicole leaned away from the island. "Daniel?"

Seconds later he'd pushed through the doors and was at her side. "What's up?"

"I was wondering how you'd feel about making a run to the store."

"Sure. What do you need?"

"I had a sudden craving for Häagen-Dazs® caramel corn ice cream. And maybe sprinkles to go on top. And chocolate sauce. Would you mind?"

"Of course not." He leaned a hip against the island. "Any news from our intrepid campers?"

Christina refilled her mug. "Not really. Holden and I have talked a few times, but it doesn't sound like they've made much progress. I keep thinking he'll tell me they've abandoned the idea of camping and booked into a hotel, but so far they seem to be hanging in there."

Nicole laughed. "I think you give them too little credit. Mikayla says it's been going all right. That it's a little cold at night, but they're at a nice campground and enjoying nature and stuff." She wrinkled her nose a little at the end, and Daniel grinned.

"City girl."

Nicole lifted slender shoulders. "I do prefer the bright lights of the big city, that's true. Probably because it's all I've ever known. I've never gone camping in my life and I have no desire to start now."

"No, I doubt it's anything we'll be doing anytime soon. Maybe someday."

"We'll see."

Daniel pushed away from the island. "I'll go get your ice cream. I'll be right—" He frowned as he swung his gaze to Christina. "Wait a minute. I seem to recall Holden telling me a story about running all over town one night looking for that flavor." He pointed at her. "This was your idea, wasn't it?"

She pressed her lips together. "I might have mentioned it. Although the sprinkles and chocolate sauce were all Nicole."

He shook his head. "And like a sap, I was about to fall for it."

"Does that mean you're not going?" Nicole stuck out her lower lip.

"Of course I'll go. But I want you both to know that I'm going because I want to, not because you have tricked me into anything."

"Duly noted."

Daniel leaned in and kissed her before starting for the doors.

Christina shifted on the stool. "Daniel?"

He stopped and turned around. "Yeah?"

"Congratulations on your amazing news. I'm happy for you guys. And Holden will be too."

He wrapped his arms around her. "Thanks, Chris, that means a lot to us."

"I mean it."

"I know you do." He ruffled her hair lightly. "That's why, in spite of your shameless attempt to use my wife to play me, you're still going to get your ice cream."

Christina laughed as he strode from the room. It felt a little rusty rising in her throat, but not as much as before. Another step forward? Maybe. If she could string enough of those together, she might be able to find her way out of the dark hole she'd been in and return to the life with Holden she'd been afraid was irretrievably lost.

Chapter Twenty-Seven

Holden meandered along the wall covered in bright, vibrant paintings. After they'd hung out in the park yesterday, Mikayla had staked out the school again today. Neither location had yielded any returns on the investment of their time. Since it was Friday, there was no use trying to spot Andrew coming or going from school over the weekend. Was it worth hanging out around the school again on Monday? Somehow Holden doubted it. Jax and Mikayla had to be thinking that the three of them were wasting their time, although neither of them had hinted at that. Lucky for him, Mikayla's pre-show event was tonight and the opening next week or they might have suggested by now that the three of them think about packing it in and heading home.

Luck likely had nothing to do with it. Even if he couldn't fully see it, Holden was clinging to the belief that God was behind all this and had brought him and Jax and Mikayla all the way to the windy city for some greater purpose.

For tonight, he and Jax had tagged along with Mikayla to check out the display of her artwork and to talk it up in the presence of any critics or investors. Holden moved on to another piece. That wasn't difficult to do. Like he'd told Jax, Mikayla was extremely good, and it was awe-inspiring, seeing her pieces of work all together like this. The space itself felt like it had come alive and radiated with energy. He could understand why Daniel had been blown away the first time he'd seen it.

Jax had stopped in front of a large, particularly vivid painting of a field of poppies. Two small girls, blond heads bobbing above the flowers, strolled through the field arm in arm. Holden wandered over to stand beside him. For a moment, neither of them spoke then Jax pointed to the artwork. "I am guessing this is Mikayla and Nicole."

Holden checked the date. "Likely, since it was painted shortly after Mik found out she had a sister and flew to Toronto to meet her."

"I wonder what that must have been like, a reunion after so many years."

Holden shot him a sideways glance at the melancholy tone in his voice. Was Jax thinking about the brother he had lost? If so, he understood completely. There wasn't much he wouldn't give to see Gage again. Thankfully, he knew he would one day, but Jax likely didn't have the same hope.

Jax shrugged and the melancholy appeared to slide off of him, like a cape he'd untied at his throat and allowed to drop to the floor. "It's something, isn't it?" He turned in a half circle. "All of this. So much … life."

"Thank you, Jax." Mikayla walked toward them, her cheeks a little flushed. "That's exactly what I hope people see in my paintings."

He smiled at her. "I am not sure how they couldn't. Your paintings, they practically have a pulse."

She laughed lightly. "That's a new one. I think I like it."

"You should. It's a compliment. And it is both kind and true."

The small white card bearing the name of the piece with the girls walking through the poppies—*The Stolen Years*—was slightly askew and Holden tapped the top corner to straighten it. "So when is the official opening?"

She wrinkled her nose. "A week from tonight, so Friday, May 14th. No idea how many people will come, but I should at least put in an appearance."

Jax frowned. "An appearance? You should be here all night. Everyone will want to meet the woman behind these works of art."

She tipped her head from one side to the other, weighing his words. "Maybe."

He pressed his lips together as if he wanted to say more but was restraining himself. Holden cast one more glance at the pictures on the wall. An ache spread through his chest. He'd give almost anything to have Christina here with him. She had always loved art galleries, and they'd spent a lot of Saturdays wandering through every one in Toronto they could find. The smaller ones, showcasing new and rising artists, were her favorite. She would have been captivated by this show. Not only because Mikayla was a close friend, but she'd always been partial to bright paintings that teemed with life. And since, as Jax had pointed out, these works practically had their own pulse, a heartbeat of their own, she would no doubt have been powerfully drawn to them.

And the joy and hope in them was particularly poignant, given that these ones had all been painted after Mikayla had lost her parents in such a sudden, shocking way. Christina would no doubt have been impacted by that, by the hope that life and joy could return after a tragic loss. No wonder Mikayla seemed a little hesitant to allow herself to believe that others could see that in her work, when it was so deeply personal, such a reflection of her own journey from grief to hope. That had to be tough, allowing yourself to be that vulnerable and transparent.

Jax was likely right about all the people who would flock to the gallery to experience that, but Mikayla needed to see for herself that people wanted to see her work and meet her in person. Holden had no doubt the place would be packed on opening night, once reporters had spread the word in the media. It would be fun to see that, even if the one person he wanted to be with wouldn't be there.

His throat tightened and he swallowed. "I think I'll go give Christina a call. Can I meet you guys later?"

Jax looked at Mikayla. "I wouldn't mind grabbing dinner, if you know of a place near here."

She nodded. "There's a nice Italian place on the other side of the street, about half a block west. Gallo's." She turned to Holden. "I'm through here, so Jax and I could get a table and you can join us whenever you're done."

"Sounds perfect." Holden kissed her on the cheek. "Seriously, Mik, the pieces look amazing."

The flush on her cheeks deepened as she glanced around the intimate gallery. "Thanks."

He lifted his phone in their direction. "I'll see you in a bit." When he stepped outside, a cool spring breeze greeted him, carrying with it the smells of damp earth and the aroma of garbage that never seemed to completely dissipate from the air in the city. Holden rounded the corner of the gallery and stopped halfway along the alleyway between it and the building next door. Leaning against the wall, he bent his knee and pressed the bottom of his shoe to the bricks as he dialed his wife's phone number. After three rings, her voice came over the line. "Hi, Holden."

His stomach clenched. She sounded better than the last time he'd called, less despondent. Had something happened? "Are you doing okay?"

He didn't like the slight hesitation before she answered. "I'm all right. I went to Nicole's yesterday. Daniel's sister Becca was there with her youngest. Ava is such a sweetie."

His stomach twisted at the wistfulness in her voice. "I'll bet. I haven't seen Becca and Austin's kids in a long time. They must be getting big."

"They are. Ava is anyway. And …"

Holden waited. And what?

"Nicole and Daniel are expecting."

He closed his eyes. He'd suspected it, and part of him was thrilled at the news. The other part had hoped he and Christina might have a bit more time before they had to deal with their closest friends having a baby. He opened his eyes and fixed his gaze on an old tire lying on the ground a few feet away. "They must be excited."

"They are. And I told them you would be excited for them too."

"I suppose I am, but …"

"It's good news, Holden. I'm happy for them."

"You are?" Was that possible, or was Christina only saying what she knew was the right thing in a situation like this?

"Yes, I am. Honest. Like I told Nicole, a baby is always good news." Her voice caught a little, but she did sound sure of herself.

"I agree. I'll text Daniel and congratulate him."

"You should." The breath she drew in shuddered a little, but when she spoke, the heaviness that had threaded itself through everything she had said the last few months was still missing. "How are things going there?"

"Still no sign of Matthew Gibson. I just came from the gallery where Mikayla's paintings are on display. Reminded me of all those weekends we spent touring galleries in Toronto."

"We should do that again."

Was that a smile in her voice? Holden was almost afraid to speak again, in case he'd inadvertently say something to drive it away. "I'd love that." Would she remember that she had suggested going? Suggested they leave the safety of their home and venture out into crowds of strangers? He prayed she would.

After a few seconds of silence, she spoke again. "I better get some sleep. Work's been crazy."

He frowned. "You're not overdoing it, are you?"

"I don't think so. It's good to be busy."

"I guess. Please take care of yourself."

"I will. Good night, Holden."

"Good night, love." She didn't disconnect the call before he had a chance to press the button this time. After he had, he dropped the phone into the inside pocket of his jacket and rubbed his palm over his chest. As good as it was to hear Christina's voice, it hurt too. Made him miss her even more. But she'd sounded good, hadn't she? Maybe it was wishful thinking, but even Daniel and Nicole's news hadn't seemed to flatten her like it would have a few months or even weeks ago. Was she finally beginning to emerge, even a little, from the grief that had shrouded her since Tristan's death?

A flicker of hope ignited in his chest. Jax was right—life really could kick you in the butt. But maybe, because of that, when something good happened, the joy of it felt that much greater.

Chapter Twenty-Eight

Mikayla played with the white cloth napkin in her lap. The aroma of tomatoes and spices hung in the air and she breathed deeply, trying to calm her nerves as much as to inhale the tantalizing mixture. A couple at a nearby table caught her eye and her breath hitched. They were older, maybe in their sixties, and the man held one of his wife's hands on the table as he leaned close to talk to her in a low voice. She laughed softly and he smiled at her. The two of them reminded her, with a sudden, dagger-like thrust to her chest, of her parents. So strongly that, although the scene was intimate, she couldn't tear her gaze away for a long moment. When she did, she scrambled for a topic of conversation to take her mind off of the two of them. "So, Jax."

His eyes met hers above his menu. "*Sí.*"

"That doesn't sound like a particularly Spanish name."

He closed the menu and set it on the table. "It is not. My name is actually Juan Miguel Rodriguez. When my parents came to Canada, they wanted to give me a name that sounded more English. Someone my dad worked with told him that John is sometimes changed to Jack. They liked the sound of that and started using it, but my older brother always called me Jax, and that is the name that ended up sticking."

"Got it." Mikayla straightened the knife and spoon beside her plate. "How did you become a PI anyway?"

Jax pursed his lips. "It is a long story, Grant. Are you sure you want to get into it right now?"

"I am. Holden will probably be a little while yet."

His smile was more of a grimace. "All right, if you insist." He tapped his spoon on the tablecloth a few times. "Like I said, I have an older brother. At least, I think I do. I have not seen him for a long time."

She tilted her head. "Why not?"

"My parents immigrated to Canada before I was born. My brother Diego was two years old. A year after they arrived in Toronto, I came along. As far as I know, things were good for a while, but when I was nine, my parents divorced. My father returned to Puerto Rico and …"

He tapped the table with his spoon again until Mikayla reached across and covered it with her hand. "And what?"

He blew out a breath and let go of the spoon. "And he took Diego and me with him."

"Legally?"

Jax shook his head. "No. My mother had been awarded full custody. He kidnapped us, basically. He was supposed to take us out for one last dinner before he left, but he drove us to the airport instead and we fled the country. My mother nearly went out of her mind trying to find us and get the Puerto Rican government to send us to Canada."

"How long did it take?"

"Two years."

Her chest squeezed. "Your poor mother."

"Yeah, it was rough. My father drank a lot and could not keep a job, so Diego and I had to learn to scrounge for ourselves or we did not eat. Between that and our father moving us around often to evade the authorities, it was not a good two years. When we were finally returned to Canada, Diego struggled. He was fourteen and had no idea where he belonged any more. He had been my dad's drinking buddy, and not only were his loyalties divided, he was already heading down the path of alcoholism. We had been close when we were younger, but he did not want anything to do with me by that time. He started staying out later and later at night and friends of mine would tell me about the kinds of kids he was hanging around with and the trouble they were getting into. I was genuinely scared for him. I did not tell *mi mamá* for a long time because life was hard for her and I didn't want her to worry. The stories I was hearing kept getting worse. When Diego was sixteen and someone told me my brother had sold his older sister drugs, I finally went to *Mamá*. She and Diego had a huge fight and he stormed out of the apartment."

Jax had told the story quickly, almost without breathing, as if he had to get it out before he lost his nerve. Mikayla touched his arm. "I'm sorry, Jax."

He shrugged, as though it didn't bother him, but the pain roiling in his eyes told a different story. "It was a long time ago."

"And you haven't seen him since?"

"No. We have not heard anything from him for almost twenty years."

"Do you think he's alive?" As soon as the words were out, Mikayla wished she could snatch them out of the air. "I'm sorry, I shouldn't have asked that. Don't—"

"No, it is all right." He drove his fingers through his long hair. He wore it loose tonight, and it hung, dark and shimmering, to his shoulders. "The truth is, I have no idea. After I graduated college I became obsessed with finding him and spent years following every lead I could find. I never did track him down, but I learned a lot about dealing with missing persons cases. When I met Daniel at church one Sunday, we got to talking. I found out what he did, told him my story, and he invited me to join him and Chase in their business." He picked up the spoon again but only clutched it tightly, didn't hit the table with it. "So I got my license with the Ministry of Community Safety & Correctional Services and that is how I got into the PI game. Which is probably a lot more than you were looking for."

"No, it was exactly what I was looking for." She bit her lip. "So you met Daniel at church?"

"Yeah. I was in London following yet another lead— someone had seen a guy matching my brother's description in a shelter there—which turned out to be a dead end. I was out walking the streets all Saturday night and the next morning I had given up and was on the way to my motel room when I passed a church. *Mi mamá* had taken Diego and me to mass when we were kids, and although I didn't understand a lot of it, I missed going sometimes. On a whim, I ducked inside. They were serving lunch after and I was hungry, so I went to the basement, loaded a plate, and got talking to the guy in front of me in line. Turned out to be Daniel and a conversation that changed my life."

"What do you think that was, a coincidence?"

"What else?"

"I don't know." Mikayla ran the white cloth napkin through her fingers. "God, maybe?"

He hesitated. "Maybe. I'm not ready to rule out that possibility. Still, I find it hard to believe that God would care about me or what kind of work I do. Don't you?"

"No." Mikayla released the napkin. "I don't."

He contemplated her, his eyes serious. "So you buy into all of it—God creating the world, sending Jesus to die and raising him from the dead, wanting a relationship with all of us, preparing a place where we can be with him for all of eternity?"

A small smile played around her mouth. "Yeah, I do. I buy into all of the above. And I also buy into the fact that God cares about all the details of our lives, even where we work or who we meet and"—she met his gaze—"how much we're hurting over losses or disappointments in life."

"I am not sure I do. When Diego was getting in all that trouble and then when he disappeared, I did pray. I mean, I prayed a lot. I would lie in my bed and stare across the room at the moonlight falling on my brother's empty bed in the corner, and I would clasp my hands together and pray my heart out, begging God to keep him safe and to bring him home." He held out the hand not gripping the spoon, palm up. "You can see how much the prayers of that scared little kid worked."

Mikayla's throat tightened. The confusion in Jax's eyes was raw and real. What could she possibly say that would comfort him in any way? "I'm so sorry you had to go through all that. I know it's hard sometimes to see how God is working in our lives, but I believe he has been working in yours. He led you to the church that day and to Daniel."

"What about my brother?"

"I hope you find him. I'll pray that you do, but God has

given all of us the freedom to make choices. If Diego's choices led him away from God and are keeping him from reaching out to you, maybe the time isn't right for you to find him. Sometimes the only thing we can do is trust that the people we love are in God's hands and then let them go."

"Maybe." He didn't look too sure.

"And now he's brought us into your life. No matter what happens from here, you're not alone—we care about you."

One eyebrow quirked. "Oh, yeah?" A mischievous glint sparked in his eye, the pain banished as completely as if it had never been there.

"Well, yeah, I mean, you've become a good friend to … all of us." *Seriously, could you be any lamer?*

"That is good. I consider you a good friend too." His lips quirked. "All of you." Jax tossed the spoon onto the napkin still folded at his place and opened the menu. "Should we order?"

Mikayla contemplated him. Clearly the subject was closed. She wouldn't push him on it any further, only pray for him, that God would somehow make it clear how much He cared for him and the rest of his family. The guilt she'd felt the day before, after making him work so hard to start the fire, churned in her stomach again. She'd clearly misjudged him, thinking he'd become a PI because it was easy, or because he wanted to stick his nose in other people's business. It hadn't occurred to her that a tragedy in his family might have driven him into the profession. That every day he helped other people do what he hadn't been able to accomplish. What was that, a kind of penance? A tribute to his brother? An offering to his mother? Whatever it was, searching for strangers had to be a constant, incredibly painful rehashing of the loss of Diego. And every joyous reunion a stabbing reminder that he might never see his own brother again.

Mikayla pressed a hand to the base of her throat in an attempt to ease the ache there. She hadn't considered, either, that the flirty, trouble-making Jax she'd been so dismissive of could be a mask hiding that hurting kid crying out to God in his bed.

Jax's fingers brushed lightly over the hand she'd clenched on the table and she swallowed hard. *Focus, Mikayla. He is helping you with a job and then he's leaving town. Do not fall for him like every other female who's crossed his path likely has.* Guaranteed he would break her heart before he disappeared, and then where would she be?

"Grant?"

Mikayla blinked. Jax was watching her, an amused look on his face. "You were far away, no?"

She cleared her throat. "Not really. I was thinking about the art show opening next week, and everything I need to do to get ready for it."

"Ah. I see." He tapped her closed menu with one finger. "You better decide what you want then so you can return to the camp and think about *work*."

The gleam in his eye rankled. He knew as well as she did that she hadn't been thinking about work. The man was infuriatingly perceptive. Which, in contrast to her initial, baseless assessment of his talents and abilities, obviously made him an exceptionally good private eye.

"Hey." Holden tugged the third chair away from the table and sank onto it. "Sorry that took so long."

Jax handed him a menu. "No problem. Christina is okay?"

"Yeah." Holden opened his menu but didn't look at it. "She sounded pretty good tonight, actually. In spite of the fact that …" He shot a look at Mikayla.

Her shoulders slumped a little. "Nicole told her."

He nodded. "Yes."

Jax tilted his head. Mikayla tried hard not to notice how the movement sent his hair cascading down one arm. "Nicole told her what?"

Mikayla sighed. "That she and Daniel are expecting."

"Ah." He winced. "That must have been hard for Christina, on some level." He clasped Holden's forearm. "And you."

"I guess it is. But we're both happy for them at the same time. At least, Chris told me she was, and she sounded sincere."

Mikayla smiled. "That's good, Holden. That sounds like a huge leap forward for her."

"I thought so too."

Jax flicked a finger at her menu. "Shall we eat?"

She picked it up. "Please. Everything smells so good. I'm starving." After a quick perusal of the choices, she lowered her menu slightly. Both men appeared to be reading theirs intently, and she took advantage of the opportunity to study them. Her heart swelled a little. The two of them had been through so much, but they had turned out to be good, honorable men. Tragedy and trauma could affect a person for good or evil. Jax had chosen one path, his brother the opposite. She bit her lip. *Father, I don't have any idea where Diego is, or if he is even alive, but you do. Watch over him, please. And maybe you could help Jax find him? Whether or not he does, please help him to find you, because that's what he needs the most.*

Part of her still ached for the pain she'd seen in his eyes. It shocked her, how much she wanted to ease that pain. How had he gotten to her so quickly? Mikayla swallowed. She couldn't start down that path. It was too dangerous, too unpredictable, and she already had enough to deal with in her life. Besides, her career was only beginning to take off, and she had to concentrate on that. There was absolutely no room in her life right now for a relationship, especially not with someone who called her on it whenever she tried to get away with the slightest little thing.

Jax closed his menu abruptly, catching her staring. "Do you know what you want?"

Startled, she nearly dropped her menu and it caught the rim of her water glass. Jax grabbed the glass before it could spill. The laughter in his eyes when they met hers sent butterflies cart-wheeling through her stomach, and she lowered the menu to her plate so she could clasp her fingers in her lap.

He let go of the glass. "Well?"

She lifted her chin. "Yes, I know what I want. And what I don't." Two could play at the double entendre game. Jax's dark eyes didn't leave hers, even as the laughter faded from them.

Holden closed his menu with a snap. "Well, then. Let's order." He raised a hand for the server. "I know what I want too."

Mikayla didn't doubt it. Holden had wanted the same thing for a long time—for Christina to be well and happy again, and for the two of them to be as close, or maybe closer, than they had been before they lost their child. But what about her? *Did* she know what she wanted? She'd always believed she did, but ever since the night of the dinner party, everything had felt scrambled in her head. The path before her was not as clearly laid out as it had been before Jax Rodriguez walked through those French doors into her sister's kitchen.

If Mikayla was being completely honest with herself, she had no idea what she wanted any longer. And she wasn't sure she liked that one bit.

Chapter Twenty-Nine

Mikayla pressed against the cold brick side of a stationery shop a block south and across the street from the school. From her vantage point, she could barely see the kids streaming out the front doors. She and Jax and Holden had discussed various options to minimize the risk of getting called out for loitering in the area around the school, but when no other ideas seemed promising, Mikayla had insisted on coming here again today.

The heavy stream of children gradually thinned to a trickle and she'd caught no sign of Andrew. Mikayla sighed. For all she knew, his family could have moved away from Chicago in the last few months, which would mean that they had lost any chance they might have had of finding Matthew Gibson.

Every day when they came for her, Holden looked so hopeful that it caused her physical pain to have to report that she had seen nothing. *Father, please. One glimpse, a small sign, anything.* Holden needed something positive in his life right now, and she'd give anything to be the one to help make that happen.

She scanned the front of the school. The double doors at the top of the stairs were closed. A handful of kids milled about in the yard, but most had either climbed into waiting cars and driven off, or wandered along the sidewalk on foot in either direction. She waited another fifteen minutes, until the last kid had left the yard, longer than she had ever stuck around before. Holden and Jax, waiting for her in Jax's car a few blocks away and around a corner, would be wondering where she was, but Mikayla was reluctant to leave.

They'd already been in the States two weeks, which meant that the clock was ticking on Jax's allotted time. Thankfully the gallery opening was this Friday evening, four days from now, barely in time for them to attend before they had to leave the country on Saturday. Holden needed to get back to Christina too, and he had to be running out of vacation time. If she didn't see anything today, she might not have many more chances. So she waited, the cold chill of the bricks and the nip in the air seeping through her jacket and into her bones. After another ten minutes, she pushed away from the wall with a sigh. *Sorry, Holden. I tried.*

She took a step toward the opening between the two buildings and stopped. A burgundy SUV was pulling slowly away from the school. It had come from the far side of the building, where signs had been posted warning parents not to park to wait for their children. So why had this vehicle been there? She couldn't remember seeing one like it around the school before. Of course, she wouldn't have if it always stayed out of sight until well after the final bell had sounded.

The SUV turned onto the street, gliding in her direction. Mikayla leapt across the small alleyway to press against the other wall where it would be harder for the driver to spot her. She kept her eyes glued to the road until the vehicle appeared in her line of vision and crept past. The driver had short, sandy-brown hair. Another adult sat in the passenger seat, but Mikayla couldn't see anything other than the flash of a blue jacket. As the SUV passed her, she drew in a sharp breath. A boy sat in the back seat, behind the driver. He didn't glance her way, but even from the side she recognized him and his mop of blond hair. Andrew Thompson.

Mikayla snatched the phone from her pocket. The battery was low again, but she sent a text to Holden, describing the vehicle to them. Would he and Jax be able to follow it without being seen? She hit send and returned the phone to her jacket pocket. That was on Jax. The man was a professional. If he was half as good at following a suspect without being seen as he was at reading people, no doubt he could follow the SUV for miles without arousing suspicion.

In any case, there was nothing she could do now but try and get comfortable here and wait.

Holden read the text and whipped his head toward Jax. "She saw him." His heart pounded. Were they actually about to confirm that Matthew Gibson was here in Chicago? He'd started to abandon hope that he was even in the area any longer, but now …

Jax leaned forward to turn the key in the ignition. "Where?"

"Driving out of the school parking lot in a burgundy SUV, two men in the front seats." His phone buzzed again and he glanced at it. "The driver had light brown hair and the passenger wore a blue coat—that was all she could see. But she definitely recognized Andrew Thompson in the back seat. They're headed this way."

Jax nodded to the end of the street a half a block from them. "There they are." He signaled and pulled onto the road. For several minutes they followed the vehicle. Occasionally Jax would turn onto a side street, go around the block, and emerge onto the road again. Holden guessed it was a good way to throw off anyone who might be watching the rear-view mirror, but each time he held his breath until they turned onto the path the car they were pursuing had taken and spotted it ahead of them.

"Can you make out the numbers on the licence plate?"

Jax leaned closer to the windshield then shook his head. "No. They've smeared it with mud or something. Old trick."

Holden sighed. That would have been too easy. The vehicle didn't travel directly to Mikayla's old neighborhood, but circled around and drove in from the far side. Eventually, they passed the park the three of them had waited in a week and a half earlier. Two blocks ahead, Holden caught a glimpse of the SUV turning left onto a side street. Jax continued past the street. Holden gritted his teeth. Would they lose them? He had to trust Jax—the man seemed to know exactly what he was doing. He turned left at the next corner, drove three blocks, then turned left and left again, onto the street the burgundy SUV had taken.

Fifty yards from the corner, the vehicle they'd been following sat in a driveway. Jax didn't slow or glance over, but continued past it and turned at the next corner. Holden followed his lead, trying to catch as much as he could in his peripheral vision as they drove by. No sign of any movement in front of the house, but they would have had time to whisk the boy inside if they were attempting to avoid detection.

They drove for five more minutes until Jax lifted a hand. "There you go. Address was 64 Sprucedale."

How on earth had he seen the number on the house? "You think that's his place?"

"I didn't actually see anyone, so I can't be positive, but it makes sense that they were there to drop him off after school, right? Let's get Mikayla, grab dinner, and charge our phones somewhere. Then we can drive back and do a little surveillance outside the house—see if anything happens."

Everything in Holden wanted to go straight to the house they had driven by, march to the door, and demand to see Matthew Gibson, but Jax was right. They had to proceed with extreme caution. Given the lengths whoever was driving the SUV was going to in order to keep Andrew from being seen, he was obviously under protective custody. Was the organization Gage had worked for still involved, even though Daniel was pretty sure they had disbanded it years ago?

His stomach tightened. If it was, their quest had just gotten a lot more dangerous.

Mikayla stepped out of the alleyway and waited at the curb until Jax pulled over. Holden had only texted to let her know they were on their way, not whether or not they had found Andrew, so as soon as the vehicle stopped moving and Holden got out, she jumped into the back seat and leaned forward. "Well?"

Holden shifted around to face her. "We think we know where he lives."

"You do?"

"Yeah. Jax followed them to a place on Sprucedale Street, number 64. Do you know that area?"

"I know Sprucedale Street. Did you actually see Andrew going into the house?"

"No. We stayed a few blocks behind them, so by the time we drove by no one was around. But it was definitely the SUV we had followed from the school. Jax suggested we grab dinner and then stake the place out for a while, see if we notice anything or anyone."

Mikayla fastened her seatbelt. "That makes sense, I guess, although I'd love to go ring the doorbell right now, since he's likely home at the moment."

Holden grinned wryly. "I had the same thought, but Jax is probably right. They're being extremely careful about sneaking him out of the school, so either his parents are overly protective or someone else is still watching out for him. Waiting a while means we're less likely to arouse suspicion."

"Exactly." Jax pulled away from the curb. His eyes met hers in the rear-view mirror. "Nice work, Grant."

It was ridiculous, how quickly a few words of praise from him drove the chill from her. "Thanks," she mumbled, brushing away a speck of dust from the door frame in order to escape the penetrating gaze still regarding her from the front seat.

Holden rested an arm on the top of the seat. "You must have been well hidden if they didn't see you."

"I was. I waited in an alleyway a half a block away. Neither of the men glanced over as they drove by, so I'm sure they didn't see me."

"Did either of them look like Andrew's father to you?"

"I can't say for sure. I couldn't really see the passenger, and the driver's hair was light. I seem to recall Andrew's dad having dark hair, but if they're being this careful about staying hidden, he could have altered his appearance by now."

"I suppose. If not, I wonder who those guys are." He glanced at Jax. "Any theories?"

Jax tapped his fingers on the steering wheel. "I don't know a lot about the kidnappings, but I gather Gage was working for some organization that Daniel and his colleagues were able to mostly shut down after Matthew Gibson was taken, right?"

Holden nodded. "That's right, but it was a pretty powerful organization with a lot of connections and money. It's entirely possible there's a remnant left, people who are still keeping an eye on these kids."

"I think we should assume that. In which case, they may not be at all happy if they find out we tracked one of them here."

Mikayla ran her fingers along the seatbelt that felt suddenly restrictive. Crossing an underground organization wasn't exactly what she had bargained for when she agreed to come on this trip. Still, Holden had been through so much. If it gave him peace of mind to find Matthew and know that Gage hadn't sacrificed his life for nothing, it was worth the risk the three of them were taking. Her gaze shifted to the front. Jax was still watching her, a small smile on his lips as though he'd followed that train of thought. He nodded slightly before switching on the signal and turning into a Denny's parking lot.

Mikayla repressed a sigh. Given her reaction to that intense gaze, it appeared that more than her physical safety might be at risk on this trip. Her heart was also very much on the line, and at the moment, she couldn't have said with any degree of certainty which threat worried her more.

Chapter Thirty

"They're watching the boy's house."

Panic flared in Natalya's chest, but she wrestled it into the box in her mind where she compartmentalized any emotion that could interfere with clear thinking and slammed the lid. After making her way around the desk, she lowered herself onto her plush leather chair. "Are you sure?"

"Yes. They're driving a black Porsche 928—we confirmed the licence is registered to a Juan Miguel Rodriguez, the one they call Jax. He and the other two parked in front of the house next to the Thompsons' at 6:47 this evening and didn't leave until 9:32 pm."

"How were they able to pinpoint the location?"

After a slight hesitation, the man said, "We're not sure. We followed the usual protocol in bringing the boy home from school and didn't detect anyone following us. When they didn't return to the campground by 6 pm, Fernandez contacted me, and we switched out vehicles and returned to the neighborhood. We parked three blocks away and spotted the Porsche arriving shortly thereafter."

Natalya drummed her fingers on the arm of the chair. So they'd managed to track down Andrew Thompson. The net was tightening. "Do you think they spotted anyone?"

"I don't know how they could have. As you requested, the man and the boy stayed inside the entire evening with all curtains and blinds drawn."

Natalya stopped drumming and gripped the leather arm of the chair. "That's something, anyway." At least Doug Thompson was following her instructions. Still, it appeared that might not be enough. "Did Kelly or the others contact Daniel Grey?"

"Not yet."

Hmm. Did that mean they still weren't sure they had the right place? Or the right person? "Let me know right away if they do, and whether or not Doug Thompson will come willingly, we will remove the two of them from the city." Natalya hoped they wouldn't have to resort to that, for Matthew's sake, but she would do whatever she had to do, and so would the others.

"I will. Anything you want us to do in the meantime?"

No clear answer crystallized in her head. From the very beginning of this journey, she'd been clear about the decisions that needed to be made, and she'd made them without second thoughts or hesitations. Every mission they had executed in the States and the early ones in Canada had been meticulously planned and carried out. If any extenuating circumstances arose, the entire organization looked to her to handle them, and she had.

Then Gage Kelly had walked into her life. From nearly the first moment, nothing had gone as smoothly as it had in the past. Not that he hadn't been capable—he'd effectively rescued the children they'd assigned to him. He'd even managed to ensure that Matthew Gibson was safely in the care of the organization seconds before he was gunned down in the street. But *she* had changed. Somehow, meeting him had eroded the foundation of every barrier she had erected to prevent any doubt, hesitation, or emotion to cloud her judgment. In fact, her judgment had been seriously impaired since the day she'd met him, and exponentially so after he had been killed.

And now that lack of judgment could result in their years of work crumbling into dust around them. Every sacrifice she had made, every sacrifice every member of the organization had made, would be rendered null and void if she could not manage to pull herself together and effectively deal with their current crisis.

Natalya's jaw tightened. Enough. It was time to deal with this situation—swiftly and decisively. When she spoke, the coldness that had thawed inside her after meeting Gage solidified again, stabbing through her like stalagmites forming in a cave.

"The house is to be completely shut down. No one goes in or out until I give the all-clear." She reached for a silver letter opener and clasped it in her hand, turning it over and over against her palm. "As for the three from Canada, watch them. I need to know if and when any of them are alone. Report to me the moment that happens and we will move in. Be ready."

"Always." The coldness in the man's tone matched her own. Good. He would do what he needed to do, as would she.

Natalya flipped the letter opener until she gripped it in her clenched hand like a dagger. Then, in one swift movement, she drove the sharp tip into the wooden surface of the desk, deep enough that it stayed there when she let it go. Light from the desk lamp glinted off the metal blade. Yes, more would be hurt. But after that, any threats to the children would be neutralized. The organization could gradually rebuild and get itself on track.

And so could she.

Chapter Thirty-One

"Chris?"

Christina typed the last word of her report on the call she'd gone out on that morning and spun her chair around to face her office door. She'd left it open a crack and one of her co-workers, a friend of hers and Holden's, had pushed it open and stuck his head into the room. "Hey, Karl. What's going on?"

"I'm heading out on a domestic—two young kids involved. Are you free to join me?"

Christina glanced at her phone. 4:40. She was supposed to leave the office in twenty minutes and had been counting the seconds until she could retreat to their house and slip into a hot bath ever since the call she'd been on earlier. Of course, it wasn't as if anyone was waiting at home to rub her feet or ask about her day. She powered down her computer and pushed to her feet. "Sure."

Karl filled her in on the few details he had as they maneuvered the streets of Toronto and stopped in front of a house in one of the ritzier neighborhoods in the city. A neighbor had called the police to complain about a loud fight going on and two small children left in a vehicle in the driveway for an hour and a half. According to the police, they'd been called to the place once before, but hadn't contacted Children's Services before today.

Christina contemplated the limestone house that, given the size and the surrounding houses, likely had a market value of somewhere around two or three million. She sighed as she pushed open the car door. Wealth and status were no indicators of domestic bliss. They were called to houses like this nearly as often as those in less desirable areas of the city. It wasn't always as easy to ensure the safety of the children if the parents had a lot of money to retain a big law firm, though. She braced herself as they walked toward the house. Two cars sat in the driveway—a Tesla and a Prius. At least the people who lived here cared about the environment, if not their own children.

Christina rejected that sentiment. She didn't know the situation yet—she shouldn't rush to judgment until she had all the facts. At least neither of the kids was still in either vehicle, which she confirmed as she peered into the windows as they strode past. They climbed the three stone steps to the red double front doors. Karl hit the bell and a low bong echoed through the house. They waited for two minutes with nothing appearing to happen behind the thick wooden doors. Then Karl pushed the doorbell again. After thirty seconds of silence, he turned to her. "Should we—"

One of the red doors opened a foot or two. A professional-looking woman in a gray fitted suit, blond hair pulled into a bun at the nape of her neck, stood in the small opening, gazing at them with a wary look on her flawlessly made up face. "Yes?"

"Karl McCormack, ma'am. From Children's Services. This is my colleague Christina Kelly."

A muscle twitched in the woman's temple, but otherwise she didn't react to the pronouncement. "What can I do for you?" Her voice had dropped several degrees.

"We'd like to speak to you and your husband, if he is at home. Could we come in?"

The woman hesitated. She bit her lip, but otherwise displayed no hint of nervousness. "What is this regarding?"

Karl glanced behind him. "We'd prefer to discuss that in private, if you don't mind."

"I do mind, actually. We're getting ready to go out for the—"

"What is it, Karen?" The door she'd clearly been using as a shield swung open. A man in a navy pinstriped suit stood behind her, glaring at Christina and her colleague.

Lovely couple. Christina considered them both for a moment. The man was handsome, but the coldness in his eyes suggested that he wasn't someone you wanted to cross.

"He says they're from Children's Services and they want to talk to us for some reason."

Her husband frowned. "I think you might have the wrong place."

Karl pressed a palm to the frame as if he half expected the man to slam the door in their faces. "I don't think so, sir. Could we come in for a moment?"

The man hesitated before stepping out of the way. "If you must, but you're wasting everyone's time."

"That's what we're here to determine." Karl held out a hand for Christina to go through the door first.

As she stepped onto the marble-tiled floor of the expansive entryway, the wail of a baby broke the silence of the house. Her throat tightened. Karl hadn't mentioned a baby.

His eyes met hers as he joined her in the entryway, and a mortified look crossed his face. Clearly he hadn't been informed of the ages of the children. Christina scanned the entryway. A table along one wall held a large crystal vase of fresh flowers beneath a piece of expensive-looking artwork. The faint scent of orchids drifted from the bouquet. Karl tugged a notebook from his pocket and glanced at it. "From the report we received, two minor children live in the home?"

"Report?" The woman pressed a hand to the lapel of her suit jacket. "What report?"

"The police notified us that they investigated a domestic dispute call at this residence a couple of hours ago."

The baby's wails grew louder and Christina balled up both hands to steady herself.

The man rested a hand on his wife's back. Was he supporting her or warning her? "Yeah, the police were here earlier. We explained that we'd had a minor disagreement in the driveway, but we'd worked it out. Nothing physical. They didn't charge either of us with anything. So what are you doing here?"

"The police got in touch with us because someone called them to report that the children had been left in a vehicle in the driveway for an hour and a half this afternoon."

The woman's features remained neutral, but she twisted her fingers together in front of her. "They were asleep when we got home and it wasn't hot outside, so we cracked the windows open, locked the doors, and left them to finish their naps. We checked on them several times and brought them in as soon as they were awake."

Christina nodded toward the stairs. "Could you bring the children here for us?"

The man glanced at his wife. When she nodded slightly, he lowered his arm. "I'll get them."

The scent of orchids was overtaken by the slightly acrid smell of something burning. The woman unclasped her fingers. "I need to check on dinner. Feel free to make yourselves comfortable." She gestured toward one of the rooms that led off the entryway. After she disappeared through another door, Christina followed Karl into a sitting room and the two of them settled on a soft leather sofa.

The room appeared to have been professionally decorated. A large mirror loomed above an oak mantel covered in candles. Lamps on several tables cast a warm glow over the room and the thick carpeting lent a peaceful hush to the space. An armchair by the window, a cashmere blanket tossed casually over an arm, was so inviting that Christina found herself gripped by an urge to sit and read that she hadn't experienced in months.

Before she could analyze that sensation further, the man came into the room holding a baby in one arm and clutching the hand of a young girl who looked to be about three years old. He stopped in front of the couch, on the far side of a large glass coffee table. "This is Sophie." He let go of the little girl's fingers and rested his hand on her strawberry-blond curls before touching his forehead lightly to the baby's. "And this …" he bounced the child a little on his hip and she giggled, "is Olivia." The face that had softened as he gazed at his daughters tightened a little when he met Christina's eyes. "As you can see, they are perfectly fine."

Karl leaned forward slightly. "Will Sophie come over here and say hi to me?"

The man hesitated, then his hand slid from his daughter's head to between her shoulder blades and he guided her forward. "Come say hello to this nice gentleman, Soph."

Christina stood. "May I hold the baby for a moment?" She held out her arms. The man's jaw clenched, but he came around the coffee table and handed the little one to Christina. It likely wasn't necessary for her to examine the child this closely. Clearly both girls were fine and had never been in any real danger. The neighbor's concern about the girls being left in the car had no doubt been exacerbated by the sound of the man and woman fighting and he or she had jumped to conclusions. Still, it wouldn't hurt to make sure.

The woman had returned from the kitchen and stood in the doorway, watching what was going on with an apprehensive look on her face. Christina shifted her attention away to focus on the soft warm body cradled in her arms.

The baby—Olivia—leaned away from her slightly, her blue eyes, framed by impossibly long, auburn lashes, fixed on Christina's face as though she was trying to figure out who this stranger was that had taken her from her daddy. Christina smiled at her. When she touched the little one's hand, the baby's fingers curled around her thumb, and the tightness in Christina's throat became almost unbearable.

"Are you satisfied?"

Christina had been lost in the feel of the soft baby skin against her fingers, the tiny dimple in the chubby cheek, and she jumped when the man spoke. When he reached for the baby and tugged her from Christina, she didn't protest. Her arms felt emptier than they had when they had entered the house, and she crossed them over her abdomen. Karl had been murmuring something to Sophie, and he nodded at the man who took his daughter's hand again and pulled her to his side. Karl rose. "I think we're finished." He glanced at Christina, who nodded.

Her colleague came around the coffee table and stopped in front of the man. "We appreciate your cooperation. Everything seems to be fine here. I'm sure you understand we need to check out every call we receive."

The man sighed. "Yeah, we know. The police told us the same thing. A woman on the street feels it is her civic duty to report her neighbors to the authorities every time she feels we have stepped out of line. Pretty much everyone in the neighborhood has been subjected to a visit from the police at one point or another. Calling in you guys is a new low, though."

Christina stood and smoothed the front of her shirt. "Likely bored and lonely, a bad combination. Still, you might not want to leave the kids in the car again. People are sensitive about that nowadays since there have been deaths as a result. We'd prefer not to have to start a file on you."

The woman's perfectly manicured eyebrows rose. "So you're not now?"

Karl shook his head. "I don't see any reason to at this point."

Her shoulders sagged a little. "Thank you." She walked over to her husband and lifted little Olivia into her arms, pressing a hand to the tiny back to hold her daughter close to her chest. The nervousness she'd displayed earlier had probably been exactly that—concern that anyone would think she or her husband could cause their children harm as opposed to guilt over doing anything wrong.

The husband followed Karl and Christina to the door, his daughter's hand still clutched tightly in his. When he pulled the door open for them, his gaze connected with Christina's. Now that she'd spent a few minutes with him and seen how he interacted with his family, the coldness she'd thought she detected earlier was gone. Could have been her own cynicism projected onto him, something she needed to keep a check on. Just because she'd walked into more horrific situations than she cared to remember didn't mean she should automatically assume every parent she encountered was an abuser or neglected his or her children.

Most loved their kids every bit as much as she had loved Tristan—loved him still—and would never do anything to hurt them. And from what she'd observed, every parent made foolish mistakes. If and when she and Holden did have kids, she'd pray every day that she wouldn't make one that could cause harm to their child. She slid onto the front seat of Karl's gray Kia.

They rode in silence for a few minutes, Christina staring out the window at the street lamps and trees streaming by in a blur of brown and green. That bath was starting to sound more and more appealing.

Karl tapped his palm on the steering wheel, drawing her attention over to him. "You didn't see anything that concerned you, did you?"

"Not at all. No red flags to indicate anything other than what they mentioned—a busybody neighbor causing trouble. Sophie didn't seem afraid or withdrawn, and the baby was perfectly fine. Did you see anything?" So much about the calls they had to make were based on gut instinct. Had Karl detected something she'd missed? Entirely possible, since she could easily have been distracted by the fact that she was holding a baby for the first time since the terrible night they'd lost Tristan.

"No, I agree. No red flags." Karl winced. "I am sorry about the baby."

"Why?"

"From what I was told, it sounded like both kids were older. If I'd known one was a baby, I wouldn't have asked you to come with me."

Christina shook her head. "It's fine."

He shifted his attention from the road to her. "It is?"

"Yes. I'm glad you didn't warn me because I don't know if I would have gone, but I was okay holding her. Better than I would have expected."

"That's good, right?" His gaze lingered on her a few more seconds before he returned his focus to the front.

"It is, actually. I'll never get over losing our baby, but I feel as though I've been moving forward a bit lately. It's encouraging."

"That's great to hear. When does Holden come home?"

She bit her lip. The mention of her husband's name sent mixed emotions coursing through her. "I'm not sure. He'll likely be gone another week or so."

Karl reached over and squeezed her arm. "If you need anything while he's gone, don't hesitate to call Amy or me, okay?"

She managed a tired smile. "Thanks." Before their world had been upended, she and Holden had spent a lot of time with Karl and his wife, Amy. She missed those carefree nights out.

He returned his hand to the wheel. "I'll take care of the paperwork on this when we get to the office. You head home and relax."

Christina wasn't about to argue. "If you insist." She laid her head against the seat again. One more hour and then she could lock the door on the world and take a long, hot bath.

But there was one thing she needed to do first.

Chapter Thirty-Two

Holden stretched his legs out as far as they could go on the passenger side. He was getting a little tired of being crammed into the front seat of this car. If something could happen with this case soon, he'd be extremely happy. They'd been trapped in Jax's Porsche for hours today, since tracking the SUV to this address yesterday afternoon. Not only was he sick of sitting here waiting for something to happen, the fact that they were running out of their allotted time in the States was hanging over all of their heads. They needed to leave the country this weekend or Jax risked getting into trouble, and Holden didn't want to be responsible for that.

"You okay?" Jax shifted his seat back a few inches. Mikayla was sitting behind Holden so she could peer out the window at Andrew's house, which meant that Jax had a little more room to maneuver than Holden did.

"I'd be better if I was about six inches shorter, but yeah, I'm okay. How can you stand doing stakeouts in this car?"

"I don't, usually. It is too small and way too conspicuous. I normally use one of the two clunkers Chase and I keep for this type of thing. Obviously, I did not have them with me in Toronto, and would not have trusted either of them to get us here safely if I did." He patted the top of the gear shift with his palm. "It is a fun car to drive, but the down side is there are no modern features such as a place to charge a phone or a built-in GPS. In any case, the end is in sight. If we can confirm that Andrew Thompson is here and snap a few pictures, we can send that information to Daniel and see what he wants to do with it."

Mikayla leaned forward. "What do you think he'll do if we tell him we've found Andrew?"

Holden sighed. "Hard to say. Everything in him wants to tell his DS. I hate putting him in the position of keeping this information to himself. If we're convinced there's a good chance that Andrew is here and that he and Matthew Gibson could be the same person, I'm sure he'll notify his boss, which is likely for the best."

"You don't sound too sure about that."

Holden twisted the cap off a bottle of water. "I'm trying to be okay with it. If Andrew has a good home here with parents who love him, I'd hate to see him taken away, especially since he doesn't have any siblings for support."

Jax nodded. "How old did you say he was when he was abducted?"

"Four."

"So he may have a vague recollection of his real parents, but this home is pretty much the only one he's known. That is tough, being taken away from everything you know, from family you love, and being thrust into a situation that is strange and unfamiliar."

Mikayla reached between their seats to squeeze Jax's arm and he offered her a sad smile. What was that about? Jax sounded as if he knew what it felt like to be in a position like Andrew's. Had something similar happened to him as a kid? Before Holden could ask, the phone in his jacket pocket buzzed, and he tugged it out and glanced at the screen. His heart skipped a beat. A text from Christina. She hadn't been the one to contact him in months. Was something wrong? He scanned the message.

Hey Holden–no, nothing is wrong.

He managed a grin. In spite of everything that had happened the last few months, she did still know him.

I wanted to check in to see how your day is going.

His fingers tightened around the device. From the time they started dating until six months ago, she'd sent him the same text almost every afternoon. He'd lived for that simple message—the affirmation that she was thinking about him and cared about what was going on in his life. Were they inching closer to that place?

Holden ran his finger over the keys. *Doing great—thank you for asking.* Could she read in those words the depth of his gratitude and how much it meant to him that she had reached out? *We may have found the person we're looking for. Waiting outside his house now to get confirmation and then we'll let Daniel know. How are you, love?*

He hit send and waited, his throat tight. Was he pushing her, asking for more? A few seconds later, his phone vibrated again.

Interesting day. Went on a call with Karl to check on two little girls. All fine. Held the baby for a few minutes.

The message struck Holden with the force—and stabbing pain—of an arrow through his chest. That was the problem with technology. The words came across as casual, matter of fact, when he knew they were anything but. She'd had to hold a baby? What had Karl been thinking, letting her go on a call like that? Karl knew what they'd been through and how hard that would have been for Christina. Holden hesitated, his finger hovering above the keyboard. How much would she share? Biting his lip, he typed in his response. *Was that okay?*

The few seconds he had to wait seemed interminable. Finally her answer flashed across his screen. *It was fine, actually. Don't blame Karl. It was good for me. Baby steps. No pun intended* ☺

Holden blinked. Was she actually making a joke? Waves of emotion crashed over him in such a tidal wave he could barely begin to sort them out. Hurt for Christina, sorrow, love, compassion, and an intense longing to see and hold his wife that made it almost impossible for him to draw in a lungful of the stale air in the car. He hit the button to lower the window. Nothing happened, but before he could ask, Jax turned the key to ignite the battery. "Thanks." Holden lowered the window and leaned closer to breathe in the fresh air.

When the feelings roiling through him settled a little, he slid his finger over the keyboard again. *I'm proud of you. And I miss you more than I can say.*

Her answer came right away this time. *I miss you too. Heading to the bath now. Be careful.*

I will. Enjoy your bath and sleep well. xoxo

Holden dropped the phone into his jacket pocket. Trying to analyze how Christina was feeling through a few typed words on his phone was a challenge, but he couldn't stop himself. If she'd been able to hold a baby for the first time since Tristan had died without freaking out, that was huge, wasn't it? He grimaced. Who was he asking? Was she doing as well as she sounded, even if, in her words, her steps forward were baby ones, or was he only hearing what he wanted to hear? *God, help her to feel you with her tonight. Protect her heart, please.*

Would God hear him this time, when he was asking nothing for himself, only for his wife? No peace filled him, but for tonight he'd done all he could do for Christina. He straightened and hit the button to raise the window. Mikayla rested a hand on his elbow. "You okay?"

He realized suddenly that both she and Jax were watching him intently. Like it had the first time he'd called home to his wife, Jax's silent presence helped relieve some of the angst still flowing through him. "Yeah, I'm good, thanks. Christina texted to ask about my day."

"I figured it was her. It's good of her to text you. Does she do that often?"

"That's the first time in six months."

Her grip on his elbow tightened. "Then that's amazing, right?"

"I think so."

"Is she okay?"

Holden angled himself to see her face. "Sounds like it. She went on a call today and held a baby and she said it was all right."

Jax turned off the battery. "That is huge, Holden."

"It is, right? I mean, I thought so too, but I want her to be okay so badly I don't always trust my own judgment when it comes to figuring out how she is."

Mikayla squeezed his arm before letting go. "It *is* huge. She's making a lot of progress. I know it's hard for you, but maybe she needed this time on her own to process what she's been going through so she can move forward."

"Yeah, maybe. You're right—it has been hard, not being there with her, knowing she's going through all this alone."

"She's not alone." Mikayla spoke quietly, but the words struck him squarely in the chest. Hadn't he asked God only a minute ago to help Christina feel His presence? Even those words suggested that, on some level, he knew God was there.

Jax grabbed the binoculars he'd set between the two front seats and held them to his eyes, leaning forward a little to peer through the front windshield. "I am thinking that window on the second floor, the second one from the left, is likely Andrew's bedroom."

Grateful for something to focus his whirling thoughts on, Holden leaned forward too. "Why do you say that?"

"The curtains are open a crack and I can see a poster on the wall that looks like a baseball player. Here."

Jax passed the binoculars to Holden. He pressed them to his eyes, squinting to see better through the small opening between the blue curtains. Jax was right. It did look like a player in a Chicago Cubs uniform, although he couldn't tell which one. "I see it."

"Gives us something to concentrate on anyway."

Holden nodded and held the binoculars over the seat for Mikayla. After a few seconds, she returned them to Jax. "Looks like the second baseman, Javier Baez."

When Jax shot her a look from the front seat, she laughed. "What? I'm a fan too. And actually, that reminds me. I talked to Andrew when he was walking through the park with his dad one day. He was wearing a Cubs jersey, so I asked him what he thought of the team and how they were doing. He was very polite when he answered me, but then his dad took his arm and almost hauled him away. I'd forgotten about that until you mentioned the poster. At the time I assumed they were in a hurry to get somewhere, but maybe his dad never wanted Andrew to talk to anyone because they were trying to keep a low profile."

"Could be." Jax lifted the binoculars to his eyes again. "They are definitely doing everything they can to keep anyone from seeing inside. That tiny crack in the curtains in Andrew's room is the only opening in any covering on any window. They were all blocked the last time we drove by as well. Whoever lives there is either intensely private or they are trying to hide something from the world."

"Or both." Holden studied the house. It was nearly nine-thirty and they'd been sitting out here almost three hours. No one had come or gone the entire time, and now that darkness had fallen completely over the neighborhood, it wasn't likely anyone would tonight. He contemplated the small opening in the curtains. A slight movement behind them caught his eye and he straightened. "There."

"I saw it." Jax bent closer to the windshield. "Too tall to be Andrew, but it could have been his dad."

A moment later the light in the room went off. Holden nodded. "Likely telling Andrew it was time to go to sleep."

The main floor of the house was also dark. The only light shone dimly around the blinds almost completely covering a window at the opposite end of the second floor from Andrew's. Ten minutes after the boy's light had gone off, that one did as well, encasing the entire building in darkness.

Jax lowered the binoculars. "I would say that is it for tonight. Might as well call it."

"I agree." Holden reached for his seatbelt, anxious to get to the campground and stretch his legs.

"Fine with me." Behind him, Mikayla's seat belt clicked into place. "Let's head to our site and maybe have a campfire. We still have those marshmallows we bought the night we arrived."

"Sounds good. As long as you allow me to use the lighter

tonight." Jax twisted in his seat to throw her a look. "I do not have the energy to start one with sticks."

"Of course. I don't want to wait half the night to get a marshmallow."

Jax shifted around and reached for the key to start the engine. He glanced at Holden. "You are good?"

"Yeah. Thanks." He was surprised to realize it was true. Even if the text exchange with Christina had been brief, it had filled him with hope. Baby steps were still progress, and he'd take every bit of that the two of them could get these days.

Chapter Thirty-Three

Jax stoked the fire with a long stick until the flames leapt high. Mikayla stared into the embers, glowing red at the base of a teepee of logs.

The thoughts that had catapulted through her mind during dinner at the Italian restaurant Friday evening returned now, spinning around and around like leaves caught in a breeze. Holden sat on a stump across the fire from her, appearing to be equally transfixed by the dancing flames.

Jax lowered himself onto the stump beside her. "What are you thinking about?"

"That Italian restaurant we ate at after the pre-show at the art gallery."

"Ah. You are remembering that couple, right? What was it about them that interested you so much?'

She blinked. His habit of jumping into potentially explosive conversations without warning still unnerved her. "What couple?"

He cocked his head and she sighed. How did he even see her looking at them? He'd been immersed in the menu at the time. "You mean the older man and woman sitting near us."

"*Sí*. They reminded you of your parents. No?"

She swallowed, reminded again of how useless it was to try and keep anything from him. "Yes."

"How so?"

Mikayla's eyes met Holden's across the flames. His smile held sympathy, but he didn't jump in to save her. Her shoulders sagged. "The closeness, I guess. The intimacy, as if they were the only two people in the room. And the way he looked at her."

"As if he adored her."

"Yes." He'd seen it too? She'd never even caught him glancing in the direction of the man and woman. Maybe he had assessed the room as they walked in and had taken the measure of every other patron before they'd taken a seat. She wouldn't be a bit surprised.

"It is still painful, thinking of them."

And talking about it. Although maybe healing, as well. Is that why he forced her to do it? Her throat had gone dry, and she leaned forward to grab her water bottle and take a swig. Still clutching the bottle in one hand, she swiped the back of the other one over her mouth to wipe off the drops. And buy herself a few seconds. "It is. A little less as time passes, maybe, but yes, it still hurts."

Jax tossed a piece of wood onto the fire. "How are you not angry with God?"

She rubbed her thumbs over the glass water bottle. "I *am* angry with God. Sometimes I'm furious with him. I yell and scream questions at him. After my parents were killed, for the first time in my life I started to wonder if he actually was good."

"And?"

"I told my pastor that I was questioning God's goodness."

"What did he say?"

"He asked me if, the day before my parents died, I'd believed God was good. I said yes, because I had believed that all my life." One of the logs Jax had propped against the others fell over, sending a shower of sparks into the air. Mikayla watched, mesmerized, as they drifted upwards toward the branches of the trees, eventually flickering and dying against the night sky. "So he asked me what had happened in those twenty-four hours. Had God changed? Was he no longer good because something had happened to me personally?"

Jax stared into the fire. "Something he allowed to happen."

"That's true. But the thing is, as my pastor reminded me, God isn't good because of what he does, or what he allows for reasons we can't understand. He's good because of who he is. He can't be anything else or he would no longer be God."

Holden poked the end of a stick into the fire, releasing another cloud of sparks. "That helped you to get to the place where everything was fine between you and God again?"

Mikayla set the water bottle on the hard-packed earth. "It helped, but I have a long way to go. I can still get mad when I remember what happened or when I forget and think about how nice it will be to go home for Thanksgiving or Christmas, or when I read a great quote and start to text it to my dad before I stop myself. And there are lots of days when, even if I'm not angry, I'm also not feeling particularly loving towards God."

She tugged the blanket she'd thrown over her shoulders tighter around her. "I'm pretty sure that's why we are commanded to love God with our hearts, minds, souls, and strength. We can love with our hearts when we're feeling it, but when we're not, when our hearts are completely broken and not functioning, we can trust what we know in our heads and deep in our souls to be true. That God is still good, he is sovereign, and whether or not we can feel him, he is still with us. On the truly bad days, it takes every bit of physical, emotional, and mental strength to cling to that and not let go. It's still a constant battle."

Holden nodded slowly. "I get that."

"I know you do." His eyes met hers through the flames and she offered him a small smile.

The three of them sat in silence for a few minutes. Mikayla tilted her head, listening to the sound of the frogs croaking by the river and a breeze rustling through the new leaves on the trees. The smell of wood smoke drifted from the pit, evoking memories of her childhood and evenings spent around the campfire with her dad.

Holden tossed the stick into the fire and stood. "I think I'll call it a night."

Mikayla nodded. She probably should too, but the warmth of the fire and the blanket around her shoulders was so comforting, she was hesitant to leave and go into the cold tent. Maybe a few more minutes. "Good night, Holden."

"Good night."

She watched him until he disappeared into the tent he shared with Jax and zipped it closed. Beside her, Jax stretched out his long legs and crossed one ankle over the other. "So, Grant, it is as good as you remember, no?"

She shifted a little to look at him. "What?"

"Camping."

Was she that easy to read? "How do you do that?"

"Do what?"

"How do you always know what I'm thinking?"

He shrugged. "You are easy, like a book. For me, anyway."

Mikayla wasn't sure if she liked that. Not so much because she wanted to keep her thoughts from him, but because him being able to read them so easily felt disconcertingly intimate. "It is, actually. As good as I remember."

"And it also hurts to remember that?"

"A little. But that's okay. It's better than forgetting all the wonderful times I had with my parents." She shoved the water bottle out of the way with the side of her running shoe so she could turn on the stump to face him. "Do you have any good memories of Diego?"

He stared into the fire for so long she began to think he wouldn't answer. Then he exhaled and ran a hand over his head. "What I told you about camping with the boy scouts, that was true. Except that I only did it once, the summer before our dad took us to Puerto Rico. I was eight years old. Diego was eleven and he and I were in the same group. When they dropped us off and told us we had to find our way to the base camp, there were ten of us. Somehow Diego and I got separated from the rest of the group. It took us four days to find our way back to the camp."

A piece of wood, blackened by the fire and smoking, fell across the stones ringing the pit. Jax shoved it into place with a stick and propped the stick against another stump. "The first night I was terrified, but he told me we would be fine, that as long as the two of us were together, nothing could happen to us. We could do anything. He had been a boy scout for three years, so he showed me how to make a trap and catch a rabbit. When we did, he skinned it with his knife and we made a spit and roasted it over a fire. To this day, that meal was the best one I have ever eaten. I can still remember sitting there, tearing off pieces of meat and drinking water we had filled our bottles with from a river. We told each other ghost stories and we laughed for hours. For those four days, I believed with all my heart that my brother was right. That as long as we were together, we could conquer the world. Nothing bad could ever happen to us."

The sorrow in his voice tore at Mikayla's chest. How had things gone so horribly wrong between the two of them? She reached for his hand. "I'm sorry, Jax."

He uncrossed his ankles and slid around to face her, clasping her hand in both of his. "So am I. I am sorry I could not stop my brother from leaving and that I have never been able to find him. I am sorry I could not save him like he saved me in those woods."

She shook her head. "It wasn't your job to save him. You were a kid. Nothing that happened was your fault."

In the light of the flickering flames, their eyes met and for a few seconds she couldn't draw in a breath. Then he leaned forward and rested his forehead against hers. Neither of them moved for a moment, until he lifted his head. "*Gracias*. Thank you for saying that."

"I mean it."

"Coming from you, I almost can believe it."

"I hope you can fully believe it someday."

"Maybe." His smile was sad.

Mikayla could barely take it when he looked at her that way. Like he had Friday night, at the restaurant. She had hurt him when she told him she knew what she didn't want. Clearly he'd taken that to mean that she didn't want a relationship with him. *Was* that what she meant? Even if it was, she could have found a kinder way to say it. "Of course, you don't always read me perfectly."

The sorrow cleared from his eyes as a smile played around his lips. "When have I not?'

"The other night, in the restaurant, when I said I knew what I didn't want."

"Ah." He lifted her hand and pressed the back of it to his mouth. "You were not saying that you did not want to be with me?"

Tingles of electricity prickled across her skin. "Not exactly, no."

He lowered her hand but didn't let go of it, only rested their clasped hands on his knee. "Then you do want to be with me."

She exhaled loudly. "I'm not saying that either."

He studied her, the amused look in his eyes again. "Are we having a language issue, Grant?"

In spite of the fact that the way he was looking at her—and the feel of her hand in his—was making it difficult to think clearly, Mikayla laughed. "No. I'm sorry. *Lo siento.* The issue isn't us, it's me."

"In what way?"

"The thing is …" How could she put it so that he would understand?

"You do not know what you want. Or do not want."

That worked. "I thought I did. Now I'm not so sure."

"Because?" He rubbed his thumb over the back of her hand.

"Because I've always liked planning out my life, knowing where I'm going to be in a week or a month or a year, and what I will be doing. After my parents died, that became even more important to me. Losing them was more than a bend in the road. It was a landslide that almost washed me away. It definitely forced me to stop in my tracks and take a major detour. A few months ago, I hit another massive curve in the road that I didn't see coming when Daniel came to Chicago and told me I had a sister I didn't know about. I'm still trying to deal with that, and to chart my course all over again. I'm not sure I can handle another hairpin curve."

"The kind you cannot see around, you mean."

"Exactly."

He squeezed her fingers. "Sometimes what lies around the bend is the best and most exciting thing that could happen to you."

"And sometimes it nearly destroys you." She gently tugged her hand from his. "I'm not ready to take that chance."

For a moment he didn't speak, only searched her face. She felt his gaze like fingers brushing across her cheek. Then he nodded, slightly. "*Entiendo*. I understand. Truly. Still, I hope you find the courage to do so one day. For your sake. Staying on a familiar road is safe and comforting, I know, and leaving it is a risk. Still, it is only in taking great risks that we can experience great joy. And I believe that joy is what your parents would have wanted for you."

Her throat tightened. Jax took her face in his hands and pressed his lips, soft and warm, to her forehead. When he spoke, his voice was as tender as his touch. "It is what I want for you too."

When she didn't answer, he smiled and lowered his hands. "*Buenas noches, bonita*."

Mikayla nodded. "*Buenas noches*." She watched him as he rose and crossed the site. For a long time after he had gone she sat without moving, staring into the fire until it burned down to embers and the ashes had grown cold.

Chapter Thirty-Four

Holden lay in the tent, arms crossed beneath his head as he stared at the small opening in the roof. Mikayla's words echoed over and over in his mind. Even with everything he had gone through the past few years, he did understand that God hadn't left him. That He was still good. Only in the rational part of his brain, though. All these months, he'd struggled to *feel* as if that was true.

If what Mikayla had said was right, then maybe it was time to stop putting all his stock into what his emotions were telling him, since those shifted every day—sometimes every minute— and start trusting what he knew in his head. He didn't feel his prayers were getting through, but he knew God heard him. He didn't feel that God was walking through this with him, but on some deep level he recognized that God hadn't abandoned him. Holden wouldn't have made it this far if He had. Not through his childhood, or Gage's death, or the loss of his son, or this terrible place he was in with his wife.

He would have checked out a long time ago if God hadn't been walking alongside him, supporting him when he was too weak to stand. Like gravity, he couldn't see it, but he was deeply aware that God's power was real and that its invisible force acted upon him every second of every day, keeping him from being flung off into a vast nothingness.

He rolled onto his side, facing the canvas side of the tent, and rested his head on his bent arm. *Christina.* Every cell in his body longed for his wife. Nights were the worst. Now, when she wasn't here beside him, but even when she had been. When he could hear her soft breathing, feel the warmth of her body, but couldn't reach out and touch her any more than he could in this moment. He pressed his eyes shut, replaying in his head every conversation they'd had since they had lost their son. Was there something more he could have said or done to help her through that, to keep her from drifting so far away from him?

The words she'd said to him before he left, the question she'd asked, still haunted him. *Why haven't you left me?* How could he have made it any clearer to her that he would never do that? That their lives, their hearts, were so inextricably bound together that to walk away from her would have been to rip out part of himself and leave it behind? A wounding he would never heal from.

A revelation struck him then and his eyes flew open. When his prayers had fallen around him—or he'd felt like they had—hadn't he accused God of leaving him? Of abandoning him?

Was God's answer to his anguished cries the same as Holden's response to his wife? It was, Holden knew, because he'd felt the words press gently into his heart and deep into his soul, even if, until this moment, he had refused to acknowledge them.

Don't you know me better than that?

The dream he'd had over and over as he chased that little boy through the woods came to him, playing in his mind as vividly as if he was asleep and experiencing it now. *Don't give up.*

The sound of the tent being slowly zipped open interrupted that thought. Jax eased through the opening and closed it behind him before changing and crawling into his sleeping bag next to Holden's. Not nearly as good as his wife's presence, but it did help still his tortured thoughts a little, having another human being close by.

Holden didn't move until Jax's breathing deepened and evened out, but his mind continued to race. What did that mean, don't give up? Was that Matthew Gibson, imploring him to come after him and rescue him? Was something wrong with the home he had gone to? Were the people who had taken him not good to him? Whoever they were, and whatever their home life was like, it couldn't be worse than the home he had left. Holden's fingers tightened around the top of the sleeping bag.

Matthew's father was vermin. He'd beaten his young son, shot and killed Gage, and kidnapped Jordan. His nephew's kidnapping had plunged them all into hours of uncertainty and terror, especially Nicole. For all Holden knew, that trauma had contributed to Christina's premature labor and the death of their son less than two weeks later. Even if they did find Matthew, Holden would do everything in his power to make sure he wasn't returned to that sorry excuse of a man.

The thought pricked his conscience. Yes, in human terms, Troy Gibson was garbage. But was that how God saw him? In light of how God measured sin, had Holden been any less broken than Matthew's father before God had plucked him out of the pit and rescued him? Was Troy Gibson any further beyond the redemptive power of the blood of Jesus Christ than Holden had been?

Holden wrestled to free the answer from the stubborn nature inside him that didn't want to release it. Didn't want to acknowledge that no, Troy was no more lost than he had been. And, like him, the man was not beyond the reach of redemption. Which didn't say anything about either Holden or Troy. It only spoke to the incomprehensible grace and mercy of God.

For the first time in months, Holden felt that grace flowing over him now, and he relaxed into the warm embrace of it. As much as he missed the intimacy he and Christina had shared, he realized suddenly that he had missed this even more. This closeness with God. Only God hadn't withdrawn from him like his wife had. Holden had withdrawn from Him.

Don't give up.

Was that what the dream had been telling him? That it was this—the presence he felt so strongly in this moment that he could nearly reach out and touch it—that he shouldn't give up on? That God would always be there waiting for him when, like the prodigal son, he chose to turn and run into His arms?

Whether that was the message or not, Holden knew the truth now, in both his head and his heart. God had not abandoned him. And, whatever happened with Matthew Gibson or Christina in the future, He never would.

Chapter Thirty-Five

Christina rapped on the door of Nicole and Daniel's condo before pushing it open and stepping inside. The place was completely quiet, which was unusual. She twisted her arm to glance at her watch. 5:30. She'd expected everyone to be home having dinner. Had they gone out to eat? Strange that they would leave the condo open if they had.

Christina crossed the living room and dropped onto the sofa. She'd wait a few minutes and if no one came she'd head home. The stillness waiting for her there wasn't appealing, which was why she'd come here. She rested her head against the couch cushions. The hot bath she'd taken the night before had helped her sleep well, and she hadn't heard a thing until nine that morning. Even so, exhaustion tugged at her eyelids. Could be that one good night's sleep wasn't enough to compensate for months of restless nights.

She'd started to drift off when the sound of the front door knob turning and the door creaking open woke her. Nicole strolled into the entryway, clutching an overflowing basket of clothes under one arm.

Christina jumped to her feet and jogged across the room to take it from her. "Nic, you shouldn't be carrying something heavy like this."

Nicole ran a hand across her forehead, swiping away a strand of hair that had come loose from her ponytail. "You sound like Daniel. I'm perfectly capable of carrying a few clothes."

"Neither of us wants you taking any chances." Christina carried the basket over and set it on the coffee table in front of the couch.

"I know. And I actually am trying to take it easy, but I don't like feeling helpless."

Christina definitely got that. Helpless had been the emotion that had assaulted her the most violently the last few months. She'd been helpless to save her son. Helpless to find her way back to intimacy with her husband. Helpless to feel like herself again. The night she'd smashed all the glasses she'd had to confront the truth. She *was* helpless to do any of those things without God. It was only when she figured that out that she'd been able to see the hand reaching out to her, offering to pull her out of the deep hole she'd fallen into. Had the hand always been there and she'd refused to see it? Somehow she knew that it had been. "I understand, but it's okay to accept help, you know."

Nicole hugged her. "Good advice."

When she let her go, Christina contemplated her friend. "Was that a dig at me?"

Nicole laughed and dropped onto the sofa. "No, not an intentional one, anyway. I meant that it's good advice for both of us." She reached for a navy T-shirt of Jordan's and folded the arms.

Christina sat beside her and tugged a towel from the basket. "Where's Jordan?"

"Alex's mom took the two of them to a movie and then out for pizza. He'll be gone until bedtime. And Daniel's working, so your timing is perfect. How are you doing?"

"Pretty good. I went on a call yesterday to check on a little girl and her baby sister."

Nicole stopped folding. "Define *check on.*"

"Karl was with me and he spoke to the little girl while I held the baby."

Her friend's green eyes widened slightly. "And?"

"And it was okay. Better than okay, actually. She grabbed my thumb with her little fingers and it felt … good."

Nicole lowered the shirt to her knees. "Chris, that's great."

"Yeah, it surprised me. Gave me hope too. I texted Holden to tell him."

"I'm sure he was thrilled to hear from you."

"Kind of hard to tell from a text, but I'm sure he was surprised. He's usually the one to text or call me." Her eyes met Nicole's over the top of the towel she'd folded in half. "Okay, he's always the one to text or call me. The last few months, anyway. Before that I was far more likely to text him to ask about his day or tell him about something that had happened to me."

"So things are slowly starting to return to the way they were."

"Very slowly, but yes, a little. Maybe. They'll never be exactly the way they were—too much has happened and we're not the same people we were before …" Her throat thickened and she stopped and swallowed.

Nicole took the towel from her, finished folding it, and set it on the coffee table before reaching for Christina's hand. "I know you're not, and I know your relationship may never be exactly the same, but that doesn't mean it can't be as good as it was. Better, even. That's what happened to Daniel and me after I broke up with him and then Jordan was kidnapped. When we got together again, we were even closer than before. I know these past few months have been incredibly difficult, but it's the hard times that mold us and shape us, right? That can make our relationships deeper and stronger than before."

Christina nodded slowly. "I think I'm coming to see that. And I hope you're right about me and Holden. It's been hard, starting to move on. It's felt a lot like letting go of Tristan. And not only of him but of all the dreams I had of being a mom, of seeing what a great dad Holden would be, and of raising our son together." Her voice broke and she bit her bottom lip.

Nicole squeezed her hand. "I know it has. But you're not letting your son go into some black void or even the cold ground. You're placing him in God's hands. And God is a good Father.

He will love him and care for him and watch over him until the timing is right for you to be there with him. You can trust Him, Chris, that He will give you the strength to let your son go. And you can trust Him with Tristan."

Christina drew in a shuddering breath. "Not very long ago, I'm not sure I would have agreed with you. But I'm starting to think you might be right about that."

"I am, I promise. And you don't have to let go of your dreams of being a mom and raising kids with Holden. Even though no child you might have in the future could ever take Tristan's place, and even though part of you will always miss him and long to see him, I believe God will bless you with other children who are going to bring you and Holden tremendous joy."

The tightness in her throat eased. Was that possible? Could she and Holden actually still have the kind of future, the kind of family, that Nicole was describing? The thought of trying again still frightened her. What if they lost another child? Could she survive that? Could they? Not on her own, the way she'd tried to get through this loss. But if she'd learned anything in the last few weeks, it was that she wasn't alone. "Maybe."

A smile broke across Nicole's face. "That's the first time I've heard you even admit that such a thing could be possible, so I'll take it."

Christina managed a weak grin. "Me too." She helped Nicole fold the rest of the laundry and put it away in their dressers and the linen closet.

When they returned to the living room, Nicole rubbed a hand over her stomach. "I'm starving. Want to order Chinese food and watch a movie?"

The mention of food made Christina suddenly ravenous. When was the last time she'd actually felt like eating for the sheer enjoyment of it as opposed to ingesting it as sustenance to get her through the day? She couldn't remember. "Sounds perfect."

Nicole's gaze lingered on her a moment, as if she was asking herself the same question Christina had. She didn't comment, only grabbed her phone from the coffee table. "The usual?"

Those two simple words—the normalcy of them—struck Christina. Nothing had been usual for so long. She and Nicole had ordered Chinese food all the time in the past, whenever they had a girls' night. Those times seemed so far away now. With everything she had been through, as hard as she had pushed everyone in her life away the last few months, they were all still here. They were waiting for her, loving her, grieving with her, and ready to resume doing life with her as soon as she was ready.

And if Holden and Nicole and Daniel and Jordan and Mikayla—all flawed human beings—could be that faithful, then maybe it was time to accept that God could be too.

Chapter Thirty-Six

"No good?" Jax inclined his head toward Mikayla's plate.

Mikayla blinked, only realizing now that Jax and Holden had finished their burgers while hers sat largely untouched. "No, it smells amazing. But …" She propped her elbows on the picnic table and rubbed her temples with the fingers of both hands.

Holden stuffed his empty plate into the shopping bag they were using for their garbage. "Headache?"

"Yeah." Two straight days of sitting in the back of Jax's car staring at the second floor of Andrew Thompson's house had resulted in a pounding in her head that so far two aspirins hadn't been able to touch. "I'll be all right." Mikayla contemplated her burger. Normally one of her favorite meals, tonight the aroma was doing nothing but cause turmoil in her stomach.

Jax wiped his fingers on a paper napkin and tossed it on his plate, his dark eyes lasered in on her. "Did you take something for it?"

"A couple of aspirin. Should kick in soon." She nabbed a sesame seed with the tip of her finger and stuck it in her mouth. "I'm fine. I get headaches sometimes if I've been concentrating on something too hard for too long."

"Why don't you give your eyes a rest and stay here tomorrow."

Holden had grabbed the ketchup and mustard and he tipped the ketchup bottle in her direction. "Good idea. No need for all three of us to sit there staring at the house with nothing happening. Probably smart for us to start taking shifts."

The idea of a quiet day at the campsite was incredibly appealing. Mikayla bit her lip. "Are you sure?"

Jax screwed the lid on the relish jar. "Absolutely. We can

handle it. Besides, your big opening is in two days—you should be getting ready for that."

Oh yeah, the opening. Nerves threatened again, but Mikayla willed them away. Holden lifted one leg and then the other over the bench before carrying the condiments to the cooler. "I'm going to hit the shower. Mik, let me know if you need anything."

She would have nodded, but she knew from past experience that would not help her head any. "I will, thanks." Her gaze followed him as he grabbed his towel and headed for the public washrooms. Wildflowers lined the pathway and crept along the ground between the trees, full green branches casting shadows over the gravel road that ran along the perimeter of the camp. It was a beautiful spot. If she had a day to spend here before they had to leave on Saturday, she might be able to do a little sketching or painting.

"Will that hurt your head?"

Yanked back to the real world, she shifted on the bench to face Jax, trying not to wince at the movement. "What?"

"Drawing. Painting. Whatever you were planning in your mind to do tomorrow."

Mikayla exhaled. "You know, it is possible that you are not quite as smart as you think you are."

"That is not what you were thinking?"

She pursed her lips. "Do they teach you that in private eye school?"

"What?"

"Mind-reading."

He grinned. "Not exactly. They do teach us to read body language and how to use what we know about our subject to predict possible actions. When I see you, a talented artist who creates amazing paintings of the natural world, contemplating the beautiful trees and flowers around us, I do not need to use my PI training to figure out that you are thinking about drawing them."

That made sense. Even so, it was maddening that he could read her so easily—"like a book" as he'd put it. "All right, I guess I was."

"Will that bother your head?"

"I don't know. This headache is more from my neck, I think. I've had my head tilted back watching Andrew's house for the last two days. I won't have to do that if I'm drawing. Should be fine."

"Will you remember to eat and drink?"

Her eyes met his. It was entirely possible that she wouldn't, if she got deep into her work and no one was there to pull her out. "Probably."

His lips twitched, but the eyes that studied her still held concern. "I might have something that will help the headache." He climbed over the bench and disappeared into his tent. When he emerged, he was clutching something that he carried over and held out to show her. "Peppermint. Good for the stomach and the head."

Mikayla stared at the bottle. "You're into essential oils?" The man was full of surprises.

Jax twisted off the cap. "*Mi mamá* is. She is a big believer in their healing powers. Me?" He held up the small green bottle. "I always try to keep an open mind."

"Hmm." Her mother had been a big proponent of essential oils, too. Since her parents' deaths, Mikayla hadn't given much thought to the collection of bottles in the box of her mother's things that she'd kept and brought to Toronto with her. She swallowed the sudden lump in her throat.

"Here." Jax shook a few drops onto his fingers, set the bottle on the table, and moved around to stand behind her. "Rub it on your head, like this." He massaged the oil into her temples. The soothing aroma of peppermint filled the air around her and Mikayla breathed it in, trying to focus on the calming scent and not the strong fingers rubbing against her skin.

After a minute, the pain in her head abated a little. Jax's hands moved from her head to her neck and he kneaded the tight knots that were more than likely the cause of her headache. Although his touch sent shivers whispering along her skin, it wasn't at all provocative. Clearly his goal was to relieve her pain and not to take advantage of the situation. She should probably tell him that she was already feeling better and there was no need for him to keep going, but the massage felt so good she couldn't bring herself to.

What was it about this man that drew her to him so strongly? Mikayla couldn't deny that she was attracted to him, not when his intense gaze or briefest of touches tightened her stomach muscles and made it difficult for her to breathe. If that's all it was, this whole thing would be considerably less terrifying and much easier to walk away from.

More and more now when they spoke or interacted, the cocky, teasing Jax persona was swept aside like the curtain in her bedroom had been the night of her prom, and she was able to catch glimpses of the real Jax Rodriguez. A man who cared deeply for his family and who was haunted by his failure to save them. Whose wounds from the past still caused him pain on a soul-deep level. Who was searching for answers from a God he struggled to understand but who he clearly wanted to believe cared about him and the pain he still wrestled with. Mikayla bit her lip, wishing she could massage that pain away from him as easily as he was vanquishing her headache now.

His hands stilled on her shoulders. "Better?"

If she said no, would he keep going? Mikayla mentally kicked herself for considering taking advantage of the situation herself. "Much. Thank you."

His fingers slid from her neck and he rounded the table to face her. "Good." He replaced the lid on the bottle and set it in front of her. "In case you lose yourself in your work tomorrow and the pain returns."

"Thanks, Jax."

His smile was warm. "You are welcome." He glanced around the grounds. "Not many other people are camping. You will be okay all alone here?"

Mikayla waved a hand through the air. "I'll be fine." A little time away from him was likely a very good idea. Might help her to gain perspective on their situation. She would definitely be able to think more clearly if he wasn't standing there looking at her like he was now. A look that she could feel against her skin as clearly as she had felt his fingers a moment earlier. She would be able to remind herself that after they arrived in Toronto on the weekend he would be leaving for London and they could both get on with their lives.

She swung her legs over the picnic table bench and stood. "I've seen a few groundskeepers around, so I won't be alone. Unless a squirrel or raccoon decide to go rogue and come after our supplies, I will be perfectly safe here until you and Holden return."

Chapter Thirty-Seven

Mikayla flopped onto her back and moaned. Someone was crying. The sound filled the air around her and made her tummy hurt. Like when they were having a fun time with ice cream and swinging and laughter in the park and it started to rain and Mommy took them home.

Today was like that. They'd been hurtling down the slide over and over, chasing each other and Daddy was catching them and she never wanted it to stop. But then her sister toppled off the slide before the bottom and Daddy couldn't catch her and she bumped her head and now it wasn't fun anymore.

She took two steps toward her sister, wanting to help. Her new shoes squished in the sand around the slide. Pink running shoes with sparkles and rainbow laces. Her sister had new shoes too, only hers were purple.

She swung her leg forward, taking a giant step, trying to get to her sister. For some reason, her sister was as far away as she had been before. No matter how many giant steps she took, she couldn't get to her. And she needed to get to her. Sometimes she could make her feel better. Like the time her sister's ice cream fell on the ground and she shared hers. The wails grew louder and she stopped and held her hands over her ears.

A hand grasped hers. "Ella," someone whispered. She looked up. A lady, she thought, but she was all shadowy and Ella couldn't see her face very well. Whoever it was held something up. A red sucker. Her favorite kind. The shadow spoke again. Her voice sounded funny—loud and then soft and then loud again. Ella took one hand off her ear to hear her better. The lady said something like, "Come with me. We'll go for a walk while your mommy and daddy are busy."

She looked over. Mommy and Daddy were crouched next to her sister, who was still crying a little but not too much anymore. The lady's hand was soft and red suckers were her favorite. She reached for it, but the lady pulled it away. "You can have it when you get in the stroller."

Ella climbed in and the lady gave her the sucker. They crossed the park to a car and a man got out. He looked all fuzzy too but she could tell he wasn't smiling like the lady. He glanced up and down the street then pulled open the door of the car. The lady stopped the stroller by the door and came around to take her hand.

She didn't want to go in the car. Not without her sister or Mommy or Daddy. She yanked her hand from the lady's. The man made a hissing sound before lunging for her and picking her up. The sucker fell onto the street and shattered into pieces. He bent and tossed her into a car seat. He did up the buckle but the straps were too tight. Ella squirmed and tears filled her eyes. "I want Mommy."

The man laughed but it didn't sound like Daddy's laugh that always made her tummy feel better. "You're going to have a new mommy now, kid. And no crying. If I hear you crying I will stop the car and you will be sorry. Do you hear me?"

She didn't understand everything he said because there were a lot of words and they were quiet and loud too, but she knew he wanted her to be quiet. Maybe, if she was, the lady would give her another sucker. And maybe, if she was really quiet, they would take her back to her sister. She wiped a tear away with her hand so they would put her in the stroller again and they could go to the park.

The man straightened and slammed the door. He and the lady got in the front and the car started to move.

Ella stared at her shoes. *Don't cry. Don't cry.* The rainbow colors had made her happy when Mommy brought the shoes home from the store but they didn't make her happy now. The pink shoes and the purple shoes had to go together. They weren't pretty when they weren't together. A sob rose in her throat. She tried to hold it in but she couldn't. The man slammed on the brakes.

"Are you going to keep crying?"

She could see the man in the mirror. His face was still fuzzy but she could see his eyes and they were angry. Pressing her lips together, she shook her head. He stared at her for a minute then started going fast again. Did he say she was going to have a new mommy?

She didn't want a new mommy. Where was her sister? Was she still crying? Were Mommy and Daddy looking for her?

Ella couldn't help it. Another sob burst out of her mouth.

The man stopped the car.

Chapter Thirty-Eight

Her own cry wrenched Mikayla awake, and she bolted upright in her sleeping bag. Her heart pounded so hard that her chest hurt. She touched her cheek, feeling the stinging slap, even now. Her fingers came away wet. Giant hands had clenched around her lungs and she labored to draw in a breath. *You're okay. It was a dream. It isn't real. You're okay.*

Except that it was real. It had happened. The woman had taken her away from her family that day in the park. And the man had been waiting for them …

Mikayla struggled to picture their faces. She'd had the dream before. Lots of times. When she was young, she would often wake up crying and her mom would come into the room and hold her and rub her back until she calmed down. Her new mother, not the one who had given her those pink shoes—one of the few things she could picture clearly in her mind after she woke up.

Her mother wanted her to tell her about the dream, but Mikayla could never remember it. Bits and pieces, fuzzy faces, loud and quiet talking, and the crying. That was the clearest thing of all. Someone was crying. And her tummy had hurt. That was all she could tell her mom. She had the dream a lot when she first went to the new house. Then she had it less and less until she didn't have it at all for many years.

After her parents died, the dream came back. She'd described it to her therapist, but she could never call to mind the faces of the man or woman or any concrete details. Only vague recollections of a stroller and a car seat in the back of a dark-colored car and the man's eyes in the mirror. Except she couldn't remember what the eyes looked like, what color they were, only the way they made her feel. They hurt her more than the man had when he had yanked open the car door and showed her what would happen if she didn't listen. She didn't cry anymore after that.

The therapist had lots of theories about what every element of the dream could mean, but none of them made sense to Mikayla. Not that she had any idea what the man and the lady could represent, or the park, or the sister, or the shoes, or the sucker. Not then.

The thin canvas walls of the tent closed in around her. She couldn't breathe in here. The fists around her lungs clenched tighter and she fumbled to free herself from the sleeping bag. Her trembling fingers couldn't undo the zipper and, blind panic gripping her, she wriggled out of it. Somehow she managed to open the door to the tent and crawl out onto the damp ground. Reaching through the opening, she snatched her flip-flops and shoved them on.

After scrambling to her feet and brushing the dirt from her hands, she stumbled across their site, not caring that she still wore her black and silver flannel bottoms and black T-shirt. This early in the morning no one was around to see her anyway. The sky to the east had lightened to a dull gray and she wandered past several empty campsites, heading for that faint light. Mikayla followed it as far as she could go, until she had crossed the gravel road, made her way down a small incline, and stopped at the edge of a narrow river. She could barely make out the rippling water in the dim light of the fading moon and stars, but the soft sound of waves lapping the shores soothed her. After a minute or two, she drew in her first deep breath since she'd woken in her tent, terror assaulting her.

Clasping her hands behind her head, Mikayla gazed at the sky, lightening below a heavy layer of cloud. Why had she had the dream now? She'd had it a few times in the months after her parents' accident, but after working through it with her therapist, sharing the maddeningly few, unhelpful details she could remember without the two of them getting anywhere with trying to interpret it, it hadn't returned in nearly a year.

So it had come in the months following her abduction, when she had been torn from her family and deposited with a new mother and father. And again, when she'd lost those parents. Major, traumatic disruptions in her life. During both those periods, the emotion that had overwhelmed her, crashed over her like a suffocating wave, had been fear of the unknown. The life she had been living had changed dramatically and irrevocably and she'd had no say in what had happened to her.

A realization struck Mikayla and she drew in a quick breath. Was that why she wrestled with a deep, driving need to know where she was going? Because, as a toddler, she'd been deposited in a strange car and driven away from everything she had ever known and thrown into a new home she didn't recognize? Was the psychological fear that gripped her rooted in a literal event in her life, one she barely remembered but that had impacted every aspect of her existence from that moment on? And what did it mean that she'd had the dream now, when she stood at another crossroads in her life, an unknown destination somewhere in front of her? Was the dream telling her that taking that journey would result in another trauma in her life?

Mikayla unclasped her fingers and ran the side of one hand across her forehead. *Wait.* She'd had that dream one other time. When Daniel had come to Chicago to tell her about Nicole, the sister she had forgotten she had. Which made sense, since Nicole was the one crying in her dream.

Ending up in that strange home had turned out to be pretty amazing, even if she hadn't known when she'd first arrived that the people who greeted her, claimed her as their own, would become such an important part of her life. And finding out about Nicole had been amazing too, even if that night, with Daniel, she'd had no idea what her relationship with her sister would be like, or whether they would even have one. Sort of like now, with Jax.

She bit her lip and tipped her head to gaze at the last of the stars managing to break through the cover of clouds. *Is the dream from you? Are you trying to tell me something? Protect me from starting down that road? Or from being too afraid to?*

No answer whispered through her, but as she watched, slender tendrils of rose and violet and orange drifted across the sky above the horizon. Tendrils heralding the advent of the sun, shimmering red and yellow as it rose, dripping color, from the water. A new day dawning.

A small smile crossed Mikayla's face as she stood, reveling in the beauty a few moments longer. Frosty morning air brushed over her skin and bumps rose on her arms. She turned to head to her tent and stopped. A man sat on a picnic table fifteen feet from her, the sneakers he'd tugged on over bare feet propped on the bench, his forearms resting on his knees. Jax.

Mikayla walked over and stopped in front of him. "Hey."

"Hey." Jax grinned, but lines of concern grooved his forehead. "Are you okay?"

The breath she took, checking, still shuddered a little, but slid a bit easier down her throat than when she'd escaped from her tent. "I think so."

He scrutinized her, assessing the truth of that statement.

"How did you know I was here?"

"I heard a cry. When I came out to see if you were all right, you were walking away from the site, so I followed you."

"I never heard you."

"Of course not." He pulled back in mock affront and in spite of the terror still lightly prickling her skin, she laughed. Jax patted the table top beside him.

Mikayla climbed up on the bench, soaking in the solid warmth of him next to her, a barrier against the early morning chill and the cold fingers that hadn't completely unclenched from around her lungs. A shiver moved through her and she rubbed her upper arms.

"Here." Jax shrugged off the navy zip-up hoodie he'd been wearing over a white T-shirt and held it as she slid her arms through the sleeves. The sweater gave off a faint hint of the cologne she'd smelled that night in Nicole's kitchen, and she had to resist the urge to bury her face in the sleeves that hung well past her hands and inhale. "Thanks."

He wrapped his arm around her shoulders. "What happened?"

"I had a dream, a recurring one I haven't had in a while."

"Want to tell me about it?"

"It's about the day I was taken from the park when I was a kid. Nicole was crying and my parents were helping her. I started toward her, but a woman took my hand to stop me. She called me Ella and offered me a red sucker."

"Ella?" His breath was warm on the top of her head.

"That was the name my parents gave me when I was born. Ella Hunter. My adoptive parents changed it to Mikayla."

"Ella." Jax said the name softly, trying it out the way she had when she'd first heard it. "She knew your name?"

"In my dream, she did. Maybe she'd been watching us for a while and had overheard it."

When he nodded, the hair that hung loose to his shoulders brushed against her cheek. "So you went with her?"

Mikayla swallowed. She'd been too young to know any better, but that simple decision had radically changed the course of her life. Why hadn't she cried out? Called for her mother or father? How different would her life—and the life of her birth parents and Nicole—have been if she had?

She sighed and rested her head on Jax's shoulder. No wonder she hesitated before taking a step—the smallest of decisions could have far-reaching ripple effects not only in her life but in the lives of countless others.

He tipped his head, lightly touching hers. "What happened?"

"She put me in a stroller and gave me the sucker. My parents were still distracted, and otherwise the park was deserted, so she was able to simply walk away with me. She took me down a street where a man was waiting in a car."

A shudder rippled through her and Jax tightened his hold. "You do not have to talk about it if it upsets you."

"It's okay. He climbed out and put me in the back, in a car

seat. The woman got in the front and we started driving." The fingers were tensing around her lungs again, but something compelled her to keep going. She wanted to tell Jax about the dream, about what had happened to her. Maybe it would help him to understand. "When I realized they were taking me away from my family, I started crying. The man told me to stop. When I didn't, he …" She glanced down at the hands clasped tightly in her lap.

Jax's muscles had tensed, but he didn't speak, only waited patiently for her to go on.

"He stopped the car and got out." Colors blazed across the sky now, and the sun had risen well above the horizon. Mikayla stared across the water, drawing comfort from the rays of sun falling softly across her face, the arm holding her tight. "He opened the door and slapped me on the face." She touched her cheek again, absently. "When I wake up, I can still feel the stinging and the shock of being struck for the first time in my life. And see my shoes."

Keeping one arm securely around her, he reached for her hand and twined his fingers through hers. "The shoes?"

"Yes." She almost smiled, remembering. "They were new, and pink, with rainbow-colored laces. I loved those shoes."

"What else do you remember?"

"Nothing. That slap seems to wake me every time. And while I saw him in the rear-view mirror, his eyes anyway, I can't remember any details about him. Or the woman. I wish I could. When I came to Toronto to meet Nicole, I went to the police station and told the detectives everything I told you. I'm pretty sure the vague details I was able to provide didn't help much."

"Is there any chance the organization that took Matthew Gibson had anything to do with your abduction?"

"No. I asked Daniel about that, and he told me they only started operating ten or twelve years ago, long after I was taken. Also, those kids were all only children taken from their homes where they lived with an abusive single parent, so I don't fit that profile. The police consider my abduction a crime of opportunity.

The woman, whoever she was, must have been waiting for the chance to take any child whose parents weren't watching them, and I happened to be in the wrong place at the wrong time."

Jax pressed a kiss to the top of her head. "I am so sorry you had to go through all that."

"I am too, although …" she lifted her free hand, palm up. "If I hadn't, I wouldn't have known my parents and had the wonderful relationship I had with them. I have no idea what my life would have been like."

"No, I guess we can never know what will happen to us, how our choices or the choices of others will affect us. We can only keep making those choices and trusting it will all turn out right in the end."

"Trusting whom?"

He ran his thumb over the back of her hand. "Ourselves, I guess. The people who care about us. God."

The admission warmed her as much as the arm clasped around her shoulders. They sat in silence for a few minutes, watching the sky until the sun rose higher and the colors faded. Then she lifted her head and contemplated him. "The case has grown ice cold by now."

"I know it has."

"So there's no use you running all those details I gave you through your mind, looking for clues."

For a moment he didn't speak, only gazed at her. Amusement flickered in his eyes, tempered by something deeper she couldn't quite name. Then he lifted her hand to his mouth and kissed the back of it. "You are right. That is disconcerting."

"What, being read like a book?"

"Yes. Although," he lowered their clasped hands to his knee, the track pants he wore soft beneath her skin, "it is nice, as well."

"What is?"

"Being known."

The last of the tightness around her lungs eased and she exhaled. "I guess it is." Neither of them moved for a moment. Finally, unsure how to handle his intense gaze and the emotions it sent coursing through her, Mikayla gently extricated her fingers from his. "We should get back. Holden will be awake soon and he'll wonder where we are."

Jax's arm slid from her shoulders and Mikayla repressed a shudder as frigid air brushed across the back of her neck. "Thank you for coming after me." She jumped off the bench, landing in a clump of damp grass, cold against her bare toes.

"It was no problem." He climbed off the table. "How is your head, by the way?"

"Much better. Whatever you did last night helped a lot."

"Good. I still think you should stay here today and relax."

Mikayla started picking her way across the rocky shoreline. "I think I will. I likely wouldn't be able to stay awake anyway." A stab of guilt shot through her. "You'll be tired too."

Jax waved a hand through the air. "I will be fine. Often when I am close to breaking a case I do stakeouts on very little sleep."

"Maybe something will happen today." The memory of Jax's arm around her, his strong presence driving the cold from her faster than it had ever been banished after she'd woken from one of her dreams, sparked a revelation. Even if she couldn't define what it was that had shifted inside her as they'd sat there gazing across the river at the fading sunrise, her fingers clasped tightly in his, something definitely had.

Chapter Thirty-Nine

"The woman is alone."

Natalya stopped pedaling her stationary bike and reached for the small white towel she'd flung over one handlebar. "Where?"

"At the campground. The two men are watching the Thompson house, but she stayed behind at their site today." Natalya swiped the towel over her face. "All right then. It's time to put an end to this."

"So we bring her in?"

"Yes, but as we discussed, you must not arouse suspicion when you take her. Somehow you need to get her to come with you willingly."

"I have a plan. I've been studying the campgrounds, and Mikayla Grant. It's a bit involved, but if it goes smoothly then no one will know we were there. Even she will not know that anything is amiss until it is too late for her to alert anyone."

"Do you think the others will follow?"

"I know they will. Given what we heard in Toronto and what I have seen here, Gage Kelly's brother appears to regard her as a sister. From what I've observed, the relationship between her and the PI is considerably less … familial."

Natalya grinned wryly. "Will they know where to find her?"

"We'll leave enough clues for the investigator to figure it out."

"Excellent. Let me know when you are on your way to the warehouse."

"I will."

"And do not hurt her. Drastic action may be required, but before that, I need to find out from her how much they know, if they have any proof, and who they might have passed it along to."

Then we will decide what we are going to do with the three of them."

"Got it."

Natalya disconnected the call and dropped her phone into the slot between the handlebars of the bike. So it had come to this. For the first time in the history of the organization, they were being forced to take action against people who were getting too close to finding one of the children. It was entirely possible that they would be called upon to end lives today as part of their ongoing mission to protect those children and keep them from being removed from the homes where they had found happiness and security.

Her throat tightened, but she climbed off the bike and tossed the towel around her neck, clutching an end in both fists as she fortified herself to do what she had to do.

Natalya drew a steadying breath, willing the ice-cold that had always given her the ability to do whatever needed to be done to settle in her core again. When it did, she tossed the towel into the laundry hamper and strode toward the shower.

She would go to great lengths to protect any one of those children, but there was nothing she wouldn't do to make sure that Matthew Gibson was kept safe. Gage Kelly had given his life to rescue Matthew, and she would not allow his sacrifice to have been for nothing.

Whatever the cost to ensure that was the case, she would pay it. And so would anyone who got in her way.

Chapter Forty

Mikayla stretched her arms above her head and yawned. As happy as she had been to help Jax and Holden track Andrew Thompson to his house, stakeouts were not the interesting or glamorous activities they had appeared on TV or in the movies. She'd been relieved when Jax suggested she stay here today. The offer had sounded altruistic, but she suspected it had as much to do with the fact that if she wasn't in the car the two of them could stretch out a little and get comfortable. More comfortable, anyway.

And it wasn't necessary for all of them to be there watching the house. In fact, since nothing was happening, it might be time for them to let Daniel know what was going on. They could see if there was anything else he thought they should do before they went to the art show opening tomorrow night and then left for home the next day. She was pretty sure Jax and Holden wouldn't argue with her about that, since it was starting to feel that they might all be wasting their time here. Maybe Holden could give Daniel a call after the three of them had dinner together tonight.

In the meantime, Mikayla definitely didn't mind having a few hours to herself. Everything that had transpired between her and Jax, and the conversations she'd had with him and Holden, had occupied her thoughts for days. Today she was hoping for a bit of time to get ready for the art show, like Jax had told her she should. Even if the other shows Leigh had arranged for her had gone well, it still freaked her out a little, the thought of all those people standing around analyzing and critiquing her work. She wasn't sure it was something she would ever get used to.

The positive reviews and the public exposure did make it worthwhile. Still, a little peace and quiet would help prepare her mentally and psychologically for what was to come. While she felt a little guilty, she was going to relax and enjoy it. Thankfully, the headache that had abated after Jax had applied the oil and massaged her head and neck hadn't returned.

Somehow, after crawling into her sleeping bag again, she'd been able to block out the chirping and calling of birds that had accompanied her and Jax to the site after their early-morning trip to the river and fall asleep. Mikayla reached for her phone and glanced at the screen. 10 a.m.

With Jax gone, she'd have to make her own breakfast. And coffee. She grimaced. Should have gotten him to show her how he did such a good job of making it in the French press. She'd never been able to master that and relied on her Keurig at home. Mikayla kicked free of the sleeping bag, tugged jeans, a T-shirt, and a hoodie on, and slid her feet into her sneakers for the trip to the public washrooms.

A few minutes later, refreshed and feeling almost human after her shower, she trudged along the pathway to their site. When she approached the picnic table, a piece of paper, held in place by the French press, captured her attention. She moved the glass container enough to read the words scrawled across it. Jax had left explicit instructions on how to make the coffee. He'd even put water in the pot and set it on the cook stove for her and ground enough coffee to make four cups. Should be enough. Smiling, Mikayla studied the note. She hadn't seen Jax's handwriting before and was intrigued by the neat but fairly large, looping letters. What did that mean again? Open and friendly? Cocky and self-confident, more likely.

Don't do that. The way the laughter had died in his eyes when he thought she was telling him she didn't want to be with him, or how he had withdrawn when she'd forbidden him to share details of his love life with her, had already shown her that he wasn't cocky and arrogant like she'd originally believed. He felt things deeply. And now that she knew more about his past, she could understand that.

With a sigh, she dropped the paper onto the table and lit the cook stove. Even with the instructions, the coffee she produced in the press didn't come close to Jax's—not that she'd ever tell him that—but it was passable and pumped energy into her veins, which was the minimum she required from it.

She directed a wary glance at the cooking supplies but settled for a peanut butter and jam sandwich and an apple. When she finished eating, she brushed off her fingers, tugged the phone from the pocket of her hoodie, and hit the power button. Nothing happened. Mikayla frowned. *I should have sent it with the guys today to charge while they were in the city.*

With a sigh, she shoved it into her pocket and contemplated her surroundings. The beauty of the woods that lined the far side of the road—tiny flowers beginning to poke through the ground at the base of the trees, leaves bursting out of the buds lining the branches above her head—sparked something inside her like it had the evening before. Mikayla jumped to her feet and hurried to her tent to grab the sketchbook and the container of brushes and paints she'd tucked into her overnight bag.

In minutes she was lost in her work. The scenery imprinted itself in her mind like a photograph before flowing through her arm and out her fingers, appearing on her page through the lens she'd used to interpret what she'd seen in her head. She had no idea how much time had passed before a sound penetrated the distance between the real world and the one of her imagination.

Mikayla's head jerked. What was that?

Another scream split the air and she dropped the brush onto the paper and hopped off the bench. *Is that a kid?* She'd only seen a few other people since they'd arrived here, mostly the maintenance workers in dark green coveralls. No children.

The scream had come from the direction of the river and Mikayla hurried toward it. When the sound of rushing water filled the air, she heard it again, more of a wail than a scream this time. Was the child hurt? Drowning? She left the main road to follow the footpath leading to the river that she'd taken that morning. Around a slight bend in the path below her the sight of a small hand on the ground cut off the air to her windpipe.

Mikayla scrambled down the slope until she reached the bend. A young boy, maybe nine or ten, lay in the grass, blood dripping from a gash on his forehead.

Mikayla dropped to her knees beside him. "It's okay. I'm going to help you." She pulled her arms out of the sleeve of her hoodie, slipped off her T-shirt, and tugged it free before sliding her arms back into the sleeves. Balling up the T-shirt, she pressed it to the wound. The young boy stared at her. She attempted a smile, hoping to ease his fear as she reached into the pocket of her hoodie for her phone. "What's your name?"

"Spencer."

Mikayla nodded. "I'm going to call an ambulance, okay? You need to go to the hospital so a doctor can look at your head." The memory of the blank screen on her phone sent her heart plummeting. How could she make the call?

The kid grabbed her arm. "Use mine." He slid a hand into his jacket pocket and withdrew a gleaming I-Phone. "My parents already programmed in 911. Hit the 1."

When he held it out to her, Mikayla grabbed it and stabbed at the keyboard.

A man answered. "911. What is the nature of your emergency?" As quickly as possible, Mikayla explained the situation. When she tried to tell the man where the campgrounds were and how to get there, he cut her off. "I know where you are. We have a station not far from there. It won't take long for us to get to you."

"Okay, thanks. We're by the river that runs along the east side of the grounds." Thankfully, she'd seen the sunrise over the water that morning so she knew how to direct him.

"Got it. Hang tight and keep applying pressure. I've already notified the station. Should only take the EMTs a few minutes to reach you."

"Great, thanks." Mikayla tucked the phone into the kid's jacket pocket, praying the man was right. Blood had soaked through the T-shirt onto her fingers. How much had he lost? She touched the boy's arm with her free hand. "What happened?"

"I was running and I fell. Hit my head on a rock."

She glanced around. No rocks lay nearby. Had he walked for a while after hitting his head, trying to get to his campsite, then collapsed? When had he screamed, when he first hit his head or when he realized he wouldn't make it to his site?

Someone should notify his family. Mikayla started to reach for the phone he'd given her to call for the ambulance. "Are your parents in the campground?"

Spencer's eyes drifted shut. Alarmed, Mikayla left the phone in his pocket and grasped his shoulder, shaking it lightly. "Spencer? Stay with me, okay? Do you know your parents' number? I could call them, tell them to come here."

He moaned a little but didn't open his eyes.

Oh God, help me. Keep him alive until help can arrive, please. Mikayla craned her neck to look behind her. Where was that ambulance?

Jax. Had his extensive outdoor training included a first aid course? He'd likely have been able to help if he'd been there. *Well, he isn't. You'll have to handle this one on your own, Grant.* She might have smiled, grimly, if she wasn't so concerned about the boy lying in the grass in front of her.

For several minutes she kept the T-shirt pressed to his head, praying that he would be okay and that help would arrive soon. After what felt like an eternity, footsteps thudded on the trail behind her and she spun around. Two uniformed men, one carrying a white medical bag, loped down the hill toward them.

Relief flooded through Mikayla. Seconds later the two male paramedics, one a short, stocky thirty-something man with a shaved head, the other tall, blond, and lean, had reached them. Mikayla moved out of the way as they crouched on either side of the boy. In less than a minute, they'd tossed her T-shirt into the long grass by the river, cleaned the wound, and the shorter man had pressed a strip of gauze over it and taped it in place.

"We need to get him to the hospital." The blond EMT scooped the boy into his arms.

Spencer let out a yelp and held his hand toward Mikayla. "Please come.'

"I don't know if I can." She glanced at the paramedic, who shifted the boy in his arms.

"It's okay. Parents are allowed to ride in the ambulance. We should go now, before he loses any more blood."

"I'm not his mother. I heard screaming and came to the river and found him. I could go around the campground, see if I can find his family."

Spencer groaned again. "My parents aren't here. They went into town for groceries. I want you to come. Please."

The shorter EMT gestured to the road. "We can't stand here talking. He needs medical attention. Would you mind coming? We'll notify his family after we get him to the hospital."

Without waiting for a response, both men started along the trail.

Mikayla stared after them for a moment before hurrying to catch up. If it made the boy feel better, she could go with him. She'd call Holden from the hospital and he and Jax could come and get her.

They reached the ambulance parked at the top of the hill, its rear doors hanging open. Strange she hadn't heard a siren, although they likely didn't need it to clear the almost-deserted road leading into the campground, especially this overgrown one that didn't appear to be used much anymore. The blond man stepped onto the bumper and into the ambulance where he laid Spencer on a stretcher.

Mikayla climbed in and the other man slammed the doors behind her. The EMT gestured toward a bench along the side of the vehicle and she sank onto it, clutching the blood pressure monitor attached to the wall to keep from losing her balance when the vehicle lurched forward. They sped through the field and onto the bumpy road that appeared to be a back way off the grounds. It definitely wasn't the road she, Jax, and Holden came and went from, the one that passed the security guard's booth. Too bad, as she might have been able to let the guard know what was happening so he could pass it along to Holden and Jax if they returned before she could use a phone at the hospital to call them.

They rode in silence through the campground. In spite of all the jostling around, Spencer's eyes were still closed and she touched his arm lightly. "You doing okay, buddy?"

"It's not him you should be worried about."

Mikayla lifted her gaze to the EMT, sitting on the other side of the vehicle, and her entire body went cold. He held a pistol in one hand, the barrel pointed directly at her. "Give me your phone."

"What are you—?"

The man lowered the weapon to Spencer's temple and the boy whimpered.

"Phone. Now."

Mikayla fumbled in her pocket for the device and held it out with trembling fingers to the man. *What is happening?* The EMT, or whatever he was, leaned forward and used the gun to rap on the glass separating them from the cab. The vehicle slowed and veered onto the shoulder of the gravel road where it came to a stop. Seconds later the rear doors flew open.

The blond man grabbed a container of wet wipes and jerked two or three of them out through the hole in the top. He ripped the bandage off of Spencer's forehead. Mikayla winced. What was he doing? Using the wipes, he swiped the red liquid away from the skin and dug a fingernail under the corner of the gash and lifted it off. Mikayla pressed her knuckles to her mouth. The wound was fake? Why would they do that? Was this all some elaborate scheme to get her to go with them?

"All right, kid, you can get up." The blond man tossed the piece of fake plastic and the wipes into the corner of the vehicle.

Spencer sat and swung his skinny legs over the side of the stretcher. He dug the phone Mikayla had used to call the ambulance from his jacket pocket and held it out to the man. "I got her to use the phone you gave me instead of hers. That's fifty points, right?"

The man shrugged as he shoved the device into his shirt pocket. "Yeah, sure, kid. Fifty points."

"Where's my money?"

The man tugged a twenty out of his shirt pocket and tossed it to him. "You did good. Fun game, right? Can you find your way to your campsite from here?"

Mikayla's mind spun. Fifty points? What did that mean? Who were these people and what did they want with her?

The boy nodded and hopped off the stretcher. Slightly bent over, he made his way to the exit and jumped onto the road. The other EMT gripped his shoulder. "Remember, don't tell anyone, okay? That would ruin the game."

"I won't." Spencer waved at Mikayla cheerfully. "Good luck. I hope you win."

She tried to swallow, but her throat had gone dry. Game? That gun looked pretty real, not that she knew much about weapons. If this was a game, she was not having fun yet. And somehow she doubted she was going to win anything. Except her life. Maybe. She scrutinized the opening. Should she try to run? Before she could move, the man cocked the pistol. "Don't even think about it."

The doors slammed shut and she jumped. "What do you want with me?"

"We don't want anything with you. We've been hired to bring you in, that's all. What they do with you after that is none of our business."

"Who is *they*?" Her voice shook and Mikayla gritted her teeth.

The man leaned against the wall of the ambulance. Obviously he had no intention of giving her any more information. The vehicle pulled out of the campground and onto the road. She hated not knowing where she was going, but obviously she'd have to wait to find out their destination and who wanted to see her so badly.

Mikayla surveyed the interior of the vehicle. Was there anything she could use as a weapon? Cubbies held sheets and towels and bandages, nothing that appeared remotely lethal. "This looks like a real ambulance."

The man smirked. "It is. A practice one, anyway. Buddy of mine runs an EMS school in another city and loaned it to me for the day."

"Does he know you're using it to commit a federal crime?"

The smirk disappeared, and he tightened his grip on the gun resting on his knee and aimed at her stomach. "He doesn't ask any questions. That's why he's still alive."

Blood pounded in her ears, making it hard to think. The words Jax had spoken to her when they couldn't find the tents in the Great Outdoors Adventure Store drifted through her mind. *Stay calm. The most important thing to do when you don't know where you are is to keep your wits about you. If you don't, chances are good you will not survive.* A shudder moved through her. Was there a chance she wouldn't survive this bizarre situation?

She stared at the gun clutched in the man's hand. At this point, anything was possible.

Chapter Forty-One

Christina opened her eyes and glanced around the spacious room. Where was she? It took a few seconds to remember that she had fallen asleep on Nicole and Daniel's couch the night before. Even when Jordan had bounded in from the hallway, she'd only been able to rouse herself enough to say goodnight to him and give him a quick hug before lapsing into sleep again.

At some point Nicole had laid a blanket over her, and for the second night in a row Christina had slept soundly, unhindered by racing thoughts or dark dreams that yanked her from her slumber with tears in her eyes and a thin sheen of perspiration on her forehead.

The rich, nutty aroma of coffee brewing drifted into the living room from the kitchen and she inhaled deeply. When the desire for a cup of the real thing became too strong, she swung her legs over the side of the couch and pushed to her feet, bracing herself on the coffee table. After folding the blanket and tossing it over the arm of the couch, she freshened up in the guest washroom before stumbling through the living room in the direction of the kitchen. Sunlight streamed through the windows and she squinted as she pushed through the French doors. Nicole and Jordan sat at the island in the center of the room.

Nicole flashed her a smile as she stood, pulled the carafe out from under the coffee maker, and poured her a big cup of the steaming liquid. Christina settled onto the stool beside her and wrapped her fingers around the blue ceramic mug. "Bless you." She closed her eyes and inhaled a deep breath of the rich scent, then took a mouthful and let out a sigh of pure bliss. Only then did she open her eyes and glance over at her nephew. "Morning, Jord."

He giggled. "You sure do like coffee."

"Yes, I do. I don't start the day with all the energy you do. I wish I did. I'd get an awful lot done."

"Like me."

"Exactly. What do you have planned for today, anyway?"

His face fell a little. "Mom says I have to clean my room before I do anything else."

Christina met Nicole's gaze over the rim of her mug. Nicole looked completely unrepentant. "Such a mean mother."

Christina grinned and looked at Jordan, who was shoveling a spoonful of Cheerios into his mouth. "Actually, Jord, I think your mom is very wise. I'm going to head home and do my cleaning too before I do anything else. That way I can enjoy the rest of my day."

"I guess." He brightened. "Daniel said he'd take me to the park to play catch after I'm finished."

"That sounds like fun. Definitely worth cleaning your room for. If I were you, I'd hurry and get it done. Looks like a beautiful day outside." *Hopefully it's as nice in Chicago.* She winced, thinking about Holden and Mikayla and Jax sleeping outside when the temperature still dipped pretty low at night.

Jordan's spoon clattered into his bowl. "Can I go do it now, Mom?"

"Umm, yes. Do a good job, okay? Inspection before you and Daniel go to the park."

"I will." Jordan jumped off the stool, grabbed his bowl and spoon, and dumped them in the sink before heading for the door.

Smiling, Christina watched until he had disappeared, leaving only a swinging door in his wake. When she lifted her mug to take another sip, Nicole was watching her, a look on her face Christina couldn't quite identify. She lowered the mug to the island. "What?"

"You're so good with him. I've been trying for an hour to get him enthused about cleaning his room."

"He's a great kid."

Nicole nudged the jug of cream closer to her. "Are you missing Holden?"

Christina splashed a little of the cream into her coffee, shocked at the intensity of her reaction to the question. She'd missed Holden for months, but their time apart had shown her how deeply she ached for him, how much she needed him to be home, with her. For the two of them to be close again. "I definitely am. Far more than I thought I would. I'm hoping and praying they can find what they're looking for and get home soon."

"Praying?"

"Yeah. I've been talking to God a lot, figuring things out, letting things go. It's been good."

Nicole squeezed her arm. "That's amazing, Chris."

Christina finished her coffee and carried the mug to the dishwasher. "Is Daniel home?"

"Yes, he's in his office working."

"I think I'll pop in for a minute before I go, see if he's heard anything from Holden or Jax or Mikayla."

"All right."

She hugged her sister-in-law. "Thanks for last night. I needed that."

"Anytime."

Christina waved before pushing through the kitchen doors and making her way across the living room and through the hallway that led to Daniel's office. When she reached it, she rapped lightly on the door. "Daniel?"

"Come on in."

She pushed open the door. Daniel was typing something on his laptop. When she sank onto one of the armchairs in front of him, he closed the lid and folded his arms on the desk. "Hey, Chris. What's going on?"

"I wondered if you'd gotten any updates from Chicago."

"Actually, I haven't heard from anyone in a couple of days. Why don't I give Jax a call, see if anything's happening."

"That would be great." Should she mention that Holden had

told her they might have discovered where Andrew lived? He hadn't told her not to, but if none of them had let Daniel know that yet, maybe they weren't ready to do so. She clasped her hands in her lap as he grabbed the receiver of the phone sitting on his desk and punched in a series of numbers.

After several seconds of silence, he made a face and mouthed *voicemail* to her. "Hey, Jax, it's Daniel. Christina's here and we're checking in to see if you have any news for us. Give me a call when you have a chance." He hit the disconnect button and set the receiver on the base. "I'll let you know if I hear from him. Hopefully he'll be able to understand what I said. I've been having trouble with this phone lately. It glitches once in a while. I have a call in to the phone company and they're supposed to be sending someone to—" His head jerked and his blue eyes met hers.

Christina's stomach tightened. "What is it?"

"It struck me suddenly that the phone trouble we've been having might not be a technical issue." He rubbed the side of his hand across his forehead. "I can't believe I didn't think of this before."

"Think about what?" She stood, her legs trembling slightly.

Daniel came around his desk and stopped in front of her. "The phone could be bugged."

Her eyes narrowed. "Who would bug your phone?"

"The only ones I can think of who might want to—and who would have the money and the means to do it—are the people who belong to the organization Gage was working for when he was killed."

"I thought you dismantled that organization."

"We did arrest a number of people, yes, but we've long suspected there were others involved who managed to elude us."

"But why would they come after you?"

"Maybe they know that I'm one of the few cops still investigating the disappearances of those children." Daniel rested his hands on her shoulders. "I don't want to worry you, Chris, but if it is them, and they did bug the phone, they know that Jax and Mikayla and Holden are in Chicago."

Horror swirled through her. "And they won't want them to find Matthew Gibson."

She fumbled in her back pocket for her phone and dialed. "I'll try to get in touch with Holden, let him know that they could be in danger."

Daniel let go of her and snatched his own cell phone from the desk. "I'll try Mikayla and then Jax again. But let's take this out of here." He grasped her elbow with his free hand and guided her to the door. "Until I can do a sweep of the office, we should assume there could be a bug in this room too."

She stepped into the hallway, listening as Holden's phone rang and rang. When his voicemail clicked on, she left a message for him to get in touch with her. "I can't get him, either."

Daniel shook his head as he stabbed at a button. "Mikayla's not answering. Could be they don't have a good place to recharge their phones at the campground." He strode toward the kitchen and Christina followed him, nearly jogging to keep pace.

Nicole was washing lettuce at the sink, but she looked up when they came into the kitchen. "You two look serious. What's going on?"

Daniel strode toward her. "I think I need to fly to Chicago."

She dropped the lettuce into the sink and reached for the towel on the stove. "Why? Is something wrong?"

"Probably not, but remember how the phone in my office has been glitching sometimes?"

She nodded. "Yes, you mentioned that. What does that have to do with Chicago?"

"It should have occurred to me earlier, but it hit me when I tried Jax a minute ago that it might possibly have been bugged. Which means that, if someone was listening in, they'd know Holden, Mik, and Jax went there to try and find Matthew Gibson."

Nicole's cheeks paled. "Can you call them?"

Christina shook her head. "We've been trying. None of them are answering their cell phones."

Daniel pulled out his phone again. "I'm going to check flights. If I can get something in the next couple of hours, I'll head to the airport now."

"I'll take you." Christina pressed her palms to the island to keep her fingers from trembling.

"You don't have to. I can call an Uber."

"I want to. I have to do something, Daniel."

"All right." He scanned the phone screen. "There's a direct flight out at two this afternoon. I'm getting a ticket."

Christina exchanged a worried look with Nicole as he entered his information and credit card number. When he stuck the phone into his pocket, Daniel lifted a hand. "Don't look so concerned. I'm sure they're fine. They've been in touch a few times since they got there and didn't say that anything had happened that felt off to them, right?"

"Holden didn't mention anything like that to me."

"Okay, then. Jax is good at what he does. I'm sure he'd pick up on any signs that they were being followed or watched."

Nicole grabbed his hand. "If you're not worried, why are you going there?"

Daniel didn't answer.

"You have a feeling about this, don't you?"

He wrapped his arm around her. "It's likely nothing, but I would feel better if I could get there in case anything happens and they need me." Daniel pressed a kiss to the top of Nicole's head. "I'll only be gone a day or two."

"And you'll keep in touch?"

"Absolutely."

She exhaled. "Okay."

"I'll get someone to check the phone and the rest of the condo for bugs." Daniel let her go and started for the door. "I'm going to shove a few things in a bag. I'll be ready to go in ten minutes, Chris."

"Okay." She concentrated on drawing in several deep

breaths. Everything would be fine. Likely the glitch in the phone was a technical problem that the repairman would be able to fix. Besides, like Daniel said, they'd been there for nearly two and a half weeks and nothing bad had happened. *But Holden said they might have found Andrew.*

Fear gripped her. If the glitch was more than a technical issue and someone actually had been listening in on them, they knew the three of them were in the States. Given the power and resources these people had, no doubt they'd been watching them since they arrived.

Had she finally realized how much she wanted and needed her husband only to have him taken from her? An intense cold worked its way through Christina, but she forced herself to speak calmly. "I'll see you later, Nic."

"Why don't you come here after you drop Daniel off? No sense in both of us worrying alone."

"That sounds good. I will." Offering her friend a wan smile, she turned and made her way on unsteady legs out of the kitchen. It wouldn't serve any purpose to add to Nicole's concern, and it wouldn't be good for the baby.

But once out of her sister-in-law's sight, Christina propped a shoulder against the living room wall and pressed a hand to her chest in an attempt to slow the rapid beating of her heart. If the people behind the disappearances of those kids knew that Jax, Holden, and Mikayla were closing in on Andrew Thompson, no doubt the organization was closing in even more rapidly on the three of them.

And what, exactly, would they do to them when they did?

Chapter Forty-Two

Holden checked his phone screen, concerned about how low the battery bar was getting. "Before we head to the campground today, we need to find a place to recharge our phones. Mine's almost dead."

Jax nodded. "Mine too. I shut it off earlier to conserve what I have left."

"Good idea." Holden powered his off too before setting it in the cup holder between them. He peered out the side window of the car as Jax lifted the binoculars to his eyes. Other than that quick glimpse three days ago of someone in the room they had assumed was Andrew's, and the lights that blinked off shortly after, nothing had moved behind the heavy drapes that covered every window. They hadn't seen any other lights coming on or going off. Was the family away? If not, why didn't they ever leave the house?

He and Jax had arrived and parked a ways away before the burgundy SUV should have come to take Matthew to school, but it never did appear. Like it hadn't appeared any of the days they'd staked out the house. Had the organization somehow figured out that the three of them had tracked Matthew down? If so, they could have spirited him away from Chicago in the night. Which would mean he and Jax were wasting their time, sitting here staring at an abandoned house.

Cold fingers of apprehension crawled along his spine, but he shook his head. There was no way they could know. Except that it was possible they had seen Jax's car parked near the house more than once and started to get suspicious. Holden set the paper cup of coffee he'd ordered from Michelangelo's in the cup holder. "See anything?"

"Nope."

"That's weird, right? That there's been no movement for days, no one going in or out of the house?"

"It is a little weird. I am starting to wonder if they have gone away on vacation or something. Although that one bedroom window on the second floor is open two or three inches. I suppose they could have left it that way on purpose, but it seems strange."

"What do you think about going to the door and inventing some excuse for being there?"

Jax lowered the binoculars to his knee. "I have been thinking about that. I hate to do it until we have to, as it is pretty hard to devise something that does not sound bogus. I do not want to raise any more suspicions than we might have already."

"So you think it's possible that they've noticed—"

A young girl on a pink bicycle rolled along the sidewalk. Holden shifted his attention to her, his muscles tightening. The front wheel wobbled wildly for a few seconds before the bike crashed onto its side. The girl was wearing a helmet, fortunately, but it appeared that her knees took the brunt of the fall. She let out a wail and Holden reached for the door handle.

"Wait." Jax grabbed his arm. With his free hand, he lifted the binoculars to his eyes again. "A curtain in the room we think is Andrew's moved. Give it a minute, and if nothing happens, we can help her." He let go of Holden and grasped the binoculars with both hands.

Holden snatched his phone and hit the on button. While he waited for it to power up, he leaned closer to the front window so he could peer at the second story. He couldn't see anything moving, but ten seconds later, the front door of the house cracked open. His chest tightened when the blond boy from his dreams slipped out and closed the door behind him, quietly, as if he didn't want anyone in the house to know he was leaving. Holden snapped a series of pictures before dropping the device into the cup holder again. Andrew trotted over to the girl. As Holden watched, he spoke to her, too quietly for Holden to make out the words, although he had lowered his window a few inches a while ago to let in a little fresh air.

When the girl stopped crying, Andrew Thompson took her arm and helped her to her feet. Blood dripped from one knee and he pulled a tissue from his pocket and wiped it off for her. She smiled at him as she climbed onto the bike and pedaled it along the sidewalk. Andrew watched her until she reached the corner and disappeared from sight. Then he jogged up the walkway, pushed open the door, and slipped inside, closing it as carefully as he had when he'd come out.

Holden stared at the closed door. "Did that actually happen?"

Jax tossed the binoculars into the back seat. "It did, and now we have confirmation. Andrew Thompson is here, and for some reason he isn't supposed to be leaving his house."

Holden straightened. "It did appear that way. Do you think they're onto us, then?"

"Could be." Jax leaned forward and started the car. "In case they are, we better not push it. We found out what we wanted to know."

Holden's stomach tightened. Was Jax saying he would report the sighting to Daniel so he could call the Chicago P.D. and let them know where Matthew Gibson was?

"No." Jax spoke without taking his eyes off the road ahead of them.

"No, what?"

"I am not going to tell Daniel. Not yet. We can talk to Mikayla tonight and decide where to go from here."

Holden studied him. How did the guy do that? "Good plan. Thanks."

Jax nodded. "I know you want to make sure that Matthew Gibson is okay, so I do not want to rush into anything. I will say that something seems more than a little off in that house. And if that is the case, it may be the best thing for him to be brought to Canada and placed into the system. There are a lot of good foster homes, you know."

"I know there are. I've dedicated my life to finding them. Unfortunately, they're not all great. Gage and I experienced both, and I definitely don't want that for Matthew."

Jax shot him a sideways glance. "I get that. And Daniel does too. The fact that he let us come to Chicago at all shows that. He is taking a pretty big risk here, and I do not want to make things any worse for him."

Holden blew out a breath. "Neither do I."

"Okay." Jax smacked him lightly on the chest with the back of his hand. "Why don't we buy a few steaks to throw on the grill. The three of us can discuss the situation over dinner."

"Sounds good." Holden gazed out his window. A woman pushed a stroller along the sidewalk and, a few houses down, a kid stuffed a newspaper into a mailbox before jogging back to the wagon he'd parked at the end of the driveway. Everyone they passed was innocently going about their business, no idea that a kidnapped child lived a few blocks away. What was going on in *his* own neighborhood that he had no clue about? He rested his head against the glass, unable to summon the mental energy to process that question.

What Jax had suggested did sound good. Both the idea of grilled steaks and talking about their situation and figuring out the best way to proceed from here. Whatever they decided, they needed to do it fast. If anyone from the organization had been watching them and knew they had spotted Andrew Thompson, they might move quickly to remove the boy from the home.

Or—a cold chill swept along Holden's spine—they might decide it would be easier to take whatever steps they had to in order to ensure the three of them didn't let anyone else know what they had found out.

Chapter Forty-Three

Christina gripped the steering wheel so tightly her knuckles gleamed white. Daniel reached across the console to touch her forearm. "Relax, Chris. I'm sure they're fine."

"I'm not so sure."

He frowned. "Why? Do you know something I don't?"

"Actually, I do." She exhaled. "I'm not sure if Holden wanted me to tell you this, but we were texting a couple of days ago and he mentioned they might have found Andrew. They were waiting to confirm it and then they were going to let you know."

Daniel appeared to mull that over for a moment. "Even so, I don't think there is cause for alarm. From the research I've done, the organization existed to help people, not hurt them. I haven't read of anyone other than Gage being killed, and that was by an angry parent, not a member of the organization. There's no reason to believe they're violent."

She relaxed her grip on the wheel slightly. "I hope you're right."

"I'm certain I am. Either way, I'll be there in a few hours. If I suspect any of them are in danger, I'll order them to leave Chicago right away, and I'll get the P.D. there to take over. I may do that anyway."

"I'd feel better if you did. I know Holden wants to do this himself, but if someone is determined to stop them …" Her voice broke and she bit her bottom lip.

Daniel squeezed her arm before letting her go. "I'll make sure he's okay."

"I wish I could go with you, but I guess that wouldn't be any help."

"I'd love the company, but it's better if I go alone. You can help me a lot more by praying and by staying with Nicole. I don't want her worrying about this as it won't be good for her."

"I don't either. And I will. She invited me to go to your place after I dropped you off, and I plan to do that. I have no desire to sit in my empty house wondering what's going on and feeling helpless to do anything about it."

"Praying isn't nothing. In fact, it's the most important thing any of us can do right now. God's with Holden and Mikayla, Chris. And with Jax, even if he doesn't know it yet. And God is far more capable of protecting them than any human being is."

Christina signalled and veered her car onto the ramp leading to the airport. "I know. And I will be praying, every minute." She followed the departure signs for the terminal Daniel's plane would fly out of and stopped in front of the entrance. Shoving the transmission into park, she shifted to face him. "Please make sure nothing happens to Holden, Daniel. I'm not sure what I would do if I lost him too."

He leaned across the console and kissed her on the cheek. "I'll do everything in my power to make sure all three of them get home safely, I promise."

"Thank you."

He nodded, reached over the seat to grab his bag, then pushed open the door. "I'll keep in touch."

"Please do." Christina watched him until he disappeared through the doors of the busy airport. *Father, watch over him. Watch over all of them, please.* Someone honked behind her and she pulled the car away from the curb. Daniel was in God's hands now, and so were Holden, Mikayla, and Jax. All she and Nicole could do was pray.

But like Daniel had reminded her, and as her journey over the past few months had slowly taught her, that was far from nothing.

Chapter Forty-Four

The blond man had kept the pistol trained on her the whole time they'd been driving. Mikayla risked a look out the window. Where were they going? And what did these men want with her? Was this a targeted abduction or did she simply happen to be in the wrong place at the wrong time like she was that day at the park when she was a little kid?

Jax's face flashed through her mind. How good a private investigator was he, anyway? Would he be able to track her? As far as she could tell, the men hadn't left many clues for him and Holden to find. Her T-shirt, maybe, if it occurred to them to search by the river. And it was possible that someone in the campground had seen the ambulance drive in or heard the boy scream. Her jaw tightened. Who was that kid? Was Spencer his real name? If he was staying on the grounds, maybe he'd tell someone what happened. Although he seemed pretty convinced that all of this was only a game and that he would ruin it if he told anyone what had happened.

Mikayla rested her head against the side of the ambulance. A few short months ago she'd found out she had a sister. Now, as they were growing close, she might never see her again. And Nicole would have lost someone else she cared about. Would the trauma of that affect the child she was carrying? Mikayla pressed her eyes shut. *Father, help me get out of this. Too many people will be hurt if I disappear. Again. I need to get back to my family. And I need to see Jax.*

Her eyes flew open. While they'd had good conversations lately, somehow she always managed to say or do something to push him away. Mikayla had always considered herself a sensitive person, but something about Jax Rodriguez brought out a side of her she didn't particularly like. Which, even if she did see him again, might resolve the situation on its own. He had to be getting tired of the sharp edge she'd flashed at him several times already, an edge she didn't even realize she had. Why did it come out around him?

Because he scares you.

She frowned. That couldn't be right. Jax didn't scare her, did he? He would never hurt her. Not physically, anyway. And not intentionally. But he very much had the power to hurt her in other ways, she couldn't deny that. Not when something deep inside of her reacted so strongly to him.

The ambulance shuddered to a stop. The knot in her stomach tightening, Mikayla glanced out the window. They appeared to be in an industrial area. The ambulance had parked in an empty gravel lot near the door of a warehouse. Dust-covered windows lined the wall as far down the side of the building as Mikayla could see. She swallowed. Whether or not she could overcome her fear enough to get involved with Jax Rodriguez might be a moot point. If she didn't survive whatever she was about to encounter inside the warehouse, she would never know whether or not they could have made it work. *Father, help me. Keep me safe. And give me courage.* The tightness in her muscles eased slightly, replaced by an inexplicable peace. She wasn't alone.

The man with the shaved head yanked open the rear door. The blond one gestured in his partner's direction with the gun, his eyes still fixed on Mikayla. "Let's go."

She hesitated, until he started toward her. Then she lifted a hand to stop him and stumbled to the opening. The bald man grabbed one arm as she landed on the first step, and yanked on it so hard she nearly stumbled and fell to her knees on the gravel. She managed to brace herself with her free hand against the open door and stay on her feet. He tugged a plastic tie from his pocket and reached for her other arm. When Mikayla resisted, the blond man jumped to the ground beside her and grabbed both arms, yanking them behind her and holding them so the other one could wrap the zip tie around her wrists and pull it tight. Mikayla winced as they each grabbed an elbow and practically dragged her to the front of the warehouse.

A huge, burly man with a beard shoved open the door. Mikayla gulped at the sight of the serious-looking assault rifle he lowered from his shoulder and pointed out into the yard as he pressed his back against the door to hold it open for them. The leer on his face as he looked her up and down sent fresh tendrils of fear winding through her, but she lifted her chin and met his gaze with a hard one of her own, gratified when he glanced away. The men directed her through the door and into the building. Mikayla counted at least three others strolling between pallets loaded with boxes and in the aisles that ran between rows of floor-to-ceiling metal shelving. All were armed and none appeared to actually be doing any kind of factory work. *What is this place?*

At the clicking of high heels on the cement floor, the fake EMTs who had taken her from the camp stopped abruptly. All the other men in the warehouse stopped moving as well. Mikayla swung her gaze to the aisle the sound echoed from. After a few seconds, a woman emerged and strode toward them. Mikayla studied her. She was beautiful, with porcelain skin, dark gleaming hair pulled into a sleek ponytail, and high cheekbones. Her lips were full and red and her runway-model walk and short navy skirt showed off her long legs to full advantage. For a moment, Mikayla started to relax. Then her eyes met the woman's gun-metal gray ones, and she straightened, nerves on high alert again. Who was this person?

The men on either side of her dipped their heads when she stopped in front of Mikayla. Clearly she was the one in charge. The woman contemplated Mikayla in silence for several seconds, her intense gaze scanning her like an MRI machine, as if she could see deep inside. Mikayla forced herself to stand still, to not shift from one foot to the other, as tempted as she was to do so. Finally the woman offered her a smile, completely void of warmth or humor. "Welcome. I trust these gentlemen have been treating you well."

What was she supposed to say to that? They hadn't shot her, if that's what the woman was getting at. Still, Mikayla couldn't bring herself to agree that being forced to go with them at gunpoint and then dragged from the ambulance and into the warehouse was in any way treating her well. "Those aren't the words I would use, no."

The woman's gaze swung to the blond man. He scuffed the cement floor with the toe of his boot. "We didn't do nothing to her, only transported her here like you told us to."

The woman exhaled loudly and inclined her head toward the aisle where she had appeared. "Bring her." She spun around and strode in that direction. The men yanked on Mikayla's arms, compelling her to follow the woman to the aisle. The four of them walked the full length of the building, until they reached a wall of doors. The woman opened one and pushed through it and the men followed her, Mikayla still between them. The three of them stopped on one side of the desk as the woman strode around to the large leather chair on the other side. "You may leave her. Wait outside the door until I call for you, please."

The men nodded and let go of Mikayla before retreating from the office, closing the door behind them when they went. The woman nodded at the armchair beside Mikayla. "Have a seat."

When she hesitated, the woman's features hardened slightly. "Now, please."

Gritting her teeth, Mikayla strode to the front of the chair and sat. The plastic tie dug into her wrists and she shifted a little to ease the pressure. "What do you want with me?"

The woman smoothed the navy skirt beneath her with both hands as she gracefully lowered herself to the chair. "I will ask the questions." She clasped long, slender fingers together on the desk in front of her. "What are you doing in Chicago, Mikayla Grant?"

Mikayla's head jerked. "How do you know my name?"

The woman contemplated her in silence. Mikayla held out as

long as she could beneath the intense scrutiny, before she blew out a breath. "I'm here for a gallery showing of my work."

"I realize the Windsong is showing your pieces, yes, but I asked you for the real reason you came to the city."

A sick feeling struck Mikayla. The woman already knew, didn't she? What would she do to her if she refused to give her the answers she was looking for? And she had to refuse. To tell her the truth, if she didn't actually already know everything, would be to throw Holden and Jax into these people's line of fire, whoever they were. Assuming that this had something to do with their search for Matthew Gibson, which she was beginning to suspect it did. "That is the real reason. My agent requested that I—"

The woman hadn't moved, but her eyes, already cold, hardened to steel. "If you lie to me, things will go very badly for you, Ms. Grant. Tell me the truth, and you and your two friends may be allowed to live."

Mikayla forced herself not to react. So she did know about Holden and Jax. Then what did she need Mikayla to tell her? Whether or not they had found Matthew? What they were planning to do about it? Whatever it was, she couldn't do it, not if it put Jax and Holden in more danger than they likely were already in. Lying wouldn't get her anywhere either, except maybe into a hole in the ground. Cold shivered along the length of her spine. Silence, then. At the moment, it seemed her only recourse. She forced herself to meet the woman's steely gaze without speaking. The two of them stared at each other for a full minute before the woman slowly pushed her chair away from the desk and stood. "Very well. We will play it your way."

She stalked to the door and yanked it open. "Take her to the cellar."

"Yes, ma'am." The blond man nodded and he and his partner strode into the room and grabbed her arms again.

The woman held the door as they passed by. When Mikayla reached her, the woman lifted a hand and they stopped. "When you are ready to talk to me, and I do not think it will take long, let one of these gentlemen know and we can try this again." She gestured for them to go and the men tugged Mikayla through the doorway and along the wall to a double set of swinging doors.

They hauled Mikayla into an industrial-sized kitchen and over to a door leading off of it. When the bald man opened it, Mikayla's mouth went dry as she stared into the murky darkness. The light from the kitchen illuminated the first few stairs, but the rest were swallowed in thick blackness. A jerking on her arms startled her, until she realized one of them had sliced through the plastic tie and loosened her hands. The bald man grasped her elbow and hauled her down the steps. At the bottom, he yanked on her arm, catapulting her a few feet away from the stairs. Before she could steady herself, the man had retreated. Mikayla scrambled up two of the steps before the door at the top slammed shut. A darkness so thick she could almost feel its weight dropped over her.

The distinct grating of three different locks sliding into place stole the last of her defiance. Turning, Mikayla lowered herself carefully onto a step and gripped the wooden railing. A minute later, a scratching sound brought her head up sharply. Was that a rat? Her chest muscles clenched. Maybe she should tell that woman what they were doing here. What harm could it do? She already seemed to know everything.

No. Her jaw tightened. If there was any chance the woman didn't know as much as she seemed to, or wanted Mikayla to think she did, Mikayla couldn't give her any more information than she already had. Not for Holden and Jax's sake, or for Daniel's, or Matthew Gibson's, or anyone else who could be hurt if the wrong people found out whly they were here.

She scrambled a few steps higher, away from any rodents that might be wandering around, feeling her way in the darkness until she settled on another stair and gripped the railing again. How long would they keep her here? What would they do if she continued to refuse to tell them anything? And what would happen if Jax did figure out where she was and he and Holden came after her? Mikayla almost hoped they wouldn't, since they would obviously be walking into …

She jerked upright, everything suddenly becoming clear to her. The two men who had abducted her likely *had* left clues at the campground. No doubt they hoped Jax and Holden would figure out where Mikayla was being held and come looking for her. The woman with the gray eyes had set a trap for the two of them.

And Mikayla was the bait.

Chapter Forty-Five

"Something is off, Holden." Jax scanned his phone screen.

Holden tossed a plastic bottle of barbeque sauce into the cart. "What do you mean?"

"I have been trying to get a hold of Mikayla to see if she wants us to get her anything at the store and there is no answer. And now my phone is almost completely dead."

"Maybe hers is too."

"Yeah, maybe." Jax didn't look too sure as he shoved the device into his pocket. "Still, let's pay for these things and get going. I will drive into town tonight with all three of our phones to charge them. I don't want to take the time now."

"Okay." As much as Holden hated not having his phone in case Christina tried to text again, Jax's words—and the look on his face—had him concerned now too. Better to head to the site, confirm that Mikayla was okay, and take care of their phones after dinner.

They checked out quickly and jumped into Jax's car. When they reached the campground, Holden climbed out of the low-slung vehicle, pressed a hand to the small of his back, and stretched.

"I will check on Mikayla then fire up the grill if you want to get a few of those potatoes ready for baking." Jax grabbed the paper bag of groceries from the trunk and slammed it shut.

"Sounds good. I'll be there in a minute." Hoping to work out the kinks from being cramped inside Jax's car for hours, Holden half-walked, half-jogged a little ways along the road before returning to the campsite.

Jax stood at the picnic table. As Holden approached, he turned. The look of concern he'd had on his face earlier had morphed into something much stronger. "Mikayla's art stuff is here, but I do not see any sign of her."

"She's not in her tent?"

Jax shook his head. "No. When I called her and she did not answer, I looked inside. She is not there."

"Maybe she went for a run or she's taking a shower."

"Possibly." Jax didn't look convinced. "But something definitely does not feel right. Her paints are all open, but nothing looks like it has been touched in at least an hour, maybe more. The picture she was working on is completely dry." He ran a finger over the half-finished field of daisies to prove his point. "If she knew she was going to be away from it that long, why would she leave the paints open?"

Holden drove his fingers through his hair. "Okay, that is a bit weird. If she'd been planning to be gone a while, I'd think she'd have left us a note or something. Did you try texting or calling her?"

Jax tugged the phone from his back pocket. "I texted her like ten times." He scanned the screen. "Nothing."

"Let's take a look around the campground, see if we can find her."

Jax nodded. When they reached the road that circled the perimeter of the grounds, he pointed to the left. "Why don't you head that way and I will go to the right. Holler if you find her. Otherwise, when we meet on the other side of the grounds we can figure out where to go from there."

"Sounds like a plan." Holden started off at a light jog, scanning the grounds as he passed by. It was still cool enough that very few people were crazy enough to be sleeping in tents overnight. He saw one kid, a boy around ten or so, climbing the monkey bars in the small playground, but no one else. And no sign of Mikayla anywhere. When he spotted Jax coming toward him on the road ahead, his heart sank. Obviously Jax hadn't found her either. He'd already pulled his phone out and was checking it by the time Holden reached him.

Holden pulled his out and checked it. His pulse rate

increased. Christina had left a message. Everything in him wanted to listen to it immediately, but doing so could use up the rest of his battery. If Mikayla was in trouble, he needed to conserve that so she could reach them. He'd play Christina's message as soon as they figured out what was going on with Mikayla and he'd had a chance to recharge his phone.

Jax looked up from the device. "Nothing?"

"Nope. And I have to admit I'm getting a little worried."

"Me too." Jax inclined his head in the direction he'd come. "I walked by the path that leads to the river a minute or two ago. I think we should check that out. Maybe she went there to get inspiration for her paintings and fell asleep or something."

"Sure." Holden trailed after Jax as he retraced his steps. It seemed unlikely Mikayla would have fallen asleep this long, but maybe she hadn't slept well last night. And she had been suffering from a headache, so she could have decided to rest, hoping it would help. It was worth checking out, anyway. They reached a worn pathway leading off the main road and Jax started down it.

They'd only walked along the river for a minute or two when Jax pointed at something. "There." A pink T-shirt lay crumpled in the grass near the edge of the water. Jax grabbed a stick and used it to lift the shirt. Holden's stomach clenched at the red stains covering it. "Is that Mikayla's?"

"Could be. I've seen her wearing one like it." Jax's tone was grim.

Holden scanned the area. Was she lying near here somewhere, hurt? Had someone done something to her? The tightness in his stomach escalated to churning. "Should we call the police?"

"Wait." With his other hand, Jax gripped the stick near the shirt so he could bring it closer to his face. He took in a deep breath before lowering the stick. "It is not blood."

"Are you sure?"

"Yes. Definitely fake, but clearly someone meant it to look real."

"Why?"

"Good question." Jax crouched on the pathway and set the stick on the ground. "The grass beside the path here is flattened, as if someone was lying on it. And there are more drops of paint."

"Could it have been her?"

"I don't think so. The area that is flattened is fairly short, like maybe a kid was lying here, not an adult. And a lot of the grass surrounding it has been disturbed too, as if people have been walking here."

"Which could have been her."

"Maybe, but it looks like more than one person tramped around whoever was lying on the ground." Jax took out his phone again and snapped a bunch of pictures. Finally, he straightened. "That is it for my phone. Hopefully yours will last a little longer."

"I wouldn't count on it."

Jax blew out a breath. "When yours is gone, we will have to do this old school. For now, let's walk a little farther along the path, see if we notice anything else."

They hiked for another five minutes without coming across any sign that anyone had been there recently. Finally Jax stopped. "Pretty sure she did not come this far. I think we should investigate the fact that it might have been a child lying in the grass. Except that I do not remember seeing any here."

Holden's head jerked. "I saw a kid in the playground. He looked to be about ten—would that be right?"

"Could be." Jax was already striding toward the road. "Let's go see if he is still there."

When they reached the park, the boy Holden had seen was sitting on a swing like he was waiting for someone. Jax touched Holden's arm. "Why don't you sit on the bench there while I talk to him. Two strange men coming toward him might freak him out."

Holden nodded. "All right." He took a seat on the bench ten feet away, close enough to see and hear everything without crowding the kid.

Jax approached him slowly, smiling. "Hey, buddy."

The kid didn't look freaked out, but he didn't smile, either. "Hey."

"Do you mind if I ask you a few questions?"

"Sure." The kid swiped at the dirt at his feet with the toe of his running shoe.

"We are looking for a friend of ours, a woman with short blond hair, really pretty. Have you seen anyone around here like that?"

The boy shrugged. "I don't know."

"You do not know?"

"That's right." His gaze shifted to Jax's. "The last guys who asked me questions offered me twenty bucks."

Holden's eyes widened. Little scammer. And who were these guys who had offered him money?

Jax crouched in front of the boy. "When was that?"

He shrugged again.

Jax shot Holden an exasperated look before reaching into his back pocket and pulling out his wallet. He removed a bill and held it up to the kid. "Will this help you remember?"

Another shrug.

Holden caught Jax's hiss of disgust as he shoved the ten into the wallet and pulled out a twenty. "I hope this helps jog that memory of yours, because it is as high as I am going to go."

The kid held out his hand and Jax smacked the money onto his palm. "They told me not to tell anyone about the game, but that was a while ago, so the game is probably over by now."

"How long ago was it?"

The boy shoved the money into his jacket pocket. "Three hours, maybe."

Holden winced. A lot could happen in three hours.

"What did they ask you?"

"If I wanted to play a game with them."

"What kind of game?"

"They said it was a race to get to the pretend hospital, and the person who got into the ambulance and took a ride there first would be the winner."

Holden frowned. That didn't sound like any game he'd ever heard of.

"So they wanted you to get into the ambulance?"

"Yes, but only for a few minutes. I wasn't playing the game. The lady was."

Holden swallowed. Was he talking about Mikayla?

"What lady?"

"The one you said you were looking for, I think. I mean, she had short blond hair and I guess she was pretty."

"What did you have to do?"

"They put something on me that made it look like I'd hurt my head. I had to lie on the ground by the river and scream until the lady came to see if I was all right. Then I had to convince her to ride in the ambulance."

"And she did?"

"Yes. She said she'd come with me to the hospital, only I wasn't going there. They let me get out before they left the campground because my mom and dad would have been mad if I had gone off the grounds."

"Did the lady try to get out with you?"

"No. The man with the pretend gun told her not to."

Holden's mouth went dry. He'd bet quite a bit of money the gun hadn't been pretend, or Mikayla wouldn't have gone with them without a fight.

"Can you tell me what the men looked like?"

The kid glanced at the wallet Jax still held in his hand. Shaking his head, Jax opened it again and ripped out the ten. "This is all I have."

The kid snatched it from his fingers and shoved it into his jacket pocket with the other one. "One was tall and had blond hair and the other one was kind of short and bald. But not like an old guy, like he had cut his hair all off. And he talked funny. Like you."

Jax ignored that. "And they said they were going to a hospital?"

"They said a pretend hospital, but when one of them was talking on the phone he said he was bringing the lady to a warehouse."

Holden didn't like anything he was hearing. At least the kid was smart and could remember a lot of details, which meant that Jax was getting his thirty dollars worth, anyway.

"Did they say which warehouse?"

"No, but he told the person he was talking to that they would be there in fifteen minutes."

"Do you know if either of the men hurt the lady?"

The kid tilted his head, his face incredulous. "Of course not. They were playing a game."

"Okay, good." Jax pushed to his feet. "For the record, you should never go anywhere with strangers, or even talk to them when your parents are not around. Especially if they give you something like candy or money."

"Like you did?" The kid peered at him, screwing up his face as the light from the setting sun caught his eyes.

Holden winced. A little too smart.

Jax nodded. "I guess, yeah. But I am not trying to get you to go anywhere. And I do appreciate you telling me all that."

"Are you going to help the lady win?"

"We are going to try."

"Good. I hope she does. She was nice."

"Yes. She is nice." Jax shoved his wallet into his pocket. "Are you going to be camping here much longer?"

"A few more days."

"Okay. Have fun. And thanks for your help."

"You're welcome." The boy pushed off the dirt with his shoe and started swinging.

Holden jumped to his feet as Jax strode toward him, his jaw tight. "You get all that?"

"Yep." He fell into step beside Jax as they started for their site. "Should we call the police now?"

"Why don't you contact Daniel, see what he'd advise. For one thing, we do not really know where to send them. And for another, I would hate to see Mikayla get caught in the middle of a gunfight between the cops and whoever these people are. I would prefer to scout the place out for myself first, see if we can get a handle on what is happening. But if Daniel thinks we should go ahead and call them, we will."

"That makes sense." Holden pulled out his phone as they strode for their site. He punched in Daniel's number but it went to voicemail. Quickly, he relayed everything that had happened and what the kid had told them and promised to let Daniel know the exact address if they found the place. When he hit the disconnect button, the battery level indicator showed almost no juice left. He returned the phone to his pocket as they reached Jax's car and jumped in.

The steak dinner would have to wait. First they needed to find a random warehouse in the midst of however many other warehouses might be within a fifteen minute radius. Then they would have to try and get Mikayla out of it before it was too late.

If it wasn't already.

Chapter Forty-Six

Gravel spewed out from beneath the tires as Jax pressed on the accelerator, ignoring the five miles per hour speed limit signs on the campground road. Holden reached for his seatbelt. "I wonder if the groundskeepers saw anything today."

"Good question. I have seen a couple of them working near our site, so maybe one of them—" Jax muttered a swear word under his breath.

Holden's eyes narrowed. "What is it?"

"The kid mentioned a tall blond guy and one with a shaved head."

Holden pondered that. He'd seen those guys too, but he hadn't paid them a whole lot of attention. His stomach tightened. "So, not groundskeepers."

"How did I not figure that out?" Jax pushed harder on the gas and roared up to the security booth at the front entrance. He stabbed at a button on the door to lower the window.

A man in a light blue uniform and black cap slid open the glass. "How's it goin'?"

Jax propped an elbow on the window frame. "Not great, actually. There's a woman camping with us and we are worried she might be missing."

The man frowned. "When did you see her last?"

"This morning. She was at our site—14a—when we left the grounds at seven-thirty. When we returned an hour ago, she was gone. A kid on the playground told us that she may have been taken in an ambulance by two guys, one blond and one with a shaved head. Did you see an ambulance come into the campground this afternoon? The kid said it might have been about three hours ago."

He shook his head. "Nope, and I've been here since one. 'Course, there's an old entrance that isn't monitored at this time of year. They could have come that way."

"Would any of the groundskeepers have seen them?"

"We only have one guy getting the grounds ready at the moment. His staff will join him in a couple of weeks to start preparing for the season."

Holden leaned forward. "I've seen at least two different guys in dark green coveralls working near our site."

The man pursed his lips and shook his head again. "That's not our staff. Our coveralls are gray. And like I said, John Carpenter's the only guy on staff right now. Hold on."

The man turned and spoke into a walkie-talkie. Jax shot Holden a look. "They have been watching us from the minute we arrived. Right out in plain sight. I do not like that level of cockiness."

Holden felt sick. He and Jax had walked away and left Mikayla completely vulnerable. "Me neither."

The man in the booth clipped the walkie-talkie to his belt and leaned closer to the opening. "John's been painting the inside of the cabins on the property this week, so he didn't see an ambulance on the grounds or anything else unusual. And he hasn't noticed whoever it is who's wandering the property in green coveralls either. He's going to take a walk around now and look for them."

"Tell him to be careful. They could be dangerous."

Not that they're around anymore, if they took Mikayla somewhere else. Holden drove his fingers through his hair, kicking himself for putting her in that kind of danger.

The lines across the man's forehead deepened. "Have you called the police?"

"No. Do you mind doing that? We are heading into the city to see if we can find her."

The man nodded. "Let me know what happens."

"We will." Jax hit the button to close the window as he

accelerated and turned onto the road leading away from the camp.

As they sped toward the city, Holden's mind raced. Why would someone take Mikayla? The story the kid had told them sounded bizarre, as though it had all been some elaborate scheme to lure her into the ambulance so they could take her away. Who would have gone to that much trouble? A sudden sick feeling struck him. The men in green coveralls had to be working for the organization. Which meant that all of this was about Matthew Gibson. And it was his fault that Mikayla was in danger, since this whole crazy quest had been his idea.

Jax clenched the steering wheel with both hands. "How could they possibly have known we were staying at that campground? Somehow they have been following our movements." He let go of the wheel with one hand and swiped the side of it across his forehead as though trying to ward off a headache of his own. "We only talked about our plans at Daniel and Nicole's that night and the next day on the phone." He flexed his fingers. "I am guessing they bugged Daniel's place, maybe a while ago, knowing that he was still investigating the abductions." He returned his hand to the wheel. "If that is the case, they knew we were coming before we even left Toronto."

"And they posted guys here to keep an eye on us, meaning they saw us leave this morning and knew Mikayla was alone at the campground."

Jax nodded, his face grim. "Try to get hold of Daniel again, let him know his place could be bugged so they can watch what they say, especially if it has anything to do with us and what we are doing here."

Holden snatched the phone out of his pocket. The battery level had reached red. He tried calling again. When it went to voicemail, he glanced over at Jax. "Should I leave another message? They might be listening in on his calls, right?"

"Quite possibly. Leave it for now."

Holden disconnected the call as they reached the outskirts of

Chicago. "It's been nine minutes, not including the time we were stopped."

"Okay, makes sense that the place could be somewhere around here, since this is an industrial area."

Having Jax with him made Holden feel better about this situation. There was definitely a lot more to Jax Rodriguez than he'd given him credit for at the party at Daniel and Nicole's. All he could think about at that dinner, besides Christina, was that he hoped Mikayla wouldn't get involved with this guy. Now he wasn't sure that would be a bad thing at all. He cleared his throat. All of that may be meaningless if they couldn't find Mikayla, or if something happened to her. He straightened in his seat. He couldn't think that way. They had to find her. If not, he would be completely to blame.

Holden's gaze swept every industrial building on his side of the street as they drove by. "Do you think there's any chance they'd have parked the ambulance in their lot?"

"I certainly hope so." Jax peered intently out the window on his side. "It is the only way we are going to be able to tell if it is the place or not."

Darkness had fallen over the city as they'd been driving. Thankfully, most of the lots around the buildings were well-lit with lampposts or lights on the sides of the factories. He glanced at his watch. "Fourteen minutes."

Jax didn't answer. They drove in silence for another five minutes. Had the kid been wrong about what he'd heard? The timing was the only clue they had as to where exactly the warehouse they'd taken Mikayla to was located. If that was off, trying to find a building that could be located anywhere in or around the city of Chicago would be like trying to find the proverbial needle in a haystack.

"There." Jax jerked his head toward the lot they were passing by but didn't touch his brakes.

Holden caught a quick glimpse of an ambulance parked in the shadows along the side of the building before they drove past the lot. "Where are you going?"

"I will stop a little farther along the road. No sense announcing our presence by driving to the front door."

That made sense. Obviously Jax had been at the sneaking around game a lot longer than Holden had. Jax pulled into an empty parking lot a hundred yards away and drove around the far side of the building to park. After he'd turned off the engine, Jax turned to Holden. "Ready?"

"No."

Jax offered him a grim smile. "Me neither." He pushed open his door and Holden did the same. Whether or not they were ready, they were going in.

The two of them crept across three parking lots before reaching the edge of the one they were targeting. They stopped behind a bush and surveyed the building. Jax let go of the small branch he'd tugged on to make an opening he could see through. "Hmm."

"What?"

"I am getting a bad feeling about this."

"What about this entire situation could possibly have given you a good feeling?"

Jax snorted softly. "Nothing. But I mean a really bad feeling. It has all been a little too easy, finding the place. I mean, there is hardly anyone at the campground. They would have to know there was a good chance we would figure out that little mercenary was somehow involved and be able to bribe him into giving us information, right? And leaving the ambulance in plain view …"

"You think they wanted us to show up here."

"Yeah. Which means they're using Mikayla as bait." His jaw clenched tightly. "Man, I wish I had my gun."

Holden did too. A weapon would help immensely at the moment. "Why didn't you bring it?"

Jax shot him a look. "Can you imagine how that would have gone over at the border?"

Oh yeah, probably not well. "Should we notify the police now?"

"Probably. But I would still prefer to let Daniel make that call. I have seen way too many hostage situations go terribly wrong when the cops come in shooting. Text him the address so he knows where to send the PD if he calls them. Then let's scout around a little, see if we can find Mikayla or figure out where they are holding her. We can decide what to do next at that point."

Holden nodded and reached for his phone. Nothing happened when he hit the power button and he bit back a curse word of his own. "It's dead." He shoved the worthless device into his pocket.

"We are on our own then. After we talked to the kid, you gave Daniel as much information as we had and we found the place, so if he calls the police and tells them that much, maybe they will too. In the meantime, let's go find out what we are dealing with."

Holden scanned the property. The ambulance was the sole vehicle in the lot, which was promising. Maybe the two men the kid had described were the only ones in there with Mikayla. At least the three of them would outnumber the abductors. Of course, they would still have to contend with the *pretend* gun the kid had seen. And maybe others that he hadn't seen.

Regardless, he'd gotten Mikayla into this, so he'd have to do everything in his power to get her out of it. Even if he had no idea what he was doing. He did get called to hostile situations occasionally, but Holden had been trained to let the police go in first and secure the area before he and his colleagues followed. Had Jax ever found himself in circumstances like this? From what he'd said, he had, and it had often not gone well. Still, would he have any idea what to do if they were confronted by people wielding guns? Holden didn't bother to ask in case he didn't like the answer.

Jax crept around the edge of the bush, Holden at his heels. Jax followed the edge of the lot until he was even with the corner of the building before jogging across the open space and slamming his back against the side of the building, next to a window. Holden fell into place beside him.

Jax leaned forward slightly to peer through the glass into the dimly-lit interior. A minute later, he shifted around to face Holden. "I do not see anyone, and the front door is slightly ajar. Let's sneak in. Once we are inside, we can separate—you go to the right and along the far side of the building and I will go to the left. We will stay ten minutes. If we have not seen any sign of her by then, we will make our way outside and find a way to contact the police. Sound good?"

Good? Not particularly. But it sounded feasible, which was enough for Holden at the moment. He nodded curtly. "Let's do it."

"Okay. Be careful. Anything happens, yell and I will come."

Holden's heart thudded against his ribs as Jax crept toward the front door. He took a deep breath and followed.

Here went nothing.

Chapter Forty-Seven

After losing track of how long she sat there in the dark, Mikayla forced herself to stand. This was ridiculous. She couldn't keep sitting here while Jax and Holden might be putting themselves in danger trying to find her. They could only do that if they found Spencer and got him to talk. But how would they know that he had anything to do with this? Even if they did think to look for her at the river, and even if they did find the T-shirt one of the men had tossed into the grass, they wouldn't have any idea that the kid was somehow involved.

She gritted her teeth. All the more reason for her to stop waiting around for something to happen. If no one was coming for her, she had to get out of here herself, preferably before the lady with the gray eyes summoned Mikayla into her presence again. Shoving the vision of rats out of her head, Mikayla grasped the railing and made her way slowly down the stairs. At the bottom, she stopped and slid her foot forward a ways, feeling for anything that might be in her path. When she couldn't sense anything, she took a few more shuffling steps forward, her arms out in front of her. It was so dark. She hated not being able to see where she was going, but she couldn't sit around refusing to move forward any longer.

The conversation she'd had with Jax, about not wanting to take a step down a road when she couldn't see what was around the bend, replayed through her mind. This journey across the basement floor in total darkness felt a lot like that, as if anything could happen, any number of things could hurt her, especially since she was completely and utterly alone. Her knee banged against something hard. Mikayla pressed her lips together to keep from crying out. She stopped and rubbed her knee with one hand, reaching for the object with the other. A dresser, maybe? Or possibly a wooden storage unit. She felt her way around it and took a few more steps. Another scratching sound froze her in place. Okay, maybe she wasn't completely alone. Although that would be better than being trapped down here in the company of rats or any other critters she couldn't see.

Of course, rodents or no rodents, she wasn't truly alone. *I do know that. I know you're here, even in this dark place. Keep me safe, please. Give me courage. Help me to find a way out. And please keep Jax and Holden safe.* She shuffled forward another seven or eight steps. Her shoe connected with something and shock reverberated through her as a deafening clatter filled the air. She crouched to feel around for the objects. Paint cans.

For a moment she stayed in place, straining to hear any noise at the top of the stairs that would indicate they'd heard her moving around and were coming to get her. The irony that cans of paint could be the death of her sent a wry smile twisting across her lips. When she heard nothing after thirty seconds, she pushed to her feet. There had to be windows set into the walls somewhere, right? If there were, why wasn't even a glimmer of light filtering through?

Keep moving, Mikayla. Another few steps and the hands she was holding straight out in front of her bumped against cold, damp concrete. A wall. If she could feel her way along it, she'd have to come to a window at some point. Assuming there were any. The dampness was a bad sign. Had this basement been built completely underground? If so, it was entirely possible that the only way out was the stairs. And given the loud clinking of the locks she'd heard being shoved into place, she wasn't going out that way until someone came and got her and forced her to go with them. She swallowed hard and continued her journey around the room for several minutes, running both hands over the chilled stone, shivers rippling through her. There wouldn't be bats flying around the cellar, would there?

Stop manufacturing trouble, Mik. Her mother had always cautioned her against doing that, whenever her imagination would get the better of her. A picture of her mother formed in her mind and Mikayla bit her lip. If she didn't get out of this situation, if the people holding her hostage ended up killing her, at least she knew where she was going. And she would see her parents. That hope brought a small degree of comfort, even as her instinct to survive kicked in, warring against the desire to be with the ones she had loved and lost.

Something slammed into her stomach, knocking the air from her lungs. After a moment, she reached out and patted the top of a wooden surface. A work bench? She made her way carefully around it to the other side and continued to the corner of the building. Turning, she started along the next wall.

Two minutes later, her fingers brushed against something and she paused, running her hands over whatever it was for a few seconds. A board had been attached to the wall here. Why would that be? A light went off in her mind. "A window." She whispered the words as a thrill of hope shot through her. They must have boarded it over, which would explain why no light was getting in. All she had to do now was pry the board off and see if the opening was big enough for her to slip through.

She dug the tips of her fingers beneath the wood and tugged for several seconds before abandoning her efforts with a loud exhalation of breath. Too many nails. There was no way this board was moving unless it was pried off with some kind of tool. Which meant retracing her steps to the work bench. Why hadn't she checked for tools when she was there? *Think, Mikayla. You have to do better than that if you want to get out of here alive.*

Lifting her chin, she started in the direction she had come. After turning the corner again, she made her way to the work bench. Bending over it, she felt along the wall. If whoever had installed the table was anything like her father, he would have hung at least a rudimentary set of tools on the wall above it. Her fingers brushed over something flat and metal, a ruler, maybe.

She continued her search. A screwdriver or a hammer would be perfect, but if she couldn't find either of those, she would check the ruler to see if it was solid enough to use as a lever. Her fingers brushed across several empty hooks, but the tools, if they had ever been there, had clearly been removed. Which made sense if the plan was to use this room as a dungeon or holding cell for whatever reason. Chills swept over her. *God, please. Help me find something, anything that would help.*

Tears threatened but Mikayla blinked them away impatiently. *Think, think.* Her mind raced as she tried to remember being in the workshop with her father. Memories of him dropping a tool once in a while, or knocking one off a hook, crossed her mind and she knelt down and felt around the hard cement floor. In the intense darkness, she found and tossed away a nail and several screws. Crouching lower, she patted her hand along the floor, moving closer to the wall and refusing to think about any creepy crawly beings whose nests she might be about to swipe a hand through.

She was about to quit looking when her thumb bumped against something smooth. Was that metal? The bottom of the wooden bench dug into her shoulder as she strained to grasp hold and pull the object out. The tip felt like a screw, only longer and thicker. Finally she was able to grip it hard enough to yank the object out. Mikayla felt along the length of the round metal rod until she reached the hard plastic handle. A screwdriver. She almost cried with relief as she hefted the tool in one hand. If this didn't work to pry off the boards, or if anyone came after her before she could finish that job, at least she might be able to use the tool to stab anyone who got close enough.

Clutching the screwdriver in her right hand, she trailed the fingers of her left along the wall, to the corner and around it. Not much farther now.

By the time she reached the window, she felt as if she'd run a marathon. Her heart thudded so strongly against her ribs that she could barely draw in air. *Relax. You're almost out of here.* For a few seconds, Mikayla rested her forehead on the board, gathering her strength. Silence hung as thickly as the blackness in the basement.

Then several loud cracks, like a distant display of fireworks, shattered the heavy quiet. She shoved herself away from the wall and spun around, instinctively gripping the handle and bending her arm to lift the tool into the air, like a knife.

Were those gunshots?

Chapter Forty-Eight

Holden crept past a skid of boxes shrink-wrapped in plastic, making his way to the far wall. Every few steps he stopped and listened, but couldn't hear any sound other than the pounding of his heart. What was he doing here, sneaking around an old warehouse on the edge of Chicago, keeping an eye out for men with guns? It was crazy, how far his recurring dream had brought them. Worse than crazy, it was reckless and dangerous. Not only had he put Mikayla's and Jax's lives in danger, his own was in a very precarious position at the moment.

What would happen to Christina if he was killed? Would she be able to survive another loss so close on the heels of the last one? He rubbed the palm of his hand over his chest at the ache that caused. The only thing in the world he wanted to do was to help his wife, to somehow, in some small way, ease the grief hovering in her eyes. Instead, his irresponsibility in dragging the three of them here could send her over the abyss she'd been lingering around the rim of for months now.

Holden reached the last aisle. Pressing his side against the metal shelving, he made his way forward, far enough to peer into the open space he needed to cross to get to the back wall of the warehouse. How long had they been in here? It had to have been five minutes. Five more and he was supposed to head outside to meet Jax. Still no sign of Mikayla or anyone else.

He stepped around another pallet loaded with boxes. A deafening blast echoed through the warehouse, and for a few seconds his heart, thudding so hard seconds ago, seemed to stop beating. More shots rang out, coming from the direction he'd been heading. Someone was firing wildly around the warehouse. Had Jax been caught in the crossfire? Or Mikayla? The possibility made him sick.

Holden dove behind the pallet. What if the guy came after

him? He was defenseless against a weapon. Wildly, he searched around for something he could use to hit someone with if they discovered him. A board lying on the bottom shelf of the metal unit a few feet away caught his eye and he started to crawl toward it.

"Don't."

Holden froze at the harsh command then flipped around to face the man. The round barrel of a handgun was pointed at his chest. The short bald man he'd seen wearing green coveralls and raking the lawn near their campsite gazed at him, an ugly smile twisting across his face. "Know what we do to intruders around here?" he asked with a thick Spanish accent. He cocked the gun.

God, be with Christina. Help her through this. Holden sent up the frantic prayer, deeply aware that he was living the last few seconds of his life.

A gunshot thundered again, and he braced himself for the impact but felt nothing. The man in front of him stumbled a few feet before dropping onto the concrete floor. A pool of dark crimson spread out from under his side. Holden scrambled to his feet.

"Get down." Daniel appeared around the edge of the stack of boxes and grabbed his arm, pulling him to a seated position on the floor beside him, their backs pressed against the pile of boxes Holden had taken cover behind.

Holden stared at him. "How did you get here so fast?"

Daniel peered around the boxes. "I was talking on the phone in my office this morning when it glitched and I realized it had been bugged. I guessed that meant the organization is still functioning, to some degree, and had been tracking my progress with the investigation, which meant they likely also knew about you guys coming to this area."

"Yeah, Jax figured that out while we were on the way here."

"I jumped on a plane and got your text about Mikayla being taken in an ambulance to a warehouse fifteen minutes north of the campground. As soon as I landed, I managed to get my gun back from customs and rented a car. Took me a few minutes to orient myself using the GPS on my phone, but when I did, I drove this way, spotted the ambulance parked outside, and here I am." He peered around the boxes again.

"Well, I'm extremely glad to see you. Did you call the Chicago PD?"

"No. I planned to do that as soon as I got here and figured out the exact address to give them, but I was about to call from outside the door when I heard gunshots and decided I better check those out first."

"Lucky for me you did."

"Yeah." Daniel fumbled in his coat pocket and retrieved his phone. "Can you call them?"

"Sure." Holden reached for the device.

"Here. Take this too." Daniel flipped around his Glock and offered it to Holden, handle first.

Holden's eyes narrowed as he took it. "Why are you giving me your gun?"

"Because I haven't checked yet, but I'm pretty sure I just took one in the leg."

They both looked down. Daniel was holding a hand against his thigh, about two inches above his knee. When he lifted it, blood had seeped through a hole in his jeans and his hand was covered in red. Holden inhaled sharply. How would they ever get out of this situation if Daniel was out of commission?

Daniel grimaced. "Oh man." He returned his palm to the red patch spreading across his leg. "I'm going to hear about this when I get home. Nicole hates it when I get shot."

"I can't say I blame her." Holden forced himself to take slow, deep breaths as he set the weapon and phone on the cement floor and tore off his sweatshirt and then his T-shirt. He slid the sweatshirt back on before ripping the T-shirt from top to bottom. After folding the cloth over three or four times, he wrapped the strip of material around the wound on Daniel's leg and tied it tightly. His friend winced but didn't speak.

Holden sank onto his haunches. "That will have to do until we can get you to a hospital."

Daniel offered him a grim smile. "Optimism. I like it." He waved a hand toward the Glock. "Do you know how to use that?"

Holden nodded as he reached for the weapon. "Gage and I used to go to the shooting range sometimes. Great way to get rid of pent-up frustration."

"Tell me about it." Daniel jerked his chin toward the gun. "Of course, shooting a person's not the same as shooting at a target. Think you can do it?"

Absolutely no idea. Holden gripped the handle of the gun. Somehow they had to get out of this mess. He had to see Christina again, make things right with her. He couldn't die and leave things the way they were between them. "If I have to."

"You won't."

Holden started to spin around at the sound of the woman's voice, close to his ear, but the cold metal pressed to his temple stopped him. In his peripheral vision he could make out two men standing next to the woman.

Another man came around the other side of the pile of boxes, his weapon trained on Daniel.

The woman spoke again, in an accent that suggested an eastern European background. "Set the gun on the ground and send it over to my friend there or the detective will find himself with yet another hole in him."

Holden's eyes met Daniel's. Daniel nodded slightly. Gritting his teeth, Holden set the Glock down and sent it spinning across the concrete floor toward the man holding the gun on Daniel. He stooped to grab it and shove it in the back of his jeans.

"Now your phones."

Holden tugged his from his pocket and gave it to the man. It wasn't much good to him at the moment anyway. Daniel's he would have very much liked to have kept, though. He blew out a breath as he swiped at it with the side of his hand, shooting it across the floor toward the man. They'd surrendered their last life line. If Jax couldn't find a way to get them out of this situation, then the extra time Daniel had bought Holden when he shot the man who was about to put a bullet in him could run out fast.

Chapter Forty-Nine

Mikayla slid the end of the screwdriver under the side of the board. Whether or not they were shooting upstairs, she had to do what she could to get herself out of the building. *Father, keep Jax and Holden safe, please.* The idea of anything happening to either of them made her stomach writhe, but she pushed away her fear and concentrated on pulling off the board.

For a few seconds, nothing happened. Mikayla leaned on the handle of the screwdriver as hard as she dared, and finally the board began to groan. One nail popped away from the wall and then another. She tugged the tool loose and felt along the board, searching for another spot to slide the tip under. Before she could, the sound of locks sliding open sent prickles of shock racing along her arms and legs.

She spun around again. Were they coming for her? Heavy footsteps sounded on the stairs and she clutched the screwdriver tightly. Even if the thought of stabbing someone sickened her, she wouldn't go without a fight. Not this time. The door at the top of the stairs slammed shut, leaving the basement in total darkness again. The grinding sound of locks sliding into place confused her. Whoever was on the stairs thumped down two more. Mikayla gripped the handle tightly in one fist, bent her arm, and lifted the tool until her hand was level with her shoulder, ready to drive it into whoever was making his way toward her.

"Mikayla?"

Relief poured through her and she lowered the screwdriver. "Jax."

"*Gracias a Dios.*" He sounded as relieved to hear her voice as she was to hear his. "Where are you?"

"Across the room, against the wall."

"Can you come this way?"

"No. I need to stay where I am. I'll show you why when you get here."

"Okay. Keep talking so I can follow your voice."

"Careful. There's a dresser or something in the way and a few cans of paint that I already knocked over."

She heard a thud, followed by a soft grunt. "Thanks for the heads up on the dresser. Only a couple of seconds too late."

"How did you find me?"

"We found your shirt by the river and the spot where a kid had been lying on the grass. We went to the playground and found the one who had helped those guys trick you into getting into the ambulance. Thirty bucks later and he gave us enough information to lead us here."

"And how did you know I was in the cellar?"

"I didn't. I was making my way to the back of the warehouse when I bumped into two guys with guns who helpfully directed me to your location."

She winced. "Is Holden okay?"

"I think so." His voice was closer now, only a few feet away. "When I heard gunshots I headed toward him, but Daniel appeared before I could reach Holden. Last I saw, the two of them were together so I kept going, trying to find you." Strong hands gripped her arms. They traveled down to her hands and Jax caught the one holding the screwdriver and lifted it. "Good thing I let you know who I was or I might have a hole in my chest about now."

She managed a weak grin. "You would have. I was ready for whoever might come for me."

"Of course you were. Should have known you would not need to be rescued."

Jax let go of her hand and pulled her into his arms. "I am glad you are okay." For a moment he held her, then he stepped back, his hands lightly grasping her upper arms. "You are okay, right? And you might want to answer quickly, because I am about to pat you down all over to check for myself." He let go of one of her arms.

Mikayla's laugh was shaky as she grabbed his hand. "Yes, I'm okay."

"You are trembling."

"I wasn't, until a minute ago."

"So it is not because you were abducted?"

"No."

"Then it is …?"

"The rats, I think."

He didn't answer for a few seconds. When he did, his voice held a hint of laughter, in spite of their dire situation. "You cannot give me that much even now, eh?"

What if they didn't get out of this alive? Was that how she wanted to leave things with him? Mikayla grasped his forearms. "You're right. You deserve more than that, after risking your life to come after me. It's not the rats. Not entirely."

He cupped the back of her head with his hand, pulling her to his chest. "I will take that. For now."

For a moment Mikayla allowed herself to give in to the feeling of being held by him, of reveling in the suggestion that they might survive this and be able to think about a future for themselves. Then she remembered Holden and Daniel and what might be happening upstairs and forced herself to move out of his arms. "You're trembling too."

"Yeah, Grant. I was scared."

"Bullets flying and men with guns will do that to you."

"That is not why I was scared. Not entirely."

A weak smile touched her lips. "Touché. Or whatever you say in your country." Mikayla tightened her grip on the handle of the tool. "We need to get out of here. I found a board nailed to the wall that I think might be covering a window. That's what I was doing with the screwdriver, trying to pry it off."

"How did you manage to find the screwdriver in the dark?"

"I was feeling along the walls for the window and discovered a work bench. When I found the window, I returned to it and felt all around for tools. Nothing was hanging on the hooks, but I remembered that my dad or I often dropped something and it would roll under the bench, and that's where I found this."

His fingers brushed lightly across her cheek. "So what you are saying is, even though you could not see what was in front of you, you managed to find your way."

His quiet words pattered over her like a gentle rain. "I guess I did."

"Here." He felt for the screwdriver and took it from her. "Might as well do something useful, since I came all this way." His arm brushed hers as he reached out, likely feeling for the board. A second later the screwdriver scraped against wood and the board creaked again.

"So Daniel's here?"

"Yeah. Him and his gun. No idea how that happened, but I was never so happy to see anyone in my life. Not until …" Jax ripped the board from the wall and soft light from the street lamp in the parking lot filtered through the dust and cobwebs covering a window. His eyes met hers. "This minute."

She swallowed. "Good job."

"Think you can fit through?"

"I think we both can."

In the dim light, he contemplated the window, judging the size. "Not sure if I will be able to."

"You better, because I'm not leaving here without you."

Jax exhaled. "I will give it a shot. But you have to go first." He tugged on the window, but it didn't budge. The locks had rusted in place and he couldn't flip them when he tried. With a glance toward the stairs, he gripped the screwdriver like a knife, the way she had, and tapped the glass with the tip of it, hard enough to send cracks spider-webbing across it. Three more taps and a piece fell out.

"Here." Mikayla snatched a pair of wool gloves from her

pocket and handed him one. Clutching the other one, she helped him work the pieces of glass out until the frame stood empty.

"All right. Let's go before anyone comes." Jax linked his fingers together and bent forward so she could stand on his clasped hands. When she did, he lifted her toward the window. The space was plenty big for her to wiggle through and out into the cool night air, and she prayed it would be big enough for him too.

"Wait."

Jax disappeared from the frame. Mikayla's throat tightened. He was coming out, wasn't he? There was nothing he could do to help Holden or Daniel if he stayed locked in the basement. A few seconds later, something clunked onto the cement floor and Jax appeared again in the frame. "Paint cans." Pressing his palms to the window sill, he levered himself through the opening. For a few seconds it looked as if it might be too tight a squeeze, but he managed to shimmy out by crawling across the gravel on his elbows and belly like a soldier at boot camp.

"We did it." Michaela held a hand to her chest in an attempt to slow the pounding of her heart.

"You did it, Grant. Well done." He clambered to his feet and held out his hands to help her. "I do not suppose you still have a phone?"

She shook her head as he tugged her up. "No, one of the fake EMTs made me give it up before they brought me here and handed me over to the woman."

Still holding her hands, he cocked his head. "The woman?"

"Yeah. I have no idea who she is, but she appears to be in charge."

"All right. We can sort out all that later. For now we need to call 911 and get help for Holden and Daniel. My car is a few lots over. They took my phone too, but we can drive somewhere and find a place that will let us use theirs." Letting go of one of Mikayla's hands, he took a step forward. Mikayla started after him.

The shick shick of a gun being cocked, deafening in the thick silence of the industrial park, stopped them in their tracks. The big, bearded man with the assault rifle stepped out of the shadows along the side of the building, the weapon pointed directly at them.

Jax reached his arm across the front of Mikayla and drew her partly behind him.

The man stalked forward several paces, stopping a few feet in front of them. A cold smile crossed his face. "Going somewhere?"

Chapter Fifty

"You will come with me, please." The woman spoke calmly but in a tone of voice that didn't leave any room for argument. The gun still shoved against Holden's temple underscored the command.

The two men with her grabbed an arm each and hauled Holden to his feet. They bent his arms behind him, and one of them wrapped a plastic tie around his wrists and pulled it tight. Holden winced. He sent Daniel one last look before the men yanked on his arms, forcing him to follow the woman along the aisle between shelves until they reached a small office. They shoved Holden through the door after her. The woman walked around a desk and nodded at the men. "Leave us. Keep an eye on the other two."

Which must mean that Jax and Mikayla were alive, at least. Before the men could move, she added, "And whatever happens, no more shooting until I give the order. Tell the others."

Holden's stomach lurched. *Until* she gave the order? She was planning on killing them, then. So what was she waiting for?

The men nodded and left, pulling the door shut behind them. The woman held out a hand to the armchair in front of the desk. "Please, sit."

Awfully polite for someone who was holding them all hostage. Holden banished the thought. He needed to stay focused. Whoever this woman was, she was clearly in charge. If he could get through to her, maybe he could convince her to let them all go. At the very least, he hoped to be able to talk her into allowing Daniel to get medical attention.

When she inclined her head toward the chair, Holden sat, the tie around his wrists digging deep into his skin. She sat too, and for a moment the two of them merely contemplated each other. Who was this woman? She was beautiful, exotic looking. Her steel-gray eyes were mesmerizing, and Holden had to force himself to look away from them or fall under their spell, like a cobra's.

A shadow crossed her face. "You look so much like him."

"Like who?"

"Your brother."

Holden's head came up sharply. "You knew him."

"Yes. Gage worked for me, helping us to rescue those children in Toronto. Including Matthew Gibson, whom we know you have come to Chicago to find."

"So that's why you took Mikayla? Because you're still trying to protect the kids who were taken?"

A slight smile touched the corners of her mouth. "Yes. After Ted Stiller was arrested, he provided the police with enough information to take the majority of those involved in the rescues into custody."

"But not you."

"No. I managed to elude them, and have dedicated myself in the years since to rebuilding a smaller network of individuals committed to those children, as I continue to be. Our mission has shifted, from rescuing those still in need to ensuring that those we provided safe haven for are not found and returned to the deplorable conditions from which they were removed."

Holden got that. Still, the parents of those children deserved to know what had happened to them, and those who had adopted them needed to be held to account for circumventing the law.

Didn't they?

Clutching the gun in one hand, the woman rose gracefully and came around the desk. Holden straightened. What was she planning to do? She stopped in front of him and leaned against the desk, crossing one slim ankle over the other. "Your brother was a remarkable man."

Heat rose in his chest. "Yes, he was. And he's dead, thanks to you."

From the dart of pain that shot across her face, that hit the mark. *Careful, Holden. You're trying to win her to your side.*

"I don't disagree. I have always held myself responsible for what happened to Gage, although he knew the risks of what we were doing and made the choice himself to accept them."

Holden nodded slightly, giving her that much. "I know he did."

"That last mission was a mistake."

His eyes narrowed. "What do you mean?"

"It never should have happened. We had already spent too much time in Toronto, more than in any other city. But Gage had only gotten started and it seemed a waste to pull out before we took full advantage of his potential. So we decided we would carry out one more rescue." She rubbed the side of her hand across her forehead, the silver charm bracelet around her wrist jangling. "It was a disaster from the start."

"In what way?"

"Well, for starters, Gage didn't want to do it."

Holden gritted his teeth. That was news. "But you forced him?"

"Of course not. We weren't in the habit of forcing our people to help save the children. And Gage had never resisted our instructions before. Only he came to me this time, before I'd had time to tell him what we were planning, to say that he was getting married and wanted out. I told him this would be our last rescue and I ... showed him a picture of Matthew Gibson."

Holden sighed. That likely would have worked with him too. "That was a dirty ploy."

Her eyes widened slightly, almost imperceptibly. "Those were your brother's exact words. Right before he agreed to do one more mission. But it had been a last-minute addition and we hadn't properly vetted the prospective parents. Last year, Andrew's mother died of cancer. Douglas Thompson has been struggling ever since. A few days ago he came to me and gave me information that would have caused us to deny them a child if we'd had it at the time."

"What information?"

"That it was his wife who wanted a child, not him. Apparently, he wasn't at all supportive of the method she chose to acquire one, but none of that came out in the pre-adoptive discussions. It didn't sit right with him to go through those types of channels. He admitted that he has struggled from the beginning with the idea that Matthew was taken illegally, and the guilt has only grown over the years, to the point where he finds it extremely difficult to have the boy in his home. So far we have been able to convince him not to make any rash decisions, but it has required a lot of hand-holding to prevent him from walking away from Matthew. I'm not sure how much longer we can keep that going. So you see—disaster."

Holden felt sick. His brother had lost his life during that disaster of a rescue mission. Had it been for nothing?

As if she could read his mind, Natalya gazed at the weapon in her hand, turning it from side to side. "The question that has consumed me since his death is, was it worth it? Did helping those children justify sacrificing Gage's life? Or," she nodded toward the door, "one more life today. So far."

"And?"

"I don't know. I believe Gage would have said yes. Several of those children likely would have died, including Matthew, without our intervention, or grown into adults who continued the cycle of abuse and neglect. We may have stopped some of that from happening. But the cost was great. Many lost their freedom, their reputations, their careers, their families. And Gage paid the greatest price of all. Or perhaps, to be more accurate, his wife and son paid."

The more she talked, the more Holden's stomach tightened. She was giving him too much information. Obviously she didn't anticipate that he would be around long enough to pass it along to the authorities. *Think, Holden, think.* How could he get through to her?

She pushed away from the desk and walked around behind him, slowly, methodically. "And now, more will have to pay.

You understand that I cannot allow you and your friends to walk away from here. As the police have not arrived yet, you obviously did not let them know you were coming here, since there is a station less than two miles away. That means that no one can tie you to this place, or to the organization. You will simply become names on that very long list of missing persons your friend Jax Rodriguez has made it his life's work to research. Ironic, I know. But necessary."

The cold round barrel of the pistol pressed into the base of Holden's skull. He swallowed hard and closed his eyes. An image of Christina, sitting in the rocking chair and kneading the tiny baby blanket, flashed through his mind. Was it actually possible that he would never see her again? And that, once he was dead, this woman would go after Daniel, Jax, and Mikayla? If not for himself, he needed to find a way to save the people he cared about, the ones who were only in this mess because they were trying to help him. The woman cocked the weapon. A frantic prayer raced through Holden's mind as he licked lips that had suddenly gone dry. *God, help me. Give me the words to say.*

He opened his eyes. "Gage would never agree that our deaths could possibly be justified. I knew him better than anyone, and he wouldn't have gotten involved with you if he believed you were capable of cold-blooded murder. That can't be what this organization is about. Everything you've done, that high price so many were willing to pay, was to help innocent people, not to kill them. You change that now and any good you might have done will be destroyed. Including everything Gage did while he was working with you."

For several long seconds he held his breath. Had he reached her?

Finally, she pulled the gun away from his neck. Her high heels clicked on the concrete floor as she walked around the desk and sank onto her seat, setting the gun in front of her. Propping her elbows on the surface, she dropped her face into her hands. Holden eyed the weapon. If his hands were free …

She looked up before he could make a move. "I'm tired, Holden."

How did she know his name? His eyes met hers. Likely there wasn't much she didn't know. "Tired of what?"

"Of fighting. Of giving up everything and asking others to do the same. Of working so hard and achieving so few results. Many, many times I have felt that we were scooping out handfuls of water as waves crashed over our ship. So much water that our paltry efforts were nothing but laughable. And now our ship is breaking apart." She lifted her hands, palms up as if in supplication. He had no idea what she was asking of him. When he didn't speak, she lowered her hands to the desk. "I'm not sure I can do this any longer."

The opening he was looking for. Holden leaned forward, resting his elbows on the arms of the chair. "You don't have to. You have done so much good. But it's time to stop now. Time to stop fighting and sacrificing. Too many people have been hurt, including another genuinely good man who's lying out there on that cement floor bleeding to death. Nicole loves him, as much as she loved Gage, and they have a child on the way, like she and Gage did. Gage would want you to help him, to keep her and Jordan from losing another man they love, another husband and father."

Her cheeks, already pale, grew ashen as she studied him. Whatever had transpired between her and Gage, he was obviously a weakness for her. Seconds ticked by in which Holden hardly dared to take a breath. Finally, her shoulders sagged and she nodded. "I believe you are right, he would." Without another word, she opened the top drawer of her desk and pulled out a walkie-talkie.

Chapter Fifty-One

"Against the wall." The man jerked the rifle in the direction of the building.

Mikayla clenched her teeth to keep from screaming. They'd been so close to freedom … Jax rested a hand on her back and guided her toward the side of the warehouse. He leaned closer, speaking low into her ear. "Do what he says. Everything will be okay."

"No talking." The man let go of the gun with one hand and shoved Jax between the shoulder blades, and he stumbled forward a couple of steps.

As much as she admired his confidence, Mikayla did not share it. This was a bad situation and, at the moment, she couldn't see any way out of it. Were Daniel and Holden okay? Had they been caught in that gunfire she'd heard? If not, why hadn't they come out of the building? She swallowed hard and pressed against the cold brick. *Stay calm or you won't survive this.*

Jax turned and leaned against the wall beside her, his arm touching hers, the side of his hand brushing against her skin. She risked a sideways look at him. Were these the last few minutes, the last few seconds, they would spend together? Why had she pushed him away so hard? Even as she had, she'd believed, somewhere in the recesses of her mind, that they could find their way to each other, given time.

Only now they had run out of time.

All her reasons, the fear that had kept her from giving him her heart, seemed weak and foolish now. As he had told her once, life was too short. How had she become someone who allowed fear to dictate what she did? Who she got involved with? Likely her recent revelation that her fear stemmed from what had happened to her that day in the park was accurate. But that fear had gotten worse after her parents' accident. And Jax was right. Her parents wouldn't have wanted her to live in fear because of what had happened to them. They would have wanted her to know joy. And Jax did too. He had offered her a precious gift and she had coldly refused to accept it. The idea sickened her.

She twined her pinkie finger around his, trying in some small way to let him know how sorry she was. How desperately she wished she could have had one more chance to let go of everything that had held her back and embrace what he had wanted to give her.

His dark gaze slid to hers, and a small smile tugged at his lips as he tightened his hold on her finger.

Some of the tightness left her muscles. He understood.

The walkie-talkie on their captor's belt crackled, and the man snatched it from the holder and held it to his mouth. "What is it?"

The woman's words were nearly lost in the static, but the man obviously caught them as his head whipped toward them. He barked, "Got it," into the unit before shoving it into the holder and aiming his weapon in their direction again. Mikayla's heart thudded painfully in her chest. Was this it?

Jax let go of her finger and clasped Mikayla's hand in his, tugging her closer. No one moved for several long seconds, until shouts echoed from behind the building and feet pounded across the parking lot. The men who had brought Mikayla here slid onto the front seats of the ambulance while four others jumped into the back. The man who'd been aiming the assault rifle at Jax and Mikayla slowly lowered his weapon, shot them a last, menacing look, then took off running toward the ambulance. The vehicle had started to pull away, but the rear doors hung open and one of the men inside grasped his hand and hauled him up. Then the doors slammed shut, the tires spun through the gravel, and the vehicle sped across the lot before squealing onto the street.

Mikayla's knees went weak, and she might have dropped to the ground if Jax's arm hadn't come around her waist. He cupped her head with one hand and pulled her to him, wrapping his other arm around her and murmuring a steady stream of Spanish into her ear. How was it possible to be comforted by someone even when she didn't fully understand him? She managed a tremulous smile. Another revelation. Mikayla rested her head on Jax's chest, reassured by the steady beating of his heart against her ear. They were alive.

Now they needed to find out if Holden and Daniel were too.

Chapter Fifty-Two

Natalya tossed the walkie-talkie into the drawer and reached for her phone. She punched in three digits and Holden waited through the silence that followed, until she spoke. "Ambulance." Her gray eyes met Holden's. "And the police."

He caught the dispatcher's voice on the other end of the line and the knots in his stomach loosened slightly. Help was coming. The woman provided the address of the warehouse. "Two people have been shot, one of them a hostage, and three others are being held against their will."

Another murmur from the dispatcher before the woman looked at Holden again. "Seven, all armed, but they may have fled the premises." After a few seconds, she disconnected the call and set the phone on her desk. "It is done. The one thing I could do for Gage. Although I do understand it does not make up for what happened to him."

"It goes a long way. Thank you."

Her features softened slightly. "You're welcome."

Holden tilted his head. "What's your name?"

She hesitated. Years of secrecy had clearly made it difficult for her to share anything. Since it didn't look as if she was about to flee, her name would likely come out in the news, but he wanted to know it now. Would she tell him?

"Natalya."

"Natalya." He tried the name out on his tongue. It suited her, as beautiful and exotic as she was.

She clasped her hands on the desk. "Would you do something for me?"

In spite of the fact that she had called for help and was clearly about to turn herself in, Holden wasn't inclined to do her a lot of favors at the moment. The woman had lured his brother into her organization. If she hadn't, Gage would still be alive. Although, as she had pointed out, he had made the decision on his own to join them. No one had forced him at gunpoint. Not like the rest of them had been forced today. He shifted on the chair, trying to relieve the pressure on his wrists. The faint wail of a siren sounded in the distance. "I can't promise you anything, but what do you want?"

"Would you take care of Matthew Gibson?"

His eyes narrowed. "In what way?"

"Whatever way you and Christina see fit."

Holden's jaw tightened. They knew Christina's name too? Fear swept through him. "My wife isn't in any danger, is she?"

She shook her head, her dark ponytail swishing across her neck. "No. Not at all. I promise you."

He still wasn't sure how much weight he'd give to any of her promises. "Why only Matthew? What about the other children who were taken? Will you tell the police where they are?"

"No." The steel returned to her voice. "Without exception, the other children are safe and happy. Only Matthew is in a difficult situation. He cannot stay where he is much longer, and he cannot return to his birth father. If he goes into the system at this point, he may or may not be placed with a good family. If he is not, all our efforts will have been for nothing." Her eyes bore into him. "Your brother's death would have been for nothing."

Holden gritted his teeth. "Another dirty ploy."

She unclasped her fingers and lifted both hands. "And yet, there it is."

The shriek of sirens filled the air. Her eyes remained steadily on him. "We are nearly out of time. I need to know that you will do this. Whether you keep him yourselves or make sure he is placed with a good family who will love him is entirely your decision, but I need you to make this promise to me."

Holden reflected on Matthew Gibson as he had last seen him before Gage had taken him from his home—the blond curls, blue eyes, and sweet smile that had always torn at his heart. Even if he'd endured more hardship in his first twelve years than most people had to in a lifetime, judging from the way he'd helped the little girl who'd fallen off her bike, he still seemed to be that sweet boy. And now his life was about to be thrown into upheaval again. If Gage had been willing to sacrifice his life to give Matthew a better one, could Holden not agree to do his best for the kid as well?

He blinked. Was that why he had been dreaming about Matthew? Was God trying to tell Holden that he was the one who needed to help him?

Shouts from outside the door tightened his chest. He waited for the sound of gunfire, but none came.

"Holden."

He met her gaze. "I'll do what I can."

Her slender shoulders relaxed. "Thank you."

A pounding on the door was followed almost immediately by it being kicked open. Uniformed officers, guns drawn, poured into the room. "Keep your hands where we can see them."

There was nothing Holden could do to comply with that request. Hopefully they could see that he was restrained and not being belligerent. Two officers pointed their Glocks directly at Natalya. "Stand up, slowly." She rose, arms in the air. Another officer swept the gun off her desk. "Hands behind your back." Her eyes still on Holden, she complied, and a female officer slapped cuffs around her wrists.

An almost imperceptible smile crossed her lips, and then two officers grabbed her arms and led her away. Holden watched until she had disappeared into the warehouse. A police officer came over to him. "Can you stand?"

Holden nodded and pushed to his feet. "Is the man who was shot okay?"

"He's being transported to the hospital."

Which didn't answer his question. "But ..."

The officer pulled a knife from his pocket. "Turn around." When Holden did, the man sliced through the plastic tie, freeing his hands. Holden faced him, rubbing his stinging wrists. The man nodded slightly. "He'll be fine."

"And the other two hostages?"

"Unharmed."

Holden took his first full breath since the moment he and Jax had figured out Mikayla had been abducted. *Thank you, God.*

For the first time in a long time, the fervent words didn't come crashing down around him.

Chapter Fifty-Three

The police talked to Mikayla for what felt like hours, making her go over and over the details of the abduction until she started to feel like a criminal herself. *They're trying to catch the guys who did this.* She reminded herself of that again and again so she could keep going, keep wracking her brain to remember any little detail she could give them. Apparently the ambulance had disappeared along with the men working for that woman who'd ordered her taken to the cellar. Only the woman had been taken into custody, so any help Mikayla could provide the police to find any of the other men from the warehouse would be valuable.

When the EMTs had brought Daniel out on a stretcher, her heart sank. Their eyes had met, and he'd attempted a weak smile as they'd loaded him into the ambulance—a real one this time— but she didn't know what had happened to him after they'd taken him to the hospital. She hadn't been allowed to speak with Holden or Jax before being brought to the station. She was dying to know if Holden was okay and what Daniel's status was, but no one seemed to want to tell her anything.

Tamping down her impatience, Mikayla went over her story one more time. *Please let me go.* To her great relief, the female cop who'd been interrogating her finally pulled a card from the shirt pocket of her uniform. "If you think of anything else, let me know immediately." She slid the card across the table to Mikayla, who took it and shoved it into the back pocket of her jeans.

"I will. Can I go now?"

The woman stood. "Yes. But please keep your phone with you in case we need to reach you."

Her phone. "The guy riding in the ambulance with me took my phone. Could you use it to track them somehow?"

The cop shook her head. "Unfortunately not. We recovered all of your phones at the scene. They were turned over to a …" she checked her notes, "… Juan Miguel Rodriguez. Do you know who that is?"

It had been worth a shot. Mikayla repressed a sigh. "Yes." She rounded the table and made her way to the door. "I'm supposed to return to Canada on Saturday. Is that okay?"

The woman strode to the door and pulled it open. "As long as we can reach you. If and when we bring these guys in, we may need you to come to Chicago to ID them."

"I can do that." She doubted the image of the two men who had taken her from the campground would ever be erased from her mind. It would give her a great deal of pleasure to be able to identify them to the police and testify against them, if it came to that. She walked out of the room. When she stepped into the hallway, Jax tugged his phone charger out of an outlet and pushed away from the wall. Mikayla wasn't sure she had ever been as overjoyed to see anyone as she was at that moment.

He closed the space between them in three strides and pulled her into his arms. Exhaustion weighed on her like an extra pull of gravity and she rested her head on his chest. After a moment, he held her at arm's length and studied her face. "Are you okay?"

"I'm fine. But what about Daniel and Holden?"

Jax lowered his arms. "Holden is good. He went to the hospital with Daniel. I drove out to the campground while I was waiting for you and grabbed a few things, including our chargers. The police gave me our phones and I dropped Holden's off to him. He did not know anything at that point, except that Daniel had been shot in the leg, but he called me a few minutes ago to say that they had taken him into surgery. The doctor told Holden that Daniel got to the hospital in time and he is going to be okay."

Mikayla's shoulders sagged. "That's good news. Does Nicole know?"

"Holden will call her as soon as Daniel is out of surgery so he can tell her how it went. He is planning to stay at the hospital tonight and contact us tomorrow to let us know what is happening."

"All right." She cocked her head. "What else did you get at the campground?"

He lifted two small bags. "A few things we might need tonight."

"For?"

He pulled two hotel room keys out of his jacket pocket and displayed them in his fingers like a hand of cards. "I booked us into a Sheridan a few minutes away. Thought you might appreciate a good sleep. And locks on your door."

The idea of a bathtub and a soft, comfy bed filled her with delight. Mikayla smiled. "That was an excellent thought."

"Kind and amazing, no?"

She laughed. "Kind and amazing, yes."

Jax slid an arm around her shoulders. "Shall we?"

"Please."

He guided her out of the police station and to the front seat of his car. Mikayla rested the side of her head against the window. Although the hotel was only ten minutes away, she had drifted off by the time they reached it, and Jax touched her arm. She jerked awake and straightened.

"Sorry."

The thought of what awaited her in the room revived her slightly, and Mikayla pushed open the car door. "It's fine. I'm more tired than I realized."

"That is understandable. It has been a long, traumatic day." Jax reached over the seat to grab their bags before climbing out of the car. When he came around to her side, he rested a hand lightly on her back as they walked to the large double doors of the brightly-lit hotel. The lobby was beautifully decorated. Mikayla studied a massive chandelier hanging above a seating area with couches, chairs, and a fireplace as they made their way to the elevator. They stopped outside her room on the third floor and Jax handed Mikayla her bag. "I am right here." He jabbed his thumb over his shoulder at the room directly across the hall from her. "I stuck your phone and charger in your bag, so do not hesitate to call me if you need anything, okay?"

"I won't." The bag in her hand felt like it weighed thirty or forty pounds. Mikayla barely resisted the urge to rest her head against the door.

"Here." Jax opened it with the key and held the card out to her. "Get some rest. You look completely done in."

"I feel completely done in." She took the key from him.

"They serve breakfast until ten, so why don't I knock on your door around 9:30."

"Sounds good."

"I booked the rooms for tomorrow night too, so we can sleep here after the gallery opening and head out Saturday morning."

Oh, right. She'd almost forgotten that her art show opened tomorrow night. Had it only been a few hours since she'd heard Spencer screaming down by the river? Somehow it seemed weeks had gone by. "That sounds good."

Jax looked as though he wanted to say more. Instead, he leaned in and kissed her on the cheek. "Sleep well, Grant."

She nodded. When he started to turn away, she grabbed his arm. "Thank you, Jax."

"For what?" His eyes locked on hers.

"For this." She waved a hand toward the room. "And for coming after me. I'm not sure I would have survived today without you."

His face softened as he ran a finger down the side of her face. "You were doing perfectly fine when I arrived. I am sure you would have made it out of there on your own. You are much stronger than you think, Mikayla Grant."

Was that true? She certainly didn't feel strong at the moment. And she hadn't since the night she'd lost her parents. Still, she had made it through that terrible time. Not on her own, though. Leigh had been there for her, and Nicole and Daniel and Jordan. But reflecting on the past months, she suddenly saw with shocking clarity that while all those people had helped, it was God's presence—His strength—that had carried her through the dark days she wasn't sure she would survive. Wasn't even sure she wanted to survive. Even when she'd railed against Him, He'd been patient and, yes, kinder and more amazing than she had realized.

Her cheek burning beneath his touch, she managed a small smile for Jax. "See you in the morning?"

He lowered his hand. "I will be here." Those words filled her with comfort as she slipped through the door, letting it close behind her with a soft click. She contemplated the locks. Jax was right—she did like the idea of being able to use them tonight. Summoning all her strength, she bolted then chained the door before stumbling to her bed. Too tired for a bath, she changed into the plaid flannel pants and T-shirt Jax had tucked into the bag for her, brushed her teeth, and crawled under the covers.

The soft mattress and high-thread-count sheets were blissful, and Mikayla relaxed into their embrace, fending off images of automatic weapons, Daniel on a stretcher, and rats scurrying across damp cellar floors as she drifted off to sleep.

Chapter Fifty-Four

"Here, Nic." Christina handed her friend a cup of steaming raspberry tea. *Sense and Sensibility* played across the big screen TV in Nicole's living room, but neither of them was paying much attention to it. The guy from the PD that Daniel had sent over had found a bug in the phone and one in his office, but none anywhere else in the condo, which made Christina feel a little better. At least the organization hadn't been listening in on everything Nicole and Daniel and Jordan had said to each other over the last few weeks or months. Clutching her own mug of tea, Christina leaned against the couch cushions. "Did Jordan settle all right?"

"It took a while. I didn't tell him everything that was going on, of course, but he did want to know why Daniel had to leave so quickly after promising to play catch with him in the park today."

Christina winced. "I forgot about that. I could have done that with him."

"He was okay with it. I told him Daniel had to help Uncle Holden and Aunt Mikayla with something, but he'd be home soon and the two of them could play then." Nicole started to lift the mug to her lips, but her hands were shaking and some of the hot liquid splashed over the top and onto her lavender sweater.

"Oh, Nic. Here." Christina set her mug on the coffee table and took Nicole's from her. She grabbed a tissue from the box on the table and swiped them over her friend's fingers. "I'm sure they're all going to be fine. Daniel reminded me on the way to the airport that the organization was all about helping those children—they didn't have a history of violence. He doesn't think Holden and Jax and Mikayla are in any real danger."

"Except that, as far as we know, they're the first to come close to finding one of those kids. These people went to incredible lengths to rescue the children—who knows what they might do if it looks like their efforts could be wasted? I'm sure they—" She stopped and took a shaky breath. "I'm sorry. That's not remotely helpful, is it? Daniel knows this organization a lot better than I do. If he doesn't think they're violent, he's likely right."

Still, her friend's words had stirred up the unease that had settled in her gut like silt at the bottom of a pond, and Christina pressed a hand to her stomach. "There's no use speculating. Daniel asked us to pray, and I've been doing that every minute since I dropped him off at the airport."

"Me too." Nicole reached for her mug. "And I should be doing a better job of trusting God to bring them through this. I do trust him. But …"

"What?" Christina took a sip of tea. The warm, fruity liquid soothed her a little.

"I can't wrap my mind around the possibility of having to raise another child on my own. If something happens to Daniel …" Her voice cracked and she lifted the mug to her lips.

"Nic, you can't think that way. It's not good for the baby. Let's try not to worry about things that are unlikely to happen. Daniel said he'd keep in touch, so I'm sure we'll hear from him soon."

As if Christina had summoned it to, Nicole's cell phone vibrated and she set her mug on the coffee table with a thud and snatched the device. After stabbing a button, she pressed it to her ear. "Daniel?"

Christina's grip on the mug tightened. *Please God, let Holden be okay.*

"Oh. Holden. What's going on, are you guys okay?"

Christina bit her lip and bent forward to set the mug on the coffee table. Holden must be all right. But why was he calling Nicole? She lifted her hands and Nicole nodded.

"Hold on. Christina's here and I'm going to put you on speaker." She pulled the phone away from her ear, tapped a button, and set the device on the couch between them.

Holden's voice rose from the phone. "Hey, Chris. I'm glad you're there."

Christina's throat tightened. He sounded all right, anyway. *Thank you, Lord.* "Me too. Is everyone okay?"

When he hesitated slightly, she shot Nicole a look. Her friend had clearly caught the pause too, as her cheeks paled.

"Everyone's going to be fine."

"Going to be?" Nicole's voice held a tinge of hysteria. "Who isn't fine now? It's Daniel, isn't it?"

"Yes, but I promise he's going to be okay, Nic."

"What happened?"

"We had a run-in with a few remaining members of the organization tonight. Daniel got shot in the leg, but he's out of surgery and the doctor said it went very well. Although they're going to keep him overnight for observation, the doctor's not concerned."

Christina reached for her sister-in-law's hand. It had gone ice cold. "He's okay, Nic."

Nicole pressed the fingers of her free hand to her forehead. "I can't believe this is happening again. What am I going to do with that man?"

"He said you wouldn't be happy with him, that you hate it when he gets shot."

She let out a choked laugh. "It's not my favorite thing."

"He saved my life, Nic. Possibly all of our lives."

Her fingers relaxed a little in Christina's. "That's good. I'm glad the rest of you are okay."

"We're fine. Jax and Mikayla went to a hotel. They're going to stay there until after the art gallery opening tomorrow night then drive home Saturday. I'll hang out here with Daniel and fly home with him when the doctors give their okay."

"All right." Nicole's voice trembled, but a little of the color had returned to her cheeks. "Please let me know the minute you have any other news."

"I will. I'll go see him as soon as they'll let me, and when he feels well enough I'll have him call you."

"Maybe I should fly there."

"No, don't. We'll likely come home in a couple of days, so there's no sense in you coming."

"I guess. Thanks for staying with him, Holden. I'll let you talk to Chris now."

Nicole hit the button to turn off the speaker and held the phone out to Christina. "I'm going to check on Jordan."

Christina nodded. As soon as Nicole disappeared into the hallway, she pressed the device to her ear. "Are you actually okay?"

"I am, honest."

"What did you mean when you said Daniel saved your life?"

He sighed. "It's a long story. Things did get a little dicey for a while there, but it ended peacefully. I'll tell you all about it when I get home."

Christina gripped the phone tighter. "Could that be as soon as possible?"

She bit her lip through the slight pause. "Of course. There's nothing I want more than to be home with you. I hope you know that."

Her throat tightened. "I do. And I want you to be here."

"That's good to hear. I have a lot to tell you."

Christina propped an elbow on the top of the couch and rested her head on her hand. "I want to hear it. I have a lot to tell you too."

"I'll come as soon as I can."

"Will you be able to sleep tonight?"

He laughed. "I doubt that a chair in the waiting room will be any less comfortable than the ground I've been sleeping on, so I think I'm good."

"You'll be glad to get back to your own bed, I'm sure."

Another short pause, then, "You have no idea, love."

Her cheeks warmed. Was he flirting with her? In spite of how worried she was for him—for all of them—she couldn't repress a small smile. "Will you call me tomorrow?"

"Absolutely. You'll stay with Nic tonight, right?"

"Yes, I was planning to anyway, but now I need to make sure she's all right. I'll talk to you tomorrow."

"Sounds good. Sleep well, okay? And don't worry."

"I'll try." Christina disconnected the call before stretching her arm along the top of the cushions and resting her cheek on it. Hearing Holden's voice—the love and the hope in it—filled her with a desperate longing to see him again. She rubbed her palm over the ache in her chest.

"You're blushing."

Christina lifted her head. Nicole had come into the living room. She settled at the far end of the couch and pulled her knees to her chest. Christina touched her friend's bare foot. "Are you all right?"

"Other than being a member of the very exclusive club of women who has now been told twice that her husband has been shot, I'm fabulous."

"Holden meant it—Daniel is going to be fine."

"I know, but I'll feel a lot better when all four of them are home again."

"Me too."

"Which brings us around to the blushing."

"Oh. That. I was hoping you'd forget."

"Why? There's nothing wrong with your husband making you blush. It's a very good sign, in fact."

"Of what?"

"That you're finding your way to each other again."

Christina reached for her tea. The mug had cooled, but she wrapped her fingers around it anyway. "Maybe. Finally. I still feel like I have a ways to go."

"There's no time frame for these things, Chris. You'll get there when you get there. You need to give yourself grace. And chocolate."

"Chocolate?"

Nicole swung her feet to the floor. "I'll see what I have. Then we can finally finish this movie."

Christina relaxed against the cushions as Nicole padded to the kitchen. Now that she knew everyone was all right, she could enjoy being with her best friend watching a good movie and eating chocolate. And sometime in the next day or two her husband would come home. She had no idea what the future held for them, but for the first time in months she was hopeful that, whatever it was, they would face it together.

Chapter Fifty-Five

Holden jerked upright in the chair beside the bed when Daniel stirred. Thin beams of light pushed through the metal-slatted blinds on the window. Morning. He leaned forward and rested his forearms on his knees. "Hey."

Daniel started to sit then winced and sank against the pillows. "Hey."

"How are you feeling?"

"Like I was run over by a truck." He glanced around the hospital room before his gaze settled on Holden again. "*Was* I run over by a truck?"

Holden let out a short laugh. "No, only shot. Again."

"Oh, yeah." Daniel gingerly touched his fingers to his leg before withdrawing them. "It's coming to me now." He gripped the bed rail. "Mikayla and Jax?"

Holden held up his hands. "They're fine. They checked into a hotel." When Daniel raised an eyebrow, he said, quickly, "In separate rooms." Then, realizing Jax hadn't exactly specified that, he added, "I think." Knowing both of them, it was a pretty safe bet.

"Did you call Nicole?"

"Yeah, as soon as you came out of surgery and the doctor said you were going to be okay."

Daniel exhaled. "All right, thanks."

Holden almost grinned at the weary resignation in his friend's voice. "Were you thinking you might be able to get away with not telling her?"

"Too much to hope for?"

"A little, yeah. Unless you want to stay in the hospital for a few weeks."

Daniel shifted, clearly trying to get comfortable. "I definitely don't."

"There you go."

"How did she take it?"

When Holden hesitated, Daniel sighed. "That bad, huh?"

"Actually, she was pretty good about it. She did say she couldn't believe this had happened again."

"I can't either." He brightened a little. "Wait until my dad hears about this."

"Why, because you've been shot twice now and he's only been shot once? Do the two of you have some kind of perverse competition going on?"

"Of course not."

His tone—almost gleeful—did nothing to convince Holden. "Anyway …" he drew out the word, "the doctor said the surgery went well and you can likely get out of here soon."

"Good."

Holden paused again. Was this the right time to mention it? He nodded at Daniel's phone. "You got a call in the night and I answered it for you in case it was urgent."

"Who was it?"

"Detective Sergeant Lector."

Daniel sagged against the pillows. "I'd ask you what he said, but I might need more painkillers first. Not that you're likely to be able to repeat most of it."

"He didn't say much, only that he wanted to talk to you. Although you're right, he may have said that a little more colorfully than I did. When I told him you were still out from the surgery he said he'd call again today."

"I'm sure he will." Daniel stared at the ceiling. "I'm pretty certain I'll be done this time. I've been living on borrowed time since my suspension as it is."

A hard knot formed in Holden's stomach. That was his fault too. "I'm sorry, Daniel. I never should have asked you to keep any of this a secret."

"It's fine. I did get it. And it's likely turned out for the best, at least as far as Matthew Gibson is concerned. Unless you found out he was in a good home and now they're going to rip him out of it." His forehead wrinkled. "Is that what happened?"

"No, actually. It turned out he wasn't in a great situation. His adoptive mother died last year and his father no longer wanted him. It's good that CAS has taken him in."

"So it's great you found him. Now they can bring him to Canada and hopefully find a good home for him."

Holden studied his hands.

"What?"

"She asked me to take care of him."

Daniel frowned. "Who did?"

"The woman who held the gun to my head yesterday. She knew Gage and had some kind of soft spot for him. Good thing she did, because I was able to use that to talk her into letting us all go, which I'm pretty sure she wasn't planning to do." Which meant that, even from beyond the grave, his brother had saved his life. Like he had the night when, lying in the street bleeding to death, he'd managed to shoot Troy Gibson before the man could fire on Holden. He hoped that, somehow, Gage knew that.

"Ah. I wondered what had happened in that office."

"Yeah. She even called the police herself, and right before they came, she asked me to either adopt Matthew or make sure we found him a good family."

"Wow." Daniel rubbed his forehead with the side of his hand. "Did you agree?"

"I did, actually. I definitely want to make sure that poor kid is well taken care of, after everything he's been through."

"Would you consider adopting him?"

Holden drew in a long breath. "I would, but it depends on Chris. As you know, things haven't been great between us for a long time. I'm feeling better about our relationship than I have in months, but I'm not sure we've made it all the way to the place where we can take on something like this. I won't know until I get home and the two of us can talk."

Before Daniel could answer, the door swung open and a tall man in pale green scrubs strolled in clutching an orange tray in his hand. "Breakfast."

"Thanks." Daniel dug both fists into the bed and hauled himself upright.

"Here." Holden hit the button to raise the head of the hospital bed.

"Thanks." Perspiration dotted Daniel's forehead as he leaned against the pillow.

The man set the tray on the wheeled table next to the bed. "Can I get you anything else?"

"No, thanks. I'm good."

When the guy had gone, Daniel reached for the cup of coffee on the tray, took a sip, and made a face. "Well, the bullet didn't kill me, but this coffee might."

Holden got to his feet with a groan. He'd been wrong when he was talking to Christina. Even sleeping on the air mattress in the tent had been more comfortable than the chair in the waiting room and then this one. Every muscle and joint in his body ached. "I'll go to the cafeteria, see if the stuff they have there is any better."

"That'd be great. I'm missing a lot of things about my wife at the moment, but her coffee is near the top of the list." Daniel picked up a piece of limp toast, stared at it a moment, then set it on the plate again. "Grab me some real food while you're getting the coffee, will you?"

"Sure." Holden headed into the hallway and followed the signs for the cafeteria. The idea of Daniel losing his job as a result of Holden's actions haunted him. Why had he ever thought coming to Chicago to chase after Matthew Gibson was a good idea? All it had done was leave Daniel unemployed, and that was the best of all the possible terrible outcomes. All four of them could have been killed because of his obsession with the blond boy in his dreams. This whole trip had been a fiasco.

He found the cafeteria and strode into the spacious area filled with tables, various food stations lining three of the walls. The clanging of dishes and hum of conversation intruded on the silent tongue-lashing he'd been giving himself, offering him a short reprieve. The rich aromas of coffee and bacon permeated the air and he breathed deeply, his stomach growling in response. When was the last time he'd eaten? It took him a minute to figure out it had to have been lunch the day before, since he and Jax hadn't had a chance to eat the steak and potatoes they'd been planning on last night.

Holden stepped into line behind several people and, suddenly ravenous, waited impatiently for his turn to order. Finally, loaded down with four breakfast sandwiches and two extra-large steaming cups of coffee, he exited the cafeteria. As soon as he stepped into the quiet hallway, self-recrimination assaulted him again. What a lot of damage he'd done, and all with nothing to show for it.

Nothing?

The quiet response echoed through his mind, so clearly that Holden stopped walking and glanced around. A doctor studied a clipboard outside a room thirty yards away, but otherwise he was alone. So where had that question come from? Holden propped a shoulder against the wall. If not nothing, then what good had come out of this escapade?

Matthew's face drifted through his mind. If God had been trying to talk to him through his dreams—putting Matthew on his heart and compelling him to go find him—that had to be for a reason, right? And maybe that reason was that he and Christina were supposed to offer him the home and the family he'd never had. If Christina agreed and they were able to wade through all the bureaucracy and actually adopt him, then the child his brother had died saving could become their son. That was definitely not nothing.

And, out of nowhere, Jax had become a good friend. Over the past three weeks Holden had not only enjoyed his company, but developed a deep respect for him. Mikayla was scared of letting anyone get close and losing them again and he absolutely got that, but he hoped she'd be able to push past that fear and give Jax a chance. And if she did, and the two of them lived happily ever after, maybe they wouldn't hold it against him for dragging them here, in spite of what they'd gone through yesterday.

And speaking of happily ever after, what about him and Christina? This time apart had been incredibly painful. She was a part of him, and being away from her was like having a lung removed—even the simple act of breathing became more difficult. But it had helped them too, somehow. As much as he hated it, it was possible that they'd needed this time apart in order to process their own grief and loss and realize how much they didn't want to face life without each other.

Whatever it was, Holden couldn't deny that they'd made more progress in the last three weeks than they had the previous six months. Maybe that was about the timing, that they'd both reached a stage where they were ready to embrace another level of healing—he'd have to discuss that with his psychiatrist the next time he met with him. Whatever the reason, they'd managed to take steps toward each other in the time since he'd left home that they hadn't been able to before that. Frankly, Holden didn't particularly care what the official explanation for that progress was—he was content to accept it and be incredibly grateful for it.

And not for one second would he say that those steps forward were nothing, or not worth every bit of the agony he'd gone through over not being with her.

He pushed away from the wall and made his way to Daniel's room, his thoughts still whirling. How could he make this up to Daniel? If he believed it would help, Holden would talk to the DS himself, try to explain and take all the responsibility. Given the stories he'd heard about Daniel's boss, he knew it wouldn't.

As he approached the door to Daniel's room, an idea occurred to him. He shoved open the door with his elbow and maneuvered into the small area next to the bed, closing the door behind him with the heel of his shoe. "Here you go." He shoved aside the toast and a bowl of what he thought might be oatmeal and set the sandwiches and coffees on the table.

"Bless you." Before Holden could resume his seat, Daniel had already grabbed and unwrapped one of the sandwiches. A look of ecstasy crossed his face as he chewed and then washed down the bite with a swig of the coffee.

Holden grinned as he sat, clutching his own sandwich in one hand and the paper cup of coffee in the other. He set the coffee on the table next to the bed and unwrapped the sandwich. "I had a thought while I was walking here from the cafeteria."

"What was that?" Daniel spoke around a mouthful of bagel, cheese, and bacon.

"If it turns out that you are out of a job, you should think about going into private investigating again."

"On my own?"

"Actually, I was thinking with Jax. After what I've seen with him and Mikayla on this trip, I suspect he might seriously consider moving to Toronto if you asked."

"Hmm. Interesting suggestion. If the conversation with my DS goes as expected, I definitely may run that idea by Jax." Daniel took another big bite of sandwich.

Holden set his on the wrapper and studied his friend. "Did something happen while I was in the cafeteria?"

"I'm stuck in a hospital bed—what could have happened?"

He cocked his head. "I'm not sure, but you seem practically giddy. They gave you pain meds, didn't they?"

Daniel looked indignant. "For your information, I called Nic while you were gone."

"Ah. I guess that would do it too."

"Plus they gave me pain meds."

Holden laughed. "Well, whatever it is, I'm glad you're feeling better. So you're not worrying about the call from your boss?"

Daniel finished the last bite of his sandwich and rubbed his hands together to brush off the crumbs. "Yes and no. I mean, I don't relish the dressing down he's definitely going to give me, but as far as losing the job, I'm not as concerned about that as I thought I might be. I love being a cop, but I loved being a PI too.

And I miss being my own boss. If I get fired, I am definitely going to seriously think about starting my own firm, even if Jax isn't interested."

"You haven't been around Jax and Mikayla the last three weeks. I'm pretty sure he is going to be very interested."

"So there's something going on between them?" Daniel slowly unwrapped his second sandwich.

"Nothing official. I'm pretty sure he'd like for there to be, but Mikayla's been more hesitant."

"Not surprising. She's had a rough time the last couple of years."

"I know. But if I were a betting man, I'd put my money on Jax being able to win her over."

Daniel took another swig of coffee and wiped his mouth with the napkin from his tray. "That wouldn't be the worst thing in the world. Jax likes to cause trouble, but he's one of the greatest guys I know. I'd trust him with my life."

Holden reflected on that. "Me too, actually."

"Interesting." Daniel lifted his paper cup in Holden's direction. "Someday you're going to have to tell me everything that transpired between the three of you on this trip. Sounds like an awful lot."

"I guess it was." Holden reached for his coffee cup, toying with the plastic tab on the lid as he contemplated Daniel. "How are you not completely furious with me right now?"

"Hey, you're the closest thing to a brother I have too. We're family. And family does stuff for each other, even if it costs them." The giddiness had leached away. Daniel's eyelids looked heavy when he set the sandwich on the tray. "I think I better get some rest."

"Good idea." Holden wheeled the table away from the bed and lowered the head of it. In minutes, Daniel had closed his eyes and his breathing had grown deep and even.

For a long time, Holden sat next to him, the words Daniel had said to him playing over and over in his head. *Brother.* That word resonated deep inside him. After Gage died, it had struck him pretty hard that he had no family left, that he was completely alone in the world. The truth of that, on top of Gage's sudden, brutal death, had dragged him into a black hole it had taken him months to crawl out of. Even then he'd only been able to do it with the help of God, his doctor, and Christina.

Then he'd married Christina, and Nicole and Jordan had become a big part of their lives. And now he had Daniel and Mikayla and Jax and possibly Matthew. If he and Christina got to the place where they were ready to try again to have a child, this family that they'd chosen, that had been pieced together by God Himself, could continue to grow stronger with every passing year. He had no idea whether he and Christina would get to that place—still had no idea where he stood with her right now—but he felt more hopeful after their last conversation than he had in months.

Holden tipped his cup to drain the last few drops of lukewarm coffee before setting it on the bedside table with a smile. His coffee cup might be empty, but his cup of life? That one was definitely running over.

Chapter Fifty-Six

The silence was the first thing that struck Mikayla after she'd slammed a palm on the top of the clock radio beside the bed to turn off the alarm. She'd managed to grow used to the sound of birdsong waking her in the morning and even missed it a little. She definitely did not miss the hard ground—or the cold.

Stretching her arms above her head, she moaned in pleasure. She'd slept like a baby all night long. A warm, comfortable, pampered baby. Thanks to what felt like extremely luxurious surroundings after weeks in a tent, and the knowledge that Jax was across the hall from her if she needed him, she'd fallen into a deep, dreamless sleep that nothing had disturbed until the alarm had gone off. Which was surprising, given everything that had happened the day before.

Her eyes flew open. Daniel. Was he okay? She grabbed the phone she'd left charging on the table and tapped in Holden's number. It rang four times before he answered with a breathless, "Hello?"

"Holden?"

"Yeah, sorry, Mik. Daniel's sleeping so I wanted to get out of his room before I answered."

"Is he all right?"

"He's fine. Woke up this morning and inhaled one and a half breakfast sandwiches and an extra-large coffee before they drugged him and he fell asleep again. The doctor thinks he'll be released soon."

She blew out the breath she'd been holding. "That's great news. Nicole will be thrilled."

"She is, although also in a bit of shock that this has happened again, I think."

"I'm sure."

"I'll fly home with him, if you're okay to make the drive with Jax."

Eight hours of the two of them alone in the car. Mixed feelings coursed through Mikayla. "I'll be fine."

"How are you doing? They didn't hurt you before we got there, did they?"

"No, not at all," she rushed to assure him. "Only locked me in the cellar for a few hours. When Jax found me, I was in the process of prying a board off a window and climbing out."

Holden chuckled. "That sounds about right."

"And you're okay?"

He sighed. "I guess, although I'm struggling with a lot of guilt over dragging all of you here and putting your lives in jeopardy."

Mikayla propped the pillow against the headboard and rested against it. "Don't feel that way, Holden. You didn't force Jax or me to come with you—we volunteered and were happy to do it. I only hope that Andrew Thompson is okay."

"I think he will be. Turns out he wasn't in a good situation here, but CAS has him now and will be returning him to Canada. So I guess, from that standpoint, it was worth coming after him."

"I completely agree. And to be honest, I needed this time away. Not yesterday, necessarily, but the rest of it. It's been incredibly good for me."

"What about Jax?"

Warmth crept up her neck. "What about him?"

"Has he been good for you?"

A small smile played around her lips. "Actually, he has been. Even while driving me completely crazy."

"For the record, I'm rooting for the two of you. So is Daniel."

The heat intensified and she pressed a palm to her cheek. The two of them had been discussing her and Jax? "We're a long way from anything definite, so don't get too excited."

"All right, but for what it's worth, Daniel and I agree that Jax is a genuinely great guy."

"It's worth a lot, coming from the two of you." She meant it. Daniel and Holden were like brothers to her—if she didn't have their blessing on this, she wasn't sure she could proceed. Not that she'd decided she was going to proceed …

"If you're concerned about his relationship with God, remember that we're all on a journey with that, and from what I've seen, Jax has taken some big steps forward with his."

"I think so too. We've had a few pretty intense discussions that have helped both of us move forward, which wouldn't have happened if we hadn't been on this trip together, so a lot of good things have come out of it."

"That's good to hear. And listen, I'm not sure I'm in any position to offer relationship advice at the moment, but if you'll allow me to offer you one piece? Don't let fear stop you from something that could be truly great, Mik."

She swallowed. "I'll try not to."

"Good. See you in Toronto?"

"Sounds great. Give Daniel my love."

"I will."

Mikayla disconnected the call and rested her head against the board, staring at the landscape hanging on the wall across from her. That conversation had taken a turn she hadn't expected. It had helped, talking things through with Holden. She still wasn't sure she could overcome her fear and step into the unknown, but at least now she knew she had the support of friends and family if she did.

She glanced at the clock radio. Nine o'clock. She'd have to move if she wanted to be ready when Jax came to her door. The thrill that shot through her scared her a little, but she pushed the fear away impatiently. *Enough, Mikayla. You are stronger than you think.*

Jax's words from the night before echoed through her head, and she smiled as she scrambled off the bed and headed for the shower.

Chapter Fifty-Seven

A gust of wind whipped a long strand of auburn hair across her face and Christina shoved it aside with a gloved hand. The wooden slats of the bench she and Nicole had settled on were uncomfortably cold, the chill seeping through her jeans and jacket. It was spring on the calendar, but someone needed to tell Toronto that. A few flakes of snow drifted from a pewter sky and the wind definitely carried a bite. Spring in Canada was so unpredictable. It could go from feeling like winter one day to summer the next. Some days it seemed as if they experienced all four seasons in a twenty-four-hour period.

It was good to get outside and to move around. Especially after the movie-and-chocolate marathon she and Nicole had indulged in the night before. The sound of children laughing and shouting in the park was good for her too—it healed something deep inside. Christina inhaled the crisp, cool air and breathed it out in a puff of white. "So Daniel sounded good?"

"He did. They'd given him pain meds right before he called, so that could have been it."

"That and hearing your voice, I'm sure."

Nicole flashed her a half-frozen smile. "Maybe."

"You still wish you could go there, don't you?"

"Absolutely. I don't like the idea of my husband lying in a hospital bed hundreds of miles away from me."

Christina got that. She'd feel the same way if Holden was the one who'd been shot and was recovering from surgery. "Of course you don't. But he's not alone. Holden is with him and they'll both be home tomorrow."

"Mom, watch me."

They shifted their attention to Jordan, waving to them from

the wooden platform at one end of the jungle gym. Nicole returned his wave and he launched himself through the air, grasping the first bar and swinging from one to the next until he landed on the platform at the other end. Christina and Nicole clapped as he punched a fist through the air in triumph. "Are you ready for that?"

Christina blinked. "Ready for what?"

"For Holden to be home."

She pondered the question for a moment. "I'm definitely ready to see him. I think I'll head home today to clean the place and do a few other things."

"Anything I can help with?"

Christina's gaze followed Jordan as he ran to the slide and climbed to the top. "Thanks, but no. This is something I have to do alone."

Nic reached over and covered one of Christina's gloved hands with hers. "You're never alone."

She managed a smile. "I know. That's something that has become pretty clear to me over the last few weeks."

"Good."

"Will you be okay on your own?"

"I would be fine, but I think I might ask Connie over for the night. We haven't seen her for a while, so I'm sure she's anxious to spend time with Jordan."

"Great idea." Connie and her husband Joe had owned the diner before Joe died and left it to Nicole. The two of them had become parents to Nic when she'd started working there after graduating from university, filling the void left by her own mom and dad.

"How are things going with your parents, anyway? Have you and Mikayla talked to them much since Mikayla moved to Toronto?"

"We've talked a little. We keep discussing the possibility of getting together, but it hasn't happened yet. We have a long way to go toward healing our relationship, but I'm hopeful that some day we may be able to."

"I hope so too."

Jordan flew off the end of the slide and landed on his bottom. He bounced to his feet and bowed in their direction with a flourish. Christina laughed as Nicole shook her head. "Exactly what I need—another man in my life landing in the hospital."

Christina smiled. "If you're good, I think I may go. I'll call you when Daniel gets home to see how he's doing."

"Or don't, if you're busy." Nicole nudged her arm and Christina's cheeks warmed.

"That's my cue to leave." She stood and brushed off the back of her jeans. "Tell Connie I said hi."

"I will."

Christina waved goodbye to Jordan before traipsing across the park to the vehicle she'd left in the guest lot at Daniel and Nicole's building. She hit the button on the remote to unlock the door of her Mazda 3 then pulled it open and slid behind the wheel. Part of her was excited at the idea of Holden coming home the next day. However, apprehension still threatened to curl around that excitement and choke the air out of it a little.

She wheeled the car out of the spot and started for home. Before her husband arrived, there was something she needed to do. All she had to figure out now was whether or not she could.

Chapter Fifty-Eight

The table by the window that Jax led Mikayla to overlooked Lake Michigan. The white caps curling over the surface of the water and the flags flapping in the breeze behind the hotel suggested a cold wind, but inside the dining room it was warm and cozy. Mikayla took a seat and inhaled deeply, even the aroma of coffee helping clear some of the cobwebs that had clung to her since the alarm had woken her an hour earlier.

Jax laughed. "I am on it." He took off and a few minutes later returned bearing two steaming cups of the life-giving liquid. He set one in front of Mikayla before sitting across from her.

She lifted the mug to her lips and took a big sip, not caring that the hot coffee stung her throat a little as she swallowed.

"Better?"

Mikayla met his gaze over the rim of the white ceramic cup. "Much. Thank you."

His face grew uncharacteristically serious. "How are you doing, really?"

"I'm good. Yesterday was bizarre, of course. It was scary when I realized I was being abducted and when I was in the basement. I could hear shots and didn't know if any of you were in the line of fire. And staring down the barrel of that weapon with you was a surreal experience. But I felt God with me the whole time, and that gave me a peace that, under the circumstances, didn't make any sense." She lifted a hand in the air. "I can't put it into words, so it probably doesn't make sense to you, either. But it's what happened."

"I am glad you did not feel alone."

"I didn't. Although I still felt a lot better after you showed up."

"Me too." He offered her a crooked smile that sent warmth coursing through her chest.

To cover the flustered feeling, she tightened her grip on the mug and took another sip of coffee. Would he ask her about that? About the way she'd wrapped her finger around his, trying to convey a silent message to him? She wasn't at all sure if she was prepared to discuss that with him, or what, exactly, she'd been attempting to convey.

"Hungry?"

Her shoulders relaxed. She *was* hungry. All she'd had the day before was a peanut butter sandwich and the coffee from the French press that Jax had given her instructions on how to make. "Absolutely."

He inclined his head toward the center of the room. "The buffet looks pretty impressive. Shall we?"

They loaded their plates and returned to the table. To Mikayla's relief, Jax kept the conversation light and fun and before she knew it her plate was empty.

"Are you ready for tonight?"

Mikayla contemplated the question. If nothing else, yesterday had been a distraction, if not the one she would have chosen to take her mind off the evening ahead. "I think so."

"Will you allow me to accompany you to this exciting event?"

"You don't have to come. You've already seen the paintings."

"Of course I will come. I have been waiting for this night since we arrived in Chicago. So will you do me the honor of letting me be the one to escort the famous artist?"

Like a date? Mikayla ran her thumb around the rim of the cup. The thought of having Jax at her side for the showing did relieve a little of the anxiety she was feeling. A lot of the anxiety, if she was being perfectly honest. "I guess that would be okay, if you're sure."

Mischief sparked in his eyes. "That I want to come or that I want to be your date?"

"Both."

"Then yes, I am sure."

Her lips twitched. "All right then."

"What time shall I come to your room?"

"Leigh wants me there early, so we should probably leave here by four-thirty."

"Done." He glanced at his phone. "It is almost noon already. You want to nap first, no?"

As a matter of fact, she did want to nap first. How did he know that? As if on cue, she yawned and covered her mouth with her hand.

A smirk crossed Jax's face. "I will take that as a yes. Why don't you go, have your nap, and get ready? I will see you at four-thirty."

Mikayla nodded and stood. "What are you going to do?"

He held up his phone. "I have a few calls to make then I will get ready as well."

"Okay." She pushed the chair to the table. "See you later."

He nodded, and she wandered through the dining hall and foyer, admiring the lighting and the artwork on the walls as she went.

In her room, she grabbed the pajamas she'd tossed over a chair and started for the washroom. A knock on the door stopped her. Jax? Who else knew she was in Chicago, at this hotel? The prickles of fear she'd woken up with after her dream sparked across her skin. No one from the organization could have tracked them down here, could they? Shaking off the trepidation, she walked to the door. When she opened it, a man in a hotel uniform stood in the hallway, holding a garment bag in the air to keep it from touching the ground.

"Delivery for a ..." he glanced at the label on the bag, "Mikayla Grant?"

Mikayla blinked. What in the world? "That's me."

He handed her the bag.

She took it from him. Had Jax stuck her wallet in the overnight bag? She hadn't even checked. Before she could, the man had nodded and walked away. Mikayla closed the door. Maybe she could add a tip to the room bill. She carried the bag over to the bed. A card had been stuck inside a plastic pocket on the side of the bag and she withdrew it and flipped it open.

Mikayla – something special to wear on your big night. I wish I could be there, but I will be thinking of you. I'm so proud of you! Have a wonderful time, Nicole

Mikayla bit her lip. A few months ago she had been completely alone in the world, with no family to celebrate a night like tonight with. Now she had a sister—a twin—who could make her feel loved and special from five hundred miles away, and she was incredibly grateful.

She undid the zipper and drew in a quick breath. A shimmering gold gown lay inside the garment bag. Mikayla lifted it out and carried it over to the floor-length mirror attached to the wall. Holding the gown in front of her, she swirled from side to side. The sleeveless dress was gathered at the waist with a two-inch wide sash. Below that the skirt fell in soft folds to the floor, swishing around her when she moved. It was the most beautiful garment she'd ever seen, let alone owned. How had Nicole pulled that off?

No matter how she'd done it, Mikayla owed her big time. She had brought the black dress she'd worn to her previous openings, but maybe it was time for something different. A little more color from the artist known for her color would probably be a good idea. She'd never worn anything so glamorous in her life. Of course, she'd never attended an opening with a date before, either, so tonight was a night for firsts.

With a sigh of happiness, she hung the gown over a wall sconce so she could gaze at it from the bed. How on earth was she supposed to sleep now?

Mikayla sent a quick text to her sister, thanking her for her thoughtfulness, before changing into her flannel bottoms and T-shirt and crawling under the covers. She desperately hoped she could sleep, because she wanted to be well-rested so she could enjoy every moment of what was shaping up to be one of the biggest nights of her life.

Chapter Fifty-Nine

The one good thing about being shot—or accompanying someone who'd taken a bullet while coming to your rescue—was that you got to board the plane before everyone else did. Holden handed Daniel's crutches to a flight attendant, gestured for Matthew Gibson to follow Daniel down the aisle, then traipsed along after both of them. Daniel hopped along the narrow passageway, supporting himself with both hands on the tops of the seats he passed by. He stopped when he reached their row and waited for Matthew to go in first and then Holden.

Good plan. That would give Daniel a chance to stretch his leg out a little. At least, it would be a good plan as long as no one tripped over him or hit him with the drink cart. Holden winced. After he'd slept a few hours, Daniel had woken up anxious to get home and refused to entertain the idea of spending another day in the hospital, so they'd booked a flight for Friday evening. Judging from his shallow breathing and pale face, another day, like the doctor would have preferred, wouldn't have been the worst idea in the world.

Still, Holden couldn't feel too badly about the fact that they were heading to Toronto. He shot a look at the young boy beside him. Matthew's face was paler than Daniel's, if possible. When Holden or Daniel had spoken to him in the cab on the way to the airport, he'd answered their questions as briefly as possible, and hadn't volunteered anything more than that. Poor kid. No doubt he'd been completely traumatized when the police officers had pounded on his door last night, handcuffed his dad and hauled him away, and taken Matthew to the police station to wait for Children's Services to figure out what to do with him.

Thankfully, they'd called Holden, since his boss remembered

that he'd mentioned he was using his vacation time on a trip to Chicago. He'd been assigned the task of accompanying Matthew to the CAS office in Toronto. Holden was still having trouble wrapping his mind around everything that had happened in the last few days because of the dream revolving around the kid sitting beside him.

Holden nudged Matthew gently in the shoulder. "You okay, buddy?"

The kid gripped the arm rests so tightly his knuckles had turned white. "Yeah."

Holden shot Daniel a look before turning to Matthew. "Have you ever flown before?"

Matthew shook his head.

"It's going to be fine, I promise." Holden's thoughts drifted to the first time he'd been on a plane. Their mother had taken him and Gage out west to visit their aunt, his mother's sister. He was seven, and every bit as terrified as Matthew appeared to be now. Too bad times had changed. Gage had been a little apprehensive too, until the pilot had invited them both for a tour of the cockpit and given them their own set of wings to pin to their T-shirts. After that the whole thing had become a huge, exciting adventure, one of the best memories he had of his childhood. Not that there was a lot of competition for that particular title.

Holden sobered. A month later his father had come home in a drunken rage and killed his mother and nearly ended his and Gage's lives as well. The next day he and Gage had been sent to a foster home they'd stayed at for six months before that family decided fostering wasn't for them and CAS had carted them off to another family. They'd lived with two other foster families after that one, the first one not great and the second one pretty good, but all of them willing to take both of them so they'd never had to be separated. Not until the night Gage had been killed rescuing the boy in the seat next to him, anyway.

Holden swallowed hard. This wasn't about him. Somehow he had to help Matthew get through whatever lay ahead. Starting with this flight. He leaned a little closer to the boy. "Do you know that flying is the safest way to travel?"

Matthew rested his head against the seat and looked up at him. "It is?"

"Yep. And it's the coolest."

"Why?"

"Because we'll get to leave the ground and go high enough to look down on the clouds. And we'll see lakes and rivers and cities below us too. It'll be dark when we land, so you'll be able to see the city of Toronto all lit up with tons of lights."

Matthew brightened. "That does sound pretty cool."

They had taxied to the end of the runway. "Here." Holden tugged a pack of gum from his jacket pocket and offered the boy a piece. "This will help keep your ears from plugging while we're climbing to the right altitude."

Matthew let go of the armrest long enough to take a piece, remove the wrapper and shove it into his coat pocket, then stick the gum into his mouth. "Thanks."

Holden held out the pack to Daniel, who shook his head. Holden dropped the pack into his pocket. "This part is the best. You're about to hear the engines kick into gear so we can get enough speed as we go along to lift into the air. You'll be able to feel all the power this machine has, plenty enough to get us off the ground, propel us through the air faster than any other vehicle can travel except for a rocket ship, and land us safely on the ground again in Toronto."

As soon as he finished speaking, the engines roared and the floor beneath them vibrated. "Here we go. Ready?"

Matthew nodded. He kept his white-knuckled grip on the arm rests as they hurtled along the runway and lifted into the air. Gradually, his fingers relaxed. "That wasn't too bad."

"I know, and did you see Chicago below us as we were ascending?"

"Yeah." He sounded subdued again. Not surprising. He'd lived in Toronto until he was four, but Chicago was likely the only city he could remember. The only home he'd known. And even if his parents hadn't gotten him legally, until yesterday Matthew had probably never suspected that for a moment.

A memory assaulted Holden, of Daniel's father, one of the cops who'd come to the house the night his mother had died, walking next to Holden as he trotted along beside the stretcher carrying Gage. Right before he scrambled into the ambulance, Holden had stopped and looked at the house he and Gage had lived in their whole lives. And he knew, with a certainty that twisted his gut, that he would never see the place again. That he would always live somewhere else now. His life—and Gage's—had changed forever.

His legs might have given out then, they were trembling so badly, except that Officer Grey had clasped Holden's shoulder. The feel of that strong hand, warm and solid through Holden's thin, train-covered pajamas, had given him the strength to turn away from the house. He'd climbed into the ambulance with his brother and refused to look back as they pulled away from the curb, lights flashing and sirens wailing.

To this day, Holden could feel that hand on his shoulder, the strength of the grip and the courage it imparted to him. Daniel had gotten that from his dad, the ability to make others around him feel safe. In that warehouse, with bullets flying around them, as soon as Daniel had materialized a calm had swept over Holden. A calm that had stuck with him after he'd realized his friend had been shot. And even when that woman, Natalya, had ordered her men to bring him to her office. It hadn't left him when she'd pressed the barrel of the gun to the base of his skull, and for the second time that hour Holden had faced the very real possibility that his life was about to end.

The strength that Daniel and his father both exuded didn't come from them. It came from their deep faith. From the unshakeable belief that God was in control and was always with them. Holden shared that faith. Yeah, it had been rocked in recent months, but this trip had reminded him of why it could never be taken from him. He'd known that, even as a kid. Had clung to it that terrible night as he'd ridden to the hospital beside an unconscious Gage, not knowing whether or not his brother would open his eyes again. And that faith had sustained him ever since. Through Gage's death and the loss of his son. And through the long, dark valley he and Christina had been traversing.

Everything in him wanted to pass that faith along to the traumatized kid in the seat next to him. God knew he'd need it in the days and weeks ahead as he processed the loss of the man he'd known as his father and started a brand-new life. Again. *Father, help him. Give him strength. Whatever happens to him now, wherever he ends up, show yourself to him. Help him to know that you love him and that, even when everyone in his life lets him down and abandons him, you never will.*

"How fast are we going?"

Yanked from his musings, Holden glanced at the boy beside him. Not a boy, really, almost a teenager. Matthew's piercing blue eyes were fastened on Holden's face. Holden blinked. "Sorry, what?"

"You said planes travel faster than anything except rocket ships. So how fast do they go?"

"Oh." Holden sifted through his memories, trying to recall what he'd read about this mode of transportation. "About five or six hundred miles an hour, I think."

Matthew's eyes widened. "Wow. My dad took me out in the country one time and no one else was on the road so he said we should see what the car could do. He pressed hard on the gas and we hit about ninety miles an hour. I thought that was crazy fast, but I guess that was nothing." He turned to face the window. "It felt faster in the car."

Holden chuckled. "I know. It's weird, right? Once we're in the air, somehow it feels almost like we're not moving at all."

"Yeah." Still looking out the window, Matthew spoke quietly, "Mr. Kelly?"

"Yes?"

"What's going to happen to me now?"

Holden shot another look at Daniel, but his friend had fallen asleep. A thin sheen of perspiration covered his forehead and

Holden frowned. Had they made a mistake, leaving Chicago so soon? He exhaled. Not that there was anything he could have done to keep Daniel there, once he'd decided he was leaving the hospital.

He angled himself in his seat to see Matthew better. "First of all, call me Holden, okay?"

Matthew nodded slightly, but continued to look out the window.

"When we land in Toronto, I'm going to take you to the Children's Services office, where I work. My job, and the job of everyone there, is to make sure that kids like you are safe. What we are going to try and do is find a good place for you to stay, maybe even a new family."

Matthew rested his forehead on the glass. Holden's heart went out to him. What could possibly be going through that poor kid's head? Even if his home situation hadn't been great, Doug Thompson was the only father he'd known. Matthew had been torn away from him only twenty-four hours earlier. And now he'd been told he was going to a new family. He'd already lost two mothers to cancer. The trauma of losing his birth mother might not be part of his conscious memory, but it was there inside him, somewhere. Like the trauma of being abducted at the age of four, of losing his adopted mother a year ago, and now his father and his home. Trauma upon trauma upon trauma.

"You won't be able to though, will you?"

The words were so quiet Holden wasn't sure he'd heard them correctly. "I won't be able to what?"

Matthew exhaled as he pushed away from the window and slumped in his seat. "Find me another family. My friend Sam is a foster kid. Since kindergarten, he's had five different families. He says no one wants to keep him because he's not a baby and everyone wants a baby. Three of his families got a baby and then they didn't want Sam anymore. That's what's going to happen to me, isn't it?" He crossed his arms over his chest, still not looking at Holden.

Someone will want you. I'll find a home for you. I'll adopt you myself. The promises floated through Holden's mind, but he clamped his mouth shut, refusing to allow them to leave his mouth. If he'd learned anything the night Tristan died, it was to never make a promise he might not be able to keep. To never pretend he had complete control over a situation when he had no real say over so many of the factors that could play into how future events would unfold.

"I can tell you one thing."

"What's that?"

"I'm going to do everything in my power to make sure I find you a good home. I'll work night and day and I won't rest until I do."

"Why?"

"Because I get it. My mom and dad died when I was seven and my brother and I went into foster care. In one night, my whole life changed. I didn't know what was going to happen to me or where I would end up either. Even though we didn't get adopted, CAS made sure we were safe and that we were living with good families. It wasn't always easy, but we made it through."

Holden reached over the arm rest and grasped Matthew's forearm. "And I can promise you this. You won't be alone. I'm going to be there, checking in on you, making sure you are okay. I'll give you my cell number so you can call me any time, day or night, if you have any problems and I'll come and help you. Okay?"

Matthew finally looked at him. The light Holden remembered seeing in his eyes as a little kid, in spite of how his own father had treated him like a punching bag, shone in them now. The muscles beneath his fingers relaxed. "Okay. Thanks."

"You're welcome."

"Can I play games on my phone while we're flying?"

Holden reached under the seat and pulled out the backpack Matthew had filled with things he wanted to bring with him. "Sure." He handed the bag to the boy.

In minutes Matthew was deep into a game, his apprehension over flying—and his future—apparently forgotten.

For the next hour, Holden gazed over the kid's blond head at the clouds drifting below the wing of the plane. His thoughts kept pace with the speed of the flight and, unlike his travel companions, he couldn't slow them enough to concentrate on anything else.

Finally, the fasten seatbelt sign lit and the sound system crackled before the pilot's voice came on, announcing that they would soon be landing. "Look!" Matthew spun toward the window and pointed into the distance.

Holden leaned a little closer to peer out the tiny window. Toronto spread out before them, the hundreds of thousands of lights that lined the streets and highways turning the city into a massive sparkling golden spider web that vanquished the darkness they'd been hurtling through.

Holden contemplated the sight. All those lights made the city glisten like a priceless jewel, but only one of those lights mattered to him at the moment. The one that gleamed on the front of his house, where Christina was.

As soon as he dropped Matthew off to CAS and made sure he was okay for the night, Holden was heading directly for that light.

Chapter Sixty

Mikayla contemplated the blank spaces on the walls where several of her pieces had hung and sighed. It had been a long evening, but well worth it. The gallery had asked her to send more work to them as soon as she had pieces ready, as they had a list of people interested in seeing more. A number of managers of other galleries had slipped her their cards as well, entreating her to please get in touch. Although the trip had been a little crazy, she wouldn't have changed a thing. Except for maybe the getting abducted part. She winced. Jax's face flashed through her mind and she swallowed. He'd be gone soon, and she could get on with her life.

The stab of pain that shot through her scared her and she lifted her chin. *That's why you can't let him in.*

She glanced around the gallery at the few remaining patrons still wandering around viewing her work. Where was he, anyway? He'd been by her side all evening and his presence had given her confidence and the ability to relax and be present in every moment. He'd disappeared a few minutes ago, and she would very much like to find him, since she was ready to leave.

Someone touched her elbow and she jumped. Leigh stood beside her, staring out the large front window. "Uh, Mik? I think you need to see this."

"See what?"

Her agent grasped her arm and tugged her to the front of the gallery. "Come look."

Mikayla followed her, the gold skirts of her gown swishing as she walked. She stopped in front of the window. Jax stood outside, beneath a street lamp. The light shone on him, illuminating the large cardboard sign he clutched in both hands. She read the words and pressed her knuckles to her mouth.

Mikayla Grant, will you go to prom with me?
Was he serious?

The limo parked at the curb behind him looked pretty serious. Jax let go of the sign with one hand and lifted his other in the air, waiting for a response.

Mikayla laughed and nodded, and he flashed her a thumbs up.

"Go." Leigh placed a hand between Mikayla's shoulder blades and shoved her gently toward the exit.

Throat tight, Mikayla made her way to the door and out into the warm spring evening. Jax met her halfway to the curb. He looked ridiculously handsome in a black tux, dark hair pulled into a ponytail. As he reached her, he lifted the flap of the jacket with his free hand to show her the white shirt beneath. "No flask, I promise."

"Then this is already the best prom I've ever been to."

He grinned and tugged something out of his pocket. "For you." He held out a slightly crushed corsage and grimaced. "Sorry. I needed both hands to hold the sign."

"It's lovely." She held out her arm. "What is all this?"

"I believe, Grant, in your country you would call it a do-over." He slipped the corsage onto her wrist, bowed slightly, and swept a hand in the direction of the sleek black vehicle. "Shall we?" He straightened and bent his arm.

Mikayla took it and together they walked to the limo. The driver stepped out of the car and opened the door for them with a flourish. She slid onto the soft white leather seat. Her disaster of a high school prom was the closest she'd ever come to being inside one of these, and she gazed around the luxury vehicle, her mouth slightly open. It was even more decadent than she'd pictured it when she'd stood by that window of the home she'd grown up in. The one she'd pointed out to Jax and where she had stood, curtain pulled aside as she peered out, trembling with excitement.

A mini bar lined one side of the car and a stereo system the other. Everything was white and pristine and she clasped her hands in her lap, afraid to leave a mark on any surface. Jax handed the sign to the driver and climbed in beside her.

"Where are we going?"

He took one of her hands in his. "*Es una sorpresa*. A surprise. Relax and you will see when we get there."

Mikayla studied their intertwined fingers. A perfect fit. Already this evening was worlds better than her original prom night had been. In fact, for the first time in years, the thought of that horrible experience didn't send revulsion shuddering through her. This memory was already pushing that one out of the corner of her mind it had occupied for far too long.

She gazed out the window, at the streetlights passing by in a stream of white. Soft classical music piped through the speakers, and the nervousness that had knotted her muscles since people started streaming through the doors of the gallery for her opening began to ease.

"See? Is that not better?"

Mikayla shifted to face Jax. "This is better, yes. Thank you, Jax. I can't believe you did this."

"It is my pleasure." He smiled and drew in a deep breath. "Absolutely no cigarette smoke or vomit smell. I specifically requested that."

She breathed in too. The air in the limo carried the hint of lemons and a faint floral scent, lavender maybe. A definite improvement over the cab she and Kyle had taken. "No, none at all. Thankfully."

He squeezed her fingers. "The show was good, no?"

"It was very good. I'm always amazed that anyone would pay money to have something I've painted hanging in their home, but somehow we did sell a lot of the pieces. The gallery wants me to send more as soon as I have them."

Jax cocked his head. "Why would you be amazed? You have a gift. People recognize that when they see it." He rubbed his thumb along the side of her hand idly, sending shivers tingling over her skin. "Did your painting change after your parents died?"

His casual way of sliding without warning into subjects most people didn't have the courage to approach still threw her. "Yes, actually."

"In what way?"

"For months after the accident, I couldn't paint at all. Everything appeared to me in black and white, no color. Then, shortly after the talk I had with my pastor about God and how he was still good, the colors returned. I grabbed a brush and started painting and didn't stop for days. What came out was far more vivid and vibrant than anything I had painted before. One critic described it as 'a newfound depth of emotion in my work.' Which made sense."

"*Sí.*" Jax nodded thoughtfully. "You had gone there, to that chasm of pain and loss, that well from which true creativity is drawn. The one good thing about pain is the way it wrenches open our souls, so that what we had previously kept locked in that place deep inside, the essence of who we truly are, has to come spilling out. Only now it has been refined and shaped by sorrow and hope. And that is what people see on your canvas. That is what I see when I look at your paintings. And when I look at you."

Sorrow and hope. How did he know? That pretty much summed up the journey she had been on since her parents had been torn from her life. And it described the two possible destinations of the path being laid out before her now. If she let go, gave in to her feelings for Jax and risked hurtling into that chasm of pain again, where would that path lead? Which of those two, sorrow or hope, would be the end result? Her chest tightened. No human could see far enough down the path to say for certain. All that was in her control was the choice to take the first step or not.

Mikayla felt his eyes on her as strongly as she felt his fingers caressing hers, but she couldn't look at him. He was silently asking her something, waiting for an answer, and she didn't have one to give him. Not yet. Her gaze shifted to the window. The streetlights had ended as they left the city. The three-quarter moon cast a glow over the fields stretching out to either side of them, giving their surroundings a mystical, otherworldly feel. She risked a glance at him. "Are we heading to the campground?"

The corners of his mouth twitched as he shook his head. "So impatient. You don't always have to know where the journey will end, you know. It is okay sometimes, better even, to simply trust that where you are going is a good place, and to rest in that."

"How can I trust in a place if I don't know where it is?"

His smile held compassion. "You don't trust in the place, *preciosa*. You trust in the one who is taking you there."

The quiet words bolted through her like lightning splitting the night sky. Since the terrible night of her parents' death, she had guarded her heart, determined to never be dragged into that gaping void of grief again. That sense of not knowing where that terrible, twisting road would take her had paralyzed her, kept her from opening herself to anyone but Nicole and her family.

But Jax was right. It didn't matter where the road took her, it only mattered that she trusted the one leading her along it. The One she'd wrestled with, cried out to, screamed at, questioned, and who was still there, pouring out love and mercy upon her.

The limo turned onto the narrow, rutted road leading to the campground. What awaited her there? She released a pent-up breath. It didn't matter what, only who.

Could she do it? Could she let go of her deep need to protect herself?

Before she could answer her own question, the limo stopped. They'd driven past their campsite, to the edge of the field in the middle of the grounds where the old wooden bandstand teetered on the brink of collapse. She covered her mouth with her hand. White twinkle lights had been strung around the edge of the stage and strands of them were draped along the curved wall of the shell. They glittered and twinkled in the middle of the dark field, turning the area into their own private fairyland. Jax had been right. The place had held potential that he'd been able to see even when she couldn't. Did he look at her the same way? Beneath her fears and the grief she still waded through, was he able to see something beautiful in her that drew him, no matter how hard she tried to push him away?

Was that how God saw her?

Jax let go of her hand and Mikayla smoothed the front of the gold gown with both palms. *I'm glad Nicole thought to …*

Her eyes widened. "Did you have something to do with my sister sending me this dress?"

His eyes glittered in the moonlight streaming through the glass. "I might have mentioned to her a few days ago that I was thinking of doing this tonight, which might have put the idea in her head that you should have a new dress, yes."

The driver opened the door and Jax slid from the seat of the limo. He held out his hand and Mikayla grasped it and stepped onto the field. "*Gracias.* Thank you," he said to the driver, who nodded. Jax withdrew something from his pocket and pressed it into the man's palm, so smoothly Mikayla almost missed it. Then he rested his fingers lightly on the small of her back, guiding her across the grassy area to the bandstand. "By the way, you look absolutely beautiful tonight."

Her cheeks warmed. "Thank you. And you are very handsome in that tux."

"*Naturalmente.* Which means—"

Mikayla lifted a hand. "I think I can figure that one out." Behind them, the car door closed and the limo continued along the gravel road until it disappeared from view. They were alone.

Jax directed her to the bandstand and they climbed the stairs. A small table set up along one side of the stage held several small bowls of chips and pretzels and a beverage dispenser that appeared to be filled with red punch. He reached inside his jacket pocket and pulled out an iPod, which he carried over and set on the table. The soft strains of "Wonderful Tonight" filled the air.

Jax held out his hand. "Would you care to dance?"

Her throat too tight to speak, Mikayla slid her fingers into his and he led her to the middle of the stage. "See?" He pointed at the sky. "Under the Stars, no?"

Mikayla tipped back her head. A million pinpricks of glowing white dotted the night sky. The sight—more beautiful by far than any school gym had ever been—stole her breath and she struggled to hold in the tears that threatened to fall. What was wrong with her? She was not a crier. At funerals, maybe, but certainly not over anything as sappy as this evening. Except—she lowered her chin and met Jax's dark, intense gaze—nothing about this felt sappy at all. Only … enchanting.

He slid an arm around her waist and tugged her close as the music drifted on the air around them, captured and enhanced by the shape of the stage. Even battered and worn, the structure could still perform the function for which it was designed. For a few, magical moments, neither of them spoke. Jax was an incredible dancer, and Mikayla felt as if she was too as they glided over the old wooden stage. The music swelled, and he lifted their clasped hands and twirled her around before wrapping his arm around her waist again. Breathless and laughing, Mikayla rested her head on his chest. His heart beat strong and steady beneath her ear.

"I am thinking of leaving London."

His words caught her off guard and she blinked. "You are?"

"Yes. I talked to Daniel this afternoon. He said his boss called and told him they would speak after Daniel returned to the city, but it sounded like he might no longer have a job. He wondered if I wanted to go into business with him again."

"So you'd be moving to Toronto?"

"*Sí.*"

Oh. She swallowed. Her arguments were being stripped away from her, one by one. Another song ended, and "Unforgettable" started.

"And, at the risk of shattering not only my mystique, but your policy of keeping our personal lives personal, I need to tell you that I am not seeing anyone else."

She murmured a noncommittal, "Mm hmm," into his shirt.

"A few years ago I lost interest in dating for the sake of dating. I vowed then that I would never get involved with another woman unless she was truly someone I could see spending the rest of my life with."

Her throat tightened. "I made the same vow awhile ago about a man."

"Good. Because there is something else I want you to know, Grant." Jax spoke the words quietly in her ear, his breath warm against her cheek. "God and I have been talking."

"You have?"

"Yes. We have been working things out. I realized that night around the campfire that I had been waiting to feel whatever nebulous thing I believed I needed to feel before moving forward. I already knew, deep inside, that God loved me, that without Jesus, my life was worth nothing. Now I have taken the first few steps forward. I am sure it is different for everyone, but for me, I needed to obey first, and the feelings are following, slowly."

Mikayla nodded, his white cotton shirt soft beneath her cheek. *I'm going to have to learn Spanish, aren't I?* She sighed.

Jax let go of her hand and slid a finger under her chin, raising it until their eyes met. When had they stopped dancing and moved apart? She still felt as if she swayed in his arms. "Sometimes, though, the feelings are there from the first moment, when you walk into the kitchen and see someone standing at a sink washing dishes."

"Jax …"

He took her face in his hands. "Do not ask where we are going, *preciosa*. Only trust. *Sí?*"

She studied his face. Could she do that? Could she trust? Trust that God would redeem the countless tears she had shed over the loss of her parents the way Jax had redeemed her terrible prom night experience? That, even if she gave her heart to Jax and lost him, she would not be alone?

Peace flowed through her. She could do it, because she already had. She trusted the man in front of her. The smile that crossed her face was certain. "*Sí.*"

Jax's eyes lit as he lowered his head and pressed his lips gently to hers.

Warmth traveled through her on a thousand sparks of light, like moonbeams on water. Mikayla wrapped her arms around his neck and, for the first time since the terrible day that her parents had died, willingly took the first step along a path not clearly laid out before her. God knew where it would lead, and He would be with her and Jax every step of the way.

That was all she needed to know.

Chapter Sixty-One

Holden climbed out of the Uber and stood in the driveway, long after the vehicle had disappeared, staring at the small house he and Christina had purchased shortly after they'd gotten married. When they were young and in love and full of hope for the future. For a long time, their home had been filled with light and laughter. And then both the light and the laughter had gone, snuffed out in an instant like the flickering flame of a candle. Would either ever return?

With a heavy sigh, Holden started along the walkway. Although trepidation filled him at the thought of what he would encounter when he went inside, he still couldn't stop the slight increase in his heart rate at the idea of being in the same room as Christina again. He physically ached to see her, to hold her in his arms. Would she allow him to touch her?

The front door was unlocked, and he stepped into the entryway and set his bag on the chair inside the door. The house was silent, as it had been for months. Holden slid off his jacket and tossed it on the chair before starting for the stairs.

The thick carpet in the hallway masked the sound of his footsteps. Christina wasn't in their room. He made his way to the doorway across the hall, the one that led into the nursery, and froze. The crib and change table were gone. Even the teddy bears in the window well had been removed. Only the small dresser—the one he and Christina had refinished—and the rocking chair remained. His wife sat on the chair in the corner to his right, her eyes closed, her breathing steady and deep.

Holden pushed away from the door frame and crossed the room, lowering himself to his knees in front of her and gripping both arms of the chair. For a long moment he watched her, his eyes taking in every contour of the face he loved and intimately knew. Her long reddish hair hung over her shoulders in gleaming strands that he yearned to reach out and touch.

Her eyes opened and she blinked. Then her hazel eyes met his. Neither of them moved for several seconds, then a small smile crossed her lips and she straightened. "You're back."

"Yes." His throat had tightened until it was difficult to speak, so he reached for her hands. Her skin was soft and warm beneath his. *Don't pull away.*

She didn't, only studied his face. "I wasn't expecting you until tomorrow."

"Daniel couldn't wait to get home." He squeezed her fingers. "And neither could I."

"Is he all right?"

"He was pretty beat by the time our Uber dropped him off, but I'm sure Nicole will take good care of him."

"Are you okay?"

He nodded. "I'm fine. But I'm more worried about you."

"Yes." Her gaze dropped to their clasped hands. "You always have been. And I've let you be, which is one of many things I want to tell you I'm sorry for."

He shook his head slightly. "You don't have to be sorry about anything."

"Yes, I do. Ever since Tristan …" she stopped, her lower lip trembling slightly.

Holden forced himself to wait, to not reach for her, as badly as he wanted to.

Christina cleared her throat. "After Tristan died, I became completely focused on myself. I forgot that you were hurting as much as I was, and I wasn't there for you. I'm so sorry."

He lifted one of her hands to his mouth and brushed his lips across her knuckles. "I understood. But if you need me to forgive you, then I do."

She exhaled. "I do, for that and for so many things."

"Done."

Her eyes probed his. "Are you here for good?"

"Of course. I told you I would never leave you, and I meant it. I love you, Chris, more now than I ever have. I'm not going anywhere. You never need to doubt that."

Her eyes misted. "I think I've always known that, on some level."

Like he'd known, deep inside, that God had never left him. "I hope so." Holden glanced around the room before his gaze settled on her face again.

That small smile played around her mouth. "I have so much to tell you. So much has happened. But for now, I want you to know that, while I've finally put everything in storage, I do want us to think about trying again for another baby. I don't want to live in fear anymore."

Holden pressed his eyes shut. He'd started to think that he would never hear those words from his wife. God had clearly been working in both of their hearts, more than he'd dared to dream or hope. He opened his eyes and tightened his hold on her hands. "Neither do I. And there's nothing I want more than to have a child with you, as soon as you're ready."

Holden considered his next words. How would Christina take them? In this moment, it felt as if they had finally taken their first tentative steps toward each other. Would his next sentence drive them apart again? He summoned every bit of courage he had. "There's something else I want you to think about."

"What is it?"

"CAS brought Matthew Gibson to Canada."

Her eyes widened. "They did?"

"Yes. Once the police realized who he was, they contacted Children's Aid. He couldn't have stayed with the family who took him in any longer anyway. The woman had died and the man no longer wanted him."

"That poor kid." She gazed at him intently. Until the last few months, they'd always been able to read each other, to practically know what the other was thinking before the words came out of their mouths. Had they gotten anywhere close to that again? "You want him to come and live with us, don't you?"

He blinked. Apparently they had. A thrill of joy shot through him. "I don't want anything that you don't want or feel that you can't handle. But, as you know, twelve-year-old boys are difficult to place. No telling what will happen to Matthew. I accompanied him to Toronto, and we had a chance to talk during the flight. He's remarkable, still full of light and joy in spite of everything he has been through. I believe, if we feel this is something God wants us to do, and it's something you want, that he could restore a lot of joy to this house. And maybe we could give him the safety, love, and stability that's always been missing from his life."

Christina nodded.

Holden rose and tugged on her hands, drawing her to her feet. "You don't have to say anything right now, but if you'd consider the idea, and pray about it, maybe we can talk about it more later."

"I will, I promise."

"Thank you."

Christina withdrew her hands from his gently and clasped them behind his neck. Holden's heart thudded in his chest. He was afraid to make a move in case it was the wrong one, terrified that pushing her would snap the fragile threads he could feel being spun between the two of them, like the gossamer silk of a web.

She took a step toward him. Unable to keep himself from doing so a moment longer, Holden wrapped his arms around her and pulled her close, burying his face in her hair and inhaling the scent of orange blossoms and spices. "I've missed you so much, love."

"And I've missed you."

Holden lowered his head and found her mouth. The feel of her soft lips on his was so right, so powerful, pinpricks of electricity skittered across his flesh. Months of keeping himself from reaching for her, from sharing intimate moments like this one, poured into his kiss as he tightened his arms around her.

When he finally lifted his head, her cheeks were flushed and the mischievous gleam he'd always loved and that had disappeared the night they'd lost their baby had returned to her eyes. "Welcome back, Holden Kelly."

The curtain that had shuttered her gaze since Tristan's death had lifted. A slow smile crossed Holden's face. He lowered his head again. Right before his lips touched hers, he whispered, "Thank you, Christina Kelly. It's good to be home."

Author Note

Dear Reader,

Creating my stories often takes a lot out of me emotionally, and that is true of *Driven* as much or more than any other I have written. Although I have never lost a child, I felt Holden and Christina's pain as I wrote, deeply aware that so many of my friends and acquaintances have experienced this inexpressible grief.

Loss is part of the human experience. We were created to be in relationship and to love deeply, as we are deeply loved. But the cost of that love, all too often, is a wrenching apart of two people so inextricably entwined that the parting requires a severing too painful for words.

And losses on a smaller scale assault us daily. They are part of life on a fallen planet where our decisions and the decisions of others have powerful, often painful, consequences. During those times of loss and sorrow, our focus inevitably shifts to God. Like King David, we cry out to him, even rail against him. And while He is patient with us, even as He walks alongside us, comforts us, and grieves with us, He often and for reasons of His own does not explain Himself or remove the pain. But He does redeem it. He uses it to refine us and to draw us closer to Him. As C.S. Lewis said in *The Problem of Pain*, "We are, not metaphorically but in very truth, a Divine work of art, something that God is making, and therefore something with which He will not be satisfied until it has a certain character."

As we walk the road of grief and loss, a road that we cannot see far enough down to know if or when or where it will end, we can trust in the promise of 2 Corinthians 1:3-4, "Praise be to the God and Father of our Lord Jesus Christ, the Father of compassion and the God of all comfort, who comforts us in all our troubles so that we can comfort those in any trouble with the comfort we ourselves receive from God." Even if we do not know where it is that we are going, we can trust the One who is taking us there.

When you find yourself on this journey, my prayer for you is that you experience incomprehensible peace, hope, and joy, whatever your circumstances, as God walks alongside you, upholding you every step of the way.

Sara

Discussion Questions

1. Holden has a recurring dream in which he believes God is trying to tell him something. Do you believe God still uses dreams to send us messages? Why or why not? Have you ever had a dream in which you believed God was trying to say something to you? What did you do with that?

2. Do any of the sentiments on the cards people sent Holden and Christina—such as God needed an angel in heaven so He took their son—strike you as particularly helpful or unhelpful? Do you agree or disagree with the theology? If you have suffered a loss like they did, what did people do or say that helped you the most?

3. Psalm 22:1-2 says, "My God, my God, why have you forsaken me? Why are you so far from saving me, so far from my cries of anguish? My God, I cry out by day, but you do not answer, by night, but I find no rest." Holden and Christina are both angry at God and lash out at him. Do you believe it is okay to get mad at God? Is there a right way and a wrong way to express that anger?

4. When Holden tells Daniel that he has encountered the "long, loud silence of heaven," Daniel counters this by saying, "Maybe God's talking, only you're not willing to listen." Could that be what is happening? Have you experienced this silence from God before? How did you handle it?

5. The C.S. Lewis quote at the beginning of the book says, "I know now, Lord, why you utter no answer. You are yourself the answer. Before your face questions die away. What other answer would suffice?" What do you think of this quote? Should God explain himself and His actions to us? Why or why not?

6. Jax is treated differently at the border than Holden or Mikayla. Does he handle the situation well? Should Holden or Mikayla have said anything to the border protection officer? Have you ever been in a situation where you witnessed racism or another form of injustice? Would you say or do anything different if you could go back in time and revisit that situation?

7. When Jax tells Holden that his *mamá* also lost a son, Holden thinks: "Shouldn't such a widespread, collective human experience somehow temper the pain of each individual loss? Instead, if anything, the pain only magnified with every story told, every heart broken. Magnified and diminished at the same time." What do you think of this quote? Do you believe it is true? Why or why not?

8. When Christina goes to church, she finds comfort in the words of the hymn they sing. "She'd struggled for months with so many questions, with a longing for answers that no one could give her. The idea that someday maybe she would understand, even if it wasn't until she was face to face with Jesus, did provide a measure of comfort." Do you have questions you'd like to ask Jesus? Does the idea that someday you may get answers bring you comfort? Why or why not?

9. When a woman at church tells Christina she has been praying for her and Holden, Christina thinks, "Those words were easy to say. She knew, since she'd said them more often to people in her lifetime than she could begin to recall. More often than she had actually prayed—she had to acknowledge that truth and the sting of guilt that accompanied it." Do you ever find yourself saying those words to someone? Do you agree with Christina that praying for someone is a way of being a stretcher-bearer for them? If so, will that change how you pray for others and how seriously you take your commitment to remember them in your prayers?

10. When they are sitting around the campfire and Mikayla tells Jax she can't start down a road when she can't see what lies around the bend, he replies, "Staying on a familiar road is safe and comforting, I know, and leaving it is a risk. Still, it is only in taking great risks that we can experience great joy." Do you agree with this statement? Have you ever taken a great risk? What was it and how did it work out?

And Now, a Sneak Peek at

Forged

Coming September 2022

Chapter One

Jax Rodriguez maneuvered the last box into place in his Porsche 928 and slammed the trunk closed. The hot June sun beat down from a cloudless sky, and he swiped his bare arm across his forehead. A car parked at the curb half a block up on the other side of the street caught his eye. The silver Matrix had been sitting there for a couple of hours as he loaded his car. Not that unusual, except that the engine had been running the whole time. Two men, both fairly large from what he could make out, sat in the front seats. Were they watching him? He frowned. No idea why they would be.

Could the attention be racially motivated? Chase Washington, his former partner in their PI firm, had been helping him move today, and it wouldn't be the first time he'd been profiled that way. Or that Jax had, for that matter. Although, now that he thought about it, he'd seen that car parked along his street before, always in a different spot. That likely meant that he was the one in their cross-hairs, not Chase.

The headlights of the Matrix flashed on briefly before dying out. Chills shivered across Jax's skin in spite of the humid day. For some reason, that had felt like a warning. But a warning of what?

A hand clapped down hard on his shoulder, yanking him from his musings. "Still can't believe you're abandoning me for the big city."

Jax whirled around. "Sorry, Chase. But you know how it is."

Chase shot a look at the apartment building Jax was vacating. "Yeah, I know exactly how it is."

Jax followed his gaze. Mikayla Grant exited the building, a garment bag filled with his dress shirts and pants folded over one arm. A smile crossed his face. He hadn't abandoned his partner for Toronto—he'd abandoned him for the opportunity to live in the same city as the woman he loved. Not to mention the chance to join his friend, former cop and Mikayla's brother-in-law Daniel Grey, who had recently started his own private investigation business in Toronto. Being in the city would also allow Jax to be close to his *mamá*. Which was a good thing. His dad had left them to return to Puerto Rico when Jax was a kid, and his older brother Diego had disappeared twenty years earlier after becoming deeply involved in the drug world. Which left Jax and his *mamá* on their own.

Jax had dedicated the last ten years to searching for Diego with no success. The failure stung, not only because he desperately missed his brother and would give anything to know if he was dead or alive, but also because Jax's specialty as a PI was missing persons. He'd been able to track down dozens of lost people over the last decade and bring them home to their families. He didn't begrudge them their happiness, but every joyful reunion he witnessed was a painful reminder that he may never find his own brother.

Jax punched Chase lightly in the arm. "Pete is a great PI—he will be a good partner for you. And you can come visit me and Daniel any time. Toronto is not that far away." Although it had certainly felt like it when he'd made the two-and-a-half-hour trip every weekend for the past year to see Mikayla. And it had felt even farther when he was driving away from her after a couple of way-too-short days together. His gaze sought her out again. Not that it hadn't been worth every second and every cent he'd spent on gas.

Her eyes met his and she smiled. The sight weakened his knees a little, and he braced himself with a hand on the trunk of the Porsche. Chase elbowed him in the ribs. "You gonna put a ring on her finger or what?"

The thought of the black velvet box he'd tucked into his overnight bag before fitting the bag into a spot on the floor behind the driver's seat flitted through his mind. "Definitely thinking about it."

"Better get my goodbye kiss in before you do then." Chase flashed him a mischievous grin before striding up the walkway.

"Do not even …" his friend had already reached Mikayla and flung his arms around her, "… think about it," Jax muttered.

"Goodbye, Mik. When you come to your senses and dump this guy, you have my number."

"I'll keep that in mind." The laughter in her voice sent warmth rushing through Jax's chest.

His former partner planted a kiss on Mikayla's cheek before taking the garment bag from her and carrying it to the car. He slid the hangers over the hook in the back seat then closed the door.

Mikayla walked over to stand beside Jax, and he wrapped his arm around her waist. Chase stopped in front of them. "Seriously, man, I'm going to miss you." He held out his hand.

Jax clasped it. "I will miss you as well. Good luck with everything, *mi amigo*."

"You too." Chase dipped his head toward Mikayla. "Take care of each other."

She slid an arm around Jax. "We will."

Jax watched his friend as he strode along the sidewalk and climbed into his car. When he drove past them, Jax lifted a hand. Mikayla came around in front of him and rested her hands on his hips. "You okay?"

He tucked a strand of short blond hair behind her ear. "Yeah, I am okay. Change is good but hard at the same time, no?"

"Sí, es difícil."

Hearing his native language on her lips did something to him deep inside. Her pronunciation needed a little work and she often used the wrong words, but Jax loved that she was trying. He framed her face with his hands and leaned in for a kiss. Before his lips could touch hers, a burst of music stopped him.

A sheepish look crossed Mikayla's face. "Sorry. I left my ringer on because I asked Nicole to call me if Christina went into labor."

Jax lowered his hands. "Better get it then." Their friends Holden and Christina had lost a baby a year and a half ago and had struggled with a grief that had driven them apart. After months of processing their loss, they had finally found their way to each other and to a stronger faith in the God they both realized had not turned His back on them. Now they were expecting another child any day, and Jax could not be more thrilled for them.

"Okay, great. Thanks for letting us know. We're on our way." Mikayla's face had lit up as she talked to her twin sister. She hit the disconnect button on the phone. "Holden and Christina have gone to the hospital."

Jax retrieved the car keys from the front pocket of his jeans. "Let's go."

"I need to grab my water bottle out of the back seat first." Mikayla rounded the trunk of the car and reached for the handle of the door behind the driver's seat.

A movement down the street snagged Jax's attention. The silver car had pulled away from the curb and was accelerating toward them. His heart-rate shifted into overdrive as the Matrix veered over to their side of the street. "Mik!" Jax lunged around the back of the car, grabbed her elbow, and yanked her behind his Porsche and out of the path of the oncoming vehicle. The Matrix roared past his car, close enough to the rear door, still hanging open, that it rocked a little on its hinges.

For a few seconds he and Mikayla stood in stunned silence, watching the vehicle until it had squealed around a corner and disappeared. Then she turned to him, her green eyes wide. "What just happened?"

"A couple of punk kids out for a joyride, I guess." He drew her into his arms. "Are you all right?"

She nodded, her head brushing against his burgundy T-shirt. "I'm fine. Thanks to you."

Jax held her a moment longer, until the violent thudding in his chest eased. If the headlights flashing hadn't been a warning, Mikayla nearly being run down definitely was. Who had issued the warning and what were they trying to tell him?

"We should head home." Mikayla lifted her head.

Reluctantly, he let her go. If someone *had* been watching him, Jax was about to leave London for good and they wouldn't have any idea where to find him. Whoever it was would have to find someone else to target.

Mikayla retrieved her water bottle from the back seat before stumbling around to the passenger side, clearly still a little shaken from her close encounter. Jax's jaw clenched. If anything had happened to her, it wouldn't have mattered to him in the slightest how big those two guys were. He would have used every contact he had to track them down and—

"Ready to go?"

Jax shifted his attention to Mikayla. She'd swung open her door and was resting her arm on the top of it. "Yeah, sorry. I just want to check my mailbox one last time. It will only take a minute."

She waved the water bottle in his direction. "It's fine. Go."

Jax shot another look down the street in the direction the Matrix had disappeared. Should he leave her alone? He stepped onto the sidewalk. Given the speed it had been traveling, the car had to be long gone. And the mailboxes for his building lined the wall inside the front door—he'd be able to see Mikayla the whole time. Plus, she had proven on more than one occasion that she was more than capable of taking care of herself. She would be fine. Still, uneasiness swirled through him as he jogged along the front walk to the entrance of the building.

He slid the tiny key into the box, yanked open the metal door, and grabbed the few items inside, likely all flyers and bills. He didn't take time to sort through the pile as he dropped the key into the superintendent's box and hurried out of the building. The street was quiet and he took a deep breath as he made his way to the driver's side of the car.

Mikayla set her water bottle in the cup holder as he slid behind the wheel and stuck the key into the ignition. "Anything interesting?" She nodded at the pieces of mail clutched in his fingers.

Jax checked the rear-view mirror. The urge to leave the neighborhood gripped him, but he didn't want to alarm Mikayla any more than she already was. He sifted through the letters quickly. As he'd suspected, two bills, a pizza flyer, and a coupon for twenty-five percent off duct cleaning. Nothing too ... The final piece of mail snagged his attention. He furrowed his brow as he tugged out a postcard with a picture of a brilliant sunset over the ocean, palm trees silhouetted against the orange, pink, and red sky. Who would send him a postcard? He searched his memory but couldn't come up with anyone he knew who might be vacationing in a tropical paradise right now.

Jax set the rest of the mail on the console and flipped over the card. He scanned the back of it, his chest tightening.

When he lifted his gaze to meet Mikayla's, his heart pounded against his ribcage as wildly as it had when he'd pulled her out of the path of the silver car. "It's from my brother."